The Summer Kitchen

LISA WINGATE

Quercus

First published in the USA in 2009 by NAL Accent,
now Berkley, an imprint of Penguin Publishing Group,
a division of Penguin Random House LLC

First published in Great Britain in 2020 by

Quercus Editions Ltd
Carmelite House
50 Victoria Embankment
London EC4Y 0DZ

An Hachette UK company

A CIP catalogue record for this book is available
from the British Library

PB ISBN 978 1 52940 252 0
EB ISBN 978 1 52940 248 3

This book is a work of fiction. Names, characters,
businesses, organizations, places and events are
either the product of the author's imagination
or used fictitiously. Any resemblance to
actual persons, living or dead, events or
locales is entirely coincidental.

10 9 8 7 6 5 4 3 2 1

Typeset by Jouve (UK), Milton Keynes

Printed and bound in Great Britain by Clays Ltd, Elcograf S.p.A.

Papers used by Quercus are from well-managed forests and
other responsible sources.

To those who serve
and those who are
served –
may we all see
that we walk in the
same circle.

CHAPTER 1

Sandra Kaye

Part of me says, *It's just a house. It's wood, and brick, and stone, nails and tar paper, weathered red shingles, a few of which are missing now. It's only a ramshackle old place that was never anything fancy.*

With luck, developers will buy it and wait for revitalization to take over the block. A quick sale to a speculator would be the easiest way . . .

The voice that says this is logical. It makes sense. It's only telling me what I already know.

Which raises the question of why those words are so hard to hear.

There's another voice, one that's smaller and quieter, timid yet persistent, like a child with something to say. *This is more than a house. This is the past. Your past . . .*

I've wondered time and again if those are the voices anyone would hear when saying good-bye to a treasured childhood place.

It's nothing but a burden, I told myself as I stood in the driveway, waiting for the real estate agent to arrive. *Maryanne was right. You should have done what she wanted. If I'd let* my sister have her way, the house would have been put on the auction block, contents and all. In Maryanne's view, the little bit it might bring wasn't worth the effort of getting an agent and waiting for a buyer. It wasn't as if Mother needed the money from her inheritance of the place. It wasn't as if anyone cared what happened to Uncle Poppy's house at all.

Anyone other than me. When the one person who always loved you the most dies a violent death, it's hard to know what should come after. There is no road map for what should be done with the possessions left behind and the memories cut short. Mother had let the house languish for months on the premise that it wouldn't *look good* to dispose of it while Poppy's murder was still unsolved. Now that the Dallas Police Department had finally admitted the case might never be closed, six months became the socially acceptable benchmark. It was time to *cut our losses,* as Mother put it.

The words stuck in my chest, too hard to swallow even now that the real estate agent was on her way. The idea of tossing this place out like an empty shoe box seemed a betrayal of Poppy and Aunt Ruth, whose breath inhabited the fading pink house even now that the contents had been sold, the porches swept, the leftover junk piled at the curb. There was nothing more to do here but hang out a sign and let go. Yet the reality remained impossible to face. Standing in the drive, I expected that the front door would creak open, and Poppy would hobble out in his bowlegged shuffle. He'd smile, and wave, and tell me to come in for coffee. The last six months would be nothing but a bad dream, a nightmare from which we'd awaken all at once.

Turning from the door, I stared down the block. There was no way to be comfortable with the silence here, no way to make peace with the painful ending of Poppy's life. I could go back a thousand times and wish I'd acquiesced when Mother and Maryanne wanted to move Poppy to a nursing home two years ago, after Aunt Ruth's death, but wishing it wouldn't change anything.

Checking my watch, I paced back and forth across the driveway. The real estate agent was a half hour late. Around me, the neighborhood had slipped into the filmy shade of evening, and even though it was warm, gooseflesh rose on my arms as a group of adolescent boys passed by on the sidewalk, their oversized shorts sagging beneath T-shirts in colors that were probably carefully selected to identify a group.

One of them kicked a plastic flowerpot from the edge of the estate sale rubbish pile. A flash of anger, hot and sudden, caused me to cry out, 'Stop it!' The boys turned my way, and I fell mute, staring at them. In a few years, would they be the ones jumping an eighty-nine-year-old man whose only mistake was to have cashed his social security check before dropping by the convenience store for a gallon of milk? 'Leave that alone,' I hissed, and hatred welled inside me. How dare those boys touch Poppy's belongings. How dare they touch anything that had been his.

Shrugging, the closest one kicked the flowerpot again, then stepped around it and left it in the street. 'Yeah, you in

3

my neighborhood now, lady,' he muttered with false bravado, and his friends laughed. 'You betta take yo' butt back home befo' dark.'

'Yeah, get in that Caddy and mojo on outa here,' another added, then slipped in a string of expletives without venturing a glance back at me.

I stood by the driveway, trapped between good sense and a blinding need to confront them.

This isn't the way, I told myself. *They're just boys. Just little boys trying to impress each other, trying to act like men.*

Poppy had always loved the kids in the neighborhood. For years, he'd fixed their bikes, patched leaking tire tubes and aired up deflated basketballs, tack welded the wheels onto broken skateboards, wagons, and tricycles. He probably knew those boys when they were younger . . .

A new red Mustang passed them on the street, and they whistled at the blonde behind the wheel. She ignored them as she pulled into the driveway. 'Kids,' she said as she stepped from her car. A high, quick laugh punctuated the sentence, and she rolled her eyes in a way meant to indicate that the boys were harmless. 'I heard they're trying to get some summer programs started up to keep young people off the streets when school gets out.'

'That's good,' I said, but I didn't ask who *they* were. I didn't care. I wanted to be done with this meeting, get in my car, go home, and put a diet frozen dinner in the microwave. Rob was working ER tonight, and Christopher would be out with friends, studying. They'd both get home late, the usual routine. It was easiest for all of us, a way to avoid the fact

4

that Poppy wouldn't be calling to check in, and Jake wasn't in his dorm at Southern Methodist University, but somewhere on the far side of the world, searching for a birth family he didn't know anything about.

Nothing was the way it was supposed to be. The little pink house shouldn't have been dark and silent. Poppy and Jake should have been inside with a bowl of popcorn, watching the Rangers play ball and cheering so loudly their voices would echo into the front yard. The two of them had loved to watch baseball together almost from the moment we adopted Jake and brought him home from Guatemala. Jake, silent and scared in a universe of strangers, had instantly latched on to Uncle Poppy. We supposed Poppy looked like someone Jake knew before – a grandparent, perhaps, or a worker in the orphanage.

Jake was always Poppy's favorite. Even after Christopher was born, there was still something special between Poppy and Jake. They never went more than a few days without seeing each other.

Now it hurt to remember that . . .

The real estate agent introduced herself, and we shook hands. My cell phone rang as she returned to her car to rifle through the backseat for paperwork.

I answered the phone, and Holly was on the other end. I should have known it would be her, checking to see how things were going. Over the years, we'd shared everything from pregnancies to caring for aging relatives. Together we'd celebrated all the major firsts of motherhood – first steps, first tooth, first day of school, first date, first car, first

5

high school graduation. But now there was a vast, dark place we couldn't inhabit together. Poppy's death and Jake's disappearance were on the fringes of every conversation, waiting to slip in like a fast-moving storm and throw dampness over everything.

'Where *are* you?' Holly never beat around the bush. She was quick and to the point, which made her great at managing a family and running a part-time catering business. 'I just drove by. Your car's been gone all afternoon. You're not out at Poppy's house alone again, are you?'

'I'm meeting the real estate agent,' I said, ignoring Holly's need to be everyone's caretaker. With six kids around the house, mothering came naturally to her. 'I wanted to get the last of the yard sale junk out to the curb before she came. She's here now, though.'

Holly coughed indignantly. 'You should have called me. I told you I'd come with you anytime you need to go down there.'

'I know you did, but there wasn't much left to clean up – a few flowerpots, some picture frames and whatnot. I'm just going to leave those boxes of dishes in the cellar, and the big roasters. Whoever buys the place can deal with them.'

Holly wasn't about to be sidetracked. 'You shouldn't go over to that house by yourself, Sandra Kaye.' I knew Holly was serious when she used my full, properly Southern, double name.

'It was broad daylight. Anyway, I thought the real estate agent would be here, but she was late.' The truth was that

Holly was probably right. Rob didn't want me coming here by myself, either. The neighborhoods south of Blue Sky Hill hadn't quite made the turn to revitalization yet. As the new residents uphill started neighborhood watch programs, put in expensive surveillance systems, and demanded greater police protection, the less savory elements of the area were forced to frequent new territories. During the estate sale, we'd engaged a private auction firm experienced at operating in older parts of town. They'd come with security attached.

'I don't care if it's high noon,' Holly complained. 'You know what can . . .' She swallowed the end of the sentence, and I pictured the blood draining from her face as we both realized she'd inadvertently pointed out that, just blocks from here, on what should have been a perfectly ordinary Dallas evening, Poppy's attack had proven that lives could collide in an instant, with painful consequences.

The real estate agent closed her car door and headed my way with a clipboard.

'Listen, Holly, I'd better go so we can knock out the disclosure paperwork while there's still enough light outside.'

Holly sighed. 'Does the real estate agent have anybody with her?' By *anybody*, she meant anybody six feet tall and burly.

'No. It's just her.' Watching the agent stagger across the lawn, her high heels sinking into the grass, I cupped my hand over the phone and added, 'She could probably poke someone's eye out with those stilettos, though.'

Holly chuckled. 'You're out of there by dark.'

'Yes, Mother.'

Holly gave the word an indignant cough. We both knew I could be on the south side of Chicago and my mother wouldn't be calling to make sure I was all right. 'Don't insult me, but I mean it. By dark, okay?'

'I'm forty-nine years old, Holl. I can handle this.'

Holly sighed. 'Call me when you're done?'

'All right. I'd better go now.' The real estate agent, Andrea, was already beginning to move around the house with her notepad. I tucked the phone into my pocket and joined her on the tour.

My mind filled with memories as I considered the reduction of family history to meaningless tick marks on a real estate disclosure sheet.

Tick . . . torn screen in the bottom left corner of the bay window. Poppy's spinster sister, Great-Aunt Neva, lived in that room, years ago. Her lanky gray cat came and went through the tear in the screen. We all pretended we couldn't see it. I was never sure why.

Tick . . . loose floorboard on the porch, just left of the door. Jalicia, a little girl from two streets over, and I played dolls under there. The loose board was our periscope hole. We watched for signs of my mother, or Maryanne. If a car rolled up, we'd slip out the side beneath the oleander bush and run around back to part ways. Mother didn't approve of my playing with a *black child*. Sooner or later, I would begin to pick up the dialect, and then where would we be? Being freckle-faced and cursed with my father's curly, flyaway strawberry blond hair, I had enough drawbacks already. Maryanne, who had been blessed by my mother's first

8

husband with normal hair and no freckles, added that Jalicia knew way too much for a nine-year-old – about sex, in particular. Mother hated that the streets at the base of Blue Sky Hill were *going mixed*. There was a time in Dallas, she said, when people stayed with their own sort, even in the working-class neighborhoods.

Mother spoke the words 'working-class neighborhood' as if she hadn't come from one, as if she hadn't grown up just down the block in my grandparents' house, where the yard was always scrappy with unmowed weeds and the holly bushes covered the windows like shrouds. If not for her fortuitous third marriage to my stepfather, she would probably still have been living in the shadow of Blue Sky Hill.

Tick . . . dent in the iron portico post, where Aunt Ruth backed the car into it when she learned to drive, after Poppy's heart attack.

Tick . . . a crumbling rock foundation in the backyard . . .

'What in the world is this?' Andrea asked, studying the square of vegetation that grew around the old foundation.

'There was a summer kitchen, back before the place had air-conditioning. They did their cooking out here, so as not to heat up the house. After they tore the building down, Aunt Ruth planted flower beds around the foundation.' Surveying the rectangle of sandstone peeking from beneath a tangle of hollyhocks and honeysuckle vines, I smiled at a memory. The hollyhocks were already taking over, forming the green walls of a living room. On long summer days, Jalicia and I had created dolls from the hollyhock blooms, turning them upside down, then adding buds for heads and

9

rose petals or dwarf mums for hats. A miniature cancan of hollyhock dancers performed summer shows atop the back fence, where in the old days Aunt Ruth had fed tramps off the train. The wanderers had scratched a symbol on the gatepost, a house blessing of sorts, a sign for the lost that this was a friendly place.

Aunt Ruth told stories about those traveling men, struggling to find their way home from the war. She said if you looked hard enough you could still see the house blessing, even years after the train had stopped running, and the men were gone, and the post had been painted over.

Jalicia and I sometimes stared at the fence, imagining we could see the carving there. We tried to decide what the symbol for a friendly place would look like. Maybe a peace sign, like the ones the hippies wore, with a smiley face in it.

Did the lost men of yesterday need a friendly place as much as Jalicia and I did?

Andrea tapped her pencil against the clipboard, frowning. 'I guess we could call it a raised garden,' she mused, and then we moved on, the remains of the summer kitchen now a sales point.

Filling out the rest of the disclosure sheet didn't take long. Andrea was fast and efficient, no time for sentiment. She wasn't certain developers would be interested in the house, particularly with everything else on the street still privately owned, but she had sold some properties a few blocks away to a development company, so a speculative buy was a possibility.

'Developers take places as is, which makes things easier,'

she commented as we stood in the kitchen, marking off leaky pipes and flickering light fixtures.

'That's good,' I said, studying the doughnut of fingerprints on the cabinet where Aunt Ruth kept kiddie cups acquired long ago in boxes of Trix, Bisquick, and Tide. An antiques dealer had bought the cups at the estate sale, the gleam of a tidy profit in his eye. I wished the cups had gone to someone who would use them.

Squinting at the fingerprints, I wondered if some of them were Aunt Ruth's, or Poppy's, or Christopher's . . . or Jake's. I felt sick all over again. I didn't want someone else to wash away the traces.

'Those could use a coat of paint,' Andrea observed when she noticed me looking at the cabinets. 'But people shopping in this price range don't expect much.'

I contemplated the idea that painting the cabinets would be preferable to washing them. Sealed between coats, the fingerprints would remain forever. It was an odd thought, considering we'd just been speculating that the house might be torn down for development.

'I think I'll get some paint and do that tomorrow,' I heard myself say. The words seemed to come from outside, as if I were in the box seats at a theater, hearing them being spoken onstage.

Even Andrea seemed skeptical. She made a note on her pad, and we started toward the door. Before stepping out, she eyed the darkened street. 'I'll come back tomorrow and put out a sign,' she said, then hurried to her car and got in. She waited until I'd locked the burglar bars on the front door and made it to my car before she backed out and wheeled away.

Looking at Poppy's place in the glare of the headlights, I felt regret settling over me like a wool blanket, itchy and uncomfortable, not right for the season. Everything in me wanted to go back – two years, ten, twelve. I could be that young mother again, driving to Poppy's house with the boys strapped in the back, the two of them fighting about who touched whom, while I threatened that, if they didn't straighten up, I'd turn the car around and we'd go home instead of visiting Aunt Ruth and Uncle Poppy.

I never did, of course. Jake and Christopher knew I wouldn't.

Closing my eyes for a moment, I tried to imagine myself back in time, tried to replace the wool blanket with a new suit of clothes and make it a reality. I could almost hear the boys in the backseat . . .

A car alarm sounded nearby, and my game of imagination popped like a balloon. I called Holly to tell her I was headed home. She didn't pick up, so I left a message, then drove away, feeling strangely numb, disconnected like a ghost not really in this world or any other.

Around the corner, the boys who'd passed Poppy's house earlier were bouncing a basketball against the side of a crumbling one-story building that housed income-assisted apartments. A teenage girl with a long blonde ponytail stepped from the end apartment and hollered at them as I waited for the car ahead of me to make a left turn into a deserted strip mall.

A police car passed in the right lane, slowed as the officer surveyed the activity. The girl on the porch and the boys froze in place, their postures deliberately casual. As the cruiser disappeared down the street, the boys picked up their basketball and moved on.

CHAPTER 2

Cass

The next time those stupid gangbanger wannabes came and threw basketballs against our wall, I was gonna do more than just go out and holler at them. I was gonna flag down the police myself.

I really was. I didn't care how much trouble it started.

A siren went off somewhere down the street, and then a car alarm in the other direction. The siren faded off, but the car alarm kept going and going. I went back inside, sat down on the sofa, closed my eyes, and tried not to hear it.

Some lady told me once that when you don't like where you are, you could close your eyes and think of the place you'd rather be – even if you've never been there and had just seen it in a movie or a magazine. If you believed it enough, she said, it'd be just like you were there. A *mind trip*, she called it. She was living in some two-trailer-park oil-field town in West Texas and working in a Waffle Shop that smelled like cow poop, so I figured she had to be on some kind of trip, just to get by.

She was nice enough, though. She showed me that if you

sat behind the hotel next door, up top of the electric box, you could look over the fence and watch the drive-in movie for free. When she was my age, she used to do it. Most of the time the wind was blowing enough you couldn't hear it, but after a while you got good at reading lips and making stuff up. I could always make stuff up like nobody's business, which is important when you're like Rusty and me. When you show up at a place too many days in a row, people ask questions, and you've gotta have an idea what to tell them so they don't start thinking they oughta call somebody official.

I don't know why people need to stick their noses in – like just because you're young means you're stupid and can't take care of yourself. The lady in the Waffle Shop was okay, but after a while she got all motherly and started poking into our business, and I had to quit going there. But before that, she'd bought me lots of French toast, so that was cool. I liked the mind trip thing, too. I used it sometimes, when we landed in places that, basically, stunk.

In my mind place, there's a field so long you can't see across it, and I'm on a white horse, just running and running, like that song 'Wildfire.' When we were in the truck and that song came on the CD, I'd turn it up loud and close my eyes, to see if I could find anything else to add to my mind place. I added the moon and the hoot owl, but I left out the early snow, because I don't really like the cold. We stayed two whole months in Fargo when Rusty got work at a feedlot, and it stunk big-time, because it snowed like crazy and the wind blew ninety miles an hour, like, all day

15

long. Rusty was gone short-hauling cattle, and I was stuck in a dumpy apartment over some lady's garage.

The lady was old and almost blind. If you weren't standing right in front of her she could hardly see you. So the good thing was she really believed I was seventeen instead of twelve, and Rusty was twenty-two, and there wasn't any problem with my brother and me being out on our own. Rusty told her some story about our parents dying in a plane crash, and she felt real sorry for us, after that. She wouldn't even take the rent when Rusty finally got it together. She just pushed it back in his hand, and folded her fingers around his, and said, 'You save that for a rainy day, young man.'

Too bad it turned rainy about two weeks later, when Mr Henry down at the feedlot got a fax from his insurance company, telling him Rusty was seventeen. The ID Rusty'd used when he got the job was fake, but Rusty had figured since it fooled Mr Henry in the job interview, we were home free. He'd unpacked his stuff in the apartment and everything. He liked Mr Henry's niece, who worked the desk at the feedlot. The funny thing was, since she was sixteen, Mr Henry thought Rusty was too old for her, and then, when he wasn't too old anymore, we had to grab our stuff and go. Mr Henry'd had a long talk with Rusty in his office. He wanted to know what kind of *trouble* Rusty was in. I'm still not sure how much he got Rusty to admit, but the only reason he let Rusty out of the office was because Rusty'd promised to go pick me up, so we could all drive to the sheriff's office together and get help.

Rusty and me were out of the blind lady's apartment quicker than you can say grab the cookie jar, and that was the end of the cold country. We headed for Texas, which was where we'd started out to go anyway. The one person who could help us was there. Somewhere.

The bad thing is that Texas is a big state, and it's not so easy finding one single person, especially when you're not sure about the name, or where to look, and you've got to make a living along the way. Rusty decided we shouldn't stay in another small town. In a small town, everybody's in your business. You can't just move in and find a job and get a place to live without everybody noticing. In a big city like Dallas, Rusty said, nobody'd know us from Adam.

He was pretty much right, but at least in Fargo we didn't have gangbanger wannabes throwing a basketball against our wall, and three little brats next door, whose mom locked them out on the steps whenever she got tired of looking at them, or when she wanted to have a man over, which was a lot. It didn't matter how much those kids whined out there, or banged on the door, or whatever. If she was busy inside, she was busy. She turned up her stupid rap music to where it'd block out the noise. Too bad that didn't stop everyone else from hearing it.

Dallas was too loud all the time. I couldn't get to a mind place, even when I tried really hard. After two weeks in the apartment, I was ready to call Child Protective Services. They could pick up those kids next door, and the gangbanger wannabes who stole the spare tire out of Rusty's truck and then spray-painted stuff all over the tailgate.

Rusty had to spend thirty bucks – which we needed for groceries – on spray paint and a used spare, so he could get to work down at the construction site a few miles away. After that, he started leaving the truck parked down at Wal-Mart, where there was security. I talked him out of killing the stupid gangbangers, and they got away with it, since we couldn't call the police on them. I thought about calling CPS, since the wannabes weren't much older than me, but I figured they might tip off CPS that the disabled mom who supposedly lived with us didn't really exist. She was just an ID number the guy who ran the place used so he could rent to Rusty and me and still get his kickback from welfare.

I gave up trying to get to a mind place and went to the kitchen. The noisy clock on the wall said it'd be a little while yet until Rusty came home. Good thing today was payday, because there was nothing left in the kitchen but some soda crackers, a tub of butter, some ketchup, mustard, a couple tortillas Rusty got leftover from someone's lunch at work, and a half bottle of flat Sprite. I ate one of the tortillas and left one, in case Rusty wanted it later, but he'd probably stop off for happy hour with the guys from the construction site. He usually did on Friday. He said it kept him in good with the rest of the bunch, which mattered, since we didn't want anybody asking questions.

I sat down with my book and figured that if my brother didn't make it home pretty soon I'd eat the other tortilla with some butter and sugar on it. He wouldn't want it by then, and we'd probably go to Wal-Mart tonight anyway.

While we were out, maybe I could trade in my book and get another one at the Book Basket, if the store was open late tonight.

In Fargo, the blind lady's apartment had a TV in it, but in Dallas TVs cost extra – a lot. Reading's not bad, though. You could take a book anyplace you ended up. A TV doesn't fit in your suitcase so good.

The woman next door was hollering at some guy and banging on the wall. It sounded like they were playing racquetball in there, but that probably wasn't what was going on. Gross. Rusty said that woman was so big she came out the door in two different time zones, and he was pretty much right.

I took my book to my bedroom, laid down, and pushed the pillow up around my ears, then opened the pages and worked on taking a mind trip. I was reading an old story about Seabiscuit, the racehorse. I always liked old books the best – like Nancy Drew, and Sam Savitt's horse stories, Walter Farley, and Marguerite Henry's *Misty of Chincoteague*. My mama and I used to read those books together, back when I was little and really believed that someone was gonna tie up a pony out in front of our house, with a big old bow on it, while I was gone to school. Every day, when the bus started around the last corner, I'd close my eyes and hope so hard it hurt, then open up and look. Every time I was bummed when there was nothing but Rusty's stupid dog chained up in the yard.

I don't know what makes somebody keep dreaming for something over and over when it ends up hurting in the

19

end. Mama used to say you can't stop dreaming just because you're afraid the dream won't come true. She said a dream's biggest enemy is being afraid. *If the mountain's big, you gotta dream bigger, Cass Sally Blue*, she told me. *Nothing's impossible if you've got enough faith. You remember that.* She might of got that from the Bible, but after a while I figured out that some kids are gonna get ponies, and some kids aren't, and whether or not you get one doesn't have anything to do with how much you wish for it. You're either born into the pony-getting crowd or you're not.

Mama probably liked the old-style books because they made it seem like life was a little more rosy than that. Those stories from way back even had the bad stuff cleaned up to where it didn't seem so real, and besides, I'd read those books with Mama, so when I laid down with them, it seemed like she was right there in bed next to me. I could still hear her voice saying the lines, her chest moving up and down under my ear, breath going in and out. She wheezed, kind of. Every once in a while her body would go stiff for a second, and she'd catch a real quick gulp of air, and I'd know she had a pain. She never said much about it, though. She'd just go on reading after it passed.

About the time I started hearing Mama's voice in my book and feeling her beside me, the baby next door got to crying. No one did anything about it. If my mama *had* been there, she'd of gone over and knocked that lady into next Tuesday. Mama was pretty quiet, and mostly she minded her own business, but she could get riled sometimes. The kids hollering on the steps and the baby crying while its mom carried on with a man would have riled her. I sure wished Mama could of been there to give that lady what for. It stinks that some kids get crappy moms who live forever, and some kids get moms who get sick and die, while they're trying to do the best they can.

I'd of gone over there to give that lady what for myself, but Rusty would of killed me. He had a heck of a time finding a place we could afford in Dallas. We didn't need any trouble here.

I wished Rusty would come on home. I hated it when he stayed out after work. As soon as the lights were on inside the apartment, it seemed dark and weird outside, like someone might be peeking around the edges where the mini blinds were too small. I didn't like being by myself.

When Rusty was gone late, I always started to think, *What if he doesn't come back?* What if he got mugged, or had a car wreck, or just decided he was sick of all this mess and left? What would I do then? How long would I sit here and wait? Where would I go, whenever I finally decided to leave?

I hated it when those questions took over my mind, so I read Seabiscuit instead. I liked the story. When Seabiscuit was a colt, he was skinny and knobby-legged. He was plain-looking – ugly, really – and he didn't run worth a flip, even though he was what the horse racers call a *blueblood*. Nobody looked at him and figured he'd amount to anything.

I could totally relate to Seabiscuit. Even though my daddy ended up in prison, so that probably didn't rank me as a blueblood, we had the rest in common. I don't think anybody ever looked at me and was too impressed, either.

People always liked my hair, because it was blonde and thick, and every once in a while someone said I had pretty blue eyes, but it was kind of like they just picked out one thing to be nice, because altogether the package wasn't so hot.

Every once in a while Rusty felt sorry for me and told me when he was a kid, he didn't look like much, either. The problem was that Rusty still wasn't too hot, if you asked me. He looked like a man-sized body with a little kid's head on top, but maybe that was because I always knew him since he was a kid. Mama said Rusty looked just like his daddy, Ray John, and Ray John was sure enough handsome.

At least my daddy didn't have red hair and freckles. Things could of been worse . . .

I was falling asleep on the lumpy sofa by the time Rusty knocked on the door. The lady'd let her kids in and got them quiet finally, and the Mexican dudes were drinking beer and playing mariachi music down in the corner of the driveway. I didn't think they meant to bother anybody. They were just loud. Most of the time they had their wives and about a million kids running around down there while they partied. As far as I could tell, there were about eighty-seven of them living in two apartments. Whatever they cooked always smelled really good, though.

I heard them hollering at Rusty, 'Hey, you wan-ee beer, amigo?'

Rusty didn't answer. He just knocked on the door again and said, 'Open up, Cass.' There was only one key to the apartment, and the stinky guy who lived in the manager's office across the parking lot, wouldn't give us another one.

I always kept the key during the day, and that way I could lock up if I went places.

I looked at the squeaky clock while I walked to the door. After midnight. Geez. Rusty was gonna be tired getting up for work tomorrow. Dope.

When I opened up, someone was with Rusty on the steps. Whoever it was tripped on the way in and just about knocked me over with something she was carrying. She stopped a few steps past me, then turned partway and looked for Rusty out the corner of her eye. She was pretty – tall and curvy, with jeans that fit good. Her skin was a soft caramel color. Her hair hung in a million long spirals down her back. It was blonde, but no girl with that color skin has blonde hair naturally.

There were little wrinkles around the corners of her eyes, *crow's-feet* my mama called them, and a tiny line that circled the side of her mouth. She wasn't as young as her body made her seem. She had on lots of makeup, thick eyeliner drawn out to the sides in a greenish color that matched her eyes, like one of those belly dancers in the *Ten Commandments* movie that's on TV at Easter.

She turned a little more, her look scampering around the room like a rabbit hunting a place to hide. She had a big fat black eye and a cut on the side of her nose that was swelled up.

The waffle lady in the oil patch town looked like that once. When I asked her what happened, she said she slipped in the bathtub and hit the faucet.

Yeah, right.

23

Rusty leaned out the door and checked the parking lot like he was watching out for someone, then he came in, did the lock, and walked right past me like I wasn't there. He stopped beside the girl and pointed across to my bedroom. 'Just put him back there in Cass's room. That door, on the left,' he said. She hesitated, shifted something under a jacket in her arms, and Rusty put his hand on her back and sort of pushed her along until she got to the opening.

She went in *my* room and shut the door, like she owned the place.

'What the . . . heck?' I said. 'Who's she?'

Rusty shrugged, watched the door a minute, then tossed his tool belt on the table in the kitchen. After the first one got stolen and he had to pay for it, he never left his work stuff in the truck anymore.

'She's gonna stay here,' he said, like that counted for an explanation. 'They can sleep in your room.'

'They who?' Rusty was such a butthead sometimes. Leave it to him to give my room away to some girl he picked up at the bar.

'She's got a little kid.' He moved to the sink and poured himself a glass of water. He swayed a little on his feet when he tipped his head back to drink it. 'I can't remember what she said its name is.'

I stood looking at Rusty with my mouth open. 'She just put her *kid* in my room? Where the heck am I supposed to sleep?'

'You can sleep in with me.'

'I'm not sleepin' in with you. Yuck.' Actually, I figured

Rusty would want to leave that spot open for the girl. 'I'm not a little kid anymore, stupid.'

Rusty let his head fall forward and rubbed his eyes. 'Sleep on the couch, then, Cass,' he said, like he didn't care if I hung from the light fixture so long as I wasn't in his way.

I got a sick feeling in my stomach, and it seemed like I was shrinking. What if Rusty got himself a little family all of a sudden, and decided I could go jump in a lake? Crossing my arms over my middle, I squeezed hard to make the hurt go away. I felt empty down deep, but it didn't have anything to do with the tortillas and crackers wearing off. 'She's way too old for you, you know. What's she, like, thirty or something?'

Rusty set the glass down hard, so that it smacked the counter. 'Knock it off, Cass,' he said, and started for the bathroom. 'Tomorrow we'll get one of those blow-up mats, maybe.'

Tomorrow? I thought. *She's gonna be here tomorrow?*

But there wasn't any point saying it. Rusty was already in the bathroom, shutting the door and then turning on the water.

I went to the kitchen, and washed the glass, and put it away where it belonged.

CHAPTER 3

Sandra Kaye

Our home in Plano sat silent and dark, as was usual lately. The days when it had hummed with life seemed both a short time ago and a long time – something I'd dreamed before suddenly awakening in this place where no one came home until they had to. I had stopped at Target and the grocery store after making the trip across town from Poppy's. I'd bought groceries we probably wouldn't use, just to occupy time I didn't want.

Maybe Maryanne and Mother were right about selling Poppy's house. Maybe without the utility bills, estate sale, keeping the lawn mowed, and sorting through family photos and other mementos Aunt Ruth had carefully placed in boxes in the hall closet, we could all move on and accept the fact that what had happened to Poppy had just . . . happened. As horrible as it was, as hard as it was to accept, as much as each of us wanted to change the decisions that led to that day, we couldn't. I couldn't go back and force Poppy to give up the house he'd built and move out of the neighborhood. Rob couldn't go back and find the time to put

Poppy's social security check on auto deposit. Christopher couldn't go back and visit Poppy more often, and Jake couldn't drive over to Poppy's house from SMU to watch Sports Center on TV. Normally on Friday, Jake and Poppy would have gone to the bank and the store together, and Poppy wouldn't have been in the wrong place at the wrong time, alone, while Jake partied with his friends at the fraternity house.

What do you say to a child when a seemingly harmless decision has terrible consequences? What does he say to himself? I wished I knew. I wished I could return to the days after Poppy's death and handle the situation more skillfully, become a rock on which the whole family could stand, rather than a confused, helpless bystander struggling to absorb the sudden impact, trying to answer the endless questions of the police detectives and news reporters, trying to will Poppy back to consciousness in the hospital, trying to decide who to blame.

In a way, I could understand why Jake had run away to search for birth parents he'd never known. Somewhere in Guatemala he was looking for a family that didn't have so much pain in it. At the same time I was angry with him for leaving and adding to our burden.

As the garage door closed, the utility lights came on, providing an electronic welcome home. I entered the house, flipped the light switch in the hallway, walked past the family pictures of basketball and soccer teams, marching band competitions, vacations to Disney World, cruises to Mexico, and ski holidays where the four of us stood bundled in colorful coats, smiling for the camera, the perfect family sharing the perfect getaway. The parents in those pictures had convinced themselves that if they packed all the right suitcases, made all the right reservations, life would progress like a carefully planned holiday, reaching the milestones at all the right times, always safe and under control. The car would never drift off the pavement, or hit an unexpected hazard, or spin into dangerous territory. Now, everything was so far off course I couldn't even imagine what we'd been thinking.

Glare blotted out the last of the photos as I turned on the kitchen lights and the TV in the media room, so that if Holly looked out she'd know I was home. Across the street, her place was lit up like a Vegas casino, every square inch of the six-bedroom brick house filled with the activities of a gaggle of semi-adult children who had never fully left the nest, and Holly's last two officially 'at home' kids, sixteen-year-old twins, Jessica and Jacey. Holly liked to joke that at the rate she was going, the nest would never be empty. *Be careful what you wish for,* I thought, but I never said it because of the awkward moment that would follow.

I checked the answering machine for messages. I'd made my weekly call to the Dallas Police Department that morning to check on Poppy's case. As usual, there was no return call. After only six months, it didn't seem that they should be letting the case go cold, but I knew they were – not because they didn't care, but because their resources were tied up with investigations that looked more promising. It's hard to solve a crime when the only witness is a woman

28

passing by in her car at forty miles an hour, a hundred feet away. Two males in hooded sweatshirts. She thought they were young – maybe teenagers. One of them had struggled with Poppy, and he fell . . .

I stopped before the scene could play out in my mind again. Bobo scratched at the patio door, pressed his nose to the glass, and wagged his tail as I walked into the media room. He whined softly, tipping his head to one side, nudged his Frisbee, then gave me a pleading look through the half-black, half-white face that had inspired Jake to name him. *Bobo,* for silly or foolish, like a clown. Jake had been studying Spanish in school the year Poppy surprised the boys with the border collie puppy on Christmas Eve. *Every boy oughta have a dog once in his life,* Poppy had said. *Good dog'll get a boy through a tough spot quicker than all this therapy they do on TV nowadays.* He had looked at Jake when he said it. Perhaps he knew that, as a teenager, Jake was beginning to struggle with the facts of his adoption.

Poppy had prevailed in the argument about the dog, even though Rob had protested that we didn't have time for a pet. There was never any saying no to Uncle Poppy, and for the most part Rob knew better than to try. If we said something Poppy didn't agree with, he pretended his hearing aid batteries were dead. On Christmas Day, Rob scoured available stores for batteries and bought Poppy an entire box, wrapped up as a joke. Rob laughed and said he wanted the hearing aid fixed before Poppy showed up with a pony. By then, Bobo was a fixture in Jake's lap, and we all knew the puppy wasn't going anywhere. The puppy grew into a dog that ate everything from pool floats to extension cords, but it didn't matter because Jake loved him so.

Now Bobo was a sad reminder of Jake's absence. Outside the window, he picked up his Frisbee, dropped it off the steps, and watched it clatter to a stop, as if he were trying to figure out why it wouldn't fly anymore.

After turning down the TV, I stretched out on the sofa, so that I'd hear Christopher and Rob if they came in. When I woke up, the garage door was grinding downward. Christopher passed by in the hall, his backpack slung over one shoulder.

'Hey,' I said, my voice scratchy.

Christopher froze midstride, his body stiff and reluctant. Lately, if he could get away with it, he went straight to his room and shut the door. These days we were all in some way toxic to each other, without meaning to be. The sadness in each of us was so palpable that there was no way to be together without seeing it, sensing it, tasting its bitterness.

'Hey.' Christopher gave a weary little smile that conveyed no bit of the gregarious high school junior who, not so long ago, had been telling knock-knock jokes and doing stand-up comedy in our living room.

'Did Dad come in?' I asked, mostly for Chris's benefit. I knew Rob would probably crash at the hospital, then get up, wash and change in his office, and go back to work. He seldom came home two nights in a row anymore. It was easier for him to remain at the hospital, entrenched in problems that could be managed. There was no managing Poppy's death and Jake's disappearance, no easy recovery plan that could be written out and carefully followed. There was only a nebulous grief that moved through the house like fog.

'Uh-uh.' Christopher shook his head, wisps of blond hair falling over his eyes. 'Want me to turn on the alarm before I go up?' His lanky body twisted as he looked over his shoulder toward the coat closet. Six months ago, it would never have occurred to him to wonder whether the alarm was on or off, because he knew his dad or Jake would handle it.

'In a minute,' I said, standing up and crossing the room to the doorway. His hazel eyes flicked away, as if he wanted to be somewhere else. 'Did you have a good study night?' Lately, it seemed as if Christopher's life was one constant homework session. His course load this semester had him cracking the books at all hours.

'Yeah.' He sighed, stretching his neck. 'Semester physics final cram.' His lip curled with just a hint of the Christopher who hated math and all things related. Music, art, literature, and a host of sports had always been more his thing. This semester, he'd switched tracks and begun working hard to get the background that would be needed for premed.

'Tough stuff,' I sympathized. Christopher came by his math aversion naturally.

'Yeah.'

'Wish I could offer to help you with that.' I felt a sudden yearning for all the times I'd sat on Christopher's bed, repeating spelling words and review questions for tests. Jake had always been an independent student, but Christopher required extra attention.

He hiked his backpack higher on his shoulder. 'I got it. It's just hard finding someone who can explain it so it makes sense.'

A flash of thought moved between us so quickly neither of us could stop it, so clearly it might as well have been spoken out loud. *If Jake were here, he could help.*

The unspoken reality made us step apart and look away.

'I'm gonna go on up to bed. I'll hit the alarm,' Christopher said, and I nodded, then swallowed the emotions in my throat.

'All right, sweetheart. Love you.'

'Love you too, Mom.'

I turned off the TV, then followed Christopher upstairs and took a sleep aid I'd gotten from the health food store, even though using it made me feel like a failure. Growing up in a house with my mother would have made anyone leery of both pills and alcohol. The herbal stuff seemed harmless enough, though, and it put me to sleep. Most nights I dreamed of Jake. He was always standing in the upstairs hall, near his bedroom door. I'd move slowly toward him, saying, 'You're home. You're safe. Thank God.'

In the dream, he nodded, his dark hair falling over the twinkling brown eyes I'd loved since the moment a Guatemalan nun had led him into a little room, stood him in front of us, and introduced us as *su nueva madre y el padre.* It was hard to tell if Jake understood or not, but he looked up at the nun and nodded, his face very serious, very wise for a three-year-old. She put his hand in mine and he stood very still. Later, he would tell me that he thought I was going to take him to the mother he remembered. When we went to the airport and got on the plane, he thought she must be a long way away, maybe living in the sky in heaven, and that was where we were going.

I fell asleep thinking of Jake and wondering where he was now, and why, six months after he'd abandoned his car at the airport and bought a ticket to Guatemala, he still hadn't called home. I prayed halfheartedly as I drifted off that tonight would be the night the phone would ring and wake me up, and it would be him. But after six months of silence, I knew better than to set expectations. A prayer that went unanswered yesterday, and the day before, and the day before that doesn't find much hope today, either.

In the morning, when I awoke, for just an instant I thought Jake was down the hall in his room, and then I came to reality. I considered staying in bed. *Sure, be just like Mother,* a voice whispered inside me. *Lie here and medicate yourself until you don't know what day it is.* As always, just the thought was enough to pull me upright, out of bed, and into the bathroom to get dressed. All of my life, there had been the underlying fear that one step down the slippery slope of substance abuse could land me in the pit of dependency and denial that had swallowed almost every member of my family. When I was growing up, Uncle Poppy and Aunt Ruth were the only normal relatives I knew. They were the reason I understood that what my family silently deemed as acceptable wasn't acceptable at all.

Downstairs, there was no sign that Rob had come and gone, and Christopher had left early again.

33

I contemplated the day as, across the street, Holly and her twins climbed into the van and headed off to school. So far, neither of the twins had shown any interest in getting drivers' licenses, and Holly wasn't pushing it. She called from her cell phone as she was threading her way through Plano traffic. Holly was always multitasking.

I told her about the meeting with the real estate agent.

'Want to grab a Starbucks this morning?' she offered.

The cabinets at Poppy's house flashed through my mind. 'I think I'm going to hang out here and climb Mount Laundry.'

'Yuck. Starbucks is better.'

'I know,' I agreed, and even as I said good-bye, I couldn't put a finger on the reason I'd lied. Holly would have willingly dropped her plans and gone with me to help paint, or act as bodyguard and baby-sitter, but I wanted to spend a last day at Poppy's house by myself. I wasn't sure why.

The question perplexed me as I cleaned the kitchen, then gathered some paintbrushes and a can of off-white semi-gloss left over from Chris's one-act play project at school. Tucking them into the trunk like contraband, I checked for signs of life at Holly's house before backing out and heading down the street.

Guilt trailed me as I drove across town. If Holly found out where I was, she'd be hurt. She would think I was taking a step backward, doing what I'd done in the first few months after Jake left – sneaking off by myself so I could drive to the SMU campus and sit on the bench across from his fraternity house. Sometimes I'd stay there for hours watching the kids come and go, halfway believing that if I waited long enough, Jake would be one of them. He'd be back in premed, studying calculus or designing rockets in his head as he walked home from class. Watching all the other kids come and go, I'd be filled with the bitter heat of envy. Their parents could pick them up for lunch anytime they wanted.

I hadn't gone to the campus to sit for three months now. Not since Holly found out about it. Having to admit what I was doing made it seem pathological and pointless. The last thing Rob or Christopher or even Holly needed was to worry that I was going off the edge. I stopped driving to the campus and filled my time stuffing envelopes and answering phones for the organ donor network, checking in with the police, and finally taking care of cleaning out and selling Poppy's house for Mother, who, thank God, remained entrenched in Seattle with Maryanne, where the two of them could share Valium and wine chasers while comparing symptoms of illnesses, real and imagined.

If anyone found out I was painting the cabinets at Poppy's house, that's the excuse I'd give. I was just filling time so as to keep from ending up like Mother and Maryanne. Poppy's house needed work, and who knew if the next residents would be able to afford renovations.

Turning the corner onto Red Bird Lane, I noticed that Andrea had put up the real estate sign. It leaned to one side, Andrea's name swinging forlornly off the bottom. The neighborhood was silent, the kids probably off to their last few days of school before summer break, the older residents locked in their homes behind burglar bars and dilapidated chain-link fences. I remembered when the neighborhood was filled with activity – children on bicycles, mothers pushing baby strollers to the little park across the creek from Poppy's house, men mowing lawns, grandmothers and grandfathers sitting on porch rockers, waving as people drove by. Now the street was cloaked in stillness, the cracked sidewalks seamed with spires of grass, the windows opaque with cardboard and aluminum foil, porches only places to dump the rotting carcasses of old furniture.

Painting the cabinets in Poppy's house was probably pointless, truth be told. The people who moved in here most likely wouldn't care.

A lump rose in my throat, and I swallowed hard. Poppy loved this home, where he'd built a life with Aunt Ruth. He would have wanted it to go to a new owner looking as it had back when he and Aunt Ruth had the showplace of their little street.

In all reality, I didn't have anything better to do than paint cabinets today anyway.

I took my supplies into the house, set them on the kitchen counter, and stood surveying the interior. The front parlor and the dining room lay soft and golden beyond the doors on either end of the kitchen, the wood floors warming in the languid morning light. The house looked larger with nothing in it, but even though the rooms were empty, they seemed full of the things that used to be there – Aunt Ruth's old upright piano, the umbrella stand with the lion head carved on top, the game table where we played Parcheesi, Scrabble, and Hand 'n Foot, the recliners where Aunt Ruth and Poppy sat watching the old console TV that was always turned up so loud your head rang with sound long after you left the house.

Every corner was filled with benevolent ghosts. On the walls, the shadows of pictures and furniture remained, baked in by the passage of years. *Those could use a coat of paint, too,* I mused, then laid out some newspaper and opened the partial gallon. Inside, yellow liquid and white pigment melted together in a strange swirl, the surface iridescent. I pushed in a stick and stirred it. Poppy would like that I was making use of leftovers. Having lived through the Depression era, he believed in waste not, want not. The garden shed outside was a testament to his thriftiness – so filled with old tools, pieces of lawn-mowers, bicycle parts, wheels, axles, chains, gardening supplies, and other bits of memorabilia that we had given up trying to clean it out for the estate sale, and just locked the door.

My reconstituted paint looked usable after a few minutes of stirring, but the paintbrush I'd brought from home was impossibly stiff. One of the boys had probably employed it for a science fair project and then failed to properly wash it out. Clumps of bristles sealed together left a streaky white mess across the newspaper when I tested it.

I considered going out to the garden shed for another, but then decided it would be easier to run to the store. And probably safer. No telling what was living in Poppy's shed by now.

I locked up the house and the burglar bars, then drove past Blue Sky Hill to the corner where a Supercenter had been erected to serve the needs of the area's new residents. It was only a few blocks away, but the glimmering commercial corner with its clothing shops, upscale restaurants, and parking lots full of new cars seemed miles from Poppy's street.

In the hardware department, I deliberated the issue of paintbrushes until finally a young clerk offered advice.

'What kind of existing surface are you trying to cover?' he asked, and I admitted that I had no idea whether the paint on the cabinets was oil or latex.

He laughed, and something in the sound reminded me of Jake. I felt a twinge, like an imbedded splinter that rubs at the most unexpected moments. The clerk had the look of a college boy. *He might be a student at SMU, like Jake.*

'I'll take one of each,' I said, and held out my basket for the three brushes we had under consideration. 'Thanks for the help.'

'Anytime,' he answered. 'Have a nice day.'

In the self-checkout line, I paid with cash like a cheating spouse, afraid her clandestine life might be discovered by a careless charge on the credit card. I justified it in my own mind as I threaded through the crowds to the door, then stepped into the sunlight.

'Excuse me,' someone said as I fished through my purse for my sunglasses before finding them on top of my head.

'Excuse me,' the woman's voice repeated, more loudly this time. 'Could someone give me a ride to my apartment?'

I didn't know who she was talking to, but it wasn't any of my business. Shifting my sack, I pulled out the car keys.

A van stopped to drop off passengers, and a young man pushed a long line of shopping carts past the door, temporarily hemming in the crowd.

'Excuse me,' the voice beckoned again. I glanced over my shoulder and saw a woman on the bench. Her legs were strangely bent, and two walking canes rested beside her. 'Could anyone give me a ride to my apartment? It's close by.'

I looked around. There were men in business suits, a teenager with colored hair and a tattoo, a grandmother with a baby in her arms, a young woman in a pretty floral dress, an old man in leisure clothes, a mother with a little boy in hand, a pair of teenaged girls, and others – more than a dozen people altogether, and not one of them heard but me.

The woman watched one passerby and then another as they skirted her bench and walked on, as if they could neither see nor hear her. The row of shopping carts moved away, and the crowd began to clear. I stood watching, oddly fascinated. The woman's thin hands, little more than skin over bone as they lay upon her flowered dress, made me think of Aunt Ruth.

'Could *you* give me a ride to my apartment?' Her eyes, a bright polished silver out of keeping with the weary, aged look of her face, met mine.

'I . . . ,' I stammered, caught off guard. At least a dozen warnings regarding crime schemes ran through my mind. 'I don't . . .'

'It isn't far.' Lifting her cane in the general direction of Poppy's place, she smiled, her brows rising expectantly, as if I'd already said yes. It occurred to me that if I didn't pick her up, someone else might, and the next person might not have good intentions.

I thought of Poppy. If only someone had stopped to help him as he struggled with his attackers, the day might have turned out so differently. 'Sure,' I said. 'Of course I will.'

Bracing her canes in front of herself, she nodded and pulled to her feet, smiling. I noted that she didn't have any packages, and an uneasy feeling crept over me again.

She seemed to read my mind. 'They have free senior coffee and doughnuts here on Thursdays.'

'Oh, that's nice.' I tried to imagine hitching rides with strangers just for a cup of coffee and a doughnut.

'Yes, it is,' she agreed, as we walked slowly to my car. 'A little treat makes a person feel special sometimes.'

It was a sad idea, depending on a store freebie to make you feel special. 'I imagine so.' As I helped her into my car, she patted my hand, and I was glad I hadn't left her on the bench.

'You're not from around here,' she observed as I backed out of the parking space, then sat waiting for a line of traffic. 'People who know the neighborhood zip around back and go through the Jiffy Lube parking lot. It's a right turn.'

'Ohhh,' I said. 'Thanks. I'll remember that.'

She asked where I lived, and when I told her Plano, she laughed. 'I remember when Plano was just a spot in the road. Back then we thought it was a long way out of Dallas. I taught there my first two years out of college, but then I got a job closer in.'

I glanced at her, surprise obvious on my face before I hid it. No doubt she saw the question there, too. How does a teacher with a college education end up begging for rides at Wal-Mart? My mind repainted the picture of her, and I imagined myself in her place, then I pushed away the idea like an itchy sweater.

A million years ago, I was going to be a teacher. I planned to be the one who recognized the children growing up with family secrets. I'd find the bruises, even the ones on the inside, and I wouldn't look the other way. I would be a confidante whom children could talk to, because I knew how the bruises felt. As an adult, I wouldn't be powerless to confront things that were wrong, and as a teacher, I'd be in a position to make a difference.

Instead, I met Rob, and getting married at twenty seemed so much easier than sticking out another three years, working at the hospital reception desk and going to school, trapped at home with my mother and my stepfather. Rob was my white knight, and somewhere between putting him through medical school, struggling through the crushing disappointment of three miscarriages, and finally navigating the challenges of an international adoption, our life together eclipsed everything else. I had a son to raise, and then, after a miracle pregnancy with Christopher, two sons. Rob's work was demanding. Someone had to be there to make a home and create a family that was healthy and happy. Jake and Christopher became the focus, but I'd never really considered that, in my efforts to give them everything that was missing from my childhood – the mom who

41

scrapbooked every milestone, who showed up at the school parties with homemade treats, who read bedtime stories, drove the carpools, lined the batters up in the baseball dug-out, and planned the huge birthday parties – I'd cast aside the dream I had for myself.

It didn't feel like a sacrifice. It felt like a mission. But now, despite such careful attention to detail, the mission had gone awry.

'I had to quit work after my car accident,' the woman said, and I focused on the conversation again. 'I wasn't up to it.'

'Oh.' I pretended to be busy looking for a gap in traffic, but I was thinking that I understood how it felt to lose the very thing you thought you did so well. In a way, I was as down and out as she was. 'I'm sorry.' Shifting in my seat, I turned away from her, anxious to drop her wherever she wanted.

'I loved the kids,' she offered. 'I missed them. That's been . . . oh . . . twenty years ago now. Doesn't seem like it, though.'

I gunned the car into a gap in traffic, because I didn't know what to say.

My passenger swayed in the seat, her hands catching the armrests. 'I don't think I'd want to be in the classroom these days. Kids aren't like they used to be,' she said, look-ing out the window. 'Back then, all you had to worry about was kids copying each other's homework, and an occasional Saturday night party when someone's parents weren't home. If you had any problems, most of them had folks you could go to. Now, they live rough lives around these neighborhoods, and half the time there's no telling where the parents are, or else they're more messed up than the kids.' She pointed ahead to the narrow driveway of the shabby stucco apartment complex I'd passed last night.

'Turn left up there,' she said.

In the daylight, I read the government housing sign in front of the apartments. I'd never once given them a second thought before last night, even though we were only a few blocks from Poppy's house. Once during the estate sale, I'd stopped for a soda at the mini-mart in the dilapidated strip mall across the street. The squat Pakistani man behind the counter was obliging enough, but the specially built cage around the register area and the group of men lingering in front made me uncomfortable. As we drove away, Holly pointed out that there was strange activity in that parking lot, all hours of the day. She surmised that, aside from possible drug deals and prostitution, it was a place where illegals hung out waiting for construction trucks to drive by with potential job offers. After that, we bought our sodas and filled up with gas on our own side of town.

Holly would have died of shock if she'd seen me calmly waiting to turn left into a place that looked even worse than the strip mall. The apartment complex seemed to belong in some third world country. I tried not to give an outward reaction as we bumped over the entranceway, and I drove between the buildings, pretending not to notice the piles of refuse lying windblown against the buildings. Foul words had been painted along the walls in bright colors. Three kids watched us from the front steps of one of the apartments, their mocha faces curious and slightly suspicious as we passed. I looked at them in the side mirror – a toddler wearing only underpants; a boy with sleek, thin limbs hanging loosely from an oversized T-shirt and a pair of shorts that were too large; and a girl who probably should have been in elementary school today. She stood twisting a braid around her finger, watching my car.

My passenger directed me to 9B. Behind us, the kids descended the steps and scampered toward the corner, the two older ones first, and the toddler following in a stubby, barefooted run.

Where in the world were they going?

'They wander around here all the time,' my passenger informed me, motioning to the kids as she opened the door and swung her legs around. 'Be careful when you back out.'

I put the car in Park, intending to help her, but she braced her canes and hauled herself from the seat before I could get there. After thanking me for the ride, she moved across the parking lot in a stiff, swinging gait, then disappeared into an apartment with lace-edged curtains that looked out of place against the clouded windows and weathered stucco.

Opening the driver's-side door, I checked the alley to make sure the children were out of the way. A young woman in tight flowered shorts, high heels, and a tank top came out of the end apartment. She balanced a laundry basket on her hip, her blonde hair swirling in the breeze as she teetered down the steps, the shoes not suited to the heavy load. She was thin, long-legged, and gangly, her body hardly seeming strong enough to carry the overflowing basket.

When she reached the bottom step, she looked over her shoulder and saw me watching. The wind lifted her hair, and in a freeze-frame of an instant I remembered her from the night before. Up close, it was obvious that she was much younger than the clothes made her seem. She looked like a contestant in some beauty pageant gone too far, a child dressed up in the trappings of a woman.

Lifting her chin, she leered at me silently, as if saying, *What's your problem, lady?* Then she tottered toward the street on her high heels, waited for the traffic to clear, and crossed to the strip mall parking lot, where the men whistled and catcalled as she passed the convenience store.

I stood watching, feeling sick to my stomach, thinking perhaps I should drive over, just to make sure she was all right, but she quickly disappeared behind the building, and the men returned their attention to the street. I climbed back into my car and scanned the rearview mirror, waiting for her to reappear. Finally I gave up and put the car in Reverse, letting it drift along the narrow pavement. Movement caught my attention as I passed the end of the building, and I hit the brake, looking around for the children. The smallest of the three was a few feet away, trying to shinny up the side of a Dumpster surrounded by a tumbledown fence. His dark hair caught the light, making a raven halo as he slipped and hit the concrete. Frustrated, he scrambled to his feet and kicked the Dumpster, ringing it like a metal drum.

What in the world . . .

The mother in me sounded a note of alarm and reacted.

Cutting the steering wheel, I bumped onto the curb, threw the car in Park, and got out. The little boy saw me and froze where he stood.

'You get out of there,' I scolded. 'This isn't a good place to play.' As I moved between him and the road, he withdrew, then sidled up to the apartment wall and stood with his back pressed against it.

A head popped out of the Dumpster, then vanished again. The toddler's wide dark eyes followed me as I walked to the edge and peered inside. In the narrow strip of light, the two older children were playing in the trash, their thin brown legs buried in offal as they tore open sacks and spread the contents around. A sickening smell assaulted me, and my stomach roiled. The myriad of potential dangers flashed through my mind – germs, rats, disease, broken bottles, used syringes. This was no place for children to play.

'You two get out of there.' My voice echoed into the Dumpster, and both children stopped moving at once. They turned to me, their hands rising from the trash bags, still gripping the contents, their faces moving from the shadow to the light. For an instant we stared at each other, motionless like figurines in a shoe-box diorama.

The toddler squealed and ran away, the sound of his footsteps disappearing around the corner of the building. 'You two kids come on out of there,' I repeated. 'Come on out, now. You shouldn't play there.' I tasted the odor of trash, and bile gurgled up my throat. Pressing a wrist to my lips, I backed away as the kids scrambled up the corner of the Dumpster. They exited on the other side and peered at me from behind the smelly metal box, like stray cats trapped in a corner, then bolted for the service alley, and disappeared. I walked back and forth, checking the alley and the parking lot, but wherever they'd gone, they weren't coming back. Even so, I sat in my car watching for a few minutes longer.

The rows of apartments remained silent, providing no clues, but as I turned my car around, then sat waiting for a gap in traffic, I had a feeling someone was watching.

CHAPTER 4

Cass

The lady couldn't see me, but I could see her. The Laundromat behind the convenience store had mirror tint on the windows, so if you didn't know better, you'd think it was just an old closed-down store. I saw the lady chase those kids out of the Dumpster. She looked for them after they ran off, which was weird, I thought. Maybe she was from welfare, or Child Protective Services, or someplace. That Cadillac SUV didn't look like social-worker wheels, but it could be. Maybe she was gonna pick up those kids and take them away. Their mama'd locked them out again, and they'd been banging on the door for, like, two hours, which was why I'd decided to go do the laundry, finally. Rusty'd stuck me sleeping on the sofa, so no matter how hard I tried to plug my ears, I could hear their noise the minute their mama shooed them out the door in the morning.

Before he left for work, Rusty didn't even say he was sorry for giving my room to some girl and her kid. He just dropped a little change on the counter, which meant he forgot to cash his check last night, which also meant that sometime today the big sweaty guy from the office would come tell me we hadn't paid the rent yet. He'd stand right in the doorway and give me a creepy look, like he thought I was gonna invite him in or something.

'Cass,' Rusty said after he put the change down, 'go do some laundry today, okay? I'm outa work clothes. Here's some money.' He kept his voice low, like we had the princess and the pea sleeping in the next room and we shouldn't bother her.

'Did you cash your check?' I knew the answer. If he'd cashed the check, he wouldn't be digging through his pockets for money.

'Nah, I'll do it today.'

'Rus-teee. The rent was due yesterday.' A lump came up in my throat, and I told myself I wasn't gonna cry, and I didn't.

Rusty opened the lock and then let in the smell of morning air, and pavement, and the sound of cars passing by.

'Wait.' I sat up, and got tangled in something, and I knew that during the night Rusty'd come out and wrapped me in one of the sleeping bags we used when we were on the road. 'Are you gonna get that girl out of my room?' Surely he wasn't planning to, like, just go off to work and leave some girl and her kid in my room.

The hinges squealed, and the slice of light from outside got thinner. 'Don't worry about it, Sal. Just let her sleep.' His voice was soft, like he felt a little bad for leaving me with his mess in *my* bedroom. Whenever he called me Sal, I felt warm inside. When I was born, Rusty wanted my name to be Sally, after some girl he liked on a cartoon. My daddy wanted Cass, and he won out, but Mama gave me Sally for the middle name. Sometimes I liked Sally better. Sally sounded like someone sweet and perfect, who wore dresses with lace, and little white shoes, and lived in a house with a painted fence.

'I gotta go. I'm late.' Rusty was out the door before I could say anything else.

I tried to go back to sleep, but once the kids next door were outside, you might as well be trying to sleep next to the hyena cage in a zoo. I sat there wondering when that girl was gonna come out of my room. Finally I decided to just go do the darned laundry. I washed my face and put on makeup, gathered up my dirty clothes from the bathroom floor and Rusty's from his room, then looked at myself in the mirror. Not bad. I could be sixteen, maybe seventeen, at least. If the girl woke up, I'd tell her that's what I was. She'd probably buy it, because I was tall enough. It helped to be tall. I didn't used to like it back in the fifth grade, when I got taller than all the boys, but Mama promised me I'd be glad one of these days. Turned out she was right. Like she always said, God's got a purpose for everything. He must of known I was gonna need to look sixteen pretty soon.

I piled the laundry in the basket and went out, and then there was the might-be-a-social-worker lady looking at me from her Cadillac SUV. The way she watched me was creepy – like she was staring right through me and could see everything. I squinted back at her, like as in, *Who do you think you are, anyway? Driving around in a fancy car – you think you're somebody?*

I hurried across the street and out of sight as fast as I could get there in the high-heeled shoes that used to be Mama's, which wasn't easy. The green sandals were still kind of big at the back, and my feet slid too far over the front, so I could feel little dots of hot pavement under my three middle toes.

The guys in the parking lot whistled and called me Blondie when I went by. They didn't care if the shoes were too big, or I wasn't so good at walking in them. They just wanted me to turn around and act like I noticed them. I thought about it, but then I was afraid to, so I didn't. I just walked on by like guys whistled at me every day. I didn't look back to see what the social-worker lady was doing – not even once – until I was behind the mirrored window in the Laundromat. Then I watched her chase the kids out of the Dumpster, look around for them, and finally drive off.

Once she was gone, I crammed all the laundry in one washer, so I could have some money left over to go to the convenience store for a pack of powdered doughnuts and a Coke. Rusty would probably come back at lunch with dollar burgers, or a Wendy's value meal. Sometimes he did that when it was payday, and we hadn't been to the grocery store and there was nothing left in the kitchen.

While I walked back to the convenience store, I watched the kids from next door head to the Dumpster again. They'd probably heard the mariachi music in the parking lot last night, and they figured there was something good in there to eat. Sometimes those Mexican guys got so drunk on Friday night that, along with the beer bottles, they threw away containers with tortillas, fried pies, rice, and beans still in them. The stuff looked pretty good, if you could get past where it came from. I'd watched the kids sit on the steps and eat it before. I warned them you could get sick eating out of the trash, but they didn't care. I told Rusty about it the next day, and he told me to stay out of the Dumpster. Duh. Like I would really crawl around in there and eat food that'd been sitting next to old diapers and beer bottles. Sometimes Rusty could be such a dope. It didn't bother him that the fat guy came to the door and hung around asking me for the rent, or that the money on the counter this morning wasn't enough for laundry and break-fast, *and* that he left some strange girl in my bedroom, but he did tell me not to eat out of the Dumpster.

The kids were finished looking for food by the time I got the laundry done, had my doughnuts, and went back to the house. Rusty's girl was still in my room. Her kid had moved to the couch, though, and was sitting with its arms twisted around its legs like a little pretzel. After looking a minute, I pretty well figured out that Rusty might of been wrong last night when he called it a boy. It had braids with little red rubber bands at the end, and it was wearing a pink T-shirt and girl underpants. And sitting on my sleeping bag.

'I hope you're, like, potty trained and stuff,' I said, and the kid just looked at me with wide eyes that were like drops of pistachio pudding in the middle of big white saucers.

The kid sat still as a statue as I pushed the front door shut and dropped the laundry basket on the chair.

'Geez, that's heavy,' I said. My feet hurt like crazy. I pulled

52

off the green sandals and dropped them by the chair, then locked the door and flipped on the light. When I turned around, the kid was still staring at me. Its eyes were too big for its face, like one of those nighttime animals you see on PBS – a three-toed sloth, or a lemur, or something.

The eyes followed me across the room. I went and looked through the crack in my bedroom door, to see what its mom was doing. She was still passed out on my bed, her long arms and legs tangled up in the sheets. Her milk-and-coffee skin made the material look white, when normally it was brownish gray. Her arms and back, and her legs where they came out from under the sheet, were covered with a thin layer of sweat that made her glisten like plastic where the sun fell from the window.

The door creaked and she took a big breath, then sighed. She had pretty lips, even with the lipstick smeared. The air came in and out between straight white teeth that looked like they'd be pretty, too, if she smiled.

The little lemur whined on the couch, and I looked over my shoulder at it. Three or four years old, maybe. No telling if it talked or not. It had its thumb in its mouth right now. It whined like it knew I was wondering, but most of the sound got caught in the fist. Whatever it said sounded like 'Gun-ungwee.'

I stared at it, and it said it again, 'Umm-ungwee,' then rubbed its stomach.

I'm hungry. Oh, geez, it wanted food. Good luck, considering there was nothing in the kitchen.

I pushed the bedroom door open some more. 'Hey,' I said,

but the lady in the bed didn't move, so I said it louder. 'Hey, your kid's hungry.'

She rolled over, grumbled something, then turned toward the wall and went back to sleep.

'Hey!' I said, but she didn't move. She told me to leave her the heck alone, and not in real nice words.

Something touched the back of my leg, tickled there real light. I jumped and turned around, thinking it was one of those huge roach things that came up the drain sometimes.

It was the kid, and I scared it. It ran back to the sofa and jumped into the corner, then stuck its thumb in its mouth again. The huge eyes got bigger and filled up around the edges. 'Unnn-unnngweeee,' it mumbled again, unfolding its fingers over a cheek, so that it pulled the skin down on one side.

'Ssshhh,' I said, and tried to think. What in the world was I supposed to do with the kid now? Ignore it? Stick it back in there with its mom and hope she'd wake up? Go in and try to get her out of bed again? Go back outside, lock the door behind me, and just leave?

Its lips trembled, and its nose wrinkled, and a big ol' tear rolled down its cheek. It had pretty skin like its mother, a soft color like milky tea.

I wished I wouldn't of eaten the whole pack of sugared doughnuts while I was doing the laundry. The kid probably liked doughnuts. Judging from the looks of things, there wasn't much chance its mom had carried in any food with her last night. As far as I could tell, there wasn't anything but the coat she had wrapped around her kid.

I went into the room and looked around anyway, just in case she had a purse, or a little money, or something, but of course she didn't. I checked the whole room, and there was nothing – not even some change in the jacket pockets or in her jeans, which were on the floor in a pile with some silver platform sandals. Cool shoes. Seemed like if she could afford those, she could feed her kid.

I grabbed my book and went back out to the main room. Sitting down on the couch, I told myself maybe Rusty would show up after a while with something for lunch. The kid sniffled and whimpered on the other end of the sofa.

'You wanna see my book?' I said. 'It's got pictures in it.' That was another thing I liked about old books. They had drawings in them. This one had drawings, and then right in the middle there were some actual racehorse pictures. 'It's about Seabiscuit. He was a big racehorse, and he won lots and lots of money.'

The kid sniffled some more, then untwisted her arms and scooted over toward me. She was kinda cute, actually. Lots cuter than the kids next door – and lots quieter.

'Unn-ungweee,' she said again, checking my face like she was hoping I'd finally get the point.

'I know,' I told her. 'But let's look at the book a minute, 'kay?'

Nodding, she scooched her rear into the ripped spot in the cushion right next to me. She didn't smell so good – kinda like she'd wet her underpants and then it'd dried a while back. We looked at the book, and I showed her the pictures. She could make the horsie sound, and a sound for

55

the trucks in the picture, and the train engine, which was cute.

When we ran out of pictures, I went back and started reading her the story. Her braids felt soft against my arm, and I got used to the way she smelled. She seemed to like listening to the story, and it was sort of cool to have someone to read it to.

After a while, I heard a car door close, and I figured it was Rusty home with some lunch, but it was just the fat guy from the office, coming back from someplace with a new box of cigarettes under his arm. He saw me looking out the blind and headed my way.

Shoot, I put on the green sandals real quick. The taller the better, I figured. It was a lucky thing that when we'd left home I'd brought some of Mama's clothes. Grown-up clothes are important, sometimes. The shoes hit my feet in all the raw spots as soon as I stood on them. I didn't know how Mama wore those things all the time, working down at the packing plant. She took care of the reception desk before she got so sick, so she needed to look good.

The guy checked me out like he thought *I* looked good. He went all the way up and down, from my shoes to my hair, then licked his nasty lips like I was a piece of pie on a plate.

'Rent's due yesterday,' he told me.

'Oh,' I said, and blinked and smiled, like I didn't notice he was wearing a greasy old T-shirt with the sleeves ripped off and his big fat hairy arms sticking out. The hair went all the way up into the shirt, a solid line, and then it came out the neck hole. It grew up his head and stopped around a big shiny circle, like a golf green, only white. 'I thought my brother gave it to you. He must of forgot to cash his check.' *He was too busy picking up stray girls and kids.* 'He'll bring it today.'

'He better,' he said, and then all of a sudden he turned friendly. He took a step forward and leaned against the door frame, and I didn't have much choice but to move back into the apartment. 'You doing okay here by yourself all day?'

A sweaty feeling broke over my skin and itched under my shirt. 'Yeah, sure. Why wouldn't I be?' I wrapped a hand around the doorknob, figuring that if he tried to come in, I'd act like I got off balance, and swing the door shut, and clobber him with it. 'I can take care of myself.'

He looked me over again, which was sick considering he was old – like forty, probably. If Mama were here, she'd of punched his lights out. 'I bet you can. You need anything, though, you just come on over and ask Charlie.'

Charlie, right. That was his name. 'Yeah, no problem. My brother'll be by as soon as he gets home. He might be here in a minute for lunch.'

The guy pushed off the door frame. He was a little scared of Rusty. Even though Rusty was skinny as a rail fence, he was six foot four. Guess *Charlie* didn't figure he'd like to take that on.

'Unn-ungweee!' the kid whined on the sofa. I'd forgot she was there.

Charlie leaned in and looked around the room, then frowned at the kid. 'That come from next door?' Figured, he wouldn't know one kid from another. The littlest one next door was a boy with a mini-Afro.

'I'm babysitting,' I told him, and I was actually glad the kid was there, which meant I wasn't alone in the apartment with Charlie crowding the door.

Charlie laughed, letting his head fall back a little, then nodding as he turned around and waddled off. 'It's probably good practice,' he muttered. What the heck he meant by that, I had no idea.

I closed the door and turned the lock.

'Unnn-ungweee!' the kid said, like that was the only word she knew.

'Yeah. Let's read the book some more, okay?' *We wouldn't want to wake up your mom or anything.*

I sat back down on the couch, and we read again. After a while, Rusty came zooming in and pounded on the door so loud I thought he was gonna knock it down before I could get to the lock.

'Geez, just a minute!' I finally got the thing opened, and Rusty about bowled me over on his way in.

'Is Kiki ready?'

'Kiki who?'

'Real funny. Is she ready?' He looked around like he expected to see the kid's mama sitting there all dressed up in her Sunday hat and gloves, with a purse in her lap.

'Well, she's still in my bed, if that's who you mean. She doesn't look like she's ready for much.'

Rusty cussed, which Mama would have smacked him for. 'Kiki, let's go!' he hollered across the room.

'Good luck,' I said. 'I tried to get her up before, and she wouldn't budge. Her kid's been wandering around here all day. I don't know who she thinks is gonna take care of it. And we don't have anything to eat here, either. Did you bring me a Happy Meal?'

Rusty glanced toward the kitchen, then he looked at the kid. She scooted back into the corner of the sofa, pulled the sleeping bag around her shoulders, and watched Rusty with her big green eyes.

'Kiki, let's go!' Rusty hollered again, then squinted at me. 'I didn't have time to go by McDonald's. I gotta take Kiki to her old man's house so she can grab her stuff before he gets back in town. He's out on a long-haul job to Idaho or someplace.'

Grab her stuff? I didn't like the way that sounded. 'What's she need her stuff for?'

There was movement in the bedroom, and Rusty checked it out where the door was cracked, then came back to me. 'She's gonna stay here with us for a while.'

'Excuse me?' I said, and I didn't care who heard it. 'Not in *my room* she's not. She got makeup all over my sheets, by the way, and now I'm gonna have to wash again. With bleach. That's fifty cents extra.'

Rusty wasn't paying me any attention. He was too busy watching the bedroom.

I was on a roll, though. 'Not much chance *she's* gonna pay for it. She doesn't have a purse or anything in there. I looked. And her kid's hungry, too.'

Rusty's face turned red behind the freckles, and he

checked his watch. If he got back even five minutes late after lunch, they cut his pay a whole half hour. The foreman told him if he didn't like it, he could find a new job that paid nine dollars an hour.

'Mind your business, Cass,' he snapped, and I felt sick and cold in my stomach. My brother cared more about some girl he'd just met than he cared about me.

I couldn't think of what else to say.

The kid sniffled and started to whine, and I went over and picked her up so they wouldn't forget her. Besides, I didn't want her to cry.

She needed a bath, bad.

'Make sure you get her something to eat,' I said. 'She's been asking all morning.'

The bedroom door opened and Kiki stumbled to the bathroom with her jeans unzipped. She went in and slammed the door.

'I told Kiki you'd babysit. I have to drop her at her job after we get her stuff,' Rusty said.

'I'm not babysitting. I'm not the one who asked them to come here.'

Rusty turned on me, his eyes narrow brown slits curled up around the edges like a dog's when it's growling. 'Knock it off, Cass. Yes, you are.'

'I'm not watching her kid!'

He sighed, like he was tired. 'She's gonna pay you, all right?'

'Yeah, I bet.'

'And she's gonna help pay rent, too.'

'With what?' In the bathroom, Kiki flushed the toilet, then turned on the water. 'She hasn't got any money.'

The kid decided she needed to use the bathroom, too, I guess, because she wiggled away from me and went and beat on the door until Kiki let her in.

'Kiki gets paid every night,' Rusty said. Rusty could be so dumb. He'd believe anything anybody told him, especially if she was hot.

'Yeah, sure.' I waved a hand toward the bathroom door. 'Then why didn't she have any money *last* night?'

'Her old man beat her up. She couldn't work a couple days.' Rusty's face turned hard and determined. It went through my mind that if Kiki's boyfriend beat her up, he might do the same thing to my brother. If Rusty got hurt and lost his job, we were dead in the water. 'Where does she work?'

'Down at Glitters,' Rusty answered, looking at his watch again.

'She's a *stripper*?' The words came out so loud the lady next door probably heard them.

'Shut up.' Rusty leaned over me and pointed a finger in my face. 'You just shut up your smart mouth, Cass. That's enough. Kiki needs a place to stay, and we need the extra money. It's time you did something to help out, instead of sitting on your butt every day. I'm tired of doing it all!'

I just stood there with my mouth open. Who did he think washed the dishes, and cooked supper, and made his sandwiches for lunch, and cleaned his nasty work clothes off the bedroom floor, and lugged the laundry across the street?

Kiki came out with her kid on her hip. She set the kid on

the sofa and gave it a kiss on the head, then she and Rusty started for the door.

'I need some money.' My voice was a little thin line choked in my throat, so I didn't really feel it. 'The kid's hungry.'

Kiki blinked at the kitchen, like maybe she was seeing more than one of everything. The shiner had turned an ugly shade of brown and yellow and was almost swelled shut.

Rusty dug in his pocket and came out with a dollar bill and a wad of change. 'I'll go cash my check after work,' he said, and then the door closed behind them.

I stood there for a long time, not sure what to feel. Finally I went over to the kitchen and counted the money. Two dollars and eighty-nine cents. That'd buy a couple more packs of doughnuts.

The kid came and wrapped her arms around my leg, which she didn't need to do. I wasn't stupid. I knew you couldn't, like, lock a little kid in an apartment and just leave her there alone.

She didn't even have shoes on.

I'd have to carry her across the street in her shirt and underpants. That'd be fun.

CHAPTER 5

Sandra Kaye

The street lay in the long shadow of afternoon by the time I'd finished putting a coat of paint on the cabinets. Outside, children were returning from a day at school. I watched as they disappeared behind windows and doors shielded with the heavy iron burglar bars that had become a fixture as the neighborhood declined. It occurred to me that after months without maintenance, the bars on Poppy's house might not be in good working order. I made a mental note to check them. I'd buy some new padlocks, too, and hang the proper keys inside each window. If a family came to live here, they might not think about the burglar bars. They might not be able to afford locks that were easy to open. A few new smoke detectors would be a good idea, too . . .

On the back of a crumpled receipt, I started a list of items to pick up at the store. Jake would have been proud. At kids' summer camp and the rec center where he'd volunteered, he'd taught a fire safety course. Jake loved kids.

'Spring and fall, change them all,' I muttered, and in my mind Jake echoed the reminder about replacing smoke detector batteries. I had the painful sense of losing him all over again and not knowing if he was ever coming back.

What if he never did? What if he found the peace he was seeking on the other side of the world, in some mythical connection to his birthright among the lush forests and thick humidity of Guatemala? What if he erased us, and his guilt over Poppy's death, like a long dream that fades in the light of a new day?

I wanted to grab him and say, *Stop this! What happened to Poppy wasn't your fault. You couldn't have prevented it.*

But deep inside me, the tiniest voice, unwanted yet determined, said that if Jake had been where he was supposed to be that night, if he'd been *responsible,* none of this would have happened. Poppy would still be rambling around this house. Jake would still be a few miles away in his dorm, and our lives would be normal again . . .

It was easier to focus on the kitchen than to consider what might have been. Unfortunately, the paint job wasn't turning out well. The cabinet surfaces were rough and greasy. My brushstrokes had dried over the old moss green paint in a thin streaky layer that would definitely need a second coat. I should have washed and sanded the surfaces first, but I couldn't bear to remove the shadows of Jake, and Poppy, and Aunt Ruth. I'd painted carefully over the smudgy doughnuts of fingerprints, sealing them safely in places only I would know about.

Right now, my hard work looked like pea soup left on the counter so long it had congealed and separated.

'Yuck,' I muttered, and it occurred to me that hours of

64

watching the home decorating channel doesn't necessarily qualify you to paint cabinets. The thought made me laugh, a strangely sweet sound, like a favorite food you hadn't eaten in so long you'd forgotten you liked it. *If Jake were here, he'd laugh at this.*

Who turned Mom loose with the paintbrush? His voice seemed so real, I looked for him.

'Don't count me out yet,' I told the quiet house before returning to the cabinets. When Rob and I married, I'd painted an entire married-student apartment by myself. My mother was mortified that we were planning to live in the aging brick building on the edge of campus, but she eventually acquiesced. She forgave Rob for our meager accommodations, because he was, after all, in medical school. Mother was looking forward to being able to say at cocktail parties, *This is my son-in-law, the doctor.* Rob came from a long line of Dr Dardens, which made him *a catch* according to Mother. I'd finally done something right.

She'd hate that I was at Uncle Poppy's house, up to my elbows in paint, which, now that I thought about it, made the job that much more appealing.

When one coat doesn't work, try two, I told myself, and decided to come back tomorrow. Preparing to leave, I felt like a child who'd sneaked off to visit a forbidden friend and stayed too long. As I left the house behind and headed across town, I tried to imagine who might move in and what their lives would be like. Maybe there would be little girls who would slip through the wall of hollyhocks to discover the hidden room where I'd passed so many childhood hours . . .

Our neighborhood in Plano was quiet when I arrived, the house empty. That was probably fortunate, since my clothes and I were spattered with paint.

Rolling the sweat suit into a ball, I tucked it in the linen closet while the whirlpool filled. As I sank into the water, I felt good about the day. Tired, but good. It had been too long since the waking hours had passed with happy thoughts instead of painful ones.

The phone rang as I sat with my mind drifting. Someone answered it before the machine would have. A few minutes later, Christopher came to the bathroom door. 'Mom, you in there?'

'Hi, sweetheart,' I said, slipping from the water and grabbing a towel. 'Hang on a sec. I was just getting out.'

'It's okay,' Chris preempted. 'I just need a check for Mr Hengerson before tomorrow.'

'What's up?' I asked, to keep him from hurrying off to his room. We were always delivering checks to Chris's band director for marching shoes, contest fees, extra lessons to help Christopher further excel in solo competitions.

'My purse is on the dresser,' I said, putting on a robe and opening the door.

Chris crossed the room in three long strides, grabbed my purse and brought it back to me. Sitting on the edge of the bed, I pulled out my checkbook.

'How much?'

'A hundred and seventy-five.' Christopher yawned and stretched, swaying on his feet, exhausted from another study night.

'A *hundred* and seventy-five?' I repeated, surprised by the amount.

'Mr Hengerson sent my sax in for repair. The check goes to Cruize Music.' He combed a shock of overly long blond hair out of his face. Normally the coaches would have made him cut that by now, but lately they'd been tolerant with Chris, in consideration of our family's grief.

'I didn't know your sax was broken.' Propping the check-book on my knee, I started filling in the numbers.

'Yeah.' He blinked, then rubbed his eyes. 'It's been screwed up for a while.'

'It has?' At one time a problem with his sax or his guitar would have been an immediate cause for alarm – *somebody call 911.* 'Why didn't you get it fixed?'

He shrugged, his yawn fading into a sigh. 'It was no big deal. I played one of the school instruments this semester. Hengerson said if I didn't bring a check and get my sax back before summer break, he wasn't going to release my grade, though.' He punctuated the sentence with an eye roll and a sardonic laugh. 'Bust my butt in physics and advanced English, and now I'm gonna flunk band.'

My motherly sixth sense came out of hibernation and perked up. 'You left your sax in the repair shop? All semester? You hate playing the school instruments.' Nothing the school owned was even close to the quality of the saxophone we'd given Christopher his freshman year.

Stuffing his hands into his pockets, Chris looked at the floor. 'I've been busy. You know, the online college class and all.' Oddly enough, Poppy's death and Jake's sudden departure seemed to have awakened in Christopher the need to push himself harder academically. In the past, he'd been satisfied to be the prankster, the easygoing athlete who was Jake's second fiddle, and admittedly not the most stellar student.

'Oh,' I said, then tore out the check and extended it to him. 'Chris, your music is important, too. There's no rule that says you have to graduate from high school with twenty hours of college credit racked up.'

Chris grabbed the check and tucked it and his fingers back into his pocket, ready to exit the conversation now that he'd gotten what he came for. 'It'll get me through to med school applications quicker.'

It bothered me to hear him talking about premed. Six months ago, he'd been determined to study music, even though his father hated the idea.

The sudden change in Chris was a subject I hadn't found the energy to take on. On the surface, he'd held it together remarkably well this semester, but I wondered what was happening underneath.

'Just make sure you're taking time to enjoy being where you are right now,' I said. 'Next year is your senior year, Chris. I don't want you to miss out.' My mind filled with milestones of Jake's graduation year – senior pictures, college visits, scholarships, awards, watching Jake step from the dressing room in his prom tuxedo, the class ring, the cap and gown, packing his things for college, buying new sheets, a towel, a laundry basket, which he ended up using to haul his laundry over to Poppy's. Poppy taught him how to do wash. Poppy was suddenly the expert even though he'd never washed clothes until Aunt Ruth passed away.

My throat ached with unexpected yearning. I swallowed hard, pushing the emotion away. *Christopher's milestones shouldn't be overshadowed by what happened with Jake*, I reminded myself. Christopher deserved his own life. He deserved normalcy, yet no matter how much I tried, I couldn't seem to will life, or myself, back to normal.

'Mom, I'm all right,' he insisted, as if he'd read the feelings I'd tried not to share. His voice was a mix of whiney teenager and tender concern. 'I've got it handled.'

'I know,' I choked out, and realized I'd done it again. I'd shown him my brokenness. I'd let him know how far I was from *back to normal*. What was wrong with me? Why couldn't I control the sudden emotional storms sweeping in and raining on everything? Maybe I was more like Mother than I wanted to admit. Maybe I'd end up lying in bed for days at a time, or padding through a dark house, searching the medicine cabinets for the right pill to make me functional again, telling myself that because they were prescriptions instead of bottles of scotch or vodka, it was all right.

Christopher felt the change in me and backed away, just like I had when I saw my mother's moods swinging unpredictably. Mothers are supposed to be rock-solid, always.

'Mrs Riley called,' Chris reported without looking at me. 'She wanted to make sure you were all right. She tried to call your cell all day, but you didn't answer.' He didn't wait for me to explain why Holly hadn't been able to contact me. 'G'night, Mom. Thanks for the check.'

'Good night, Chris.' I didn't say *I love you*. If I did, I'd start to cry, and Christopher would feel as if he'd caused it, just by being.

When he was gone, I sat staring into space, thinking about the day – the paint job at Poppy's, the trip to the store, the woman asking for a ride, the girl with the long blonde hair, the kids in the Dumpster. For an instant, I had the urge to go down the hall and tell Chris about it, to see how it would sound out loud. Perhaps his reaction would tell me if I'd lost my mind completely – hiding out in a house no one cared about.

I care, though. I care about that old place. What else was I supposed to do? Sit all day in an empty house my family avoided coming home to? There was nothing wrong with wanting to spend time at Poppy's, to do a good deed. It was preferable to trying the prescription antidepressants Rob had discreetly brought home and suggested I take. *I know how you feel about medication, Sandra*, he'd said. *But sometimes it's necessary . . . on a short-term basis. It doesn't make you anything like your mother or Maryanne. There's a difference between using a medication and abusing one.* In some sense, I knew he was trying to help, but in another, I wanted him to help by being here, by talking about it, by checking the e-mail and the answering machine for news of Poppy's case or Jake's whereabouts. I didn't want him to make letting go look so easy. For Rob, it seemed to be as simple as burying himself in work until he was so exhausted he fell asleep the minute he sat down.

Crawling into bed, I listened for the chime on the burglar alarm and wondered if he would come home tonight. My body was stiff and leaden, and for once I didn't feel the need for the herbal sleep aid. I turned on the TV, but before *Late Night* was halfway over, I sank into the most peaceful sleep I'd experienced in months. I dreamed of Jake and Poppy. They were on a lakeshore fishing. Jake was just a little boy, and I knew it was a memory, not a dream.

In the morning, the house was quiet, as usual. Christopher had left early. Warm coffee in the coffeemaker testified to the fact that Rob had been home, as well. No one had awakened me to ask about clean clothes or lunch money. In the past, I couldn't have slept through their morning routines if I'd wanted to, but now everyone tiptoed past. Rob must have come and gone on cotton feet, getting a change of clothes. His side of the bed was still made, which meant he'd crashed on the sofa again to avoid having to dutifully tune in to the latest rundown on Poppy's case, the sale of the house, the absence of news from Jake. More than once, Holly had pointed out that men process grief differently. I should give it time, she said, allow him space to work through it in his own way. But it didn't feel as though we were going through a *process*. It felt as if we were separating into two different planes of existence.

In spite of the empty house, I began the day with the energizing feeling of having something to do. Sunlight was pressing against the window as I slipped into my paint suit and called Holly. Her twins were bickering at the breakfast table, and she refereed while inviting me to go to decorating day for a cheerleading fund-raiser dance at school. 'I know how much you *love* all the craftsy stuff,' she said, and

I looked down at my paint-spattered clothes with a strange sense of irony. Good thing Holly hadn't come to the door to collect me. I would have looked like a mind reader. 'Anyway, there are signs to make, and big glittery figurines to put together, and a giant tunnel with about a million lights that need to be poked through the cardboard.'

'No *way*,' I said, and a chuckle tickled my throat. 'I did my bit with all parent projects Jake's senior year. I get a free pass this time, thank you.'

Holly groaned. 'Come on, Sandra. You know what those women are like. They're all so into it. I need moral support. This is my third time to be a cheer mom. I can't take it anymore!'

'That's what you get for having so many kids,' I quipped, and laughed again as I put another can of off-white latex in the back of the SUV and peeked out to see if Holly had left her house yet.

'I should get an exemption on all the crappy parent-volunteer jobs this time around,' Holly defended. 'These last two were an accident.'

I scanned the storage shelves for masking tape. 'You and Richard ought to know what causes that by now. But you could try pleading your case at the next PTA meeting.'

Holly coughed indignantly. 'Well, aren't we the little smart aleck so early this morning? You sound like you're in a good mood.' Her surprise was evident. More than once she'd come over in the morning to bring me coffee, and drag me out of bed to take me somewhere – anywhere – because getting out would be *good for me.*

'I slept well last night.'

'Great. I guess the melatonin supplement worked.' Holly read every alternative health magazine known to man. 'Want to ride over to the school with me? We could stop at Comera's for a latte and a pastry.'

'Can't.' I realized I'd just created a situation in which I'd have to lie outright. 'I'm volunteering this morning.'

'At the organ donor network?'

'Mmm-hmm.' Guilt slipped over me. Lying to Holly was so incredibly wrong. And if you're doing something you have to hide from your best friend, it probably isn't healthy. 'Anyway, we're swearing off Comera's, remember?' My stomach rumbled at the idea of sharing a pastry with Holly. Afterward, we'd vow to go to Curves tomorrow to make use of those memberships we'd bought a year ago. I needed to get in better shape, and Holly still wanted to take off the extra thirty pounds she'd been carrying since the twins were born.

Holly sighed. 'You sound like my doctor.' The sentence ended on a down note that wasn't Holly's usual.

'Everything okay? You're not pregnant again, are you?' After six kids, accidental pregnancy was a running joke. This time, she didn't laugh.

'No.'

'What's wrong?'

She paused long enough to raise a note of alarm. 'The doctor said I'm halfway through menopause. Can you believe that? At forty-five. How is that fair? And he picked on me about my weight again. Someone needs to teach that guy a little bedside manner. The last thing you want to hear is you're never going to have any more babies, *and* you're fat, *and* it's probably not going to get any easier to lose the weight.'

'Well, Holl, you two don't want any more babies.' I meant that to seem like a positive statement, but it came out sounding insensitive. No woman likes to face the fact that she's turning a corner in life.

Holly's breath trembled in and out. 'I don't know. Lately I've been thinking about it ...' She left the sentence open-ended.

'About a *baby*?'

Holly's response was a forced laugh, strangely ragged and sad. 'Yeah, I know it's silly. We'd practically be on social security by the time we got it raised. It's just hard to think about no kids in the house, you know?'

Something painful prickled in my nose. I knew what an empty house felt like. I rattled off the stock response. 'But, Holl, remember all the fun you and Richard were going to have? All those plans to go along with him when he travels for work? Think of how great it'll be to do that without having to worry about the whole high school showing up at your house for a party while you're gone.'

Holly's giggle was genuine this time. We both remembered the one screwup of Jake's teenage life – the time Rob and I went away overnight and left him in charge. Jake was naïve enough to mention our trip during football practice, and the next thing he knew he was hosting a teenage luau. Fortunately, Holly ratted on him from across the street before it could go too far, and Rob ended the party with a phone call.

Rob came down hard on Jake for breaking the rules. In hindsight, I guess I did, too. We couldn't believe our perfect son had let himself get caught in an imperfect situation. If I'd had it to do over again, I would have lightened up a little, let him know that everyone stumbles – it's only how you get up that matters . . .

I realized Holly was talking again. '. . . and with all the other ones in college, we probably wouldn't be able to afford to feed another kid anyway. We'd be like those freegans on the morning show. They hunt for food in Dumpsters behind stores and restaurants. Did you see that? They're regular people with college degrees, and nice houses and stuff. They go Dumpster diving to see what they can discover that's still consumable for . . . I don't know . . . the challenge, or to cut down on world waste, or something. They're having a seminar on freegan-ing someplace downtown. I have to admit, they come up with pretty good finds – still in the packages and everything – but, yuck!'

'Yuck,' I repeated absently, grabbing a package of paper towels the cleaning lady had left on the workbench. A partial roll of masking tape lay underneath, so I tossed it into the car as well. 'Hey, Holl. I'd better sign off now and head to work.'

'How come you're on two days in a row at the donor network, anyway?' Her cautious tone said I shouldn't push myself. With the next breath, she'd be telling me I should keep busy, so as not to get depressed.

'They're redoing a few offices. I'm helping with some painting.' How easily the lie rolled off my tongue.

' *You're* painting offices?'

'It needs to be done.'

'Ohhh-kay.' Holly stretched out the word as if she smelled a rat, but couldn't figure out where it was hiding. 'So, have you heard anything from the real estate agent? About your uncle's house, I mean?' It was a loaded question, as if some sixth sense had her picking up my vibes from across the street.

She couldn't possibly know, I told myself, peeking out the garage window as I closed the hatch on the SUV. I was relieved when the argument over a missing T-shirt escalated in Holly's kitchen, and she had to sign off to get the girls straightened out and off to school.

Tossing the cell phone in my purse, I headed into the house. All the talk about Comera's had made me realize I should take along some food, so I wouldn't have to leave Poppy's for lunch. In the kitchen, I ferreted out lunch meat, bread, soda, chips, and some peanut butter and jelly, just for emergencies. In the bathroom, while grabbing a towel, washcloth, and soap, I had the vague realization that I was making plans that extended beyond today – setting up Poppy's house like a hideaway I intended to return to repeatedly. There was probably something bizarre in that, but I felt more anticipation about the day than I'd felt about anything in months. Even Bobo seemed to notice the change in me as I took a scoop of food out to his dish. Instead of whining and regarding me with his sad mismatch of one blue eye and one brown, he barked and wagged his tail.

He misses Jake. The observation flashed through my thoughts like a bolt of lightning, the harbinger of a storm that would change the outlook for the day, if I let it. Bobo had always been Jake's dog. Both of them loved a challenge. They'd spent hours in the yard, perfecting Frisbee-catching acrobatics, stalking sticks and squeaky toys as if they were prey, and performing a routine in which, during a mock showdown, Jake pointed a finger pistol at Bobo, and Bobo fell over and played dead.

Staring into Bobo's sad, soulful eyes, I recognized something of myself. He couldn't understand what was happening, couldn't figure out how life had come from there to here without so much as a warning note. One day things were fine, and the next they weren't.

He whined as I headed toward the garage. I turned back, and he perked up his ears, then barked and picked up his Frisbee. 'You know what?' I said, and he stood wagging his tail, his head cocked to one side. 'Come on. We're going for a ride.' *Ride* was a word Bobo understood. Before Jake had left for college, he hardly ever went anywhere without his furry black-and-white sidekick.

Dropping his Frisbee, Bobo scampered to the door, then stood wiggling in a way that said, *Finally, something different is happening today.* As soon as I opened the garage, he squirmed past me, jumped into the car, and took up a position in the passenger seat. Panting happily, he checked out the view as we backed out of the garage, wound quietly through the neighborhood, and left Plano behind us.

CHAPTER 6

Cass

The last time Mama got sick, and we got behind on the bills, and she had to marry creepy Roger, she sat on the edge of my bed and said, *Cass Sally Blue, you can spend all your life thinking you ought to be in a better place than you're at, but the problem with that is, you'll always be miserable where you are.*

She went on talking about how Roger was a good man, and he was lonely, and maybe we could add something good to his life, too – maybe it was all part of a plan God had to take care of us. But if God was looking out for us, why didn't he keep Mama from getting sick in the first place? Being as she only had one lung left, it seemed like she deserved for that one to stay healthy.

Mama was hard to figure, anyway. Part of the time, she was telling me to get used to the way things were, and the other part she was saying things like, *Cass Sally Blue, when the mountain's big, you've got to dream bigger. The biggest part of doing is believing you can.*

I worked hard on the believing part. Sometimes I felt real sure that sooner or later Rusty and me were gonna land someplace better. We'd live in a nice house, and Rusty would finish up high school instead of working all the time, and I'd be in the sixth grade with someone telling me I was too young to wear makeup to school.

But sometimes I looked around and couldn't help seeing that the longer me and Rusty were on the road, the worse things were. Even though we'd made it to Texas, we weren't any closer to tracking down Rusty's daddy, Ray John. We couldn't even drive over to the library and use the computers to look for him, because here in Dallas, Rusty was tied up working all the time. Usually, the foreman found some reason to hold back some of Rusty's check, because Rusty'd showed up a few minutes late, or broke some tool, or something. He knew Rusty couldn't say anything about it, any more than all the illegals who worked down there could. Some folks just have to keep their heads down and take it, even if it's not fair, because they don't have anywhere else to go.

This apartment was the worst place we'd ever lived, and now we had to share it with some girl from the strip joint, whose kid I was supposed to babysit from two in the afternoon until, like, after midnight, when Kiki got off work. At least Kiki and Rusty did bring some clothes from Kiki's old man's house, but when she came back the first night after work, she still didn't have any money. I heard her and Rusty talking in the kitchen, even though they thought I was asleep. She told him she'd borrowed ahead at work, and she had to pay it back before she could take any money home. With that shiner on her eye, all she could do was wash dishes in the back, which didn't bring in any tips, either.

'In a few days I'll be makin' *real money* again,' she said, and Rusty believed her. Rusty'd believe anything if someone who looked like Kiki said it. I bet Kiki never had any trouble getting guys to do whatever she wanted. 'I'm sorry . . . I'm sorry, baby,' she told him. 'You been ssss-so . . . good to me.' Her voice was kind of slow and sloppy, like she was out of it. I squinted my eyes open long enough to see her lean up against Rusty and kiss him on the cheek. Then she just kind of hung there, limp, like she didn't have the energy to move.

'We can get by a couple days.' Rusty cleared his throat, and I wanted to choke him, because that wasn't true at all. As soon as he'd cashed his paycheck, almost all the money had gone in rent. The guy in the office charged us a fine for being late, and we didn't have any choice but to pay it.

I snorted and rolled over, and I guess they both remembered I was there. 'We're botherin' your . . . ummm . . . sis-ter,' she said, like for a minute she couldn't think what to call me.

I covered my head and stuck my face in the sofa, because I was so mad, if I opened my mouth, there wasn't any telling what was gonna come out. I waited till Rusty got up for work in the morning before I said anything about Kiki.

'You really believe she's gonna give you money?' I asked. Kiki was locked up in my bedroom, sleeping again, of course.

'She said in a day or two.' Rusty was always so flippin' sure of things. He was born that way, pretty much, I think. It got him in trouble over and over again.

'Uh-huh, so what do we do until she hits the lotto down

there at Glitters? There's only thirty-eight dollars left after the rent and McDonald's last night.' I wished Rusty woulda skipped going by McDonald's. If he had money in his pocket, it just burned a hole until it found its way to a drive-thru somewhere.

'I'll take you to Wal-Mart after work today, and we'll get some stuff,' Rusty said. He pulled half a leftover hamburger out of the fridge and ate it for breakfast, then took a couple dollars out of the coffee can and put it in his pocket. Thirty-six dollars left for groceries now, and I needed to do more laundry today. All the clothes Kiki'd brought for her kid were dirty, and they stunk like a moldy old house and cigarettes.

'We can't buy enough stuff to last four people,' I said. 'Not with thirty-six dollars.'

Rusty shrugged, eating the last of his Big Mac and washing it down with whatever was left in a soda cup on the counter. 'We'll get what we can. Anyway, I told you, Kiki'll have some money in a day or two.'

'Yeah, I bet.' I stared at the bedroom door, wishing I could burn a hole in it like Superman, and laser Kiki's rear right outa my bed and through the front door. She was using Rusty like a big stupid toy, and he was letting her because she was hot, even with the shiner on her eye.

He crossed his arms over his chest and leaned up against the counter. 'You know what, Cass, you could cut her a break. Her old man beat her up pretty good. She's got some cracked ribs and stuff. She should probably be in the hospital.'

'Then why isn't she?' Turning my back on him, I crossed the room and plopped down on the sofa.

'She can't afford it. Same as you and me. She hasn't got anyplace else to go.'

Same as you and me. The idea stuck in my head a minute. Rusty and me were the same as some stripper who'd been knocked around by her long-haul trucker boyfriend and tossed out on the street? Mama would of had a fit. She raised Rusty and me to be decent folks, to live like normal people and have a house, and go to school, and church on Sunday, and have a kitchen with food in it. She'd be sick to see us here . . .

I didn't mean to, but I started to cry. Everything in me went soft and watery, and I wanted Mama in a way that hurt so bad I felt like I was splitting down the middle. I wanted our little house on the outside of Helena, Montana, with the flower beds, and the fenced yard, and Rusty's dog out front, and the mountains off in the distance. I wanted someone to take care of us again.

'Don't do that, Sal.' Rusty's voice bounced off the hurt like a bird hitting window glass. I felt him sit down beside me and put an arm around my shoulders, pulling me close. His chest smelled of soap and was tight with muscle, a man's chest now that he spent his days pounding nails instead of goofing off in high school athletics class. Even that seemed sad. Rusty wasn't supposed to be a man yet. He didn't need me to take care of, and he sure didn't need some stripper and her kid. He needed to be laughing and joking, running the bleachers with a bunch of boys whose biggest issue was where to party on Saturday night.

'Ssshhhh.' The sound rumbled under his skin. 'Come on

now, Sal. It'll be all right. I've gotta head off to work. Don't worry, okay?'

He kissed me on the head and squeezed my shoulders one last time, and then stood up. I heard him moving around the kitchen, getting his wallet in his pocket and picking up his tool belt. Something brushed my leg, and when I opened my eyes the kid was standing there with her arm wrapped around my knee and her thumb in her mouth, her huge eyes blinking sleepily at me.

'Come 'ere,' I said, and she crawled into my lap and snuggled against my chest, her bony knees poking me in the stomach, her skin cold against mine. I pulled the sleeping bag over her legs as Rusty punched in the doorknob so it'd lock behind him.

'See ya after a while.' He didn't look at me. He just rubbed his eyes with his thumb and forefinger, going out the door, and sighed like he was real tired.

'Oook?' the kid said around her fingers.

'We'll read the book in a little while.' It was scary, but I was starting to understand her.

I rested my chin on her head. Her hair smelled good this morning, like the strawberry shampoo I'd dumped in the bathtub last night to make bubbles. That was one thing the kid and I had in common. We both liked bubble baths. I guess everyone probably does. A bubble bath makes things seem all right, for a little while.

Today I'd have to ask Kiki the kid's name, even though I didn't want to talk to Kiki at all. Every time I asked the kid her name yesterday, she kept saying something like Popah or Popal, and I couldn't make it out, so I just called her *squirt* all day.

Squirt and I sat for a while together, curled up in the sleeping bag, and even though I didn't want to be, I was glad she was there. Yesterday, it was a pain having to take care of her all the time, but at least now that they'd brought some stuff from Kiki's old man's house, Squirt would have shoes. We could get out of the apartment and walk someplace.

'How about we go down to the Book Basket and get something new to read today?' The Book Basket was just down the road in an old gas station across from the little white church. I liked it there, because MJ, the lady who owned the store, had tons of books, and she didn't care how long you stayed and looked at them. She also took trades, which was good when you didn't have any money.

'Maybe we'll walk on down to the Just-a-Buck store, too,' I told her. 'Sometimes they've got old cans of stuff on sale for cheap. You want to go look for cans?' Squirt nodded, and her braids scratched up and down on my chest where my nightshirt hung loose. If we could get some dented cans instead of paying full price at Wal-Mart, that'd help the groceries go further. We still weren't gonna be able to get by all week on thirty-six dollars, even if Rusty stayed out of the drive-thru windows and gave up Mountain Dew, which wasn't too likely. Rusty couldn't hardly go six hours without a Mountain Dew.

'Unnn-ungwee,' Squirt whined, and after listening to it all day yesterday, I knew what *that* word meant.

'We've got McDonald's for breakfast,' I told her. At least

this morning we had food. I'd cut all the hamburgers in half last night, saved some of my fries, and put my vanilla shake in the freezer.

'Mmmmm,' she said, then sat up in my lap, pulled the thumb out of her mouth, and smiled at me. I hadn't ever seen her smile before. She really was cute, even with her hair pulled half loose from her braids and sticking up all over her head. Maybe before we went to the Book Basket we'd take out the braids and make a couple pigtails.

'Guess we should get some breakfast,' I said, then looked at my bedroom door, wondering if, while she was in there crashing out in my bed, Kiki wondered at all how her kid was getting fed. Squirt could be wandering out in the street for all Kiki knew. How could somebody's mom be like that?

I put Squirt on her feet and we went to the kitchen together. She tried to crawl up my leg when I got out the hamburgers, so I lifted her onto the counter. Pulling her knees under the big T-shirt I'd put on her last night, she sat with her chin resting on them as I got out the burgers and scooped some of the shake – ice cream now – into a couple bowls. She watched the food move from the counter to the table, like a little puppy dog waiting for a bite.

'Let's eat,' I said, and she put out her arms so I could move her to the table. I took the broken chair and gave her the good one. For a little thing, she could eat a lot, and really fast. When she was done, she wanted more. I told her that was it, and she got up, went to the refrigerator, and tried to pull it open.

'There's nothing in there,' I told her. She looked confused, so I said, 'All gone.' She knew what that meant.

A memory of our refrigerator back home went through my mind, and my stomach rumbled. Mama always kept sodas, and there was a gallon of milk on the middle shelf, sometimes two. There was butter, and jelly, and string cheese we could pull out for a snack anytime we wanted it. Usually there were leftovers – a casserole or something Mama had made that Rusty and me complained about . . .

My insides ached, and I wrapped my arms tight around myself. *There's not any point in sitting here thinking about the stupid refrigerator, Cass Sally Blue,* I told myself, but I couldn't help it. It hurt deep down, like the past was eating me up a little at a time. I wanted Mama to put a casserole in front of me, and I'd eat every bit of it and tell her it was good. I wanted her to holler from the kitchen to wait until we all said grace together. I wanted her to put a glass of milk by my plate, and push my chair up on two legs when she squeezed by . . .

'Ook?' Squirt was standing there watching me with my book in her hand. She held it up against her face and peeped over it, looking worried.

'All right.' I wiped my cheeks on the way to the sofa, and we sat down to read. It was halfway through the morning before the lady next door put the kids out, and they started making a racket. I figured as long as they were making all that noise, Squirt and me might as well head on down to the Book Basket and maybe the Just-a-Buck. On the way back, we could go to the convenience store and get something for lunch with the change from the bottom of the jar. Something cheap.

'Let's go get a new book.' It went through my mind that

Squirt was gonna need clothes, and everything was in a ripped trash bag in my room. With Kiki. Through the crack in the door, I could see her spread out across the bed, her arm bent back like it'd landed that way. That had to be uncomfortable, but she didn't seem bothered. It was creepy, watching someone so passed out she didn't even move when I pushed the door open and it squeaked. I'd heard her tell Rusty she was taking some kind of pain medicine for the cracked ribs, and it knocked her out. Flopped out in the bed like that, she looked like the dead bodies on *CSI*, except she was breathing.

I didn't want to go in there with her, but I needed shoes for Squirt.

I pushed the door some more, then looked at Kiki. She sure didn't seem worried about what her kid was doing right now. It wasn't fair that crappy people got to stay around and raise their kids, and good people didn't, sometimes. I'd wanted to ask Pastor Don about that at Mama's funeral, but the room was full of people she worked with and stuff. They were all looking at Rusty and me with sad, worried faces and telling us how sorry they were, and whispering behind their hands about what would happen to us now. Then creepy Roger made Rusty take me on home before the room cleared out and I could get to Pastor Don. I wanted to tell him Rusty and me shouldn't go home with Roger. He acted weird when Mama wasn't around. He was always rubbing my shoulders with his big nasty hands, and trying to get me to sit by him on the sofa, and watch movies and stuff. I was afraid to be with him in the house.

Since I didn't get the chance to talk to Pastor Don, I told Rusty on the way home. He said to get my things together, because he'd already made up his mind we weren't staying there. We left that night when Roger was sound asleep.

The feeling of sneaking past Roger's bedroom came back when I went in with Kiki. Rusty and me had put all our stuff in trash bags to get ready to leave Roger's house. It was only in the dark that we realized the trash bags were noisy.

Kiki's bag made a racket as I dug through it, trying to find Squirt's other pink sandal. Squirt climbed around on the bed, and Kiki stayed as still as death.

I got your kid up, fed her, read her a book, and watched her all morning. I didn't bother to say the words anywhere but in my mind. Kiki wouldn't hear, anyway. *Now I'm gonna get her dressed and haul her around town with me. Sure, no problem.* I dumped out the bag. *You can pay me later.*

From the bottom of the trash bag, a little necklace with letter beads spilled out. *O-P-A . . . something.*

''S mine!' Squirt said, and hopped off the bed. She grabbed the necklace, then closed both hands over it when I tried to look. 'My-mine.'

'Ssshhh,' I whispered, because I really didn't want Kiki to wake up. 'I just wanna see the letters. I won't touch it. I promise.'

Squirt thought about it, rocking back on her heels, blinking at me.

'Come on . . .' I sounded like creepy Roger, trying to get me to go with him for ice cream. Squirt looked like she was thinking what I always thought about him: You can't trust people who act way too nice for no reason. Finally, she opened her fingers, one by one, just enough so that I could see the beads. O . . . P . . . A . . . L.

'Opal?' I said. 'That's your name? Opal?'

Closing her fingers over the beads again, she nodded and stuck a thumb in her mouth.

'That's, like, an old lady name,' I said, and she just blinked at me. 'All right. I guess you can be Opal.' I went back to looking through the pile. 'I sure wish I could find your other shoe, because right now it looks like you're gonna have to hop to the Book Basket on one foot.

Opal scrambled around the other side of the bed, lifted the covers off the floor, and came up with a tennis shoe that didn't match the sandal in my hand, but at least it was for the opposite foot. 'Tshooo, tshoo!' she cheered.

'Yup, that's a shoe.' Even if Opal was hard to understand, she understood me real good. I was gonna have to be more careful about what I said around her.

'Come 'ere,' I told her. 'Let's get dressed. You'll be cool with two different shoes, right?'

Opal made a squeaky sound in her throat, then followed me into the other room, and laid down on the floor, waiting for me to get her dressed. 'Stand up, for heaven sakes,' I said. 'You're not a baby. You're a big girl.'

'Big gul,' she echoed. 'Popal big gul.'

'Right. You're a big girl.' We talked about what a big girl she was while I put her in the cleanest thing I found in her bag – a pink sundress that was too big for her, and two pink socks that didn't match. The shoes were a great finishing touch. One pink sandal, one purple tennis shoe. 'Perfect,' I said. 'You look like Hannah Montana.'

'Anna banbana!' Opal cheered, swinging her hands until she lost her balance, stumbled sideways, caught my hair, and almost pulled it out.

'Ouch!' I squealed. 'Hold still!' I said it louder than I meant to.

Opal stopped moving and stuck her thumb in her mouth, then pulled her chin into her neck and ducked away like she thought I was going to smack her.

'It's okay.' Was Kiki the reason Opal acted that way? The idea made a shudder go down my back. I was glad Kiki was sound asleep.

'Come on,' I said, then took Opal into the bathroom and fixed her hair into two ponytails, which wasn't easy because I don't know anything about black-girl hair, but it was pretty cute when I got done. At least she was dressed and it looked like someone had tried to clean her up.

Opal followed right behind me while I got a little money, my book, and the key to the front door. She grabbed the hem of my shorts, and hung on like she was afraid I was gonna leave her behind, then she choo-choo-trained along behind me out the door.

The parking lot was empty, but I could feel someone watching us. The Mexicans were all gone to work by now, and as far as I could tell sweaty Charlie slept until noon before opening the office, so it was probably the crippled lady. She never came out, except when the Dial-a-Ride showed up for her. Then she'd take it somewhere, and when she came back, she'd go right inside and shut the door. She sat at her window and watched a lot, though.

I stepped back and looked down there, and her curtain moved.

The kids from next door came out near the Dumpster and ran to the other side of the parking lot. They disappeared into the breezeway between the two buildings across from ours, scampering off like little mice looking for a place to hide. I wasn't sure why at first, but then I heard something hit the Dumpster, ringing it like a big drum before bouncing off the pavement. A basketball. Looked like the gangbangers were skipping school today. Great.

'C'mon, Opal,' I said, then opened the door and pushed her back inside. It wasn't so much that I was afraid of those stupid gangster wannabes, but I was worried they'd scare Opal. 'We'll go in a minute,' I told her, and locked the door to wait.

CHAPTER 7

Sandra Kaye

As I exited the interstate near Poppy's house, I turned the car radio on. 'Another clear day ahead,' Jim, from *Metro Morning with James and Jim*, predicted. 'The unseasonable cool spell continues, with a high of eighty-one, then cooling toward evening as a weak storm front pushes into the metro area, bringing lower temperatures overnight, but only a slight chance of rain.'

'That's good news for the freegans conventioning in town,' James remarked. 'You catch that on the news, Jim? If you sign up, you get a free demo.'

James chuckled, lowering his tone like a voice-over announcer. '*Dumpster Diving for Fun and Profit*,' he joked. 'Considering what they pay us here, it might be a good idea.'

'Ever wonder who caters the food for a freegan convention?'

'I don't know, James, but –'

I turned off the radio before James and Jim could illuminate the details of professional Dumpster diving. Holly had already clued me in well enough. *They go hunt for food in Dumpsters . . . to see what they can discover that's still consumable . . . yuck!*

They hunt for food in Dumpsters . . .

Hunt for food . . .

I passed the apartment complex with the crumbling white stucco walls, looked over, watched the Dumpster go by, but the vision stayed with me. I pictured the children climbing among the broken bottles and Wal-Mart sacks full of soiled diapers.

They weren't playing . . .

The image was clear now – the little girl holding a wad of foil, the boy turning over a Hostess Cup Cakes box . . .

They were looking for food.

My stomach roiled as I neared the little white church across from Red Bird Lane. It sat quiet and pastoral in the shade of a towering oak tree, a place out of keeping with the rundown buildings up and down the street. When I was little, I'd attended a neighborhood potluck there with Poppy and Aunt Ruth. There were tables full of casseroles, salads, and desserts. Was it possible that, now, just down the road, children were looking for food in trash cans?

In Poppy's driveway, I sat with the question circling in my mind. I could call the police, or CPS – someone official to check on the kids, see what was going on, get help and services for the family if needed . . .

There were organizations set up to handle situations like this – Meals on Wheels, food pantries, summer lunch programs . . .

Weren't there?

If I called someone, how long would it be before action was taken? Tomorrow? The next day?

What if nothing came of it? The headlines were full of stories of kids who slipped through the cracks of an over-burdened, underfunded social services system, kids who were living in desperate, dangerous situations.

I sat with my fingers on the car keys, thinking of the groceries in the back.

You can't just wheel in there and start handing out food to someone else's kids, Sandra. Kids should be taught not to take food from strangers, for one thing.

Just call someone . . .

That's why cities have social services . . .

But even as I tried to convince myself, I knew that if it were as simple as making a phone call, someone would have done it already. Those kids were hungry today, and they had been yesterday, and any number of days before that.

I took the groceries into the house, let Bobo into the backyard, laid out some clean newspaper in the kitchen, and started making sandwiches.

This is crazy. You can't just go down there . . .

But I kept making sandwiches. I couldn't help thinking of the story the nuns had told us about Jake wandering alone in the marketplace, just three years old. He'd come so close to disaster. If someone, a stranger, hadn't intervened, there was no telling what would have happened to him. If passersby had minded their own business that day, if everyone had looked the other way, he could have ended up in the hands of dangerous people and been sold into a life so terrible I couldn't bear to imagine it. When he was brought to the nuns, he was so hungry he would have gone with anyone who would give him food.

Those children down the street *were* Jake. Different country, different faces, but they could have been my son, all those years ago. If I didn't have the courage to help now, I didn't deserve Jake at all – I didn't deserve to have him home, ever.

I finished the sandwiches and put them in the car before I could try once again to talk sense into myself. I considered bringing Bobo for moral support, but he was covered in wet dirt from nose to tail. 'All right, buddy,' I said, before heading out the yard gate. 'If I'm not back in twenty minutes, call out the National Guard.'

Bobo barked and went back to digging in the dirt.

On the way to the apartment complex, I engaged in an ongoing mental dialogue about the wisdom of what I was doing. No telling what sort of people lived in a place like that. Hadn't the woman I'd driven home from Wal-Mart confessed that she was afraid to step out her front door? Hadn't Holly and I decided that the strip mall across the street looked like a place where all sorts of unsavory activities might go on?

It's just a bag of sandwiches, Sandra. You're not moving in. You're just dropping off some sandwiches. It won't take long.

What could possibly go wrong?

I thought of Poppy, of what had come of a simple trip to the store. A lot of things could go wrong. Life could change when you least expected it – the minute you let your guard down, made some seemingly harmless decision.

Maybe you were meant to see the kids in the Dumpster. Maybe all of this is happening for a reason.

It was an odd thought, a paradox in a voice that seemed to come from some boldly determined part of me I didn't even recognize. The voice of my mother arose to beat it down. *Who do you think you are, Mother Teresa? If there were a grand plan here, why would anyone choose you, of all people?*

I pushed her out of my head as I drove into the apartment complex. The area around the Dumpster was deserted, as was the parking lot. With the car idling, I tried to decide what to do next. There was no sign of the children, no way to know where they might be. *I could leave the sandwiches by the Dumpster. They'll find them, if they come looking.*

This whole thing was a stupid idea.

Lately, it was hard to know which voice had the better grasp on reality. Prowling around some government housing complex was completely unlike me.

I turned off the car, climbed out, grabbed the sandwiches, and hurried to the Dumpster. It wasn't until I got there that I noticed a movement behind the corner of the building. By then, it was too late. I looked up, and three teenage boys were circling the Dumpster, trying to get between me and my car.

My heart jumped into my throat, and I froze in place, suddenly aware of my own vulnerability. I recognized the boys from the day I'd met the real estate agent at Poppy's house. They couldn't have been more than twelve or thirteen, not yet fully grown, but together they had the menacing aura of a gang.

I was out of view of the road, trapped between the Dumpster and the wall of the building.

If I didn't come home tonight, no one would know where to look.

The largest of the three, a tall youth with a boyish face, drew his tongue slowly over his lips. 'If it ain't the pink house lady,' he said, his dark face nearly hidden under an off-kilter ball cap, his chin jutting out with the words. 'That yo' nice car out front? How 'bout you gimme the keys fo' that nice car?'

The smallest boy, a gangly kid with wide brown eyes and his hair hidden in a do-rag, darted a concerned glance at his friend. 'B.C.,' he muttered out of the side of his mouth.

'Shut up, Monk,' B.C. snapped, then uncrossed his arms and took a step toward me. 'We just talkin'. Ain't we, Pink Lady?'

My mind raced through the possible options – tell them to get out of my way, be forceful, confident, authoritative? Yell for help and hope it would frighten them? Threaten to call the police? If there was a police report, Rob and Holly would find out everything. They'd think I was insane for coming here. They'd think I was having some sort of a breakdown. They'd lock me up and only let me out for PTA meetings and trips to Starbucks.

The off-base thought made strange, sardonic laughter press my throat and spill from my lips.

The largest boy, B.C., stiffened. 'You laughin', Pink Lady? You laughin' at me?'

'Leave her alone!' The teenaged girl I'd seen yesterday was standing just beyond the Dumpster. She looked incongruously adult again today, in tight red shorts and a halter top, her hair clipped in a messy twist. She carried a toddler on her hip, a little girl with caramel brown skin, dark fluffy pigtails like the top knot on a French poodle, and her thumb in her mouth.

'Well, look who here.' The smallest boy, Monk, turned halfway. 'Ain't you too good to talk to a black boy?'

She returned his look narrowly and hiked the toddler onto her hip again.

B.C. laughed. 'Wanna come here and play, pretty baby?'

The girl answered with a sarcastic smile. 'Yeah, right. And then my brother'd kick your butts when he found out. He knows y'all messed up his truck, by the way. If he didn't just get out of prison, he'd of kicked your butts already. Don't mess with our truck again.'

'We didn't mess with yo' brother truck.' Monk's voice carried a hint of fear. He glanced nervously at his partners.

'I bet,' the girl challenged. 'You better leave our stuff alone.'

'Yo' brother bes' not mess with us,' B.C. postured. The volley of threats dribbled to a halt, and they all stood staring at each other, trying to decide what should come next.

'That yo' baby?' Monk asked finally.

'Pppffff!' the girl spat. 'Does it look like it's my baby? It's my cousin's.' She cuddled her chin protectively over the toddler's head.

Monk studied her. 'You cousin a stripper? Because I seen that baby down at Glitters las' week.'

The girl fluttered a nervous glance in my direction, then glared at Monk. 'No.'

Having found a tender spot, Monk grinned. 'Maybe you a stripper. You gonna take it off fo' us, pretty baby?'

Throwing out my hands, I stepped between them like a referee at a boxing match, the sandwich bag swinging from my elbow. This had gone too far. After ten years of coaching soccer and being the dugout mom for baseball, I should have been able to handle kids with attitude better than this. 'All right. That's enough. You boys go find something else to do before you end up in trouble. Get out of here. Leave her alone.'

Monk's eyes narrowed. 'What you hidin' in the bag, Pink House Lady?'

'Sandwiches. Would you like one?'

Monk's brows drew together, and B.C. gave the bag a critical frown. For an instant, they seemed tempted. They looked back and forth at the bag and each other.

'No,' B.C. finally spoke for all of them, and they moved on. Monk glanced over his shoulder just before they disappeared around the corner.

I stood there with the girl, temporarily at a loss. Up close, she looked as if she might be twelve or thirteen. She was tall and long-legged, but underneath the grown-up clothes and the makeup, her body was hard and straight, her face still rounded with a look of childhood. The boys' assumption that the baby was hers, and their questions about her working at Glitters and the toddler hanging around at a strip joint, were nothing short of obscene.

She gave me a worried look, as if she were sensing my thoughts. 'I gotta go.'

'Wait,' I said, before she could slip away. 'I brought some sandwiches. I saw the kids digging in the Dumpster yesterday.'

Her eyebrows rose and knotted in the center. She didn't come closer, but didn't step back, either. Both she and the toddler flashed quick, interested glances at the bag, then she shrugged. 'They do that all the time. Their mama doesn't care.' She studied me with obvious curiosity.

'They shouldn't be in there. It's dangerous.'

Shrugging, she let her passenger slide to the ground, then held the toddler's hand.

'Unna nan-ich!' the toddler whined, tugging the bond between them to get closer to the sack, while sucking furiously on her thumb. 'Unn-ungwee!'

'Ssshhh!' The girl's gaze flicked over the bag, then back to me. 'You from CPS or someplace?' Her chin tipped upward, her face narrowing cautiously. In the sunlight, her eyes were a deep blue. Conflicting currents swirled behind them. I had something she wanted, but she was afraid. Of what, I couldn't imagine. 'Social workers don't get high-dollar wheels, usually.' Her gaze darted toward my car.

I had a mental flash of how out of place I must look, standing there beside a Cadillac SUV in my paint-spattered sweat suit. 'I'm not with CPS. I've been down the road working on my great-uncle's house on Red Bird Lane. I gave one of the residents here a ride yesterday.'

'I saw you,' she said flatly.

'I didn't realize what the kids were doing in the Dumpster. It just hit me today as I was driving past. Do you know where they are?'

She shrugged in a way that said she didn't care if the kids dropped off the face of the earth. 'They hide places.'

'Maybe I could leave the sandwiches with their mom.' I pictured myself walking up to some stranger's door, handing her a bag and saying, *Here, have some sandwiches. I saw your kids digging in the Dumpster yesterday* . . . She most likely wouldn't give me a hug and a thank-you.

'Their mama's probably asleep. She's always asleep . . . unless she's got a man over.'

I looked down at the bag, getting a sudden sense of the complexities of the situation. I wished I'd stayed at Poppy's and minded my own business. 'Maybe I could just leave this on their doorstep. Which apartment do they live in?'

'There's lots of cats around here. They get into stuff. I could give it to 'em.'

'Unna nan-ich,' the toddler repeated behind her fist. No matter where I left the bag, it would probably go to someone who needed it.

'All right,' I said.

'I'll make sure everyone gets some and stuff.'

'Good.' I handed over my cargo with the feeling I was being sold a bill of goods. 'I'll trust you with the job, then.' As she turned her attention from me to the bag, I recognized the *You're so lame* look kids employ when they think they've hoodwinked an adult. 'I didn't catch your name.'

She focused her attention on me again, and the toddler

stretched upward, touching a jelly stain on the paper. 'Cass.' Shifting the bag in her hands, she weighed its contents.

'Nice to meet you. And what's your little cousin's name?'

With a blank look, she followed my gaze to the toddler. 'Oh . . . uhhh . . . it's Opal. Say hey, Opal.'

Opal stared up at me with a soulful expression.

'Hello, Opal,' I said, and she scooted behind Cass's leg.

Cass shifted her hips to one side, squinting against the sun as it peeked through a hole in the clouds, then faded again. 'Those kids'll get back in the Dumpster again, anyway.' Her expression was flat, pessimistic, emotionless, a dull gray mask on a face that should have been young and hopeful. She was a beautiful girl, with long blonde hair and stunning blue eyes. She should have been giggling over fashion magazines and trying new hairdos with her friends. 'They do it every day.'

I didn't know how to answer that. The sad truth was that even if I wanted to fool myself into thinking a few sandwiches could make a difference, she knew I hadn't accomplished anything by coming here. Tomorrow, the cycle would repeat again.

Opal poked the jelly drip, then brought a sticky finger to her face and tasted it. *How often does she go hungry?*

'I could bring some sandwiches again tomorrow.'

'If you want,' Cass answered, tipping her head to one side, noticeably perplexed. Perhaps she was wondering if I would really show up again.

Would I? I wasn't sure myself.

The question followed me like a shadow as I parted ways

with Cass and Opal and left the apartments behind. Back in Poppy's driveway, I stood leaning against the car, overwhelmed, the memory of the last half hour swirling through my mind. I recognized the look in Cass's eyes. I knew what it was like to be a child keeping secrets, afraid to tell. How many times had I wanted to confide in someone – a teacher, a neighbor, a pastor – about what was happening in our house? My mother's behavior ranged from vegetative to violent, depending on her mental state and what medications she was taking. If my stepfather was worried about it, it didn't show. He worked in his office off the den, every available space crowded with architectural drawings. He came and went in his black Lincoln – a new model every two years, some of which I never saw the interiors of before they were traded for replacements. He ate oatmeal for breakfast every morning, rinsed the bowl and put it in the dishwasher. He drew sketches of odd, theoretical machines in the margins of the daily newspaper. Every so often, he blew up at my mother when he came home in the evenings and found her still in bed, never having gotten up, showered, or fixed her hair, and too mellow to care. *For God's sake, Nora, you have children to raise!* he'd say, and then he'd storm away to his office, close the door, and lose himself in the hypothetical again.

In Poppy's little pink house, none of that existed. Together, Poppy and Aunt Ruth had locked the family curse outside their door. There, the newspaper was only a newspaper, not something to roll up and use as a weapon. The beds were made by nine, and the voices were soft and pleasant, like sunlight warming the rooms. There were cookies in the jar and popsicles made from Kool-Aid, and if Aunt Ruth thought my curly, strawberry blonde hair was *difficult and singularly unattractive*, as my mother had deemed it, she never said so. She only brushed it around her finger and said, *My, my, but your hair does curl up so nicely, Sandra Kaye. I've seen movie stars who didn't have such beautiful hair. . . .*

If not for Poppy and Aunt Ruth, I would never have known there was a way to live other than the one I saw at home. As a child, whatever you experience seems like what should be . . .

Voices pushed away my thoughts, and I looked up and down the street. On the sidewalk, a group of people was strolling along – a young blonde in medical scrubs, most likely a home health nurse like the ones who had cared for Poppy; an elderly woman in a wheelchair; and a bulky middle-aged man, who lumbered along in an uneven gait I recognized. He'd walked by repeatedly during the estate sale, and lately I'd seen him tending the flowers outside the little white church.

During the estate sale, he'd stopped a couple times to sift old plastic flowerpots and discarded plastic glasses out of the rubbish pile. He seemed harmless enough, so Holly and I had let him take what he wanted. *Poor thing*, Holly had whispered behind her hand. *He's probably homeless.*

It wasn't until later that we learned he lived in a house with his parents. His sister stopped by looking for him, frantic as she told us he was mentally handicapped and wasn't supposed to be out wandering alone. Now, he waved as if he remembered me from the estate sale. 'Hi-eee, lady!' he called, releasing the wheelchair handle, his arm moving in a wild sweeping motion that caused him to let the wheels drift toward the edge of the sidewalk.

The woman in the chair clutched her armrest. 'Ted-eee!' she complained, her words slow and slightly slurred. 'Watch out!' She swung a hand toward the road, and he looked down.

The nurse leaned over and straightened the chair, moving it away from the curb. 'Be careful, Teddy, okay? You need to push your mom's chair with both hands.'

'Huh-oh!' Teddy grabbed the handle securely. 'I watchin', Mary. Doin' it good, right, Mama?'

'Yes, Ted-eee,' the old woman said, reaching back, and brushing her fingers across his wrist.

Teddy turned his attention to me as they reached Poppy's driveway and stopped. 'Hey-eee, lady. I gone get pots, soo-kay?' He pointed toward the junk pile.

'Pardon?'

'Teddy wondered if it would be okay to take some of the flowerpots from the trash pile. He saw them when we drove past yesterday,' the nurse, Mary, explained, seeming somewhat embarrassed. They'd probably expected the house to be empty.

'Yeah,' Teddy agreed. 'I saw pots.'

'Oh,' I said. 'Take anything you want. It's all headed for the dump anyway.'

'Ho-kay,' Teddy answered. His mother tapped him on the hand, and he added shyly, 'Thanks.'

'You're welcome.' I had the fleeting thought that Poppy would be glad for someone to take the flowerpots from the rubbish pile. He and Aunt Ruth would have been against putting them there in the first place. *Waste not, want not.*

'He's potting . . . for the church . . . sale. He tends the . . . flowers.' The woman in the wheelchair, Teddy's mother, formed each word carefully, so that they dragged like a record playing a bit too slow. Her face drooped on one side, like my stepfather's after he'd suffered a stroke. 'We live . . . on Blue . . . Sky . . . Hill.' Perhaps she'd said that to let me know digging through rubbish piles wasn't her normal occupation. Even though Blue Sky Hill was not far from Poppy's, the stately homes there were a world away from the little houses on Poppy's street. When Teddy's sister had come by our yard sale looking for him, I'd been surprised to learn that he lived on the hill. *He's a ways from home,* I'd said to her, and she'd looked worried.

'Gon' sell some plant,' Teddy muttered, then headed off to begin his salvage project. Grabbing a box off the top of the pile, he set some empty flowerpots inside, then dug deeper, commenting enthusiastically about the junk we'd dumped on the curb.

The nurse introduced both herself and the woman in the wheelchair, Hanna Beth, as we watched Teddy sort and comment. 'We walked down from the church,' she said. 'It's such a nice day.'

'Paint-ting?' Hanna Beth nodded at my spattered sweat suit.

'Oh, just a little.' I realized I was probably a mess.

'Sell-ing . . . your house?' She helped define the words by indicating the real estate sign.

'It was my great-uncle's house.'

'Oh.' Her quick brown eyes took in Poppy's place. 'A Sears . . . house. I grew up in a . . . Sears house . . . not way . . .' Pausing, she shook her head and pressed her lips together with determination. 'Not far . . . a-way there.'

I tried to make sense of what she'd said. 'A Sears house . . . You know, I think this was a Sears Catalog house. I'd forgotten all about that, but I recall Aunt Ruth talking about Poppy ordering the house, and a railcar delivering it in pieces.'

'Yes!' Hanna Beth smiled. 'I remem-ber, too. In pieces. Like puz-zles.'

Memories of Poppy and Aunt Ruth proudly talking about the building of the house filled my mind. I hadn't thought about that in years. 'They used the boards from the crating to frame up a summer kitchen out back.'

Nearby, the trash pile shifted, and Teddy made a discovery. 'Ohhh! Sho-bel, and got hoe. Broke hoe.' He dragged out a shovel head and a hoe with a partial handle, then held them up. 'I gone take them to Pas-ter Al church, 'kay, Mama? Take the sho-bel and the hoe.'

Hanna Beth smiled indulgently, then explained, 'Ted-eee loves . . . the church . . . gardens.'

'I've seen him there,' I offered. 'He must do a good job. The plants have been beautiful lately. A lot better than these, I'm afraid.' Frowning over my shoulder, I took in the sadly overgrown flower beds around Poppy's house. Aunt Ruth would have been mortified.

107

Teddy straightened, his gaze slipping past me toward the little pink house. 'You gotta cut them rose. Ant-tigue rose, gotta cut new wood, and thinnin' iris, and di-antis takin' the deadhead off . . .'

I looked at the scraggly rosebushes along the porch, musing over what the house used to be and what it was now. 'My aunt and uncle always kept the gardens in such beautiful shape.' Impulsively, I turned back to Hanna Beth and the nurse. 'Would Teddy be interested in cleaning up the flower beds here? I'd pay him.'

'Ho-kay,' Teddy replied, then dropped the junk pile and started toward the flower beds.

His enthusiasm made the three of us laugh. 'Oh, I didn't mean right this minute. I'll be here painting for a few days yet.'

Hanna Beth smiled and called Teddy back to her chair. 'Tomorrrrow,' she said. 'Mary can . . . bring him around ten.'

'Wonderful!' I agreed.

The nurse checked her watch and suggested that they should be heading home for lunch and medication. Teddy rescued his box from the rubbish pile and set it in his mother's lap.

'I gone come to-morro, lady.' He waved as Mary turned the wheelchair, and they proceeded back toward the white church. Taking the handles from the nurse, Teddy made a motor sound and popped a wheelie. 'She a nice lady,' he said. 'She gimme some pots. Good pots. I gone clean the flowers' beds.'

CHAPTER 8

Cass

Opal and me sat on our apartment steps and watched while that lady drove away. For once, the kids next door weren't around. They were probably still hiding behind the other building in the storm ditch.

I opened the bag, and sure enough, it was sandwiches in red plastic wrap. I counted them. Ten altogether. That lady must of used a whole loaf of bread. The bag even smelled like peanut butter and strawberries, which made the back of my mouth water.

'Mmmm,' Opal said, looking into the bag. Sucking hard on her thumb, she rolled her eyes up at me and watched to see what I would say.

'You want one?' Mama would of had a heart attack about me eating sandwiches dropped off by some lady I didn't know from Adam.

Don't take candy from strangers probably included sandwiches, too. Last year, in the sixth grade in Mrs Dobbs's class, a guy from the Montana Highway Patrol came and gave a slide show about all the ways people made drugs look like candy, so little kids'd try it. Then you got hooked, and that was that. You were dealin' Jolly Ranchers, and next thing you were on the billboard about your brain on meth. We laughed when he said that, and he laughed, too, but then his face went straight and he said, 'I know that sounds funny, but there's a serious point here. It's just that easy. You think you're playing around, and before you realize it, you're into something you can't get out of.'

His look passed over me, and it seemed to stop, and we froze that way for a second. After the talk was over, while everyone was walking around the tables looking at pictures of meth people and slices of drug brains, I almost went over to him. I thought about telling him that one time when the door wasn't shut all the way, I saw dirty pictures on creepy Roger's computer, and I was afraid my mama would have to go in the hospital again pretty soon, and I didn't want to be at creepy Roger's when she did.

You're into something you can't get out of, I thought, and I left it be. I was afraid I'd make trouble for Mama, and she had enough to worry about already. Once she went to the hospital, I started going and watching Rusty's football practice after school, instead of riding the bus home. Rusty was good at football. Too bad he didn't end up getting to be in school for his senior year. Mama would of hated that, too.

I looked in the bag again, and it smelled so good. Really, why would some lady come over here to bring us poison sandwiches? She had a nice car, and she didn't seem psycho or anything. She had paint on her clothes, which fit with the story about working on some house on Red Bird.

Opal was still watching me, her eyes blinking real slow, the long lashes going up and down like paper fans.

'Oh, all right.' I took out a sandwich, and unwrapped it, and gave it to her, then got one for myself. They were pretty good, a little bit soggy, though. Mama always put peanut butter on both pieces of bread, so the jelly wouldn't soak in and make it gushy. Peanut butter was an impermeable barrier. I learned that in science class. Mrs Dobbs always had neat examples.

She came to Mama's funeral and sat in the third row, right behind Rusty and me and creepy Roger. After the service, she got me off to the side and said, 'Cass, I want you to know I'm here for you. If there's anything . . . well . . . anything you need, or if you want someone to talk to.'

I looked over, and creepy Roger was headed our way.

'Okay, Mrs Dobbs,' I said, and she hugged me so tight I thought she was trying to get the truth out of me by osmosis. Sometimes I wondered what she probably thought when I didn't show up for school the Monday after Mama's funeral . . .

Halfway through the sandwiches, me and Opal got thirsty, so we went inside for a drink. The bedroom door was still shut, of course. I was quiet with the cabinets and the glasses while I got water for Opal and me. I wasn't sure why, except I didn't want to see Kiki.

When I tried to give Opal her glass, she wanted 'Mmmm-ik,' so I poured out some of the water and stirred in the last of the ice cream from the leftover milkshake in the freezer.

'There you go. Milk,' I said, and set it in front of her. It didn't look very good, but she drank it anyway.

After we were finished with the first sandwiches, we halved another. Opal didn't really eat hers, so I wrapped it back up for later. I ate all of mine, when normally I would have saved some for later, but when you've got ten sandwiches in a bag, it seems all right to eat one and a half. Opal and me could take the money we were gonna spend on lunch and do laundry with it. Once Kiki finally cleared out this afternoon, I'd sort through their stuff and get Opal's. If Opal was gonna be hanging on my leg all the time, she needed to not smell like her clothes had been peed in.

After I cleaned the dishes and put them away, I stared into the paper bag for a minute. 'Looks like supper to me,' I said to Opal. 'The lady wanted the sandwiches to go to hungry kids. Here we are.'

Opal pulled her feet up under her and stood in the chair, so she could see into the bag, too. 'Unt nudder namich,' she said.

'You can't have another one right now,' I told her. 'You didn't finish your last half.' I rolled the bag shut because, really, it didn't smell so good anymore.

Opal made a pouty lip and sat down in her chair.

'We should go on to the Book Basket.' With everything that'd happened that morning, I'd almost forgot we were headed to the store. 'Let's go get some new books, okay?'

''Kay!' Opal quit pouting right away. I picked up the bag nd looked around for a place to put it where Kiki wouldn't see it. Kiki could find her own food, was the way I looked at it.

I heard the kids next door, and for about a half a second, I felt bad. They banged on their window, and the baby cried in the apartment, and their mama hollered at them to quit making a racket or she was gonna come out there and give them somethin' to cry about. Then there was a man's voice with hers, and the baby just kept on fussing. If Rusty'd been home, he would of pounded on the wall to make her take care of the baby.

The sandwich bag felt heavy in my arm. The jelly'd soaked through and made a little round spot on the palm of my hand. It made me think of the stained-glass window in Mama's church – big hands with little red circles in the middle and water cupped in the fingers. I sat there and looked at it the day of Mama's funeral, because I didn't want to see the casket. Mama shouldn't of had a plain brown casket. She didn't like brown. She liked bright colors . . .

The red on the window hands was too bright. It didn't look like blood, but of course, I knew the story – you can't go to Sunday school, even some of the time, without knowing the story – but with the light coming through from behind, the red spots in the hands looked perfect, and round, and pretty.

I always thought the story of Jesus's bloody hands was sad when they told it on Easter, but the day of Mama's funeral, I looked at the window and thought Jesus had strawberry jelly on his hands. Something sweet, and good.

I wasn't afraid for Mama to go to heaven anymore.

I just kept thinking about those hands touching her, leaving a perfect round stain on her pretty white robe. The preacher said there wasn't any sickness in heaven, and I thought how awesome it would be for Mama not to be sick.

Now, looking down at the spot on my hand, I thought of

the Jesus window and Mama. She wouldn't like it that I was hunting a place to hide those sandwiches. Neither would Jesus, actually. *You get back what you give, Cass Sally Blue,* Mama always said. *You just remember that.* There was a little selfish streak in me she said needed work.

I headed out of the kitchen, and Opal got off her chair and followed me. When I opened the door, light flooded into the room, and for the first time in a long time I felt like Mama was right there beside me in her white robe and angel wings.

The kids'd given up banging on their door and they were sitting on the steps, drawing on the cement with chalky rocks from the storm ditch. The littlest one had tears all over his face and snot running down his chin. He looked over at us, and that stuff was hanging like a couple of big green gummy worms. They jiggled in the sun while his chin trembled.

Gross.

I turned around and went back in the house and grabbed a stack of leftover McDonald's napkins, then headed out again. Opal choo-chooed along, holding a handful of my shorts like she thought I was gonna leave her behind.

The kids watched me when I came out. They always did that. For just a second, I wanted to do what I usually did and pretend I didn't see them. It was their lazy, stinking mom's job to take care of them, not mine. I already had one rugrat hanging on my shorts, and I still wasn't even sure how that happened.

'I've got some sandwiches. Ya'll want one?' Maybe they'd say no, and I could put the sandwiches back inside, and me and Opal could go on to the Book Basket.

The oldest girl, who went to elementary school once in a

while when her mom woke her up and got her dressed, sneered sideways at me like she figured I was pulling her leg. 'What kind?'

You little brat, I thought. *Never mind, then. Just hang out over there and see what kind of sandwiches your mom gives you.*

'Nub-bubber-nelly-nam-ich,' Opal answered, and the girl from next door gave her a snotty look.

'Where'd *she* come from?'

'She's my cousin.'

'She don' look like you cousin.'

'Well, she is.' The last thing I needed was for anyone to tell sweaty Charlie we had some stripper and her kid living in our apartment. 'Do you want a sandwich or not, because we've got stuff to do.'

The other two kids were on my steps before I could say, *Stay where you're at. I'll bring it over there.* They hadn't ever come over on our steps before. Now they'd probably be over here all the time. Opal scooted behind me and about pulled my shorts off, peeking around my leg.

I handed the kids a couple of napkins. 'Here. You have to wipe up first.' The kids frowned at me, then wiped their hands with the napkins while the oldest girl wandered on over, dragging her sneakers on the asphalt. She stopped at the bottom of the steps, and I didn't tell her to come on up. I reached in the bag instead and took out a sandwich, and the littlest kid tried to snatch it out of my hand. He still had snot strings hanging down his face. 'Oh, no way.' I pulled the sandwich back. 'You have to wipe your face, too. That's just nasty.'

115

His chin started to quiver like he was gonna cry. I guess he thought I was teasing him with the sandwich. No way was I gonna wipe that kid's face for him, though, no matter how much Mama and Jesus talked in my head. Finally, his sister grabbed the napkin, swiped it across his face, and then threw it on the ground. I handed the kid the sandwich, then gave one to the middle brother, and then to the bratty girl.

I set the bag by the door to save the rest. No telling if that lady really would come back with more tomorrow, and I still didn't know how me and Rusty were gonna buy enough food for all week. The extra sandwiches were what Mama would of called *a godsend*.

The kids plopped down on *my* steps, and the next thing I knew, we were having a picnic. Opal let go of my shorts and went and sat down next to the littlest boy, who was about her size. She had her knees folded out to her sides and her hands between them, so that she looked like a squashed frog. She watched him eat like it was real interesting. He finished his whole sandwich and then licked the jelly off the plastic wrap. Then he licked his fingers and looked at my sack.

Oh, man. I started counting the sandwiches in my head. *Ten to begin with. Opal and me ate most of three. I gave three to the kids. If they all took another one, that'd leave . . .*

Math wasn't my best subject back in Mrs Dobbs's class, but even I knew that'd leave one sandwich, and Opal's part of a half that was wrapped up on the counter inside. Not even enough for breakfast tomorrow. We'd have to eat some of the food me and Rusty were gonna buy tonight . . .

Man. I knew what Mama and Jesus would do, but they weren't the ones who'd got stuck listening to Opal whine about being hungry all day yesterday. I didn't want to end up back in that shape again.

The bigger boy finished his sandwich and eyed the bag. 'I wanna 'nother one,' he said.

I thought about telling them the bag was empty. I *wanted* to tell them it was empty.

He dropped his wad of plastic wrap on the step, which was rude. Opal picked it up, then twisted around and climbed up the steps. She opened the bag, put the plastic wrap inside, and pulled out another sandwich.

'Opal, don't . . .' It was too late. Opal was already headed over to him. She tripped and about gave him a peanut butter and jelly hairdo before she fell down hard and hit her knee. He leaned over and ripped the sandwich out of her hand while she was trying to get up. I wanted to smack him, even though he was only about five or six. Opal didn't cry. She just stuck her finger in her mouth, then pulled it out and rubbed it over the little bead of blood on her knee. I had to give her credit for being tough.

'Just a minute, Opal,' I said, then went inside and got a wet napkin with a little soap on it. When I put it on Opal's knee, she acted like nobody'd ever done that to her before, ever. 'Hold it on there a while.' I started to get up, because the kids were in the sandwich bag, but then I just left it be. They each had another sandwich, which would still leave one for me and Opal tomorrow, if the sandwich lady didn't come back.

One of the girls from the apartments where the Mexicans

117

partied at night walked by carrying a baby. She didn't look more than about fifteen, but I'd figured out that baby was hers. She had a husband or a boyfriend, and I was pretty sure they were straight out of Mexico. He'd go across the street every day and hang around the parking lot waiting for the contracting vans to come by and offer straight-cash jobs. Rusty didn't like it when people hired parking-lot help. He said the illegals worked so cheap, they made it hard on everybody else. I didn't mind the Mexicans so much. On weekend nights, when they were partying down there, it sounded like they were having fun, and they always waved at us and stuff, and they never locked their kids out all day.

The Mexican girl looked surprised to see us on my steps. She didn't say anything, just gave us a curious look, her eyes big and dark and her long black hair swinging from side to side across her hips as she passed. She was pretty. It seemed like a girl that pretty wouldn't have to come across the border and live in a crappy apartment. She could of been a movie star someplace.

As soon as the next-door kids finished their sandwiches, they lit out like rabbits. When I picked up the bag, I figured out why. Someone must of stuffed the extra sandwich in their pants, because the sack was empty. Quick as we got to the land of plenty, Opal and me were back to nothing.

Brats. I didn't say it, because I didn't want Opal to know those kids did a mean thing while she was being so nice to them. I grabbed my book from inside, and Opal and me headed out. By the time we'd walked a couple blocks down the street, I'd cooled off a little. Maybe those kids needed an extra sandwich more than Opal and me did, and besides, I *had* promised the sandwich lady that I'd give food to the kids. I'd ended up keeping the promise, even if part of me didn't want to. Mama would be happy.

At the little white church across from the Book Basket, the gardener guy was pushing a lady in a wheelchair down the sidewalk. She was telling him what to do with the flower beds, I guessed, because she'd point and he'd nod. I'd seen him there before, working in the memory garden or trimming the bushes by the door. He always waved at me, but the first few times I acted like I didn't see him. He was, like, really big, and you could tell by the way he moved around that his elevator didn't go all the way to the top. He was stuck somewhere around halfway up, like a big ol' kid. We had a few like him in my school back home. I never thought much about how they'd be when they got to be old, like forty or something.

While Opal and me walked closer, he left the wheelchair lady in the shade. The pastor dude came out of the church to talk to her, and the big guy went to work by the pole sign out front. He waved when he saw Opal and me, and I waved back at him. Today, he was digging some plants out of the flower bed and putting them in plastic pots he had in a box.

'Hi-eee!' he said, and sat back on his heels, and smiled at us. He picked a flower and held it out to see if Opal would come get it. I knew she wouldn't. She stopped on the sidewalk and looked at him.

'She's afraid of people,' I explained. 'She doesn't . . .'

Opal took a little step toward him, then she stretched as

far as she could, anchoring herself on my arm like she was trying to reach over a big pool of water. Her fingers opened and closed. She couldn't get to the flower, but she wanted it.

'Here,' I said, then pulled her back and took the flower for her. 'Thanks,' I told the dude, and he ducked his head and did a kind of honk-honk laugh that was funny.

I put the flower in Opal's hand. She rubbed it against her nose and said, 'Mmmm,' and the man honked again.

'Say thanks, Opal.' I waited for Opal not to say anything, and then we crossed over to the Book Basket. All the way there, she kept looking back at the man, and just before we walked in, she turned and waved at him.

In the Book Basket, MJ was behind the counter with an African-looking twisty turban on her head. She was wearing a long loose shirt with giraffes around the neck and down the front, and about eighteen strings of wooden beads. There was never any telling, any day you went in, what she'd have on. One day she'd be dressed like a black Mother Goose, because she'd been to some school reading to the kids, and the next in a fluffy dress like Cinderella's fairy godmother, and the next a pioneer suit, like she'd just come off a wagon train. Today she looked like the ambassador from Zimbabwe or someplace.

Like usual, she was typing on her computer behind the desk. It was an old one – so old the screen was all green print. 'Well, hello there!' she said. 'You haven't been by in a couple days. I was beginning to wonder about you.' MJ always sounded real proper. She talked like she was reading a storybook, even when she was just shooting the breeze.

'Been busy.' Before Opal and Kiki came, I'd gone in the Book Basket, like, every day the doors were open, and sometimes more than once. I could trade books and kill time hanging out between the cases, looking at pictures and reading. MJ didn't seem to mind, and it beat sitting home alone in the apartment.

You could get lost in MJ's store. It had rows and rows of bookcases. The shelves were stacked so full they sagged in the middle, which was probably why your first book was free, and then after that you could come in and trade for another anytime you wanted. I was smart about it. I picked out a really big, fancy first book. On my next trade, it was worth two regular books, so I came out pretty good on the deal. I had credit for an extra book anytime I wanted it, but mostly I just got one at a time because then I could go back to the store more often.

I couldn't figure out how MJ made any money in her store, but when the shop was closed, she went around and told stories at schools, so I figured she made a living that way. She was fun to talk to, and it seemed like she knew just about everybody that came in. One time, the little gangbangers even wandered through, and she knew all three of them. She told them they needed to bring their old books by and trade them off. She asked about their families and school and stuff, and they hung around a while talking to her. I stayed back in the bookshelves where they couldn't see me.

MJ homed in on Opal right away. 'Who have we here? A new customer?'

'This is Opal,' I told her, and MJ said Opal was cute, and I was proud in a strange way, like Opal was mine or something. I told her Opal was my cousin. 'She likes books,' I said. 'I thought she could, like, use my credit and get one.'

'No way,' MJ answered, and I was disappointed. Then MJ smiled and said, 'First-time customers get a free book of their own. That's the deal. Let's see what we have for little girls who like books.' She held her arm out over the counter, and Opal moved from my hand to hers, and they headed toward the front window, where the picture books were. I went back to my section and picked out *Black Beauty* and a book about a kid who finds a magic door in his cellar and ends up in a secret world. With Opal in the apartment, I figured two books might be a good idea.

'*Black Beauty* again?' MJ asked, when I came up to the counter to cash out. 'Didn't you just read that?'

I watched her ring up my trades. *Black Beauty* was hardback, so I thought she might tell me it was too much. 'My mama and me used to read it.' It was a second before I clued in that I'd bloopered. 'I mean, we still will, again, but she's been sick. That's all. I don't need for someone to read to me anymore anyway.'

'Well, of course not.' MJ smiled and handed the books across the counter, her eyebrows slanting upward into her funny African hat. 'And here's Opal's first book.' Leaning far over the counter, she stretched a picture book down to Opal. *Billy and Blaze.* I figured Opal picked it because it had horse pictures in it.

MJ leaned on the counter with both elbows. 'What else can I do for you girls today?'

'Nothin',' I said, but I was hoping she'd tell a story. MJ knew great stories from all over the world. 'You been somewhere telling stories today?' I squinted one eye at the turban on her head.

She laughed, her teeth a wide white line between her dark lips. 'I have. It's World Heritage month, so I've been to the festival downtown. I've been sharing stories from Africa.'

'Cool.' I hovered there a minute, because that was usually all it took to get MJ going.

She pretended to think, and then sure enough she started into a story. 'I'll tell you a folktale from Ghana. I learned this from Ifeoma, a nurse who lives nearby. She came to this country from Africa, and as soon as she has enough money, she'll return to Africa to bring her son here.'

'Cool,' I said. 'I bet he misses his mom, being way over there.' I knew just how that boy must feel, only my mom was even farther away than Africa.

'I'm sure he does.' MJ swirled her hands over the counter, then spread them out, like she was drawing a picture to start the Africa story. 'Once, a large frog and a small frog were hopping along the road. They came to a little village, and the large frog said, "Let's go into the village. There is a market on the street, and we will have an easy meal of all the bugs there."

'The small frog wasn't certain this was a wise idea. "There are many dangers in the market," he told his companion. "What if we should be trampled by people, or run over by a cart, or captured by some child and put into a box?"

'"Pah!" said the large frog. "You worry too much. Come along. We'll have an easy meal."

'The small frog, being small, was afraid to have his friend leave him, so they hopped along to the market, and straightaway found a crate with flies buzzing around. "Let's hop up there and eat some delicious flies," said the large frog, and so they did. But the crate was very tall and they could not see that it lacked a solid top. When they jumped onto it, they fell straight into a large pot of cream, and try as they might, they could not get out of the pot.'

MJ made the motions of the frogs swimming.

Opal said, 'Uh-oh,' and tried to crawl up my leg.

I picked Opal up so she could see better when MJ went on with the frog story. '"Oh!" said the large frog. "Whatever shall we do now? You should have warned me of this. You said we may become trampled, or run over, or put into a box, but you said nothing of falling into a bucket of cream! Now we are trapped."

'The small frog did not answer. He only continued to swim round and round in the cream.

'"Oh, this is the end of my life! There is no escape from here! All is lost!" cried the large frog. He stopped swimming and refused to continue, even when the small frog pleaded with him not to give up.

'Straightaway, he sank to the bottom and died.' MJ made a sad face with a big frown, and Opal caught a breath, waiting to see what would happen next.

'But the small frog swam and swam,' MJ went on. 'For a long time, he beat the cream with his feet, even though his legs burned from the effort, and his heart pounded so hard against his chest. Finally, many hours later, the cream became a ball of butter. And do you know what the little frog did?' MJ's eyebrows went up into the turban, and she waited for me to think it through.

'Uh-uh,' I answered. 'Doesn't seem like it'd be too good to be stuck in a bucket of butter, either.'

Opal nodded like she agreed with me.

MJ's lips lifted into a smile, and she raised a finger like she always did when she was about to give you the real point. 'Ah, but you see, he was a very smart and strong little frog. He climbed right onto that ball of butter and jumped out of the pot, and he did not stop again until he was safely home.'

MJ leaned across the counter, touched the end of Opal's nose, and winked at me, her eyes twinkling. 'So, you see, it is not always important to be the largest frog. Sometimes it is the small but determined one who churns the butter and hops out of the pot.'

'That's a good story,' I said, and Opal nodded. 'I guess Opal and me better go now.' Even though I liked her stories, I was always careful not to hang around at the counter talking to MJ too long. She was the kind of person who got in people's business, I could tell. Rusty and me didn't need anybody getting into our business, no matter how nice she was.

'Thanks,' I said, and we headed out the door. Opal held her book and her flower against her chest so tight you couldn't of got a toothpick between her and her new stuff. My feet were tired, so I decided to skip the Just-a-Buck store and head home. It wasn't till we were halfway there that I thought about Opal having on one sandal and one tennis shoe. MJ might of wondered why the adults in our house would let her go out like that. I'd have to look again later and see if there were more shoes anywhere in Kiki's stuff.

We took our time walking back past the white church. The flowers were all done, and the big guy was gone, and so was the wheelchair lady. The pastor dude waved at us, and I waved back. After that, we stopped at the storm ditch to look at some tadpoles. They were living in a little puddle of water where the dirt and the cement came together. I caught a couple and poured them into Opal's hands and let her see how some of them had legs and some didn't yet. She stayed with the water dripping on her dress for a long time, just watching the little pool between her fingers. I guess no one had ever showed her a tadpole before.

Rusty's truck was out front when we got home. I grabbed Opal up and hurried the last little ways, because I was afraid something was wrong. It was two hours past lunchtime.

When I walked in, Rusty was pacing by the bathroom door. Kiki must of been inside.

'What are you *doing* here?' If he kept sneaking off from work, he was gonna get himself fired.

'Geez, where've you been?' He lifted his hands and let them smack to his sides. 'Kiki was worried about her kid.'

'Yeah, I'll bet. I had to go to the bookstore, so I took her with me. It's not like her mama's gonna watch her.'

Rusty checked the bathroom door and then the wall clock, then he gave me a tired look. 'Give Kiki a break, okay? She's in pretty rough shape. The pain pills knock her out.'

Yeah, I've heard, I thought, but I didn't want to get into another argument about Kiki, because it wouldn't do any good, and besides, Opal was right there. She sat down in her favorite corner of the sofa and opened her book.

'Why are you here?' I asked Rusty again. 'It's way past lunch break.'

He yanked off his cap, rubbed his forehead, and then put his cap back on. 'Kiki needed a ride to work again.' Turning toward the door, he hollered, 'Come on, Kiki. We've gotta go!'

'You came all the way home for *that*?' I asked. 'You've gotta be kidding.'

'She couldn't get a ride, all right?' He sneered at me like Mr Snothead big brother. I hated it when he did that.

'Tell her to walk.' I sounded like a snothead, too, but I didn't care. Rusty needed to catch a clue about Kiki.

'She can't walk that far. She can barely make it through her shift at work.' He checked the bathroom door again. 'Come on, Kiki! I've gotta get back.'

'Is she ever gonna give us any money? We don't have enough to feed her and her kid, too.' On the sofa, Opal looked up from her book, and I was sorry I said it.

'She just needs a few more days, maybe a week, before she's paid off what she owes her manager.' Rusty paced to the bathroom door and back.

'A *week*?' I hollered, and in the corner of my eye I saw Opal pop her thumb into her mouth and try to disappear between the sofa cushions.

'It'll be all right, Sal.' Rusty dug in his pocket for his keys as the bathroom door unlocked. 'See ya later on, okay? We'll go to Wal-Mart.'

Kiki dragged herself from the bathroom, pushing off the door frame and looking out-of-it. She swayed on her feet as she stood by the sofa, leaned down face-to-face with Opal, and slurred out the words, 'You okay, ba-by? Mama was wor . . . wor-ried.'

Opal bobbed her head slowly up and down.

Kiki kissed her on the forehead and left a big crooked smudge of red lipstick, then swayed upright again and blinked at me with the shiner eye half open. 'Take care my ba-by,' she said, as she pulled a pair of massive, red-rimmed sunglasses off her head and put them on to hide the shiner. Staggering back and forth on her high heels, she crossed the room. 'Be good, shhhh-sugar.'

I wasn't sure which one of us was *Sugar*, but when Rusty pulled the door shut behind the two of them, I made up my mind right then and there, if Rusty wasn't gonna do something, I'd have to. Kiki needed to find someone else to leech off of before we all starved to death, or Rusty got caught sneaking away from the construction site and lost his job.

Kiki had to go.

When I turned around, Opal was all wrapped up in a ball with her arms strung around her legs. Her big lemur eyes were peeking out at me from behind her little bony knees, and then another question went through my mind.

If I get rid of Kiki, what do I do about Opal?

CHAPTER 9

Sandra Kaye

My cell started ringing just as the neighborhood filled with the sounds of kids coming home from school. Up to my elbows in paint, I didn't bother to answer. When the phone rang a second time, I stripped off my gloves and grabbed it from my purse.

Jake's phone, the ID said, and my heart jumped. I'd answered by saying, 'Jake . . . Jake, is that you?' before I realized it couldn't be. When Jake had disappeared the night after Poppy's memorial service, he'd taken almost nothing with him. As far as we could tell after searching his room, everything he'd chosen was tucked into the small backpack he used for his books at college. The cell phone, his high school class ring, the treasured Randall pocketknife Poppy had given him, and his house keys had all been placed on the desk in his room, as if he were turning them in.

His debit card had been used just three times – once to pay for an airport shuttle, once to buy a plane ticket to Guatemala, and once to withdraw the remaining eight hundred dollars of the money he'd earned working at a kids' camp over the summer. The two thousand Rob had just deposited for college expenses was left behind, as was the debit card, which we found in his car at the airport, locked inside with the keys.

If a person wanted to disappear, the young police lieutenant said after he checked the car for signs of foul play, *this is how they'd do it.*

'Mom, it's Chris.' Christopher's voice drove home the sharp thought that I might never hear Jake on the phone again. The sting of loss was followed by the rapid awakening of parental guilt. Christopher had dropped his phone in the swimming pool last week while he was feeding Bobo. Rob had told him to go ahead and use Jake's.

Rob and I had argued about it later. I'd told him he was acting as if Jake had ceased to exist.

It's just a phone, Sandra, he'd said. *We can't keep putting everything under glass, waiting for Jake to come back.*

I don't want him to get back and think we just . . . gave away his things! Tears overcame me, and I ran away, feeling split down the middle like a piece of worn fabric. Letting Christopher use the phone wasn't giving it away – I knew that in some logical part of myself. But even after six months with no word from Jake, keeping everything ready for his return seemed important. It was the only way to retain some control, to avoid the fact that we didn't know if our son was alive or dead, or if he ever intended to return, or who he'd be if he did. He wouldn't be our Jake, who smiled and laughed at everything, who knew the world was basically good, and believed that his Guatemalan mother had delivered him to an orphanage because she loved him and couldn't take care of him. He would be a young man who'd learned some of life's harsh realities. What would he do if he found out that his mother had tried to sell him in the marketplace before abandoning him there?

'Hi, Chris. What's up?' The words were overly cheerful – like a picture painted with artificially bright colors. I didn't want Christopher to think I was sorry it was him instead of Jake.

'Mom, where are you? Are you home?' The statement drifted into space, ending in an eerie pause that caused the hair to prickle on the back of my neck.

'Chris, what's wrong?' *There's been some news about Jake. Something bad.* The thought raced across my mind, leaving a white-hot trail. Surely if there was news, Rob would be calling instead of Christopher.

'Where are you?' Chris asked again. A car alarm was blaring in the background, almost drowning out the call.

'Christopher. What's wrong?'

'Can you just come . . .' A sob choked the end of his sentence. The sound grabbed my lungs and squeezed out a painful breath. This wasn't the voice of Christopher, the suddenly mature, fiercely independent young man who didn't need anyone's help anymore. This was my little boy, who ran home in tears when his friends talked him into vaulting off the edge of the culvert on his skateboard and he broke his arm.

'Christopher, where are you? What's going on?'

'Near the steak place. In the parking lot. I had a wreck.'

'Oh, Christopher.' The reproach was a knee-jerk reflex. Chris had been involved in fender benders twice already in less than eight months of driving. 'Are you all right? Is everyone all right?'

'Yes.' Christopher's voice trembled, growing faint, so that the car alarm seemed louder and louder. 'My head's bleeding. It's just a little cut. It wasn't my fault, Mom. I don't think it was my fault, but the guy says I cut him off, but I didn't, I don't think –'

I interrupted Christopher's frantic tide of words. 'Stay where you are. Just don't go anywhere. I'll be right there.' My mind snapped to reality. I wouldn't be *right there*. I couldn't be. I was all the way across town.

I tossed the paintbrush into the water bucket. What was I doing here? Why wasn't I in Plano where I needed to be? 'Chris, are you by yourself? Was anyone in the car with you?'

'No. It's just me. It's just me and the guys in the other car. They say it was my fault, Mom, but it wasn't. They called the police . . .' Chris's voice turned weepy and uncertain again, almost panicked.

Digging my keys out of my purse, I headed for the door. I imagined an officer taking statements, an adult driver making accusations on one side and my confused teenager babbling almost incoherently on the other.

'Christopher, listen to me,' I ordered, and Chris stopped sniffling and muttering about the accident. 'Have you called Dad?'

'The desk said he's in surgery.'

'All right,' I said as I struggled to open the burglar bars on Poppy's front door. 'All right, listen. I'm all the way across town. It'll be a while before I can get there. I want you to calm down and think about the accident. Tell me exactly what happened.'

'I can't, Mom. I can't. The guys are mad. They're looking at their car, and yelling and stuff. I've got to get out of here. I don't know if my car'll drive . . . I don't . . . I'm not . . . the tire's rammed in . . .'

'Christopher!' I hollered, slamming the burglar bars shut behind me. Two little girls on a porch across the street watched as I rushed to the yard gate to retrieve Bobo. 'Is the steak place open? Christopher, is the restaurant open?'

'No. It's closed. It's still closed. Mom, they're coming over here. They're –'

'Christopher, I want you to get in the car, lock the doors, and wait until the police come. Get in and lock the doors. Right now. Do you hear me?'

'All right. Okay,' he sobbed. 'Dad's gonna kill me. Oh, Dad's gonna kill me. The car's messed up. It's really messed up.'

The incessant blaring of the alarm quieted as Chris closed his car door. 'I'm in my car.'

'Good. Just take a minute to catch your breath. *Don't* try to start the car.' After getting Bobo loaded, I climbed in, backed out of the driveway, and rocketed up Poppy's street. My fingers trembled on the steering wheel as I waited to turn off Red Bird into traffic, and it seemed ludicrous that I was the one telling Chris to get his wits about him. *Calm down*, I told myself. *Calm down and watch what you're doing.*

'Dad's not going to kill you, Chris. The main thing is that you're all right. We'll figure this out. Now listen. You stay where you are. Don't get out of your car. I'll call Holly and get her or Richard to come down there, okay?'

'Okay.' Chris's voice was a thin, frightened ribbon. 'Mom?'

'I'll call you back in a minute. I'm going to get Holly now.' *Please let Holly be somewhere near home. Please. Please.*

'Mom . . . I'm sorry.'

'We'll talk in a minute. I'm sure it was an accident.' Was it? Chris's record was abysmal. So much of the time, his head seemed to be off in a cloud somewhere. By contrast, when Jake was sixteen, we hadn't experienced a moment's hesitation about letting him drive. Jake had never so much as put a scratch on the car. After Chris's first fender bender, we'd delayed plans to get him a newer vehicle. *He doesn't seem to be ready for it,* Rob had said, and of course he'd said it in front of Christopher.

I tried to convince myself to believe my son's side of the story as I called Holly. She was on the way to pick up the twins from a cheerleading meeting. She headed for the steak house parking lot instead. 'I'll tell the girls to catch a ride with Stephie's mom,' she said.

'Oh, Holl, thanks. I'm sorry to have to ask you to do this. Chris is so upset. He really needs an adult there.'

'I'm just down the road. Anyway, I don't mind. You know I'd do anything for Christopher.'

'I know you would, Holl. Thanks.' I was filled with tenderness. There was never a time Holly failed to be there when we needed her.

'No problem. Okay, I can see the steak house. It doesn't look like the police are here yet.'

'Holly, be careful.' It occurred to me that I didn't know what the situation might be by now. 'Chris said the guys were threatening him. Don't get out of the car if you're worried.'

'Hey,' Holly chirped. 'I've been to Neighborhood Ranger School, remember?' Then she added, 'Gotta go,' and hung up the phone.

I dialed Chris's number again and waited for him to answer. As I passed by the low-rent apartment complex, my mind spun off momentarily. I looked down the narrow strip of pavement between the buildings, thinking of the three boys in the alley, the kids in the Dumpster, and Cass with the toddler on her hip. Where were they now?

Christopher's voice broke up the thought. He still sounded weepy, so different from the tough mini-man who'd been hitting the books night and day these past six months, determined to handle everything on his own.

'Hi, honey, Holly's almost to the steak house. I'll be there as soon as I can get across town.'

'Okay.' Chris's relief was obvious. 'I see her car.'

'Where are the other guys now? Are they still harassing you?'

'They're looking at their car again. They're really mad. Mrs Riley just got out. She's talking to them. I better go.' Chris hung up, and when I called back, he didn't answer.

Holly sent me a text a few minutes later:

Under control. Told them I'm your lawyer. LOL!

By the time I finally got back to Plano, Holly had brought Christopher home. She was hovering over the sofa, dabbing the cut on his forehead with antiseptic, while Chris tried to protest.

'Hold still!' she commanded. Christopher looked up as I came into the media room, and Holly took advantage of the chance to swab his forehead with the cloth. 'This might need stitches.' If not for the situation, Chris and I would have laughed. Holly's first reaction to every injury was hydrogen peroxide and then, *This might need stitches.*

Chris winced as the antiseptic started to bubble, then he let his head roll back against the sofa, and closed his eyes.

'He shouldn't go to sleep,' Holly advised. 'He could have a concussion.'

'I'm fine.' Chris's voice had lowered, had once again taken on the controlled tone of an almost-man. 'I'm okay . . . I'm . . . sorry I messed up again.' A tear drifted from beneath his lashes, fell down his cheek and swirled around his ear. Dried blood had colored the tawny curls there, turning them a brownish pink.

I felt guilty and sick. I wanted to rush to him, hold him the way I had when he was little, tell him it was all right, it wasn't his fault. At the same time, I felt the need to know what had happened and who was responsible. As much as I yearned to soothe the hurt and disappointment, a third fender bender in only eight months was no small problem.

'The main thing is that you're all right, Chris,' I said.

Holly nodded and patted his arm, giving him a sympathetic look before standing up. 'Hang in there, kiddo.' She laughed softly. 'Hey, you're not even close to Cammie's record yet. By the time she made it through her first year of driving, every police officer in the city knew her by name.' Holly's eldest daughter had been our first cooperative experience with teenagers. Cammie was notoriously distractible, chronically late, and way too addicted to her cell phone. She'd been famous for backing out of parking spaces and running into things, including the Riley garage door. Twice.

Chris groaned, his lips spreading into a weary smile over teeth that had only recently been freed of braces. 'Now she's comparing my driving to Cammie's. Go ahead and just pour some more of that stuff on my head, okay? Let me die.'

'Christopher!' I said, and both Holly and I chuckled. Chris's response to dire situations had always been to go for a laugh. It was comforting to see him acting more like himself. I hadn't heard him crack a joke or seen him really smile in months. He had a wonderful smile. Rob's smile. The first time I saw Rob, I was working part-time at the hospital reception desk, and that smile caught my eye from across the room. He'd had the presence of a doctor, even though he was just a med student.

'Look on the bright side. You haven't taken out the garage door yet,' Holly quipped. 'Cammie's still way ahead of you.'

Chris's smile faded to something more forced. 'Thanks for coming today, Mrs Riley.'

'Oh, hey, anytime, kiddo.'

'You sure gave those guys heck.'

'I think they really believed me.' Holly giggled. 'It was some entrance, huh?'

The question won another grin from Chris. 'Yeah. I thought that one dude's eyes were going to pop right out of his head when you tripped and acted like you were about to fall on him.'

'For a guy whose back was supposedly injured, he got out of the way pretty quickly, didn't he?' Holly's face narrowed. 'Jerks. They saw a kid in a car by himself, and they figured they could get something out of it. I wouldn't be surprised if they hit you on purpose.' She slanted a glance at me, her expression serious. 'I got their names and license number, and the name of the police officer who did the report. If anything comes of this, y'all should research and see if those guys have been involved in scams before.'

If anything comes of this . . . 'What did the police say? Did they give Chris a ticket?'

Holly squeezed one eye shut, grimaced, and shrugged toward the kitchen. 'You get a Band-Aid on that cut, Christopher,' she instructed, her voice an airy contrast to the dark look on her face. 'That'd be a terrible place to catch staph.'

'Thanks for coming, Mrs Riley,' Chris said again, then sagged against the sofa, his mouth somber.

'Take care, sweetie.'

'I will.'

Holly waited until we were in the kitchen before giving me the details of the accident. 'I just got a weird feeling about the whole thing,' she finished. 'These guys seemed really . . . professional – like they knew exactly what to say and do. Chris told me that, at first, they acted like the wreck was no big deal. They offered to push his car off the road, and then after they got in the parking lot, they were all over him about the wreck being his fault, and they were kind of, well, prepping him for the police statement almost, trying to bully him into it while he was upset and confused. It's a good thing he called you.'

'I'm so glad you were here.' Smoothing my hair out of my face, I felt a tiny crust of dried paint. Holly seemed to notice it at the same time, then she quirked a brow and looked me over from head to toe, spattered sweat suit and all. 'Holly, thank you so much.'

'I don't mind.' She continued surveying me narrowly. 'Where did you say you were again?'

The sense of having been caught at something caused me to look away. 'Across town. So, what happened when the police officer got there? Did he say who was at fault?'

Holly's shoulders rose and fell. 'To tell you the truth, he didn't seem very . . . interested. Both cars had been moved by the time he arrived, and if there were any witnesses, they didn't hang around. He didn't give either one of them a ticket because by then you couldn't tell *what* had happened. But those guys were pretty determined. They were being careful about what they said. I don't know what statement they gave to the officer in private, but I'm afraid you'll hear from them again.'

'Ohhh, what next.' I let my head fall into my hand, feeling the weight of yet one more major issue atop the others. When was our family, our life, ever going to return to normal? When would things be good again? Right now, I didn't think we could hold up under one more straw. 'Rob's going to have a fit. He's already been frustrated with Christopher about his driving. He probably would have taken the car away by now if it weren't for the fact that Jake's . . .' I couldn't force out the word 'gone,' so I just let the sentence rest without it. 'Anyway, Holl, thanks so much for helping. It was a lot to ask.'

She gave me a perplexed look. 'You know I'd do anything for you, or for Christopher.' She laid her hand on my arm, over a spot where spatters of paint had dried when I flipped the bristles off the edge of a shelf and accidentally sent up a shower. 'Girlfriends, right?' Leaning over, she tried to find my gaze. 'That's what girlfriends do. Just like you did for me last year.'

'I know.' Was it only a year ago that I'd held Holly's hand during her lumpectomy, driven her to chemo, brought her soda crackers and Sprite, and shuttled her girls around to activities? Just last year? It seemed a lifetime ago. Jake was doing well in college, Christopher was busy with his music, all was right with the world. 'How did everything else go with the doctor visit the other day, by the way? I forgot to ask.'

Holly continued watching me intently. 'All right, except that he told me I'm too fat. What does he expect? I've got six and a half kids constantly bringing junk food into the house, and the rest of the time I'm working on catering. None of that's on Jenny Craig, I'll tell you.'

'We need to get out and walk more.'

'Yes, we do. How about tomorrow?'

Poppy's house, the mess on the counter, and the issue of sandwiches flashed through my mind. If the real estate agent brought anyone over, they'd find painting supplies and masking tape everywhere. 'I don't know about tomorrow. I may be tied up with Christopher and his car. Where is the car, anyway?'

Holly chewed her lip, then answered. 'Richard and the girls went over there to push it to the side of the parking lot. The restaurant manager said it would be all right there until you can get it towed.'

'Tell Richard thanks, okay?'

'I will.'

Holly started toward the door, then stopped and looked back at me. 'Is everything all right ... with you, I mean? Everything else?'

'Yeah, sure ... why?'

'You just ... normally wouldn't go out running errands looking like that.' She motioned to the splattered sweat suit. 'In all these years, I can't remember you ever leaving the house without looking perfect.'

The statement made me seem shallow and self-focused, but Holly was right. In my mother's home, appearances were everything, which was ironic, considering what went on when nobody was looking. 'You know what, Holl? With all that's happened these last few months, it just doesn't seem ... so important.'

'You're right.' Holly was pleased. For years, she'd been subtly trying to convince me that worrying about how things looked and what everyone thought was an unhealthy response to the subliminal presence of my mother. 'You go, girl.' Holly waved over her shoulder as she went out the door.

I poured a couple sodas and carried them to the media

room. Chris was still sitting on the sofa with his head back and his eyes closed. 'Here, sweetheart. I brought you something to drink.'

Chris shook his head, and his eyes closed more tightly, tears squeezing from beneath his lashes.

'I really screwed up.' His lips barely moved with the words.

'Sssshhhhh.' Leaving the drinks on the table, I sat down beside him, then slipped my arm around the little boy inside the nearly grown body.

'Dad's going to get the phone message.' His voice trembled with apprehension. 'As soon as he's out of surgery, he'll get it.'

'Ssshhhh,' I said again. 'Let's just sit here a minute.' I pulled Christopher closer, and slowly his muscles surrendered the resistance, gave in to the pull. He collapsed against me, leaning his head on my shoulder. A sob escaped his throat, a low sound filled with pain and grief that seemed to come from someplace deeper than just today.

'If Jake was driving, it wouldn't have happened,' he said, his sadness, his disappointment, his yearning for his brother evident in the words.

'We don't know that, Christopher. We don't know anything yet. Let's just take one step at a time. Whatever happened, your dad loves you and I love you.'

Chris sagged against my shoulder. 'I wish Jake and Poppy were here.' His voice was little more than a sigh.

'I know you do,' I whispered. 'Me, too.' It was the first time in six months that Chris and I had let ourselves openly admit how much the empty space in our family hurt.

'I wish Dad hadn't said what he did . . . to Jake,' he whispered. 'He shouldn't have blamed Jake . . . for Poppy . . .'

Outside, the garage door rumbled upward. Christopher stiffened, all the softness replaced by tension.

I left Chris on the sofa and met Rob in the kitchen. He was angry and red-faced, his jaw hard with frustration. 'Where is he?'

My stomach wrenched into a familiar knot that had little to do with Rob's outburst. A part of me rushed back in time, as always, and remembered being little Sandra Kaye, standing like a statue in the corner of the room, trying not to be noticed while my mother flew into a tirade.

'I can't *believe* he wrecked the car *again*!' Rob's teeth were clenched, his hands hard knots hanging on stiff coils. 'That's it! That's it for the car. Until he learns to be responsible, he can walk.'

A part of me cringed. *Responsible* – Rob's whipping word for Chris, one of my mother's whipping words for me. *Why must you be so irresponsible, Sandra Kaye? Why can't you be more like Maryanne? I've told you over, and over, and over – no schoolbooks on the counter. Haven't I? Haven't I? These filthy things* . . . The hand flew, the books scattered, and I dodged. My essay about reindeer in Siberia dropped quietly from my hand, the gold star suddenly one more insignificant item.

Stop, I told myself now. *Stop this. You're not a child. You're not powerless.* 'I don't think we should make any snap decisions. Holly's convinced that the other party might have hit Chris on purpose, to collect insurance.'

Rob's hand flailed toward Holly's house. 'Oh, come on. She

probably saw that on an episode of *48 Hours*.' Pursing his lips, he let out a long breath, ran a hand through his thick salt-and-pepper hair, then let it fall. His anger was burning out like a flash fire, and now he looked tired. His eyes flicked toward the doorway, as if he were considering proceeding to the media room to deal out Chris's sentence this very minute.

'It *is* possible,' I pressed. I hated fighting with him like this. Lately it seemed we couldn't have a conversation that wasn't hijacked by wild swings of emotion. Every conflict rebounded off a tightly stretched net of frustration and spiraled out of control. 'She could be right. We really don't know anything yet.'

Rob's gaze leveled and connected with mine in a sardonic way that said, *Come on, Sandra, don't be so gullible!* 'Holly's always making excuses for her kids. That's why she and Richard can't get them to move out of the house.'

'Holly did us a big favor today!' I spat, my temper rising, the words carrying into the hall. 'If she hadn't been there for Chris, who knows what might have happened? You could show a little gratitude.'

Rob's face reddened, his nostrils flaring. 'Holly's not the –'

'Stop arguing!' Chris's voice rounded the corner first, and then he followed it. Standing in the doorway, he looked out of place, sad, wounded. 'All you guys ever do is fight!' Tears spilled onto his cheeks. Sniffling, he wiped them impatiently with the back of his hand. 'I'm sorry! I'm sorry about the car. I'm sorry . . . I'm . . . sorry Jake's gone and not me!' The words crumbled into a sob. He ran from the room and up the stairs.

Rob turned to follow him, but I caught his arm. 'Leave

him be, all right? Don't say anything now while you're angry. Don't . . .' *do what you did with Jake. Don't drive him away because he messed up.* 'He feels bad enough. I'll find out more tomorrow when I can talk to the insurance company and get the details of the accident report.'

'I'm in surgery tomorrow. I can't get away.' Rob moved toward the door, grabbing his keys and wallet in a way that told me he was heading back to the hospital.

'I didn't suppose that you would.' The words were quick and bitter, a knee-jerk reflex.

'I need to check on a patient,' he muttered, then walked out, his arms stiff at his sides.

I went upstairs to Chris's room. When I opened his door, he was sitting on his bed, digging stuff out of his backpack.

Wiping his face on his sleeve, he hardened his shoulders. 'Is he coming up here?'

'No. He had to go back to the hospital. I'll check into the accident tomorrow, and then we'll talk.'

Letting out a long sigh, Chris nodded, then proceeded to spread papers out on the bed. 'I've gotta cram for history and English.' It was his way of saying he wanted to be left alone instead of getting another parent talk.

'All right.' I was suddenly exhausted by the day, too weary to try to bridge the gap between Chris and his father, or to pump Chris for the details of the accident. Rob would say I was being too much of a pushover, too willing to make excuses and smooth things out, as usual. Perhaps he was right, but I'd never wanted the boys to feel about me the way I'd felt about my mother.

145

Leaving Chris to himself, I pulled the door closed behind me and headed downstairs. A strange woman passed me in the mirror on the landing, and I took her in – frazzled hair, strawberry blonde tipped with paint in a few places, sweat suit spattered here and there, white on her index finger where she'd been holding a brush.

Rob had never even noticed.

The thought stung, pressing tears into my eyes as I settled onto the sofa.

How had we ended up here, fighting over who'd been wrong and who'd been right, and who was to blame for Poppy's death and Jake's disappearance?

If you hadn't insisted Jake join that stupid fraternity, none of this would have happened. I'd wished over and over again that I'd never said it in those dark, dizzying days after Poppy's funeral. In spite of the fact that all logic told me Rob could never have predicted what would come of his pushing Jake into the best fraternity, a part of me wanted to lay the blame in some tangible place.

What happened was nobody's fault, I should have said, but I didn't. I hadn't. I wasn't even sure why. Clinging to the blame was like clinging to Jake and Poppy. Making peace with it would be like admitting they were gone, and life had to go on without them here.

Through a rising fog, I watched the blurry image of Holly's house across the street. All the lights were on, shining into the darkness, pointing out that just a short walk away lived a healthy, lively family. No matter how hard Rob and I tried, we seemed to be drifting further and further from anything good.

I closed my eyes, and the tears came harder. I wanted to be somewhere else. Anywhere but here, trapped in my own life.

The sound of Rob coming in again roused me from a light sleep just as the evening news was signing off. I got up and went to the kitchen. 'Hey,' I said, and he stiffened, like a prowler caught in a home that wasn't his own.

He glanced at the clock on the stove. 'I thought you were asleep.'

'Just dozing,' I answered, watching as he pulled out lunch meat and made a sandwich.

'How's Chris feeling?'

'All right, I guess. He's studying, if that's any indication.' The conversation felt bland, but at least it wasn't an argument.

'Everything all right with his semester finals?'

'I think so. Sounds like physics is eating his lunch a bit.'

Rob nodded. 'Guess that's understandable.'

'Did you know his sax was broken?' I asked, even though the answer was obvious. Rob would have had to be home to know that. 'All semester, I guess. He never even said anything about it.' I wondered if Rob would pick up on the fact that our son was struggling. Music had always been the way Christopher worked out his thoughts. I could tell by the songs he played how he was feeling. After Poppy's funeral, he had played for hours.

Rob rubbed the back of his neck and stretched it from side to side. 'He's busy with other things. Too busy, if he can't keep his mind on his driving.'

147

'Please, let's not talk about the accident,' I said, disappointed. 'Let me look into it tomorrow.'

Rob's eyes, which had once seemed brown but now appeared the deepest shade of hazel with his thick, prematurely gray hair, avoided mine. 'I'm not trying to pick a fight. It's good to see Christopher getting after the schoolwork for a change. He's growing up.'

'I guess,' I agreed blandly, allowing the conversation to drift back into benign territory. 'He's really trying.'

'I know.' Rob's gaze caught mine for just an instant, then the conversation ran out, and finally he picked up his plate and started toward the door. 'I have to go sit down. Long day in surgery.' In the past, he would have shared the details – something funny that happened in the OR, or some touching moment between a patient and family.

I walked to the counter, closed the deli bags, and put the knife in the dishwasher.

'I can do that.' Rob turned back in the doorway.

'I know, but I don't mind.'

When I started toward the refrigerator, he was still there, frowning at me. 'You've got something in your hair.'

I reached up and touched the back of my head, finding a crusty line of paint. 'Huh,' I said. For just an instant, I was tempted to tell him the truth, but I didn't. 'Guess I must have brushed past something.'

CHAPTER 10

Cass

Rusty ran out of gas on his way home from work, and he had to use twenty dollars for a few gallons, so by the time he got back to the apartment he was in a bad mood. He didn't want to go to Wal-Mart. He wanted me to walk across the street and get some stuff from the convenience store, but I knew that was a bad idea. If we started buying from the Pakistani dude who had everything marked, like, three times what it was worth, we wouldn't have enough to last a day.

'What's the point in going to Wal-Mart with sixteen dollars?' Rusty asked. He stopped halfway through taking off his boots, and sat in the kitchen chair with his arms on his knees. His head sank into his hands, and his fingers disappeared into the stick-straight red hair the kids in school used to tease him about. 'What's the point in any of it? We're never gonna make it here in the long run. Everything costs too much.'

A sick feeling spread inside me, thick and black like an oil slick spilled into the ocean. Rusty looked tired, round in his shoulders, small. It scared me to see him that way. 'The point is we're gonna find Ray John, and then everything'll be okay.'

Rusty gave an angry laugh. 'We're never gonna find Ray John. We don't even know where to start.' I'd never heard Rusty talk like that. From the minute we left Helena, he was sure we were gonna track down Ray John, Rusty's daddy. Rusty could barely remember him. He recalled him coming to a birthday party once, a long time ago, and bringing Rusty a little guitar. After that, we didn't see Ray John anymore, but he was a good man, and Mama always had a soft spot for him. She said he was a welder, and a good one. He'd come up to Helena to work on a job, which was how they met. He was splitting up with his wife when Mama and him fell in love, but before they could get married, Ray John's son got hit by a car back in Ft. Worth, and he went home to take care of his family. He sent money for Rusty whenever he could, and that one time he drove all the way straight through to come to Rusty's birthday and bring him that guitar. Anybody who'd do that had to be pretty decent.

'You said the last check from Ray John had a Ft. Worth address on it,' I pointed out. I wanted Rusty to get up out of that chair and stop acting like this was the end of everything.

He snorted softly, his head bobbing up and down. 'What check?'

'The check from Ray John. The stuff that was in Mama's file box when she went to the hospital.' I felt the oil slick rising up, coming to life like a monster in a comic book. It grabbed all the good feelings I had from getting Opal a book of her own and reading it to her about twenty times while we waited for Rusty. She was curled up on the sofa now, looking at the pictures.

'There wasn't any check in Mama's drawer.'

'Well, then, the envelope. The envelope from Ft. Worth.' I wanted to throw something at Rusty, to snap him out of it. Of course the actual check wasn't still in the envelope. If Mama'd had a check there near the end, she would have cashed it, instead of us having to get everything from creepy Roger. 'You *showed* me the envelope.'

Rusty glared up at me. 'Who knows if that was from Ray John. It didn't have any return address but a P.O. box.'

'She wrote his name on the front, Rusty. She wouldn't do that if it wasn't from him.'

Rusty gave me a weird look that crawled over my skin like a mosquito looking for a place to bite. 'Yeah,' he said finally, like he really didn't care anymore who the envelope was from. Being seventeen, Rusty probably didn't have so much to worry about. Even if CPS did catch us, they'd most likely turn him loose to go his own way. They'd have me in for six more years before I finally aged out of the system. They might send me right back to creepy Roger.

The idea made tears burn in my nose, and I pinched it to make them stop. I wanted Rusty to straighten up. 'Listen, let's go on to Wal-Mart, okay? You won't believe what I can get for sixteen dollars. One thing I learned from Mama is how to stretch money. It'll be enough. I'm hungry. Aren't you?'

'Unnn-unn-gwee!' Opal hopped off the sofa and came

151

trotting over to the kitchen, her tennis shoe and sandal making lopsided sounds on the floor. I got the half-eaten peanut butter and jelly from earlier and handed it to her. I sure wished I'd kept the rest of the sandwiches. Seven free peanut butter and jelly sandwiches would make a big difference right now.

Rusty stuck his feet back in his boots, then pushed himself out of the chair, groaning and twisting his shoulder round and round while he held it with his opposite hand. He pushed his eyes shut and his lips pulled away from his teeth, like it really hurt.

'What's the matter?' I asked.

'Gob owie?' Opal added with her mouth full of sandwich. She twisted to look all the way up at Rusty's face. From her height, he must of seemed like the Tower of Pisa.

'Nah.' Rusty smiled at her, then rolled his shoulder again and made another face.

'What's wrong with your shoulder?'

He snatched his keys off the counter. 'Nothin'. I fell off a deck and landed on it. No big deal.'

'Are you sure it's all right?' Not so long ago, Rusty having any kind of hurt arm would have been something to panic about, because it'd mean maybe he couldn't play whatever sport was going on at the time. No sports meant no scholarship. The coaches really thought he had a good chance at a free ride to college. This time of year, he'd be pole vaulting and running the mile in track and playing baseball. He was good at all three.

'Yeah, no big deal. I was in a hurry, and I did something stupid, trying to make up time.'

Probably the time it cost coming here to take stupid Kiki to work,
I thought, but I didn't dare say it, because with the mood he
was in, Rusty'd jump down my throat. He had a thing for
Kiki, and whether I wanted him to or not, he was gonna
take care of her like he was Prince Charming and she was
Sleeping Beauty. But the truth was that Kiki was the reason
he had to put gas in the truck when we weren't planning to
yet. A few extra trips back and forth between the construction site, here, and Glitters could eat up twenty bucks
quicker than you could say *broke.*

'Let's take off, if we're going,' he said, then tossed the
keys up and caught them behind his back. I thought about
how many times I'd seen him do that with a baseball. Rusty
could handle a ball like nobody's business.

Opal giggled, her face all peanut butter and jelly. Now
that I looked, she was kinda dirty all over from crawling
around the bookstore and storm ditch. I stuffed a couple of
napkins in my pocket, so I could wipe her face when she
finished the sandwich.

Rusty threw the keys up and caught them again, and Opal
belly laughed. She tripped on the toe of her sandal and
almost landed on her face when we went out the door. She
did that about every three steps. Walking in two different
shoes probably wasn't so easy, but after looking through all
their stuff, sorting out Opal's laundry from Kiki's and taking
it over to wash, I hadn't found anything else to put on her.

Rusty noticed Opal's feet. 'How come she's got two different shoes on?'

'That's all she has,' I told him. I didn't want him to think

I'd done the shoe thing on purpose. 'Her mom didn't bring her anything else. I went through their stuff and took Opal's to wash. She's only got a few things.'

'Kiki had to grab what she could.' Rusty stopped to lock the door. 'Her old man threw their stuff out in the yard after he beat her up. She had to wait until he was gone before she could pick up whatever was left.'

'Geez. Where'd they go when he threw them out?' The night Rusty brought her home, the shiner on Kiki's eye wasn't brand-new. By then, it was already swole up and the blood had dried.

Rusty looked over his shoulder at Opal while he checked the door. 'They just started walking and looking for a place. They ended up in some of the condos that were almost finished down at the construction site. Security ran them out, but when I went back and checked later, they were there again, curled up on the cement under the stairs. I figured if the night guard found them, they'd get arrested, so I asked her if I could give her a ride someplace. We drove around a while, but she didn't have anywhere to go.'

'Geez,' I muttered again. I looked at Opal and thought about her sleeping on the cement in the dark. Our junky little apartment must of seemed really good after that. It's funny how when you think you've got problems, you usually don't have to look far to find someone who's in a lot worse shape. *Count your blessings, not your troubles*, Mama would of said.

Rusty picked up Opal with his good arm when we got down the stairs. With her little legs, she couldn't even come close to staying up with him. I had to jog just to keep from getting left behind while we walked. I reached across and wiped Opal's face with the napkin, then threw it in the Dumpster.

'We'll get her some shoes,' Rusty said. Opal looked excited, but I knew there wasn't any way we were gonna be buying shoes anytime soon.

When we got to Wal-Mart, all Rusty wanted to do was look for shoes for Opal. By then, he had her so worked up, she was bouncing up and down and saying, 'Tshoo, tshoo, tshoo, newww tshoo!'

While I went and picked out groceries, adding the prices up in my head until I had all we could pay for, Rusty took off with Opal. He patted her on the head and told her to 'C'mere,' like she was that dog of his back home. He liked that dog better than he liked any of his girlfriends. Missy sat right in the front seat of the truck whenever Rusty drove it. There was always a big circle of gray cow-dog hair to stick to your butt when you got in the passenger side.

After we moved in at Roger's, Missy disappeared. Roger said she ran away while we were at school, but I figured he took her and got rid of her someplace, because she didn't like Roger any better than we did. I thought Rusty was gonna kill Roger, but Mama was there on the couch sick, so Rusty just walked out the door and went all over town looking for his dog. I figured he wouldn't find her, and he didn't.

Opal and Rusty came back from the shoe department with a pair of little pink plastic clogs that were on clearance for three dollars. They had flowers painted across the straps and rhinestones on the toes. Opal hugged them under her chin while me and Rusty argued about whether or not we'd have enough money for the groceries, plus shoes. Rusty was never worth a flip at math. I told him we wouldn't have enough, and we didn't. At the checkout, I had to take off a jumbo bargain bag of Frosted Fruity O's I figured we could eat on for about three days.

'I told you we didn't have enough.' My face turned hot, and Rusty walked off while I stood looking at the groceries, trying to think what else to give up. I didn't grab Opal's shoes, because she was standing on her tiptoes watching them with her fingers wrapped around the edge of the counter.

I picked up the jelly, because it was a dollar, and we could still make peanut butter sandwiches without it. The clerk, a big black lady with her hair in about a million long braids, laid her hand over mine and pushed the jelly back into the pile, and then the Fruity O's, too. 'Here, honey.' She reached into her pocket and pulled out some folded bills. 'I figured they was some reason for that three dollars in my pocket today.'

My face got really hot when her hand put the dollar bills in mine. She covered them over with her fingers for a minute. Her long pink fingernails had little diamonds on the ends, like Opal's new shoes.

I didn't look up at her, just nodded and counted money in my head again. All I could think was that at first I didn't want to go through her line because she looked like the lady who locked her kids out on the steps. Rusty made me use her checkout because it had the shortest line.

'Things'll get better.' She squeezed my hand, and then she let go, and I had the money for Opal's shoes, and jelly, and cereal.

Opal stretched up so that her eyes poked above the edge of the counter. The lady laughed at her, then picked up the shoes and handed them over. 'Here you go, shug. You'll look real good in those pretty little shoes.'

Hugging the clogs under her chin, Opal rocked back and forth. When we left with our groceries, she turned around and waved, but the lady was already busy helping the next person in line.

I thought about that lady when I was trying to get to sleep on the sofa that night. I kept trying to think why, of all the people she checked out, she decided to give that money to us, and then I thought that I almost didn't go through her line because of the way she looked. It sure was lucky hers was the shortest, but then, luck is really just the angels blowing you a kiss.

I fell asleep feeling like there were angels all around me. Even when Kiki knocked at the door and came stumbling in from work about midnight, that soft, sweet feeling didn't leave. I didn't gripe at her and tell her to be quiet, or feel myself fill up with hate, like I normally would of. I just squinted across in the dark and whispered, 'Hey.'

'Hey,' she said softly, and crossed the room with her heels making uneven sounds on the floor. Her silhouette was crouched over, and she was holding her ribs. She lost her balance and fell against the stove as I crawled back into my sleeping bag.

'You okay?'

'Yeah.' She sighed, then disappeared into the bathroom. She must of fallen against the wall in there, because she made a crash, and Rusty got up to check on her. He had to help her off the floor. I heard her tell him she was home from work early because her ribs were hurting so bad she couldn't carry the trays, and so the manager made her leave. He charged her for some glasses she broke, and said she better get back in shape soon. He'd hired her to be a dancer, and then she got herself beat up by her old man. If she didn't get better soon, and get back on *the pole* – whatever that meant – she'd lose her job.

Rusty told her not to worry. 'It'll be all right,' he said, then helped her to bed.

I closed my eyes not feeling quite so bad about Kiki being in my room. The bed was like the three dollars in the check-out lady's pocket. I needed three dollars, and the lady had it, so she passed it on. Kiki needed a bed for her and Opal, and I had a bed. It didn't hurt me to sleep on the sofa a while.

I fell asleep and dreamed about a big circle. All kinds of people were walking in it. Every once in a while, you reached across to a person on the other side, so you could give something from your hand to theirs, and then your hand was open and you didn't have to carry extra. After a while, someone reached across to give you something you needed. There was never any telling who it was going to be or what, and you couldn't see the circle, but you could feel it, if you let yourself.

In the morning, when Opal put on her new pink shoes, and I poured the cereal, I thought about the checkout lady again. Sitting down at the table, it seemed like we should say grace. I had to show Opal how to do her hands and tell her to close her eyes, just like Mama showed me when I was little. After that, we did all right. I said grace real quick, because I wasn't sure how long Opal'd hold out, and besides, when you mix water in the milk to make it go further, your cereal gets soggy fast. 'God bless these gifts that we're about to receive,' I said, just the way we used to at home. 'And bless Mama and Rusty and me, and Opal, and Kiki, MJ down at the bookstore, and the lady at Wal-Mart.' I thought for a minute, then added, 'And the lady with the sandwiches yesterday. Thanks. Amen and let's eat.' Mama always added that to let us know grace was over. Opal wasn't used to it, so she waited until I picked up my spoon to pick up hers.

Opal liked the cereal a lot. She ate every last drop, and then she wanted more. I told her no. I'd measured it out. If I didn't pour the bowls too full, and Rusty could keep from going wild with his breakfast, we'd have enough for three more mornings. By the time it was gone, maybe Kiki would be able to bring a little money home.

Someone was playing mariachi music in the parking lot across the street. 'Hear the music?' I said, so Opal would quit whining about the cereal. 'Listen.' I put a hand to my ear, and she did the same. She got out of her chair and started doing the hippy shake.

Opal danced around while I went in the bedroom and found her a pink T-shirt and some pants that were maybe pajama bottoms, but I couldn't tell. Anyway, they looked pretty good with the T-shirt, and once Opal got her new pink shoes on, I turned her loose, and she boogied all over the living room. She'd hippy shake a while, then spin round and round with her arms in the air like a little bird. She wanted me to dance with her, and I thought, why not? I held Opal's hands and we twirled together until we were so dizzy, we fell down. It made me think of Ring around the Rosie at school. It'd been a long time since I'd played that game, but I guess you never really outgrow Ring around the Rosie.

Things felt pretty good until the lady next door started hollering about something and the baby got to crying. Opal didn't seem to notice. She just kept on dancing until the music finally quit, and we sat down to read her book. After a while there was a strange sound out front. It wasn't knocking, really. It was more like the wind rattling the door a little, trying to push it open.

'Who-da?' Opal took her finger off the picture of Billy and Blaze, and pointed to the door.

'Just the wind,' I told her. 'Or maybe the trucks going by.' We'd studied sound waves in science last year – how they could travel through air and collide with solid stuff and bounce off it, like ocean water hitting rocks and going back out to sea. The whole world was one great big ocean of sound.

The door rattled again, and I knew it wasn't the trucks or the wind. Someone was messing around out there, trying to get in. The knob jiggled, and goose bumps crawled all over my skin.

'Stay here, Opal.' I slid out from under her and tried to decide what to do next. For the first time ever, I was glad Kiki was there. If someone drove a freight train through the room, she probably wouldn't hear it, but I was still glad someone was home besides me.

I thought about the gangbanger wannabes and wondered if it was them outside. Maybe they were messing with me.

Maybe someone was trying to break in . . .

Why would anybody bother?

I stood there like one of those goofy people in a horror movie who waits for the axe murderer to jump around the corner. *Do something, Cass,* a voice said in my head, but I couldn't decide what. Holler at them to go away? Go try to wake up Kiki? Get in the bathroom with Opal and lock the door? What?

Finally, I slipped over to the window, leaned around the edge of the blind, and looked out with just one eye. Through the gap and the dirt on the glass, I could see the top half of the door. There was no one there.

'Must be the wind. Maybe Rusty didn't get the door shut good.' The words came out with a big breath I'd been holding. I went over and turned the locks, then pulled the door open to look out. Something moved near my feet, and I squealed and jumped back, then fell over one of the kitchen chairs. When I finally got untangled, the kid from next door, the littlest one, was climbing onto the sofa next to Opal.

'Hey . . . hey . . . no!' I hollered. 'Get off the . . . get away from there. Hey! You can't come . . .' The next thing I knew the two bigger kids were inside the door, and the littlest one was settling in to look at Opal's book.

'See hawsie?' Opal asked, and pointed to the horse in the book. It seemed like Opal was talking more every day – almost like she'd been afraid to when she first came.

'Ooohhh,' the boy whispered. 'Ho-see!'

'Es Bw-ades,' Opal told him, tapping her finger on the picture of Blaze. 'Bw-ades howsie.' She started pointing to the words and babbling along like she was reading. Every once in a while, I could recognize something she was saying. She had the story all messed up, but she'd been listening. When she turned to a page with another horse on it, she called him 'Eee-bit-cut,' from the Seabiscuit book we read before we got the new ones.

The other kids wormed past me and walked into the room like they belonged there. 'C'mon in.' I flipped the door shut behind them. 'You're already here anyway.'

The bigger boy and his sister with the smart mouth went over and hung around the sofa, watching Opal turn the pages of the book and talk about them. Even though it was rude the way they came in without being invited, and they smelled like cigarette smoke, I was proud of Opal. I'd sort of taught her to read, which was cool.

It was cool right up until Opal finished her book for the second time, and those kids got bored and the middle one – I'd figured out his name was Ronnie from listening to his sister saying *Sit still, Ronnie* – saw the cereal bag on the table.

'I-unt-some.' Ronnie had a weird way of talking that made him sound like he had a wad of gum in his mouth. His teeth stuck out in front so that his lips didn't close all the way, which might of been why.

The littler one caught sight of the cereal then, and he was off the sofa lickety-split. He scaled a chair, knocked it over, and was hanging off the table when I caught up to him and grabbed a big wad of his T-shirt. 'No!' I hollered.

'Let go my li'l brother!' the girl – Angel, I'd figured out her name was – said, but she didn't get off the sofa, because Opal was about to give her a turn with the book.

'Tell him to leave the food alone then.' I didn't like that girl. She was only a punky second or third grader, but she acted like the queen of the world.

'He's just hon-gry. He didn't have no breakfast,' she said, then she flipped a hand at him. 'Ged down, Boo.'

Boo didn't listen very well. He kept trying to squiggle onto the table and get the cereal.

'I'm hon-gree,' Ronnie said, and instead of looking at the book, he sat there staring at me. He had big brown eyes with long, long lashes, and round chubby cheeks that would have been cute on a teddy bear – without the stick-out teeth, anyway.

Of all things, I thought of the lady with the three dollars in Wal-Mart, and the big circle in my dream, and the Jesus hands and the dots of strawberry-colored blood. Down there at Jesus's feet, at the bottom of the next window over, there were all these kids – little kids and big kids, black kids and white kids, Mexican kids and Chinese kids, standing in a circle like the people in my dream.

'Oh, flip,' I said, and thought, *Cass Sally Blue, you have lost your mind. Yesterday it was the free sandwiches, and now they want the cereal that was supposed to last three more days. Next thing, they'll be drivin' off in Rusty's truck.* I lifted Boo off the table and set him down, then grabbed the bag. 'Easy come, easy go,' I said. The cereal was free, after all.

I unfolded three napkins and laid them out, then put two big handfuls of cereal on each one. By the time I finished, all three kids were standing at the table, watching. After I'd folded up the napkins, I handed one to each of them. 'Here,' I said, 'but you guys better go, okay? Your mom might wonder where you're at.' Not likely, but I figured if they stayed any longer, *all* the cereal would be gone.

Even though it was hard to see those handfuls of cereal going out the door with them, I felt good – like I did last night in my dream, when all the people were walking in the same circle, reaching across to each other. Ronnie and Boo looked happy, and the girl, Angel, kind of almost smiled.

Once they got down the steps, they took off. I think they headed around back somewhere to eat, because I didn't hear them outside. Later on, me and Opal went out and sat on the steps. The kids from next door came back, and they had a little Mexican girl with them. They wanted sandwiches, and I told them I didn't have any – that a lady in a car brought them yesterday. They hung around anyway, and we all sat there together looking out at the road and hoping the sandwich lady would come back today.

CHAPTER 11

Sandra Kaye

In the morning when I woke up, I heard Christopher down the hall as I rolled over and looked at the clock. After nine thirty? He was an hour late for school.

I'd gotten up and started toward Chris's room before I remembered the accident and its aftermath. Rob had chosen to sleep on the sofa downstairs again, and I hadn't argued. No doubt, he was already gone this morning – up and quietly out of the house, no time for the cup of coffee we used to share before the boys awakened. Lately, it seemed so much easier this way.

The door was ajar, and Chris was just pulling a shirt over the slim, straight waist that had led more than once to embarrassing low-rider moments with soccer and basketball shorts. Jake had some shape, but with Chris, clothes hung like samples on a wire rack. He was all bones and sinew, like a marionette slowly metamorphosing into a new creation. Still growing. Still becoming real.

'Hey,' he said when he saw me there. 'I've gotta get to school. Finals review today. Can you drive me?' The last sentence was clearly painful. It's never fun to be driven to school by your mom, at sixteen.

'Sure. Let me slip on some clothes. Why didn't you wake me earlier? You're late.'

Slinging his backpack over his shoulder, he crossed the room, then looked in the mirror, checked his hair, and brushed it down to hide the cut on his forehead. 'Forgot to set the alarm. I fell asleep studying last night.' He stopped the sentence short. I had a feeling he'd been about to say something else, but Chris was so much like me, an emotional cotton ball. His response to conflict was to take it in, pad it as much as possible, wrap it up, silence it, and quietly tuck it away. 'Is Dad here?'

Chris's need to sleep late suddenly made sense. He'd been making sure the coast was clear before coming downstairs. 'Dad's at work, I'm sure.'

'Good.' A look of relief flashed in the mirror.

'Christopher,' I admonished. 'That's not fair. Your dad has a right to be upset. He's worried about you.'

Chris's lip curled on one side. 'Yeah, right. He doesn't even listen. He just yells. He thinks we should be perfect.' Turning away from the mirror, he blinked hard and pretended to be busy cramming study sheets into a textbook.

It was hard to argue with him. Rob did maintain an idealized version of the boys in his mind. He pushed them hard, wanted them to be successful at whatever they did – sports, academics, hobbies. I'd convinced myself that since those things were intended to build the boys up, to broaden their possibilities in life, it was okay, but maybe the reality was that pressure to perform, even when it's directed toward beneficial activities, is still pressure. Maybe Rob had pushed too hard, and maybe I'd let him. Maybe I'd wanted the boys to be perfect, too – a sort of living proof that despite my mother's predictions for me, I had succeeded in this one, very important area. I had created a normal, healthy family, made a home that was calm, and happy, and steady. I'd achieved something my mother never could. I'd put an end to the family curse.

'Christopher, your father loves you.'

A sardonic puff of air passed Chris's lips. 'He doesn't even know me.' He zipped up his backpack with quick, impatient movements.

Anything I said next would have seemed ludicrous and manufactured, so I left off the conversation. 'Let me get dressed, and I'll drive you to school.'

'Thanks,' he answered, then began looking for something. Considering the layer of clothes, schoolwork, and electronic devices on the floor, he wasn't likely to find it. Finally, he gave up and finished tucking pencils and a calculator into his bag. 'Is the cleaning lady coming today?' It was an off-the-wall question.

'Not until next Monday, why?'

He shrugged. 'No reason.'

I turned and headed down the hall, thinking that if I was still working at Poppy's next Monday, I'd have to leave the key out for the cleaning service.

Chris was waiting in my car when I came downstairs. I was halfway around the vehicle before I realized that he hadn't gotten behind the wheel. Perhaps he thought I wouldn't let him. I slid in on the driver's side and backed out of the garage as if it were normal for me to drive him.

'I'll see what I can find out today,' I said as we headed down the street. 'About the accident.'

'Okay,' he answered, his gaze fixed out the window, his knee jittering by the door, his body ready for a quick exit the minute we rolled to a stop. 'Dad's probably right.' His voice was heavy with defeat.

'Holly was the one who was there.' I wanted to grab Christopher and shake him, tell him not to accept the role of family screwup just because it was an open slot. Jake was the superachiever, the perfect kid, the one we'd chosen from a handful of pictures. Christopher was the one who couldn't quite measure up, the one who'd been born too early, underweight and pale, a little behind in development, with a lisp that made him cute and funny when he was little, but that Rob worried about even though the pediatrician assured us he'd grow out of it.

Now, here he was, past the lisp and the developmental worries, yet still, in some ways, willing to accept that he wasn't good enough.

Your brother isn't perfect, I wanted to say. *He isn't perfect, either. He left, didn't he?*

We arrived at the school and Christopher climbed from the car. His body was hunched under the weight of the backpack as I watched him walk away. *What if he leaves, too? What if he finally decides it isn't worth staying?*

More than anything, I wanted to look into the car wreck

and find out it wasn't Christopher's fault. If he wasn't at fault, then this latest crisis would dissipate like a storm that threatened, then faded while still on the horizon. Chris needed absolution. We all needed it. We were drowning. We couldn't handle one more drop of rain . . .

By noon, my head was pounding and I felt like I was losing my mind. I'd spent hours navigating automated answering systems and playing voice-mail tag between the Plano Police Department, a towing service whose driver couldn't pick up the car until after lunch, and the insurance company. I still wasn't close to getting an accurate picture of Chris's accident. The other parties involved had contacted our insurance company, complaining of injuries. I told the agent of Holly's suspicions, and he seemed interested, but would only promise that the company would open an investigation. I asked him if he thought we should contact our lawyer, and he said that if Christopher were his son he probably would.

My cell phone started ringing as I was standing in the parking lot of the steak house, watching the tow truck driver load Chris's car. 'Wheeew! That's messed up,' the driver had said when he looked at the front wheel, hanging at a forty-five-degree angle like a broken arm. 'Insurance company'll probably total this thing.'

I didn't want to think about that possibility. *That was Jake's first car.* Rob had insisted on getting Jake a new one for college and passing the older car down to Chris, at least until Chris's tendency toward fender benders decreased.

When I answered the phone, Chris was on the other end.

'We're out early today because of finals and teacher training,' he informed me.

I checked my watch. How could it possibly be twelve thirty already? 'Hang around school for a little while, all right?' I said. 'The driver is just putting the car on his tow truck.'

There was a pause during which I sensed Chris working up to something. 'A few of the guys are going over to the weight room to lift, and then Coach Powell needs help cleaning up the field house.' I clued into the fact that this was what he'd had in mind all along. He wasn't calling for a ride; he was calling to test the waters – to see if he could get away with going somewhere other than home. 'Coach can drop me off after. He goes right by our house.'

'Christopher . . .' I could imagine what Rob would say if I let Chris hang out with his friends the day after he'd been in a car accident.

'I know,' he muttered, saving me the trouble of composing the remainder of my reasons for *no*. 'I'll wait out front. How long am I grounded?'

'I'm not sure, Chris. We'll have to see what we find out about the wreck. Let's just go home and relax. You don't need to be lifting weights or moving stuff out of the field house today anyway.'

'Yeah, I guess so.' He sighed, as if I'd handed out a prison sentence in making him come home. Not so long ago, our house was the place all the kids hung out. The rec room was always full of Jake's and Chris's friends. Now Chris never brought anyone over, but chose to go somewhere else. 'Can we pick up a sandwich on the way? I'm starved. I didn't get lunch because I had to go do some extra credit to bring up my physics grade, and . . .'

I barely heard the rest of Chris's remark about a failed test and extra credit to get a passing semester grade. My mind was stuck on . . . *pick up a sandwich? I didn't get lunch . . .*

The sandwiches. I'd promised to bring another bag of sandwiches to the apartment complex today . . .

'Chris, just wait out front. I'm on my way.' Exchanging a check for the towing bill, I waved good-bye to the driver and hurried back to my car.

When I turned the corner in front of the school, Christopher was sitting on the retaining wall with his backpack at his feet. His elbows were braced on his knees, and he was staring at the ground, his body sagging forward. From a distance, he looked like the first-grade boy who'd had his color changed on the teacher's behavior chart and was dreading having to come home. I wanted to do now what I occasionally did back then – just forget to check the behavior chart. If Rob mentioned it later, I'd say, 'Oh, I imagine he did okay today. I didn't think to ask him, but I can usually tell.'

Maybe I'd made the wrong decision, all those times, but it seemed that Rob set the bar so high; I didn't want Chris to give up, thinking that, no matter how hard he tried, he'd never make it over.

Seeing Chris now, I felt his despair. I wanted to ignore the behavior chart and take him out for an ice cream cone, then smooth things over with his father later.

Chris looked up when I pulled to the curb. His chest rose and lowered with resignation as he slid to his feet, then snagged his backpack. The body language said he'd given up the fight. He was ready to go home, sit in his room, and take whatever punishment came, because he probably deserved it.

I remembered how it was to be a teenager mired in that sense of defeat, to feel as if, no matter how hard you tried, you couldn't do anything right. Everything bad was your fault. Everything you did was substandard and idiotic. Really, at the core of the matter, you were nothing but trouble, and you always had been. I'd tried so hard not to pass that trait on to the boys, yet somehow, here Chris was, surrendering to his own inadequacy, admitting guilt when, in all reality, we didn't know whether or not he was at fault in the accident. I was only making him come home because Rob would expect it.

You always do this. The voice in my head was unusually clear and strangely determined today. *You always knuckle under. You always give in to what everyone else thinks is right . . .*

Chris opened the car door, tossed his backpack onto the floor and slid in, his body folding into the seat in pieces, lean and agile, apparently not suffering much from yesterday's trauma.

I kept my foot on the brake, but my mind was revving ahead, my thoughts burning. After situating his legs and his belongings, Christopher gave me an odd look. 'Mom?'

'Chris, I want an honest answer about something.'

'Okay.' He flashed a worried look in my direction.

'Do you think the accident was your fault?'

His head tilted to one side, and he shifted in his seat, as if he were trying to get a better view of me. 'What did Mrs Riley say? Did you find out anything from the insurance company?'

'I haven't been able to gather much information yet, but that's not what I'm asking.' I steeled myself with the thought that I was doing what I believed was right. I was tired of letting other people tell me what I should do, what I should believe, who I should be – as if I didn't have a brain of my own, as if I weren't capable of anything beyond making sack lunches, picking out table arrangements for the football banquet, or comparing fabric samples for fund-raiser T-shirts. 'Holly wasn't there, and the police officer wasn't there. You were. I want to know what you think, what you remember.'

'You mean, like, now? Right here?' Chris's gaze darted around the car, out the windows. He watched several boys cross the practice area, heading toward the field house. One of them climbed an old set of monkey bars and hung upside down, goofing around. The corners of Chris's lips twitched when the kid tumbled off in an ungraceful somersault.

'Yes, right here. I want to know what you have to say about it.'

He blinked, seeming surprised to be asked as he studied me for a long moment. 'It wasn't my fault, Mom.' His gaze flickered upward, then he looked away, afraid to invest himself in the idea that his word might actually count for something. 'That guy wasn't close when I turned my blinker on to change lanes. He wasn't close when I looked in the mirror. He sped up after I started to move over. I think he wanted me to hit him. There's no way he couldn't have known I was changing lanes, and the only way he could have ended up there would be to gun it like crazy.'

I sat for a minute thinking about Chris's description. It fit with what little I knew about the accident.

'Can we go home now?' Chris was probably afraid that his friends, still horsing around on the monkey bars, would see him, stuck in the car with his mom.

'No.' My heart fluttered in my neck, and my stomach filled with turbulence. An instinctive warning, one I'd known as long as I could remember, screamed in my head. In my mother's house, conflict ended in punishment that was swift, decisive – usually a whipping with whatever weapon she could get her hands on. By the next morning, she couldn't remember doing it, but I did learn a lesson. The less the waters ripple, the less painful things are. Walk softly and keep your voice low. 'No, Christopher, we're not going home. You head on to the field house, and then catch a ride home with Coach Powell when you're done. I have some errands to do, and I'll be back this evening. I'll bring something for supper.'

Chris blinked at me, then blinked again, as if I'd spoken the words in a foreign language, and his mind couldn't translate them into something that made sense. 'But Dad . . .'

'Dad isn't here.' I looked straight ahead, wrapping my fingers around the gearshift. 'I'm not saying you're off the hook. I'm just saying there's no point doing anything until we find out more about the accident. For now, we should go with what you think and what Holly's impressions were.'

Opening the door, Chris reached tentatively for the backpack, then pushed it farther into the floorboard. 'Well, what if those other guys come back and say –'

'We'll cross those bridges when we come to them,' I cut him off. In my mind, I was already heading across town, breaking free, doing something no one would have ever thought I'd do. 'If it comes down to your word or theirs, we have no choice but to take yours.'

Chris straightened, his chin tipping upward.

'Be home for dinner, all right?'

'Awesome.' Unfolding one leg, he stepped onto the curb, then stopped halfway out of the seat. 'Mom?' He waited until I looked at him before he added, 'I'm telling the truth.'

'I know you are, Chris. No heavy lifting today, all right? Just help clean up the field house.'

Nodding, he climbed out, then closed the door and hurried down the sidewalk. I watched him jog away in an easy, long-legged trot, his shoulders back and his face turned upward as he hollered at his friends. For an instant, he looked like the old happy-go-lucky Christopher I remembered.

You're doing the right thing, I told myself. *For now, he needs to know you believe in him.*

All the same, as I went home, grabbed a loaf of bread and the last of the peanut butter and jelly, then started across town, my mind cycled over and over the potential arguments with Rob. I role-played them as if we were already there, descending into a disagreement that would eventually end up with a rehashing of what had happened to Poppy, and then who was to blame for Jake's disappearance. The litany would play like a tape we knew by heart.

I considered turning around and going home, maybe calling the insurance company again. Driving all the way across town to deliver sandwiches was an unnecessary complication. By the time I got to Poppy's, it would be after two o'clock. If I stayed long, I'd be stuck in the quagmire of afternoon commuters heading back to Plano. On the opposite side of the highway, all three lanes were still moving at top speed right now. *I could get off at the next exit and go back the way I came . . .*

I pictured the kids in the Dumpster, and then Cass with Opal clinging to her leg. I remembered Cass tucking the bag of sandwiches close to her body, holding it carefully so as not to smash what was inside. I saw the look on her face when I said I'd be back tomorrow.

She didn't believe I would. Maybe I didn't believe it myself.

You have ongoing issues of your own, Sandra. It isn't smart to take on more than you can handle right now . . .

More than you can handle . . . The mollifying voice whispered a limitation to which I should surrender. It was echoed by my eighth-grade teacher's voice. *Sandra is a lovely girl, but I'm afraid she'll never be a star in school. She's going to need some extra help this year in prealgebra. It's harder for some children than others.*

Certainly, my mother agreed, putting a hand on my shoulder in an outward gesture of affection that felt foreign. *Now, Maryanne. Maryanne's another matter. She's always done well . . .*

To her credit, Mother hired a tutor to help me after school, and the tutor was good. I still wasn't Maryanne, but at least I didn't flunk out of middle school, and Mother didn't get *dragged out* to any more parent-teacher conferences.

The tutor and hard work carried me through high school and into Baylor, albeit not with accolades or academic stardom. Dyslexia, undiagnosed, isn't easy to overcome.

A girl like you should be looking for a good match, Sandra Kaye. What's the point in a teaching degree anyway? If this boy, Robert, wants you, of course you should say yes. My goodness, you're lucky he's asked, considering . . . A doctor's wife . . . Who ever thought you'd be a doctor's wife . . .?

The voices in my head droned on, and I realized an exit was coming up. One way toward home, the other toward Poppy's. A habitual surrender or a bold step toward something new?

It was now or never . . .

CHAPTER 12

Cass

Probably, free sandwiches two days in a row was too much to expect. By two o'clock, I kinda figured no freebies were gonna show up. Maybe the lady didn't mean it in the first place, or maybe she got to thinking about how the gang-banger wannabes hassled her yesterday, and she was scared to come back.

The only people that showed up all morning were a couple of Mexican guys in a truck. They picked up the pretty girl with the baby and the little Mexican kid who was sitting on the steps with us. They checked me out real good when they left. After they were gone, the Dial-a-Ride came for the crippled lady. She didn't look at us kids at all. She came out of her apartment and got in the van, acting like we weren't there.

Angel, Boo, and Ronnie gave up on sandwiches and wandered off, so I took Opal inside, and we ate a piece of bread and some cereal, dry. I sat there, thinking, *Maybe the sandwich lady forgot.* It went through my head that if she saw Opal and me, she'd probably remember about the sandwiches.

Since Red Bird Lane was right past the Book Basket and the old church, we could go get Opal a new book and then walk on down Red Bird a little, and see if there was a house with her car out front. Could be she had the sandwiches all ready, and she'd just got busy, and didn't have a chance to bring them by.

I tucked a few Fruity O's in my pocket so Opal and me could feed the tadpoles, and we headed out. The only problem with going down the street was getting rid of Ronnie, Boo, and their snotty sister. As soon as we went outside, they were right on our tails.

'Y'all go on back,' I told them when they started following us out of the parking lot. They stood looking at me, like all of a sudden they didn't know English. 'I mean it. Your mama's gonna whip your butts if you don't get back home.'

Angel huffed and poked her hips out to one side. 'She don' care. We can go wherever we want.'

'No, you can't. Go home.'

The little brat cussed at me, and then Ronnie poked out his tongue.

'You stick that thing out at me again, I'm gonna yank it off,' I told him, and his sister cussed me out again. 'Go home,' I said, but I really wanted to smack her one. Man, did she have a mouth on her. If my mama'd ever heard Rusty or me talk like that, we'd of been in soap city from now till next Christmas.

Right about then, an old tore-up car came pulling into the apartments. I could see the crippled lady riding shotgun. She'd probably caught a ride home with somebody, like usual.

179

'Hey, look, there's the sandwiches, I bet,' I said, and all three kids looked, then next thing they lit out back to the apartments. I grabbed Opal, and we took off down the sidewalk with Opal's book bouncing between us. I crossed the street and hurried all the way to Red Bird Lane, which wasn't easy because I had on the green shoes, so I was running mostly on my toes. We made it though, and when we turned onto Red Bird, I peeked back around the bushes. There was Angel coming out of the apartment complex and looking down the street for us.

Maybe that'd teach her who she shouldn't cuss at.

I took my shoes off and carried them while Opal and me started down Red Bird. There wasn't any glass on the sidewalk there, just lots of cracks with grass growing up. Opal took her shoes off, too, and she walked beside me, carrying hers like I was carrying mine. Every once in a while she'd look over at me and make sure I hadn't put my shoes back on.

'You can wear your shoes if you want,' I said, and she shook her head.

We walked on down the street, looking over the houses and watching for the sandwich lady's car. After a few houses, we passed what used to be a park with a creek running beside it. What was left of a slide, a merry-go-round, and some monkey bars were all grown up in weeds. The gate was locked, but kind of broke at the hinges, so it was just hanging there. Opal wanted to go in, but I wouldn't let her, even though we could of squeezed through the crack. When we got to the bridge, we looked down at the creek for a minute. There were little perch in the water, so I told Opal, 'Watch this,' and I threw in the Fruity O's, and the fish came up to push them around like soccer balls, then nibbled them up when they got soft.

'Tap-po,' Opal said, and tried to pull me toward the water. 'Tsee tap-po?'

'There's probably tadpoles in this part of the creek, too,' I told her. 'But those are little fishies.'

'Go tsee!' She pulled my hand harder and leaned over the cement curb.

'No, we can't go see.' It was a mess down there. The part of the creek by the apartments was cemented, but this bridge had muddy banks under it. 'It's yucky down there.'

'No nuck-ee,' Opal complained.

'Yes, it's yucky, and we're not climbing down. C'mon. Let's go.'

Opal made a mad face with a pout lip, pulled out of my hand, and plunked her butt down on the curb. Then she threw her book on the ground and crossed her arms. It reminded me of Angel, so I was annoyed right away.

'Don't you throw a fit.' I pointed a finger at her. 'If you throw a fit, I'm gonna take you home and put you back in the room with your mama. You can just sit there until *she* wakes up and takes care of you.'

Opal didn't move.

'I mean it, Opal. You get up and come on.' I could of picked her up and carried her off, but then she'd probably scream and cry, and everybody'd think I was kidnapping someone's kid.

Opal poked her lip out so far it was making its own patch of shade.

'Right now!' I sounded just like my mom. She didn't put up with any kid throwing any fits.

Opal figured out I meant business. She put her pink shoes back on, then stood up with her arms crossed and her face turned the other way. I guessed she didn't want to be like me anymore.

'Pick up your book,' I said, but she wouldn't. I told her again, and she stomped her foot, so finally I picked it up myself. 'You're not getting it back.'

Of course, then she started whining and trying to get the book.

'When I grow up, I'm not ever gonna have any kids,' I promised myself and her. *Ever, ever, ever.*

I gave Opal the book, and we started walking again, and sure enough, when we cleared all the trees along the creek, there was a pink house, and in the driveway was the white SUV. I felt real glad, because I could see me and Opal getting another bag of sandwiches, and that would help out a lot. Then I thought, *Well, what if the lady really never planned to bring the sandwiches at all? You'll look really dumb showing up at her door.*

We got to the pink house, and I stood on the sidewalk, thinking about it. Mama would be way embarrassed if she ever found out I was out, like, begging for food. She wouldn't like where Rusty and me were living, or that we had some stripper crashing in my bedroom, or that Rusty'd dropped out of high school, or that we couldn't afford food. She'd feel bad about it. She'd feel like she didn't do enough to take care of us, and it was her fault she died and left us this way.

I stood on the curb, wondering if people in heaven sit around looking at us, or if sometimes they're busy, and they just check in every once in a while. I didn't want to hurt Mama's feelings.

My tummy growled, and then Opal's growled, too. Probably Ronnie, Boo, and Angel were checking out the Dumpster by now. There wouldn't be much in there this time of the month, three weeks since people got new money on the food stamp cards, and a week until they'd get any more.

I took Opal's hand, and we started up to the door. I went kind of slow, hoping the lady would see us coming and we wouldn't need to knock, but the door didn't open by magic. There was an old-fashioned bell on it when we got there. It had a little twisty knob. I reached through the burglar bars and turned it, and the bell jingled, seeming really loud since the street was so quiet. Opal wanted to do the bell, too, but I pulled her hand away.

'Ssshhh.' I listened to see if I could hear anyone coming. There was nothing, so after a minute, I let Opal twist the bell.

When the sound died, I heard footsteps inside, I thought, but then they stopped and the door didn't open. All of a sudden, I felt weird about being there. 'We better go,' I told Opal.

Before I could grab her, Opal reached through and did the bell two more times.

'Opal!' I pushed her hand off. 'No!' Opal jerked away like

183

she thought I was gonna smack her. I wondered again if someone had hit her before. I looked into her big pistachio pudding eyes and thought, *Who in the world would hit a little thing like Opal? Would Kiki do that? Did she let somebody else do it?*

If Kiki's old man beat her up, maybe he smacked Opal around, too.

A sad feeling seeped over me and stung in the back of my eyes. Even when things were bad at Roger's, Rusty and me always had people we could of told, if we had to. When Roger started really creeping me out, I let him know that my teacher at school always asked how *everything* was at home. That worried him some, to know she was checking up.

But little bitty Opal couldn't even talk enough to tell anybody about anything. She didn't have a big brother or a teacher to go to.

'Hey,' I said, and bent down so I wasn't standing way over her. 'It's all right. I wasn't going to –'

The front door creaked, and I looked up, and there was the sandwich lady. I hadn't thought about what I was gonna say if she actually opened up. It worked out all right, though, because she was just about as surprised as I was. Opal slipped around behind me and grabbed my shorts. I picked her up, and she whacked me in the eye with her book.

'Oh, Opal!' I felt my eye to make sure it was still there.

'Gob a owie,' Opal said. 'Uh-oh.'

My eye went watery, and I rubbed it, all the while trying to look at the sandwich lady through the other eye.

'Uhhh . . . hi there,' she said finally, then pushed open the

184

burglar bars and leaned over to look at my eye. 'Are you all right?'

'Opal just whacked me with her book, that's all. She didn't mean to.'

Opal put her nose against mine, trying to see my eye. 'Uh-oh, owie.'

I felt someone's hand on my arm, and the sandwich lady said, 'Come on in here. Let's take a look at that.' I hung back a minute, and I guess she thought I was afraid to go in, but really I couldn't see anything because my other eye went watery, too. 'It's all right,' she said. 'There's no one here but me.'

I let her lead me in by the arm, and I could sort of see a room with dark wood walls, a wood floor, and tall windows. The room was empty. Our shoes echoed as we moved through it and into the kitchen, where the walls and cabinets were white, and the countertops were bright red. I let Opal slide down, and I heard her clogs squeaking across the floor, and then something rattling. I smelled paint, and maybe peanut butter also, which was a good sign.

The sandwich lady ripped a few paper towels off a roll. I heard the sink go on and off, and then she touched my hand. 'Here, let me look at that.' Her fingers were careful when she dabbed around my eye with the wet paper towel. 'There,' she whispered, and for a second my mind told me I was back with Mama. Something squeezed inside me, and I missed her all over again. It was always the weirdest thing, because I never knew when that feeling was gonna come. My eyes were already watery at least, so the sandwich lady couldn't tell anything was going on.

'Here, just hold this a minute. There's a little scrape on your cheek, but it's nothing bad. It'll feel better in a sec.' I took over holding the paper towel, and she moved back, and the wanting Mama feeling went away.

'Oh, honey.' The lady walked over to where Opal was messing with something. 'Those things came out of the cellar. They're dirty. I meant to take that stuff out to the trash pile yesterday.'

I wiped my eyes and could see Opal squatting on the floor, digging in a box. She had a little Raggedy Ann doll under her arm, and she was trying to get a Cootie game out from under an old coffeepot.

'She doesn't care . . . I mean, if you don't. That the stuff's dirty, I mean.' I could tell that if we tried to get that doll away from Opal, we were gonna have a hissy fit on our hands. The doll was old, and its dress had mold on it, but I thought if we took it home, I could put it in the sink and try to wash it. Then Opal would have a doll to play with. 'She likes dirty stuff. That way, she doesn't have to worry about not messing it up.' I didn't want the lady to think Opal didn't have anything at home, so I said, 'You know, some of her nice toys, she can't take them outside in the dirt and stuff.'

The lady gave me a weird look, but then she just smiled and said, 'Okay. Well, she can have anything she wants. It might be good to wipe it off with Lysol or something when you get home. I think that box has been down in the cellar since I was little.'

'Wow,' I said.

She chuckled. She had a nice laugh, really. 'Well, now you're making me feel old.'

I felt my face go red. I didn't mean it that way, but she had to be, like, forty or fifty, even though she looked good. Her skin was pretty and perfect, and she only had little bitty wrinkles at the corners of her eyes. I figured someone like her could afford all that laser surgery and Botox, like they talked about on *Oprah*. Anyway, she was a pretty lady with friendly goldish brown eyes and a nice laugh. She was taller than I remembered from yesterday.

We kind of stood there watching Opal pull out the Cootie game and open it. She picked up one of the Cooties that was almost put together and said, 'Wook! Bug. Big wed bug.' I didn't know she knew the color *red*.

'Yes, that's a red bug,' the lady said, and smiled at Opal. 'It sure is. It looks good with your shoes. Did you get new shoes?'

Opal nodded and smiled real big, pointing a finger and touching her shoes. 'New tshoo-s.'

For a minute we couldn't find much else to say. I wiped under my eyes again and came up with mascara smudges, then looked for a place to throw away the towel. 'Over there.' The sandwich lady pointed to a trash can full of paper towels with paint on them and junk. I tossed the towel in and noticed bread laid out on the counter, and jelly and peanut butter jars. The sandwich lady didn't say anything about them.

'So . . . anyway, me and Opal were just going by, and I thought we saw your house.' That sounded dumb, but I was embarrassed to come right out and say, *So, are you handing those out?* 'I gave the kids next door those sandwiches yesterday. They ate two each, and then they came this morning, like, knocking on the door. My mama always said, if you feed a stray, you might as well name it, because you can plan on it coming back.'

The lady smiled. It wasn't a big smile, but the kind of smile somebody gives you at a funeral, where they think it wouldn't be right to look too happy. 'Your mom sounds like a wise woman.'

'She always said things like that.' I was looking at Opal, so I didn't think about the way that sounded until after. Opal'd sat down crisscross with her doll in her lap, and she was trying to put together the Cootie bugs. 'I mean, Mama still says things like that, but she's been sick, and, besides, where we live now, we don't get any stray dogs, like we used to in Helena. We lived in the country when I was littler. My brother'd feed stray dogs all the time. A whole herd of them used to come around the back door after suppertime to see what they could get. Sometimes there'd be so many they'd eat up all the food before our dog, Missy, could get any. Missy didn't like watching those other dogs eat all her leftovers.' I hadn't remembered until right then about all the food we used to toss in the old metal bowl outside the back door. We never thought anything about it. Now it was hard to picture having extra food you didn't save for later.

It was kind of like we were the stray dogs, but I didn't want to think about that too hard.

Those sandwiches sure smelled good.

My stomach rumbled, and my mouth started to water. 'I

could help you make those.' Mama would of died, if she could see me right then. She'd of shot me the mama-eye, and said, *Cass Sally Blue! You watch your manners!* 'If you want, I mean.' I hoped up in heaven Mama was busy at a crochet class or something.

The lady didn't seem to mind. 'Sure,' she said, and we moved over to the counter. 'I'm in a bit of a hurry today, actually. My son had a minor car accident yesterday, and I don't want him to be home by himself this evening.' She picked up a knife and handed it to me, and I was glad that she'd only got to the point of putting peanut butter on one side of the sandwiches. I started taking the other sides and covering them.

'We always put it on both pieces, so the jelly doesn't make the bread all soggy. It's an impermeable barrier,' I told her, but then in my head, Mama said, *Cass Sally, were you raised in a barn? Little girls shouldn't be bossy.* 'But I don't have to. I mean, I don't want to waste your peanut butter or anything.'

'You're fine.' Her voice was gentle and nice, like she didn't think I was bossy at all. It made a warm place inside me. 'Actually, I'd forgotten that trick, I have to admit. It's been a few years since I've made PBJs for lunch boxes.'

For just a second, I was worried the sandwiches were for lunch boxes, and then I decided that was stupid. Who'd be packing ten lunch boxes at once, and besides, nobody even lived here.

It'd be cool to own so many houses that you had an extra one nobody lived in.

While I worked on the peanut butter, she started doing

the jelly and closing up the sandwiches. Strawberry again, darn it. 'We always buy the grape kind, because it's, like, easier to spread,' I said when she was mashing the gloppy strawberries around. 'No lumps.'

'I'll remember that.' She looked at me from the corner of her eye, and the tiny wrinkles there scrunched up a little.

'But strawberry's good, too. Grape's cheaper, though.'

The wrinkles scrunched a little more. 'I hadn't noticed. You sound like a good shopper.'

It was stupid, but I liked it when she said that. It'd been a long time since anybody had said anything good about something I did – since back in school, I guessed. Mrs Dobbs always said good things. 'I'm real careful about it – shopping, I mean. Somebody's got to be. My brother'd spend all the money in two seconds. You know how boys are.'

'Oh, yes, I do.'

'He's always over, like, looking at truck stuff when he's supposed to be picking up hamburger.'

'That's what they do.'

'I told him, Rusty, you can't eat a steering wheel cover, even if it is Mossy Oak camo color with rubber grips.'

She laughed. 'That sounds familiar. Boys love their cars.'

I finished doing the peanut butter, then moved back to the front of the line, and she handed me the sandwich bags.

'How old is your brother?' she asked while I was trying to get the first sandwich into a bag. Jelly was dripping on my hands, and I wanted to lick it off, but that'd be rude.

'Twenty-one,' rolled off my tongue, just like it was the truth. 'I'm seventeen.'

190

'Oh.' She looked over at me with one eyebrow hiked up.

I had a feeling I'd better change to another subject. 'How old is your son – the one that had the car wreck?' That didn't come out sounding great, so I also said, 'He's all right, isn't he?'

'Yes, he's fine.' She reached up and brushed her forehead with the back of her hand like it hurt to think about it. I was sorry I brought it up.

'I bet he's kinda upset, huh?' I remembered the first time Rusty hit somebody's car with our truck. It took him a whole three days after he got his driver's license to do it, and then another day to admit it to Mama.

The lady chewed the side of her lip and went back to spreading jelly. 'Christopher's had a hard time with fender benders since he's been driving.'

'Oh, listen, Rusty's the fender bender king of the universe. He had, like, ten when he started driving. Mama said she was sure she'd got five years older in six months. She told him he better quit showing off for girls and watch the road, or she was gonna take the keys and he could get to football practice on foot.'

'Well, Christopher's dad isn't too happy about it, either,' the sandwich lady said.

I was gonna have to ask her name, because I was tired of thinking about her as *the sandwich lady*. She looked upset about Christopher and the driving. 'Mama made Rusty go down and take a driving class at the college building on a Saturday. He had a fit, because he was gonna miss a track meet, but it turned out he didn't mind it much. He met a cute girl there, and his driving got better.'

The sandwich lady nodded like she thought that wasn't a bad idea. 'I'll have to give that some thought. That might help.' She finished with the jelly and started helping to bag sandwiches.

'I think boys just grow up slower. They shouldn't drive till they're eighteen,' I said. 'Just girls should drive when they turn sixteen.'

The lady chuckled. 'That's an idea.'

'Rusty grew up out of his driving problems, though,' I said, which was true enough. These days he knew we couldn't afford to fix the truck. 'I bet Christopher will, too.'

'I'm sure he will.' We finished the sandwiches, and she put them in a Wal-Mart sack. I didn't reach for it, but just stood there where she could hand it to me.

'Guess we got that done quick,' I said, and my stomach squeezed like the apple-shaped stress ball Mrs Dobbs used to keep on her desk.

'Guess we did,' she agreed.

'I can't think of your name.' I tried not to keep looking at the bag, just in case it was going somewhere else. If it did, it wasn't like me and Opal and Rusty would go hungry tonight. We had the food we'd bought yesterday.

I couldn't keep handing our food to Angel and Ronnie and Boo, though.

The sandwich lady gave me a surprised look. 'I'm sorry. I guess I didn't introduce myself. I'm Sandra Kaye.' She shook my hand.

'It's very nice to meet you, Mrs Kaye.' Mama would of been proud.

Mrs Kaye smiled, like she thought I had good manners, too. 'It's Sandra Kaye,' she said. 'It's all one name. Sandra Kaye Darden, but Mrs Kaye's fine. I like it.'

'Cool.'

'Thank you for helping with the sandwiches.' She started wiping down the counter. I helped her cap the peanut butter and jelly, and put things away. There was a little food in the refrigerator. My stomach growled at it. Before I really thought about it, I reached over and picked up the sandwich bag. I hoped they were for us, or that was gonna look really stupid.

'I can give you a ride back with those, if you'd like,' Mrs Kaye offered.

'Oh, it's all right.' In case Rusty was home picking up Kiki, I sure didn't want him seeing me get out of some strange lady's car, and the thing about the sandwiches might really hurt his feelings, because even with him working so hard, we didn't have enough money. 'Me and Opal are gonna go by the Book Basket and get her another book on the way home. I think she knows this one by heart already. C'mon, Opal.'

Opal started putting all the Cootie things back in the box, and Mrs Kaye squatted down to help her. 'I'm not even sure all the pieces are here.'

'She doesn't care,' I said, and really, I was thinking it'd be fun to have a game to play. We'd make some pieces if we had to.

Opal stood up and Mrs Kaye helped her hold the doll, the book, and the game box. 'I guess that's it.'

'Guess so,' I agreed. 'Opal, say thank you for the cool stuff.'

Opal smiled and showed every baby tooth she had. A couple of them were brown around the edges, like nobody had ever showed her how to brush. 'Tang-oo cool 'tuff.'

'And thank you for the sandwiches. Say thank you, Mrs Kaye.'

'Tang-oo, Mit-tay.' Opal smiled again, and I had to admit, she was really cute. I couldn't think how anyone could ever hit something that cute.

Mrs Kaye grabbed her purse off the counter, and we walked to the door together. On the way out, she had trouble getting the burglar bars to lock.

'These darned things,' she complained. 'I've got to work on these tomorrow.'

I was glad she was planning to be back. 'I could come and help you. I mean, Opal and me don't have a lot going on. I could help you do this, and make some sandwiches and stuff. I'm good at fixing things.' *What a doof.* I sounded like a total suck-up, like the little twerps next door, ready to hang around anybody who had food.

I grabbed the burglar bars and helped her pull them to where the lock would work.

'All right, then,' she said. 'Check and make sure it's okay with your parents, and then I guess I'll see you two tomorrow.'

CHAPTER 13

Sandra Kaye

When I arrived home, Chris was sitting out on the back steps with Bobo. Bobo's Frisbee rested at Chris's feet, and Bobo was lying beside it with his head on his paws, as if even he had given up on anything fun happening here. The pallor of our house struck me like a burst of cold air as I stood watching them through the glass. Christopher moved his hand. Bobo raised his head and watched, then rested his chin on his paws again.

There was life here, I thought, and a kernel of bitterness sprouted in my chest, spawning something black and ugly. It grew quickly, putting down roots and stretching upward, working its way toward forming seed. The good feeling I'd had when I handed Cass the sandwiches, the sense of purpose, was gone, and I felt the pain of loss replacing it. *Why did this have to happen? Why us? We had a perfect family, a good life . . .*

But even as the thought crossed my mind, I pulled it back, examined it. How perfect was something that could crumble so quickly? Perhaps what we had was an easy life, all the required elements falling into place. We had enough money, a big house, an adoption when we couldn't get pregnant, a miracle pregnancy to complete our family, career success for Rob, best friends right across the street. We were healthy. The boys never suffered anything more than the usual childhood ailments. They never got in any serious trouble. They succeeded in school, scored the big goals in soccer matches, and ran for touchdowns at the high school football games. We cheered them from the sidelines, then went home feeling triumphant. The sun rose again, Rob kissed me good-bye and headed off to save lives. I made sack lunches, went to mom meetings and Bible studies, made banners for next week's game, and helped raise money for disaster relief funds and families who'd suffered unfortunate turns of fate.

It never occurred to me, while I was rallying to help those *less fortunate*, that fortunes can turn at any time, and only then do you find out what you're made of, what's beneath the surface. Across the street, I'd watched Holly's crazy, chaotic family rally around her during her mother's breast cancer death, and then less than a year later, Holly's diagnosis, lumpectomy, and chemo. Holly's kids, usually dependent and borderline irresponsible, had risen to the occasion, taking care of the house and each other. Richard worked half days as often as possible so he could hold Holly's hand during treatments, or shuttle kids to activities, or cook supper. Everyone pulled together and pulled through.

I'd never asked myself whether, faced with something terrible and unexpected, we would come together or fall apart. Perhaps I'd thought that by making sure all the school papers were letter perfect, and all the toys were picked up and put away before bed, and the plates and cups were rinsed and stacked just so in the dishwasher, and the boys were studying and bringing home good grades, I could prevent life from ever taking a blind curve. Maybe Rob and I fed that idea in each other. Rob's family was regimented, formal, and strict – the training ground for a long line of Dr Dardens. Compared to the family I grew up in, they had it all together. It seemed a good road map, and it suited Rob's personality. Even basketball in the driveway took on the air of a military drill when Rob was present, but I'd convinced myself it was all right. Jake never seemed to mind. He thrived on being pushed, on consistently reaching the goals, on working behind the scenes to help Christopher achieve them, too.

But maybe Jake *did* mind. Perhaps that was why he left. Perhaps he thought if he was no longer the perfect son, if he'd failed his obligations the night Poppy was killed, there was no place for him here. While we were creating the perfect life, we'd failed to make sure Jake knew – that he and Christopher both knew – they didn't have to be perfect to be loved.

How can you teach your children something you've never believed yourself? Hadn't I always felt the need to be perfect for Rob? Perfect for everyone? The right clothes, the right hair, the carefully applied makeup and the wrinkle creams, the gourmet cake at the school bake sale?

I'd never dropped the pretenses, even after Poppy's death.

At the memorial service I'd told everyone we were fine. We didn't need colleagues and friends to bring casseroles to our door or check on us. We didn't need the pastor to set up a time for bereavement counseling. We'd be all right, and yes, of course, I'd still be able to help with the canned food drive next week. It was best to stay busy . . .

But I knew it wasn't best. I knew Jake was suffering under a load of guilt, and Chris was locking himself in his room every afternoon, and Rob blamed Jake for partying with his fraternity brothers instead of keeping his usual Friday night date with Poppy, and Jake blamed himself. It was only a matter of time before someone said it out loud. I knew we were crumbling. I knew Jake was crumbling, but I didn't confront it. I did what I'd always done. I covered everything over with a layer of frosting, so the neighbors wouldn't see the fractures.

Now, looking at what was left of my perfect life, I thought of Cass in her inappropriately grown-up clothes and overdone makeup, her body still lanky and girlish and awkward, but filled with confidence, with fire and determination. At her age – whatever her age really was – I would never have walked up to a stranger's door, come inside, and made sure I got what I wanted. I would have been too afraid – afraid I wasn't wanted, afraid someone would tell me to go away, afraid I was being impolite, afraid I'd get in trouble, afraid of what people would think of me, afraid I'd end up with my feelings hurt. I would probably have starved to death, being quiet and polite, and staying within the boundaries . . .

Christopher noticed me watching him and came inside. Bobo sat looking through the glass with a sad expression on his bandit face. I made a mental note to take him along to Poppy's house tomorrow. He would like the girls, and the girls would like him.

'Have you eaten?' I asked as Chris and I walked into the kitchen.

He nodded. 'Yeah. Coach ran me by Sonic on the way home.' He pointed to a bag on the counter, then moved toward it with a guilty look. Rob didn't like it when the boys ate junk food.

'Dad called my cell and said he'll be late,' I told him.

The tension drained out of Chris in a way that was impossible to miss. He slurped the last of his soda, then buried the contraband in the trash, while I made myself a plate of leftover chicken salad. We hovered together in the kitchen, standing at the bar.

'Everything go all right at school?'

'Yeah, good, I guess.' Pushing his hands into his pockets, he studied the ugly size-thirteen purple Converse sneakers he'd just had to have. The sneakers crossed and uncrossed. Chris had something on his mind. 'Did you find out anything more about my car?'

'I haven't checked the answering machine yet.' I realized how strange that was. Normally, I went to the answering machine first, hoping there would be a message from Jake, or possibly some unexpected news about Poppy's case.

Christopher sighed. 'I checked it. It's empty.'

I felt the sting of disappointment, a sharp edge that never seemed to dull. 'I'll check with the insurance company again tomorrow. I was tied up this afternoon.'

Chris's lips pressed together and turned downward on one side. I ate a few bites of chicken salad. I could tell he was working up to something, deciding whether to let it out or give up without trying.

'Mom?'

'Yes?'

'I have to go into school early tomorrow to make up an in-class essay I missed. I was thinking . . . Jake's car's just sitting there in the garage.'

'Christopher . . .' I drew back, surprised. The car hadn't moved since we'd brought it home from the airport. For six months it had remained parked in anticipation of Jake's return. Using it would be like admitting he wasn't coming back. 'You know how your father feels about that car.' *You know how we all feel about that car. That's Jake's car. His graduation gift.*

Chris sighed and nodded, then pushed off the counter and headed across the kitchen. 'Yeah, I know,' he said, as if he wished he hadn't brought it up. 'Can I work out at the field house, then ride home with Coach again tomorrow?'

'I don't think . . .' If Rob found out I wasn't keeping Christopher under house arrest, he wouldn't be happy. 'We'd better . . .' I thought of Poppy's place, and the sandwiches and the work I needed to do tomorrow. 'Go ahead and plan on it. Just be home before six, all right?' Rob was never home before six.

'Okay.' Chris left the kitchen and disappeared upstairs for the rest of the evening. I finished eating, passed time sitting absently in front of the television, then checked e-mail. Nothing from Jake, just a forward from Andrea, the real estate lady, showing the online listing for Poppy's house. She had copied the e-mail to Maryanne's address, for Mother.

Maryanne had replied on Mother's behalf. *Looks good. The sooner the better. – M.* Then she'd listed a fax number where paperwork could be sent, should an offer come in. At this point, the prospect of an offer seemed unlikely. So far, there had been no sign of Andrea other than the little billboard in the yard.

I hope no one answers right away, I thought, and then I realized I hoped Andrea didn't bring anyone to Poppy's house ever.

Looking at the picture, I thought again of the peanut butter and jelly sandwiches that needed to be made there tomorrow. More old puzzles or games might be hidden in the cedar chest under the window seat in the back bedroom. I hadn't thought to clean that out when we held the estate sale. Clearly, little Opal needed some things to play with . . .

I considered the idea as the evening wore on.

The next morning, the window seat was still on my mind. 'Chris,' I said as he was preparing to bail out of the car a block from the school, so as not to be seen in the drop-off lane. 'Didn't Aunt Ruth keep toys for you guys under the window seat in the back bedroom?'

He paused with his hand on the door. 'Yeah. I think she did. Some puzzles, and coloring books, and little dishes and toy cars and stuff. Why?' His eyes narrowed.

'Oh, no reason.' The answer was out of my mouth before

I realized I was once again lying to one of the people I loved most, and there was something truly wrong with that. 'I was just thinking. I don't remember cleaning that out for the estate sale.'

Loosening his grip on the door handle, Chris gave me a curious look. 'Are you going over to Poppy's today?'

'I might. We'll see.' Another lie. It got easier each time.

'Can I go?' The question came quickly, as if he'd thought about it ahead of time.

The sudden spasm of panic in my chest was startling and disturbing – heavy with guilt. 'Well, not today. You have school.'

'I could miss.'

'You have tests, Chris. And makeup work, remember?'

Deflating with a long, slow sigh, he opened the door. 'Yeah, I know.'

A strange mix of emotions wound through me, indefinable. If I took Chris to the house, how in the world would I explain Opal and Cass, the painting supplies, the food in the refrigerator, the sandwich making? 'Is there some reason you wanted to go?'

'Yeah ... well, kind of. I should've looked through the garden shed better. Some of Poppy's pocketknives are probably out there, and his woodworking tools and stuff.'

A wound opened in my chest, raw and tender. Poppy had planned to give those things to Christopher one day. Now he never would. Chris would be cheated out of the memory of receiving something treasured directly from Poppy's hands.

Instantly, I was angry all over again – angry at the neighborhood, at the police, the convenience store clerk who'd heard Poppy call out but didn't respond, the perpetrators, whoever they were. 'I'll look around, if you want.'

'No big deal.' Chris grabbed his backpack and turned away, and I knew he'd perceived the swing of emotions in me. He'd probably felt my anger, too, and assumed it was somehow his fault.

Talk to him about this, a part of me urged. *Stop right here and just talk*, but like a robot, I said, 'You'd better get in the door before you're tardy. Have a good day, sweetheart.'

'Okay. Bye.' Christopher exited the car, and I swung by the house to pick up Bobo. He cavorted happily to the door when he saw me coming, then dashed past me and stood by the car with his tail wagging and his ears perked, as if he remembered our last adventure and was eager to repeat it.

As we left Plano, Bobo paced from window to window, then finally settled down when an accident on the freeway forced me to take the city streets to Poppy's. Winding through neighborhoods of decaying homes with rotting front porches, windows opaqued with aluminum foil, front yards grown up in weeds, and sidewalks crackled like paint on old wood, I wondered about the children who lived in those houses. How many of them were like Cass and Opal, like the children in the Dumpster? How would anyone know? Ten sandwiches was a drop in the bucket compared to what was needed here.

I stopped at the store, parked Bobo in the shade and cracked the windows, then ran in for two loaves of bread, a giant jug of peanut butter, and two big jars of jelly. Grape. Easier to spread.

When I arrived at Poppy's, Cass and Opal were sitting on the front steps. Cass was dressed in a short tight pair of flowered shorts and a tank top that looked like it had been purchased for someone older, because it sagged in front. Today she'd traded the green high-heeled shoes for a pair of clogs with thick platform soles that made her long, thin legs appear even longer. She looked like a store mannequin mistakenly dressed in the wrong size clothes.

Opal, in saggy sweats and a long-sleeved T-shirt that was too warm for May, was busy playing with her doll. I remembered sitting on the steps the day Aunt Ruth gave it to me. She told me she'd picked it up at a yard sale. The little girl there didn't like the doll because it didn't *do* anything and you couldn't comb its hair. Aunt Ruth thought a perfectly good Raggedy Ann deserved a better home than that.

Watching Opal now, I recalled feeling obligated to love the doll because someone else had rejected it. I took her home, and for a while she was my secret – until Mother found her and sent her back to Poppy's because she smelled like an old house.

Cass waved as I got out of the car, but Opal went on talking to her doll and showing it how to smell the roses on an overgrown vine that twined through the porch railing.

'You're here awfully early,' I said when Cass came to the car.

'Me and Opal didn't know when you got here, usually.' She waited for me to exit the driver's seat and shut the door, then followed me around to the back hatch.

'It won't be time to make sandwiches for a while yet.' It was only a little after ten.

She sent a worried glance my way, and I had the sense that I'd hurt her feelings. 'We could ummm . . . like, help you with other stuff. Till it's time to make sandwiches, I mean. If you want.' Her blue eyes flitted upward, than sank again. 'I didn't know what time it was. Our clock's busted . . . at home.' She seemed to be making things up as she went along. 'Rusty woke me up early anyway. He was mad because all the cereal was gone. Stupid Kiki ate it. She eats every-thing.' Her lips clamped shut at the end of the sentence.

'Who's Kiki?' It occurred to me that Kiki might be a pet of some kind, and that could be where my sandwiches were ending up.

'Opal's mama.' The words conveyed a definite lack of affection, and if the tone wasn't clear, the look of teenage resentment was. Having spent plenty of time around teen-agers, I recognized the sardonic eye roll.

'Your aunt?' I opened the back hatch, and Cass watched as I gathered the grocery bags and a bucket of painting supplies.

'Huh?' She held out her hands for something to carry, and I gave her the groceries.

'Opal's mom is your aunt, right?'

'Geez, no. I don't have a aunt.'

The painting supplies rattled in my bucket as I braced them on my hip. On the floorboard, Bobo awoke and poked his head over the backseat. Cass drew back, surprised. 'Hey, cool, a dog.'

'This is Bobo. Say hello, Bobo.'

As Jake had trained him, Bobo did the whine-bark that sounded like *el-lo*, then scrambled over the seat and down the bumper to join us in the driveway.

'Cool!' Cass said, rubbing his ears. 'He talks.'

'Just about. My son taught him.'

'Awesome,' Cass remarked as we closed up the car and proceeded to the porch. Opal was preoccupied in the far corner, sticking pink rose petals in her shoe.

'The other day, you said Opal was your cousin. That would make her mom your aunt,' I said as I wrestled with the lock on the burglar bars. I was beginning to wonder if anything Cass told me was entirely based in reality. She seemed able to spin out fiction as easily as truth. That might explain why she and Opal were allowed to wander the streets anytime they wanted. No telling what story she was giving the adults at home.

After setting down the sacks, she put both hands on the burglar bars and pushed inward, trying to help. 'Oh . . . yeah . . . but on her dad's side. My uncle, like, married Opal's mom.'

'Oh, I see.'

'They don't live together anymore, though. Rusty felt sorry for Kiki and told her she could stay with us. Mama did too, I mean. Mama's that way. She wouldn't leave anybody out on the street. Even Kiki.' She spat the word with hard *K* sounds, inflicting as much verbal damage as possible. The security bars finally came loose and landed in Cass's hands as she pulled them open. 'Dang,' she said, looking up at the hinges as she dragged the sagging metal over the floorboards.

'Looks like the screws pulled right out of the wood,' I observed. 'I was going to work on the burglar bars today. I don't know if I can fix that, though. I think the door frame is rotten.'

Cass stood on her toes beside me, observing the malfunction. 'My brother does construction. He might could fix it for you.' As soon as she made the offer, she seemed to reconsider. 'I dunno. He's pretty busy all the time, though.'

'I'll bet my son could put some longer screws in it. He's handy with tools and such.'

'The one that had the car accident?'

'Yes. Christopher. He wanted to come over and look through the storage shed out back before the house sells.' The heavy wooden door creaked as I opened it. Cass stood in the gap, peering into the darkened interior, not quite sure whether she should enter. Sliding past her, Bobo trotted in like he owned the place.

'Did Christopher get okay from the car accident?'

I stopped to look at Cass, surprised she'd ask. 'He's still pretty upset, but he won't say much about it.'

'Boys are like that.' Cass spoke as if we were two adults discussing teen psychology. 'One time, Rusty hit a signpost and didn't tell Mama about it for two days. He thought he was gonna fix the truck and everything, and she'd never know. She was sure enough hot when she found it, I'll tell you.'

I chuckled. 'We're still waiting to see if the accident was Christopher's fault. Then we'll decide what to do about it.'

Cass picked up the sacks again. 'One time Rusty had a

accident that wasn't his fault. The other guy ran right into Rusty's back end, and there wasn't anything Rusty could of done about it. The guy gave Rusty five hundred bucks, right there on the spot, if he wouldn't call the police.'

We slipped through the doorway, and Cass called over her shoulder, 'C'mon, Opal.' Opal grabbed her doll and the flower petals, then dashed through the opening between us. She raced across the squares of light in the living room and disappeared into the kitchen.

'I bet she's looking for that box,' Cass surmised.

As we crossed the living room, Opal's giggles drifted from the kitchen, high-pitched with excitement. When we rounded the corner, she was getting a tongue bath from Bobo while she investigated the remaining contents of the box.

'She's probably looking for more games. We had to play Cootie, like, all night,' Cass offered. 'The neighbor kids liked it, too. We played on the steps till it got dark.' As she talked, she unpacked the grocery bags and set the supplies on the counter. 'You brought more stuff today.' Her thick blond ponytail flipped over her shoulder and swung across her hips as she looked enthusiastically at me.

'I thought we'd do two loaves,' I said. 'If you think you can give away that many.'

Counting the slices through the wrapper, she nodded. 'Oh, sure. Those kids had three more kids with them when I got back yesterday. I don't even know where they got 'em. Like, down in the storm ditch, probably, because they play there sometimes. These new three were straight out of Mexico, I think. They couldn't understand a thing except I had Spanish in Mrs Dobbs's class last year, so I can say a few things, like, *hungry,* and *stop,* and *para tu,* which is *for you,* and *lavarse sus manos,* which means *your hands are gross,* which theirs were. They were, like, slimy from the storm ditch.'

I couldn't help but laugh at Cass's enthusiasm. 'That's pretty good Spanish. Both of my sons took three years in high school. They're rather impressive with it, actually.' With Jake, we weren't surprised, given his early language history, but, interestingly, Christopher was good with languages as well.

'In Helena, we can take it in middle school.'

My mind keyed in on the words 'Helena' and 'middle school,' and almost as quickly, Cass glanced up and caught me studying her. 'But I took it in high school. My freshman year,' she added unevenly.

I pretended not to notice. 'So, is that where you're from? Helena, Montana?'

'Oh, we've lived lots of places.' She counted the bread she'd counted twice already. 'We can make twenty-two, with the heels. Are you gonna paint for a while now? Opal an' me could help, if you want. I'm good at painting, and Opal can hand us stuff, or whatever. She likes to help. Right, Opal?'

On the floor, Opal dug a tiny plastic teacup out of the box and made an appreciative sound. 'I ga a tup!' she cheered, and held the cup to Bobo's face so he could see it.

'Opal, we got work to do. You can look at that stuff later.' Cass turned to me self-consciously. 'She usually acts better.'

'It's all right. She's a little young to help with painting anyway.'

Cass chewed the side of her lip, and I had the sense that she was afraid she and Opal were about to be sent away. 'But, actually,' I added, 'I was thinking I'd start out this morning by checking all the burglar bars. It would be easier with someone to pull the latches from the inside, while I work on the outside. You could help me with that, if you like.'

'Sure,' she said cheerfully.

'I'll tell you what. First, why don't you call home and make sure it's all right that the two of you are here?'

'We . . . ummm . . . don't have a phone.' Cass counted the bread again. 'I mean, we're gonna get a phone in a day or two, but we haven't lived here very long yet. When Mama gets her paycheck, then we're gonna have a phone. She's not home, anyhow, but Kiki is. She knows me and Opal were gonna do some stuff. She doesn't care.'

I pretended to be busy unpacking the bucket of painting supplies. I had a disturbing vision of police cruising the neighborhood, looking for two missing kids and finding them with me. On the other hand, if I sent Cass and Opal away now, they probably wouldn't go home. They'd wander around waiting until it was time to make sandwiches.

Cass's fingers twisted and untwisted as she waited for an answer, and she pulled her bottom lip between her teeth.

'All right, then. But I'll tell you what. Before we get started, let's go look in the back bedroom and see if we can find something to entertain Opal while we work. There might be some old games and coloring books.'

A wide smile spread across Cass's face, and as quickly as it came, she muted it, so as not to look too eager. 'C'mon, Opal. Let's go look for some toys.'

Together, we headed through the dining room and down the shadowy hall on a quest. In the back bedroom, we discovered a treasure trove of old coloring books, puzzles, and tea party dishes, just where I'd suspected they would be, under the window seat. Opal investigated the new finds while I went outside to take a look at the burglar bars on the windows, and see what tools might be needed. After a cursory investigation, the situation didn't look promising. The burglar bar latches and padlocks, which Poppy had maintained faithfully, were rusty and uncooperative due to a rainy spring and lack of attention. Even with Cass helping from the inside, we couldn't operate most of them.

'I'll have to wait until I can get Christopher to come help,' I said finally, and headed to the front of the house. When I turned the corner, a late-model Cadillac was pulling up to the curb. I thought instantly of the real estate agent. Maybe she was meeting a customer here. The idea cast a shadow that was long and thick as the car door opened, and I prepared to make excuses for the mess in the kitchen.

'Hello, lady!' I recognized the voice before the passenger emerged. He waved clumsily. 'I comin' and cut fo-wers. Gone cut some plants, 'kay?' Without waiting for an answer, Teddy began pulling gardening tools from the car and aligning them on the sidewalk.

'Oh.' After Chris's accident, I'd completely forgotten about having made arrangements for Teddy to come work on the flower beds.

The front passenger window rolled down, and Hanna Beth waved, her fingers curled. 'Hel-lo. Nice day . . . to-day.'

'It is,' I agreed, as their driver exited and joined Teddy on the curb.

Today, their nurse was a tall woman with mahogany skin and an accent that sounded South African. 'Teddy would like to inquire as to whether he might work today, Missus. He did come yesterday as arranged, but no one was at home.'

'I'm sorry I wasn't here yesterday morning,' I apologized, thinking that, actually, the timing of Teddy's arrival couldn't have been better. Teddy was tall enough to reach the burglar bars without a stepladder, and he looked strong. 'But, yes, I would love for Teddy to work today. Actually, I need some help with the window bars. I wonder if he would mind doing that? I was trying to take off the old padlocks and make sure the latches are in good working condition, but with all the rain this spring, they're rusty.'

Teddy eyed the house. 'Ho-kay,' he said amiably. The nurse made arrangements to pick him up in a couple hours, and Teddy followed me to the backyard. On the way, he assessed Aunt Ruth's overgrown flower beds. 'Gone need lotta work,' he predicted. 'Gotta cut the rose, and thinnin' the iris, and the daisy, and cuttin' the myrtle . . . ohhh, is a hollyhocks. Lotsa hollyhock!' He admired the living walls around the old summer kitchen. ''N' honeysuckle. Them taste good.'

'Yes, they do,' I agreed, thinking of all the times my

childhood friend Jalicia and I had slowly drawn out the centers of honeysuckle blooms and touched our tongues to the stems to harvest the sweet, tiny drops of nectar.

'I'll see if there's a pry bar in the shed,' I said, and Teddy followed me, helping to pull open the door after I unlocked it.

He surveyed the interior with interest as the scents of oil, grease, and damp earth wafted out. With a gasp of appreciation, he took in the pile of broken iron furniture, rakes, shovels, rusted fencing wire and posts, garden hoses, the remains of an old swing, several lawn mowers, and countless other items in Poppy's treasure chest of might-be-useful-someday items.

The mess was even worse than I'd remembered. 'I don't know if we'll be able to find anything in here.'

'Is a shob-bel.' Slipping into the shed, Teddy grabbed a shovel near the door and set it outside. 'Good shob-bel,' he pointed out, as if to prove to me that we could find *something* in the shed.

'Unfortunately, what we need is a pry bar,' I told him. 'But that is a good shovel. It might come in handy with the flowers.'

Teddy worked his way past the tangle in the doorway.

'Be careful. There's no telling what might be . . .'

'Got wheelbarrow . . .' Teddy's voice rose from the darkness of the interior. 'And spread-der . . . and some pots . . . and cutter, cut them rosebush back . . .'

The girls and Bobo came out of the house as Teddy continued his safari.

'Who's that?' Cass asked, standing beside me. Bobo didn't

wait for an explanation. Putting his nose to the ground, he followed a scent trail of who-knew-what into the shed.

'Got dog,' Teddy announced.

'That's Bobo,' I called, then added to Cass, 'Teddy's here to do the yard. The flowers need some work.'

'Oh.' Cass shrugged. ''Kay. You want me and Opal to go back inside and try the latches again?'

'Let's see if we can find a pry bar first. Otherwise, I think we might just have to give up for now. This project is going to require some tools.'

''Kay.' Cass listened with interest to Teddy's description of the shed's contents. 'Can I go in there?' she asked finally.

'I don't think you'd better. There might be rats.'

Cass lowered a brow at me. 'I'm not scared of rats. They had 'em all over the place when Mama worked at the plant.'

'Or snakes,' I added. Actually, I could imagine a myriad of reasons not to enter the shed, which was why I'd left it alone all this time.

'I'm not afraid of snakes. You just need to make noise and they go away. A lady told me that in Marfa. She'd lived there all her life, like, where there's rattlesnakes and stuff.'

Turning to look at Cass, I laughed. 'Is there anything you *are* afraid of?'

'Not much,' she said, and I laughed again, because I could have predicted that would be her answer.

CHAPTER 14

Cass

It was pretty fun, helping at Mrs Kaye's house, even though we ended up pulling weeds instead of painting, when it seemed like painting would be better. Pulling weeds was something to do, anyway, instead of hanging around the apartment. The dude with the slow elevator, Teddy, was cool, too. Back when I was real young, my mama had a brother who'd got his head banged up in a motorcycle wreck when he was a teenager, and he was like that. We used to go visit him at the nursing home. I'd forgot what ever happened to him, but now I guessed he must of died sometime, and Mama just didn't make a big deal of it to us.

Anyway, Teddy was fun. He knew a lot about plants, and he took time to show Opal little caterpillars and butterflies, which most adults wouldn't bother with when they had work to do. He put a ladybug on Opal's hand, and she giggled at it crawling up her arm. She squealed and laughed when it flew away, and it came in my mind that Opal didn't laugh much. She was always kind of careful and quiet around people, like she was afraid they'd notice she was there. After the ladybug, we started pulling out clumps of grass and throwing them over our shoulders. Bobo chased them and beat them up like they were wild animals, and Opal laughed so hard she rolled on the ground.

Once we had the grass out from around the rosebush, Teddy cut some pieces off it. His hands were big, and must of been thick as leather, because the prickers didn't even bother him. Opal pricked her finger and got a little dot of blood, though, and I thought Teddy was gonna pass out.

'Oh, got a boo-boo, Mama!' Teddy's mama, the lady in the wheelchair, was back by then to pick him up, but she'd had the nurse get her out of the car, and come to look at the flowers. Good thing, because for a big guy, Teddy was sure freaked over a little blood. He took Opal's hand and pulled her over to his mom's wheelchair, so she could see the finger with the blood on it. Bobo got up from the shade to check what all the commotion was about.

'Ohhhh, not so bad,' Teddy's mom said, then she wiped away the blood with a hankie and smiled at Opal. 'All better. Such a pred-dee girl.' Teddy's mom talked kind of funny, and her mouth hung down on one side, but she was real nice.

Opal just blinked up at her, like she didn't have any idea what Teddy's mama was talking about.

'Say thanks, Opal,' I told her. 'She said you're pretty.'

Opal got too embarrassed to talk, like usual, and she pulled the front of her T-shirt up over her arms so that everyone could see her belly.

'Opal!' I yanked her shirt back down, so she'd know not

216

to do that again. I remembered when I was little, I thought if I pulled my dress up over my head at church, people couldn't see me anymore. My mama cured me of that, real quick. She spanked my butt, so I'd know I wasn't invisible after all. 'Go check on your caterpillars, okay?'

Opal ran off to the steps, where she had a jar of caterpillars Teddy'd caught. She'd set them next to her doll and the little dishes we found in the back bedroom. There were also a pile of coloring books, a bucket of crayons that were too dried up to use, a couple puzzles, and a Candy Land game Mrs Kaye said we could take home. Opal had a fit to bring it all outside, and Mrs Kaye let her. All day long, Opal kept looking back at her stuff and checking on it, like she thought it was gonna disappear.

Teddy's mama decided they better get going after the bloody finger. I figured out that Teddy's daddy, Edward, was at home, and they didn't like to leave him alone too long because he had Alzheimer's. I knew what that was. The waitress in the oil patch town had a uncle with Alzheimer's. Old Bab, she called him. I met him once or twice. Old Bab could tell you the same story four times in a row and not even remember he did it.

Mrs Kaye looked at the work Teddy'd done and asked if he'd keep coming and get all the flower beds looking good, and clean out along the fence. Teddy said he would, and also, he wanted to get some seeds off the tall flowers out back, because he hadn't seen any like them, ever. Mrs Kaye told him the old train tramps had brought the seeds a long time ago, and they grew just like Jack's magic beanstalks.

Mrs Kaye laughed and said they used to make dolls out of the flowers. On the back steps, Opal looked around to see if there was another doll hid somewhere.

After Teddy and the rest of them left, Mrs Kaye decided we better go on and fix the sandwiches, which was good, because I was hungry for sure, and it was after lunchtime already. We put together all the sandwiches, and bagged them up, and by then Opal and Bobo were sitting in front of the cabinet, whining for food. Mrs Kaye said we ought to go out back and have a picnic, since we'd all worked so hard. So we did. We sat on a little bench by a big old tree stump and ate sandwiches and chips, and drank lemonade. Bobo got Opal's first sandwich when she wasn't looking, so we had to give her a second one. Then she started pinching off little pieces and throwing them in the air, and Bobo would catch them. She filled her little teapot and gave him a drink in a teacup, too. I let her do it because when you've got, like, twenty sandwiches and plenty of lemonade, it seems fine to give it to the dog.

Mrs Kaye watched her and smiled. 'I'll bet we played tea party with those dishes a thousand times,' she told me while Opal and the rag doll talked a blue streak. Mostly you couldn't understand what Opal said, or what the doll said back, but they could sure carry on. Bobo sat there real quiet and watched, waiting for the next piece of sandwich to come his way.

'If you crawl through the hollyhocks, there's a little room inside where the old summer kitchen used to be.' Mrs Kaye was looking past me toward the tall spikes of flowers that grew thick like a waving green wall with dots of color all over and honeysuckle twisted in between.

That got me curious, even though there was another sandwich on the plate, and I wanted it. 'Can I go see?'

Mrs Kaye smiled at me. She had pretty eyes that were a deep greenish brown out here in the yard, like the hollyhocks. 'I'll show you.' She stood up, and stretched out her fingers and wiggled them, and I put my hand in hers. It felt strange at first, holding someone's hand, but then it was nice. Mama used to take my hand when we'd walk across the grocery store parking lot, and we'd swing our arms up and down real high, and she'd say, 'To market, to market, to buy a fat pig. To market, to market, jiggedy-jig.'

Then I'd say, 'To market, to market, to buy a fat hog. To market, to market, jiggedy-jog.' And then we'd go along with our arms swinging and the sun shining down on our faces.

I felt the sun on me when Mrs Kaye and me walked to the hollyhocks. Once we got there, she slipped her hands between the plants, and pulled apart the honeysuckle vines and the hollyhock stalks, making a little tunnel.

'Go ahead,' she said, and I stepped through. Mrs Kaye came in behind me, and then the plants snapped back together again, and it was like we were in a little room about as big as our kitchen in the apartment, but with a rock floor, and tall green walls, and blue sky for a roof. It seemed miles away from everything, a storybook place, like Narnia inside the wardrobe.

'Wow,' I whispered.

Mrs Kaye put her hands on the small of her back and

turned in a circle. 'This was our secret place. My friend Jalicia and I spent many an hour playing let's pretend here.'

'It's awesome.' I stretched out my arms and twirled until the room and the colors spun. 'Who built it?'

'Well, years ago Poppy and Aunt Ruth had what people called a summer kitchen out here. Back in those days, some houses had little kitchen buildings in back, so when you did your cooking and canning in the summertime, you wouldn't heat up the house.'

I thought maybe she was pulling my leg, but one thing I'd learned about Texas was that it got hot, even in the springtime. On the truck radio one day, the weatherman said this was a *unseasonably cool* spring, and I about fell over laughing. 'How come they didn't just turn on the air-conditioning?'

She chuckled. 'They didn't have air-conditioning. I can remember when lots of houses didn't have air-conditioning.'

'Seriously?' I looked at her and tried to decide how old she really was.

Mrs Kaye laughed again. 'Yes, seriously. And, in case you're wondering, I'm not that old.'

'I wasn't wondering.' My face turned red, so she could probably tell I was. 'It's really awesome in here, though. Maybe tomorrow I could, like, bring Opal in for a tea party.'

Mrs Kaye looked out at the wall of green for what felt like a long time, but she didn't answer me. I got that twisty feeling in my stomach I used to have on the playground when I tried to get in on tag with Tamara Powell's little snotty group of soccer girls, and they told me to buzz off.

She probably thinks you're a doofy little pain in the butt. Dork. 'I

mean, if me and Opal are gonna come help with the painting and the gardens and sandwiches and stuff tomorrow, I
just thought . . . well, she's probably never had a tea party
with anybody before – except the dog and the rag doll, I
mean, but that's not a real tea party.' I rolled my eyes, so
maybe Mrs Kaye would think I was doing it for Opal, but
really I thought the secret room was cool.

'I think that would be lovely,' she said, and I felt the air
loosen up in my chest. 'I think tomorrow we should all have
a tea party in the summer kitchen for lunch.'

'Cool. Awesome.' I heard Opal hollering for me outside,
and I knew we needed to head out anyway. Opal and me
had sandwiches to take back to the apartments, and besides,
Rusty was supposed to come get Kiki at two thirty, and I
figured we'd better be home before then. Rusty wouldn't
like it if he didn't know where me and Opal were, and of
course Kiki couldn't tell him, since all she did was sleep.
And we still had to stop by the bookstore on the way home
to get Opal a new book.

Opal hollered again, and I could hear her moving around
outside the flower wall, trying to figure out what'd happened to us. 'Hang on, Opal,' I said. 'Here we come.' Mrs
Kaye opened the tunnel, and we climbed out. Opal clapped
like we'd done a trick.

Opal and me said good-bye, and got the bag of sandwiches
and Opal's doll and book and Candy Land game, and headed
off. Opal didn't even fuss about leaving behind the little
dishes or the puzzles. So long as she could keep her doll, she
was okay.

On the way home, at the bookstore, we took a minute to show MJ how Opal had learned her book, and MJ said Opal was the best customer she ever had. Ever. That made Opal really happy, I think, because she wouldn't leave until she sat there and had MJ read the new book to her.

When we got back to the apartments, Angel, Ronnie, and Boo weren't on the steps. Opal wanted to read her book, so I put her inside and told her to stay right there. The bedroom door was open a little, which meant Kiki'd been up, but she wasn't in the bathroom, so I figured she was probably lying around in bed.

I looked at the time and figured we had about thirty minutes before Rusty would show up, so I locked the door with the key and went out back to look for the other kids. They were down in the storm ditch, like usual. They had five little Mexican kids with them. As soon as Angel, Ronnie, and Boo saw me and the bag, they came running up. The Mexican kids hung back like they weren't sure about me. But once they saw there was food, they came up, too. I gave them some, and they ran off with it, but in a minute they came back with more kids. They made a pretty good dent in the sandwiches. Angel, Ronnie, and Boo took a second one and unwrapped it, but a couple of the Mexican kids took a second one and, like, hid it under their T-shirts and stuff. I guessed they wanted to take it home, but they didn't leave.

'Some dude come to your apartment,' Angel said after a while. She stopped to lick her fingers, which was gross, because they'd been playing in the slimy water again.

'Huh?' First I wondered if I heard her right, and then I thought about Kiki. If she was having some guy in our house when my brother was busting his butt trying to help her out, I was gonna kill her. 'What guy? You mean my brother?' Maybe Rusty'd come home early today, and Kiki wasn't even in the bedroom right now. Maybe she was already gone to work, which would mean Opal was alone in there, which wasn't good.

Angel smacked her lips and wrinkled her nose at me like Tamara Powell used to on the playground. 'No. Some dude, like, bangin' on yo' door. Some big ol' white dude with long greezy gray hair. You know him? He ask was anyone there, and we keep tellin' him no, but he don' believe it. He come back beatin' down the door four time. He drive 'round the block a couple time, then he come back. Drive 'round, come back.'

'What'd he want?' Long strings of hair blew across my face, so I pulled out the ponytail holder and started to gather it up again. It felt thick and damp in my hands, a little sweaty from the walk home.

Angel wiped her mouth on her shoulder and took another bite of her sandwich. 'He lookin' fo' you brother girlfriend. If she sleepin' in there, she deaf, she cain't hear that.'

I had a brain flash of the way Kiki looked the night Rusty first brought her home. Her old man did that. He beat her up pretty good before he kicked her and Opal out . . .

If Opal was in the apartment alone right now, and someone came pounding on the door, she wouldn't know what to do. She'd think it was me. If she could work the lock, she might open the door. Maybe she'd already opened the door . . .

'See? There he go again.' Angel pointed toward the road.

In the gap between buildings, a dented red and white pickup with monster tires passed over the bridge.

'He ga' a big tuck,' Ronnie said, then called the man a word my mother would of busted my butt for.

My chest got tight and lunch rushed up my throat like dirty floodwater, and I tasted what was left of the tea party. What if Opal opened the door? Maybe he'd grab her to get to Kiki. Maybe he'd hurt her. Maybe he'd take them both off and kill them and leave them in a ditch somewhere, and it'd be some sad, terrible story on the news tomorrow.

My mind went haywire, and I had a flash of Opal's little pink shoes dumped in the mud someplace.

Dropping the sandwiches, I took off down the storm drain, my feet splashing through the puddles and the clogs wobbling with every step. I tripped where the cement was cracked, my foot twisted sideways, and I fell hard, my arm skidding into a patch of water and slime. My hand slipped when I tried to get up, and for a minute I was in one of those dreams where you want to run, you need to run, but you can't.

I have to get to Opal.

Angel hollered at me from behind, 'Hey, where you goin'? You want yo' bag?'

Kicking off the clogs, I scrambled onto my feet and took off again toward the gap between two of the buildings, where a gutter ditch ran through to the parking lot. My foot landed on a piece of glass, but I only felt it a little. All I could think was, *Please, please, please, God. Please. I have to get to Opal. I have to get there first.*

Running through the gap, I couldn't see anything but brick. I tried to listen, tried to think if I could hear the truck, or the man yelling or pounding on the door, but all I could hear was the air coming in and out of my mouth, and blood rushing in my ears, and my heart banging so hard against my ribs it felt like they'd bust. I saw the sunlight ahead at the end of the buildings. I ran toward it, and into it, and the pavement was hot under my feet, the tar sticky and thick.

The wind caught my hair and blew it over my face. I quit running, pushed the hair away, and looked around the parking lot. The truck pulled in off the road, slow, like the driver was looking for something. He stopped near the Dumpster, the brakes squealing out a sound that echoed against the walls and filled the air for a minute before it died to just the engine rumbling.

Across the street, Monk and his friends were hanging around in front of the convenience store. When the man got out and left the truck engine on, the wannabes started pointing and punching each other, like they were trying to get up the guts to come jack the truck.

The man left the door open and went to get something from the back.

I kept walking toward our apartment, acting like it was any other day and I was coming home from someplace.

The ring of metal against metal came from the truck,

and from the corner of my eye I saw the man start toward me with what looked like a crowbar. I swallowed hard as I passed Angel's apartment. For once, I wished the Mexicans were having a party, or Charlie would come out to hassle me about the rent. He probably had his TV turned up so loud, Kiki's boyfriend could bash me in the head and he'd never hear it. The wannabes would be the only ones who knew what happened, and they wouldn't care.

'Hey!' the man yelled.

I stopped at the bottom of our steps, put both hands on the rail and one foot on the step, so he couldn't go past me without pushing me out of the way. Part of me said he wouldn't do it – not right here in the daylight, and to some girl he didn't even know. He probably just beat up his girl-friends. But part of me was knotted up like one of those shoelaces you'll never get untied.

I looked over my shoulder, like I didn't know what in the world he wanted. Angel and Ronnie were standing in the shadow between the buildings. They must of left Boo some-where. Angel watched me with her arms crossed over the sandwich bag and her eyes great big. If the guy did some-thing, maybe she'd holler for the police, or run out to the street at least.

'Where'zzz she at?' The man shook the metal bar at me. He stopped a few steps away, and I was glad, because I was trying really hard not to back up. He stunk of beer and ciga-rettes, even with the wind blowing. I hoped Monk would get up the guts to jack the truck. That'd get Kiki's boyfriend and his tire iron out of here anyhow.

'Where's who at?' I gave him a snotty look, so he'd know he was bothering me, and I wasn't scared of him.

He called Kiki a bunch of sick names, then finally told me she better come out.

I acted like I heard that kind of talk every day, but I wondered if he could see the hammer pounding inside my chest. I felt like I couldn't breathe. My mind flashed a picture of Opal coming out the door.

No, Opal. No. Don't come out.

'Kiki!' He staggered backward a few steps and the tire iron caught the sun. 'You tell her ta geddd-out-here. You tell 'er if she's with some . . . body . . . I'll kill 'em both.'

A new worry zipped in my ear and buzzed around my mind. If Rusty came home, he'd get in a fight with the guy for sure. Rusty was tall and he was a lot younger, but this guy was huge, and besides, he had a tire iron. Rusty'd be just stupid enough to take it on.

'There isn't anybody in there,' I shouted, pointing to the door I hoped Opal wouldn't open. 'Except my mama, and she's sick in bed with cancer, and you're bothering her out here with your stupid noisy truck. Go away!' The man kind of looked surprised, so I went with it. 'You better leave right now, because the manager already called the police. My brother's on the police force, so we go right to the top of the list. In about two and a half minutes, you're gonna get arrested for about five different things. Leave us alone.'

He almost seemed convinced, and then the door rattled, and he looked at it. 'She'zzz-zin there!' He took a step closer, staggered around, and hollered. 'Kikiiii! Kiki! Come-mon out here, baby. I'm sor-reee. You just pusss-shed the button the other day. You just pusss-shed . . . the button. It's okay, ba-baby. It's allll right. Where's Opal? C'mon out herrr-re, Opal, an' see Uncle Len. Got sssome can-deee . . . for ya . . .' His voice turned sticky sweet in a way that was fake and sickening. 'C'mere, Opal. C'mon out nnnow. You better-rrr come.'

No, Opal. No, no, no. I glanced at the door, but nothing happened. Maybe it was just the wind that had rattled it. 'I said there's nobody in there but my mama. Go away before the police show up.'

Down at the end of the alley, a door opened on one of the apartments where the Mexicans lived. I checked over my shoulder, and the pretty girl with the baby was peeking out. Between the buildings, the Mexican kids squeezed past Ronnie and made a run for it, and the pretty girl pulled them inside with her, then stood watching. Maybe I'd get lucky and she'd call the police. They probably didn't have a phone, though, and besides that, if the police did come, they'd ask all kinds of questions. No telling where me and Opal and Rusty would end up then.

The window blind moved on the crippled lady's apartment, but there wasn't much chance she'd come out. She never did.

When I turned back around, Monk and his gang had crossed the street and they were sort of standing by the man's truck. They weren't messing with it, really. They were hanging around, looking at the truck, and *Uncle Len*, and me. Maybe they were trying to decide if they could grab some stuff and get away with it. There were papers and what looked like a wallet smushed in the corner of the dash.

I never thought I'd be glad to see those three stupid little wannabes, but I was.

Uncle Len came closer to me, and I smelled major beer breath and body stink.

Don't back up, I told myself. *Don't back up.* I pointed at the wannabes and said, 'Y'all better not mess with that truck.'

B.C. lifted his hands, grinned under his do-rag, and said, 'Hey, it's just sittin' here with the do' open. Maybe he don' want it no mo'.'

Oh, thank you, I thought. *Thank you, thank you, thank you for having such a big mouth.*

Uncle Len staggered back, fell sideways, landed against the steps, and roared, 'You little punks touch my truck, I'll knock your heads in!'

'Hey, you in the hood now,' B.C. said. 'Dis my hood.'

Monk stuck his hand in his pocket and moved it around like maybe he had a knife in there. 'Look to me like they three a' us and one a' you.'

Holding his hands up, B.C. moved his fingers like, *Come on.*

Uncle Len pushed off the steps, and for a minute, I thought he was gonna take them up on it. I wasn't sure who'd win. The wannabes would probably get their butts kicked.

'You better go before anything happens,' I said. 'There's no Kiki or Opal here. Just my mama. Go away!'

Uncle Len blinked hard like he'd got sleepy all of a sudden. He lowered the tire iron and kind of let it hang at his side, then he walked back to the truck. The wannabes moved out of reach, and stood there looking tough, which meant they were smarter than I thought. Uncle Len acted like he didn't remember they were there. He just got in his truck, backed it over the curb until he hit the corner of the Dumpster, then put it in gear and took off. On the way out, he almost wrecked with somebody. The other car spun a doughnut and hit the curb as Uncle Len drove away.

The wannabes cheered, because they thought that was cool.

I didn't wait for them to get done watching. I ran for the door, feeling like I was about to throw up. When I got it unlocked, I squeezed through, then shut it behind me, turned the lock, and made a beeline for the bathroom. I didn't see Opal, or Kiki, or anybody. I just ran for the toilet and got to it barely in time to hurl everything from the tea party. Afterward, my mouth tasted sour, and I hung there waiting for the burning to pass. I wanted someone to come put a cool rag on the back of my neck and smooth my hair and tell me it'd be all right.

Finally, I had to stand up on my own, because I needed to know Opal was okay and if Kiki really did sleep through it all, or if she was hiding.

The living room was empty and still. 'Opal?' I whispered, because I couldn't help thinking that Uncle Len might be outside again. 'Opal?'

Rusty's bedroom looked empty, and the door to my bedroom was still cracked open a little. The closer I got, the more I could tell that Kiki wasn't in the bed. She wasn't anywhere in the room, and she wasn't in the living room, either.

Kiki took Opal. Kiki took Opal and they ran off while I was down at the storm ditch giving sandwiches to the kids . . . My heart went wild again, and I started running through the house, checking the closets and under the beds, thinking, *No, no, no!*

Kiki wasn't anywhere. My eyes filled up with tears. I shouldn't of left Opal in the apartment. I shouldn't of left her, even for a minute. I'd let Kiki have long enough to grab her and run off.

Please, God. Please don't let her be gone . . .

I thought about Jesus with the red on his hands, with the strawberry jelly and all the little kids sitting on his feet. *Jesus, please, Jesus . . .*

Something squeaked in the kitchen, but all I could see was a blur, and then a pan rattled in the cabinet by the stove. I rubbed my hand across my eyes, then stood a few steps away and listened. The pans moved again, so soft I almost couldn't hear it, and then there was a little sound, just a tiny squeak. I knew what it was right away, because I'd been hearing it all day. Plastic rubbing together. Opal's little pink shoes.

Every bone in my body dropped out, and my fingers were like rubber, opening the cabinet door and letting the light in. There under the shelf in the back was Opal, curled up in a cake pan, making herself as tiny as she could. Her body was covered in shadows, but her eyes caught the light and made my throat go stiff. Kiki didn't take her after all. Kiki must of been gone before we ever came home in the first place. Maybe she ran off after the first time Uncle Len came banging on the door.

I didn't care where she was, so long as Opal was safe.

'Come here, Opal.' My voice was a dry little croak. 'It's all right.' I stretched out my hand, but she didn't move. 'It's all right now.' I sank down on the floor and let my head fall against the wood. My eyes were burning and heavy. I let them close and tried to go to a mind place. Anyplace. Anywhere but here.

The pans shifted, and Opal crawled closer, and I smelled the peanut butter and jelly she'd smeared on her T-shirt, and the laundry soap I'd washed it in, and shampoo, and plastic shoes, and her hair, and something else I didn't know at first. Her hand touched my face, and the smell was of something green, and tall, and thick. I smelled the hollyhocks, and I found a mind place.

Opal crawled into my lap, and we went to the summer kitchen, where the walls were high and solid all around us. We were safe, and the ceiling was a clear, crystal blue filled with fluffy white clouds.

CHAPTER 15

Sandra Kaye

Over the next few days, life began to take on a routine as we awaited the results of the insurance investigation of Christopher's accident. Each morning, I woke early to take him to school, dropped by the store for bread and supplies, picked up Bobo at the house, then continued across town to Poppy's in the tail end of rush-hour traffic. Cass and Opal were always waiting on the porch – Cass in the tattered high heels she would kick off sometime during the day and replace with flip-flops I'd brought from home, and Opal with her doll propped against the porch post. Usually she'd be singing to it – not a nursery rhyme or a lullaby, but melodies she seemed to make up, and words only she could understand. Every so often during the day I'd see her lift the doll's dress and put a finger on the little printed heart that said I Love You, as if she were checking to be sure it was still there. Occasionally she'd bring the doll to me and ask, 'Ut say?' and I'd tell her. Then she'd show Bobo the doll's painted-on heart and explain, 'Say wub-oo, Bobo.'

Teddy, Hanna Beth, and one of their day nurses, either

Mary or Ifeoma, came by around midmorning, and the girls went outside to help with weeding the flower beds and gathering starts of Aunt Ruth's heirloom plants. Teddy had begun the painstaking job of cleaning out the garden shed, and I took advantage of the time inside to paint.

Around noon each day, after Teddy left, the girls and I held a tea party, during which Bobo drank lemonade from a tiny cup and waited for falling scraps. On a whim, I brought a small iron table with three petite soda-shop chairs from the rec room at home. Together, the girls and I dragged everything through the wall of hollyhocks and furnished the summer kitchen.

After tea, we made sandwiches – more each day, it seemed – then we packed them into a grocery bag, and Cass took them home. Each day, I offered to drive her, and each day she declined, saying that she and Opal had plans to visit the Book Basket on the way. I took time once to look at the store she was so fond of. It was little more than a hole in the wall, just a crumbling stone structure I remembered as a gas station and repair shop, back in the day. Now, a hand-painted sign read, BOOK BASKET, NEW AND USED, with suns and moons and what looked like astrology symbols around the edges. On the portico and under a ragged tree out front, long strings of beads held glass bottles suspended, so that they waved and clinked in the dry breeze from passing cars. The old plate-glass windows were stacked high with yellowed paperbacks in all possible sizes. The place looked odd and mystical, like a fortune-teller's shop, and not the sort of place children should be wandering into alone.

I'd considered stopping to meet the proprietor, whom Cass referred to as MJ, but whenever I happened by, the store was closed. I wanted to be sure the shop was a safe place for Cass and Opal to be spending time, but I was also curious as to whether this MJ could fill in some of the blanks in the girls' living situation. Cass's story changed daily, and as bad as it sounded, I suspected that the reality was worse. There was little point in asking, because when I pushed, she backed away. She was happy to come to Poppy's and spend her days helping with chores and playing tea party, but that was it. She didn't want me involving myself in her life, and she only occasionally asked about mine – as if it were perfectly natural for two people to spend time in proximity but never move beyond the surface.

I was surprised when she inquired about Poppy as we were painting some closet doors I'd had Teddy carry out to the back porch before he left. My renovations had moved far beyond their original scope, and on some level I knew I was making excuses to keep spending time here. So far there hadn't been any indications of buyer interest in the house.

On the inside of one of the closet doors, we unearthed a growth chart of sorts, marking heights, and ages, and names. There were my mother's marks, Maryanne's, and mine on one side of the frame, and on the other, Jake's and Christopher's. There was even a growth chart for Bobo, undoubtedly put there at Jake's request. The tallies ran in neat little columns that started near the bottom of the door and moved upward as the dates evolved.

Cass was fascinated that the house had seen two generations of my family grow taller than the little closet door.

'Did Poppy build the house all by himself?' she asked.

'Is a Pop-pee-howse?' Every so often, Opal popped up and echoed whatever Cass had to say. Then she'd sit quietly with Bobo and wait for an answer, her face open and inquisitive.

'More or less, he did.' Touching the closet door, I thought of Poppy, and had the strange realization that I hadn't considered calling the detective about his case in over a week. 'Poppy could build almost anything and fix almost anything. He was always finding broken bikes, and wagons, and toys in trash piles. He'd bring them home and repair them, and then he'd give them to kids he knew, or he'd set them out on the sidewalk for whoever wanted them.'

'Cool,' Cass said. 'I asked my brother about fixing your burglar bars in front, and he said he could do it when he has some time off, if you want. Rusty's good at fixing things. Like Poppy. He doesn't fix toys, I mean, but he can fix other stuff.'

'Pop-pee toy?' Opal asked, her long lashes fanning upward in hope. Over the last several days we'd discovered toys and pieces of old board games hidden behind closet doors and tucked in the corners of upper shelves. We'd even found a naked Barbie behind the water heater and fashioned a dress from paper towels and twist ties.

'No, sweetie,' I told her. 'Poppy doesn't have any more toys around here. I think we've found them all.' I made a mental note to go through the closets at home and see if there were any leftovers Opal or Cass might like. For the most part, the boys' childhood things had either been packed away or donated to church rummage sales long ago.

Cass leaned close to the door. 'Who's Jake?'

'What?'

'Jake.' She pointed to Jake's name. 'Who's Jake?'

'My son.' I touched the marks, let my finger run along them, and was filled with memories. Poppy's house was Jake's favorite place. The summer we brought Jake home, Poppy had a garden out back. Rob was working long hours and it was lonely at home, so Jake and I often drove in to spend the day helping Poppy and Aunt Ruth with planting and weeding, harvesting and canning. Even though Jake was just three and knew only a few words of English, he understood the language of plants, and we gathered that he must have lived in one of the farming villages in the Guatemalan countryside. In the afternoons when he grew tired, we'd find him under the plants, drifting off to sleep. Aunt Ruth would bring out an old quilt, so Jake could curl up on the swing beneath the bur oak tree and fall asleep. I could still picture his tiny body, his skin brown and smooth, his dark hair falling in curls over his forehead, his lashes brushing his cheeks in inky streaks as his lips fell open with slow, steady breaths.

The swing was gone now. The rusty brackets that had held it lay with the rubbish and estate sale debris by the curb. I had the strangest urge to hurry to the pile, grab the brackets, and tuck into my car these things that had once held my son suspended above the ground. I'd show them to him and ask him if he remembered falling asleep on the old swing . . .

A slipknot of dread trailed behind the thought, and I stepped away before it could wrap around me. Of course I couldn't show the brackets to Jake. He was gone. The little boy who slept on the swing was lost in the world again, wandering the marketplaces alone, searching for something he might never find.

'Oh.' Cass's voice seemed far away, light and innocent in comparison to the dark images of Jake in a foreign country with no family and no means of support. 'I thought you just had Christopher.' Over the past few days, Cass and Opal had inadvertently listened in on so many phone calls about Christopher's accident that they talked about him as if they knew him.

'Jake is Christopher's older brother.' I dipped the brush into the paint, then wiped the bristles against the rim and watched the excess drip away in thin, white streams. 'Rob and I adopted him from Guatemala when he was three.'

Cass pulled her finger away from the door, then braced her hands on her hips and looked at me. 'Really? Like in South America?'

'In Central America.'

'Whoa. Like on TV?'

'We didn't think of it that way. We just knew we wanted children and hadn't been having any luck.'

'Pppfff.' Cass laughed. 'My mama always said all she ever had to do was look at a man and she'd get pregnant. I bet I'll be like that, too. Someday, I mean. I don't want any kids for a long time. Like after college and stuff.'

'That's a good plan.' Looking at Cass, I tried to imagine

her future. Where was the path from wandering the streets unsupervised, saddled with a three-year-old, to college and a family?

'Does he like to come here, too?'

'Who?'

'Jake. Does he like to come here, too?' As the shed cleaning had proceeded, I'd told Cass about Christopher's desire to find the pocket-knives and the wood carving tools – special treasures he remembered from his time with Poppy. I hadn't mentioned that I'd been stalling Chris because I didn't know how to explain the ongoing activity at Poppy's house. Just considering it made it all seem more absurd. I could imagine what Rob, what Holly, what everyone would say if I told them I was driving across town every day to renovate a house no one cared about, to have tea parties with two little girls I barely knew, and to make peanut butter and jelly sandwiches, which would be taken down the road and handed to whoever wanted them.

Rather than descend into self-analysis, I related the story of Poppy and Jake – their close relationship when we adopted Jake, their fishing trips and backyard engineering projects together, Jake's decision to attend college close by so he could help care for Poppy, their baseball and football nights together, and the one night Jake didn't show up, and what it led to, and Jake's disappearance after the funeral. I'd almost finished the story when I looked into Cass's face, took in her wide blue eyes, her small round nose just beginning to sharpen and mature, her lips parted slightly over two front teeth that still looked as if she needed to grow into them. I realized I was telling the story to a child, and it wasn't appropriate.

I felt the dampness of tears on my face. 'I'm sorry,' I said, wiping my cheeks with the back of a painting glove.

Frowning, Cass stretched out her arms and hugged my waist. I heard Opal's footsteps cross the porch; then I felt her wrap herself around my leg. Our embrace was awkward at first, but I surrendered to it, and we stayed there until Opal grew impatient and tried to shinny up my leg.

'Opal, stop,' Cass scolded, then picked her up and took her back to her toys. 'You can't, like, climb on people whenever you feel like it, and you're gonna get paint on your clothes. I told you to stay over here.'

Opal's pout lip made known her opinion of being left out. Cass ignored her and picked up a paintbrush again. We worked in silence for a while, painting the other doors, but not the one on which Poppy had charted family history. When we'd finished the others, we stood looking at it.

'I think we'll leave this one for now,' I said. 'I can't quite bring myself to paint it.'

Cass wiped her brush on the edge of the tray and started pouring the extra paint back into the can. 'One time when I was little, Rusty an' me made cinnamon toast, and we got in trouble because we weren't supposed to use the oven. Rusty got mad and took off, and Mama an' me drove around all night looking for him. He's such a dork, but guess what happened when we drove up home? There he was sitting on the porch because he didn't have a key to get in. What a doof, huh? He got Mama all upset for nothing. Some people – boys mostly, I think – just have to figure everything out the hard way. They don't mean anything by it.'

I realized she was trying to comfort me, trying to tell me Jake's absence wasn't my fault. It occurred to me that Rob and I hadn't even attempted to extend that level of grace to each other. We'd only sought to lay blame. 'You're a very smart girl, Cass. You have a good sense of people, for someone your age.'

She watched the last of the paint stream into the can in a long thin swirl. 'I'm not a *little girl*.'

'I know that.'

'I'm seventeen.'

'You've told me.'

Her eyes flicked upward, the brows in a worried tangle, then she concentrated on the paint again. 'People think I'm younger sometimes, but I'm seventeen.'

'One of these days, you'll be glad for people to think you're younger.' The words sounded old and tired. Sometimes I looked in the mirror, and I wondered what had happened to the college coed with freckles over her nose and not a wrinkle on her face. It seemed impossible that so much time had passed, and I hadn't done any of the things that girl thought she'd do. She thought she would finish her education degree, move someplace where passionate teachers were in short supply and change the lives of kids who needed someone to believe in them . . .

Cass blew a sardonic puff of air through her lips. 'I *wish* I were older.'

'Well, I wish I were younger, so we're quite a pair.'

Her gaze lifted and met mine, her face filled with questions. I remembered sitting on this very porch, not a child, not a woman, already afraid I'd never be good enough for anyone to love me. Without that fear, what decisions might I have made?

I smoothed wispy strands of hair over Cass's shoulder so they wouldn't fall into the paint. 'Don't be in such a hurry,' I whispered. 'You never get to go back.'

A noise filtered into my consciousness. I heard it dimly at first, then louder and louder. A bell ringing. The doorbell, ringing over and over incessantly.

Cass jerked upright and checked to see if Opal was still in the corner with her toys. Engrossed in a coloring book and the new crayons I'd brought, she hadn't moved.

'Who'd be ringing the doorbell?' Dusting myself off, I looked at my paint-spattered clothes and had the absurd thought that I was in no shape for company.

Cass picked up Opal and followed me through the back door into the kitchen. I heard a conversation outside, the rapid back-and-forth of an argument, but I couldn't discern the words, only the hum of voices, one high and shrill, one low and raspy. Neither sounded like Andrea, the real estate agent. They sounded like . . .

Children?

We rounded the corner into the front room, and there was someone at the window – just a shadow with the sunlight behind, perhaps my height or taller, but slim. The face was hidden, but I could make out dark skin and hair in cornrows. Pressing between the burglar bars, the figure put a hand to the glass and tried to block the glare to see inside.

'Oh, geez!' Cass's voice was little more than a tightly controlled whisper, but it startled me in the empty room. 'Geez! I can't believe it. They must've followed us.'

I stopped. The shadow receded from the window, and I had the eerie sense of someone, now invisible, still being there. 'Who . . . What are you talking about, Cass?'

She bolted past me, set Opal down, then pressed her back to the door. Opal mimicked her, and they looked like two of the three little pigs, trying to keep the wolf away. 'Don't answer it,' Cass whispered, and put a finger to her lips. Opal copied the motion, as if they'd been through this routine before. 'Don't let 'em know you're here. If they know you're here, they'll never go away. They'll knock on the door until you let them in.'

'*Who* will?' If I hadn't been so confused, I would have laughed at the theatrics. The girls' eyes were as wide as cue balls. Outside, the front porch grew silent, and the floorboards squeaked. 'I think whoever it is just left,' I whispered.

Cass shook her head. 'They do that. They make you think they're gone. They hide until you open the door, and then they run into your house.' Carefully, silently, she touched Opal's shoulder, then pointed toward the window. Opal dropped to all fours and crept to the glass like a spy evading motion detectors, then raised up and peeked through the bottom corner.

After checking the front porch, she shook her head. 'No see-see kibs.' Moving to the middle of the windowsill, she scanned the porch again. 'No see-see kibs.'

I couldn't help myself. I started to laugh, then crossed the room and reached for the lock. 'What in the world are you girls doing? Who's out there?'

'Nobody!' Cass spread her arms in Katie-bar-the-door fashion. 'Don't open it.'

Opal continued her surveillance work from the window. 'No see-see. No see kibs.' She stood up, braced her hands on the small of her back, and twisted from side to side, looking confident.

I put a hand on the dead bolt, and both girls gasped.

'No, don't do it!' Cass sagged helplessly. 'It's those kids. The ones next to our apartment. They'll come in your house, and they won't ever leave. They do this, like, every day as soon as me and Opal get home. They're in our house all the time, and they'll eat all your food. I think Boo ate the Cootie leg. I do. He had it, and now I can't find it anyplace. They eat *everything*.'

'Oh, for heaven's sake.' I twisted the knob. 'We have plenty of food. I bought five loaves of bread today, and there's food in the refrigerator. We'll be all right.'

'You don't understand. They won't leave anybody alone. Me and Opal have to sneak out of the apartment at seven in the morning to keep them from following us.'

'You've been coming here at *seven* in the *morning*?' Instead of amusement, I felt apprehension. It wasn't good for Cass and Opal to be out wandering the streets before the neighborhood became active.

'We have to. They tail us all the time. They're always . . .' Mouth dropping open, she gaped at the doorway behind me, leaving the sentence unfinished.

I turned to see a little boy standing in the square of light from the kitchen.

'Ere Boo!' Opal observed, pointing at the boy. 'Ere Boo.'

Cass growled in her throat and crossed the room with her arms stiff at her sides. 'Boo! You can't just go walking into people's houses.' Towering over the boy, she shook a finger. 'Where's Angel? How did you get in here?'

The little boy pointed to the front window, where someone, Angel apparently, was trying to peer through the bars again. She wasn't as tall as I'd originally thought. She must have been standing on something before. I recognized the little boy in my living room from the Dumpster day. He was the pint-sized lookout.

'Boo, did you crawl under the fence?' Cass grabbed his arm, and he blinked up at her, his. dark eyes soulful. 'He can get anywhere. Yesterday, while we were playing Candy Land, he climbed up *on top* of our refrigerator. Nobody even heard him, but he got up there because that's where the cereal was. He's like one of those frogs with the suction feet.' Huffing an exaggerated sigh, she pulled him toward the front door.

I opened it and let in the light, along with Boo's brother and sister.

Cass wasn't pleased. 'Go home and wait till I get there.' Steering Boo past me, she placed him with his siblings in the entranceway. 'I told you guys *not* to *follow* us. Go home.'

'It's all right,' I said. 'Why don't we make the sandwiches and then you can all head home together?'

'They *know* how to get home,' Cass protested. 'I bet they

245

came up the storm ditch. Did you guys come up the ditch, Angel?'

Angel jutted her hip to one side and crossed her arms. 'Maybe.'

'You'll probably get poison ivy.'

'Will not.'

'Will so, and you deserve it, anyway. I told you not to . . .'

I sensed a girl fight coming on, so I stepped in the middle and moved everyone to the kitchen. The sandwich making proceeded with far more help than was needed, and a latent but noticeable ongoing power struggle. I was reminded again of how fortunate I was to have raised boys. Boys didn't care who got the coveted job of spreading jelly. Boys just wanted to eat the sandwiches. By the time we'd finished our manufacturing process, Angel's brothers had given up helping with construction and settled on the kitchen floor with Opal, happily consuming the products as if they hadn't eaten all day. I fixed juice in Dixie cups and they drank as if they hadn't seen liquid in a while, either. Standing at the counter, I played bartender, refilling cups at least a dozen times.

When the impromptu picnic was finished, we packed a bag of extra sandwiches, and I drove the kids home. Cass was pleased to see Angel, Ronnie, and Boo deposited back where they belonged, but she made it clear that she and Opal wanted to return to Poppy's with me. She handed the sandwich bag over to Angel and sulked in her seat as she watched them disappear around the corner with it.

'Can me and Opal stay longer at Poppy's with you today?'

she asked. 'Book Basket wasn't open when we drove by just now. MJ's probably gone somewhere telling stories.'

'Why don't you check in at home while we're here?'

Cass glanced toward the apartment door. 'Rusty's at work, and Kiki sleeps all day. I don't wanna bug her.'

'What about your mom?' I knew I was pushing. Cass leaned away and pressed her body into the gap between the seat and the car door.

'Mama's at the doctor today. The Dial-a-Ride comes for her on Fridays.' She spilled the words like a street vendor popping out a bag of counterfeit Rolexes. 'It's easiest for her to take the Dial-a-Ride when she has to go to the doctor. I'd go with her, but I've gotta watch Opal, but it's no big deal. Mama's used to the treatments. She's sick for a day or two after, and then she feels better.'

'What are the treatments for?'

Looking down at her hands, she picked some dried paint off her index finger. Her lips arched into a contemplative pout. 'Dialysis . . . and she has to have blood transfusions sometimes. She had cancer, but they took it out. She's on the list for a kidney transplant, though.' Her chin trembled again. The emotion was real, not manufactured, even though the medical diagnosis didn't make much sense. 'I don't like to talk about it, okay? When she gets a transplant, she'll be better.'

'I'm sure she will.' I reached over the console and squeezed her arm.

Her hair fell forward, like a sunlit gold shield hiding her emotions. 'Me and Opal can help you put the closet doors back on.'

'I think we'd better just bring them inside and wait for Teddy to come tomorrow. They're a little hard to manage,' I said, but more than anything I wanted to break through the shell of secrets, part it like the curtain of hair and see what Cass was hiding inside.

We drove back to Poppy's house in silence. Opal fell asleep in the backseat, so we carried her inside and laid her on the rug in front of the kitchen sink. She curled into a ball with her thumb in her mouth, sighed and drifted off again. Bobo scratched at the back door, and Cass let him in. Panting, he padded across the kitchen, sniffed Opal, then settled in beside her.

We cleaned the kitchen, then brought the closet doors inside. We'd barely finished before there was a knock on the front window. Angel was back, alone this time.

Cass was not pleased. 'Go on home. You can't just come here anytime you want.'

'Anyone's welcome here,' I corrected, and I could tell I'd hurt Cass's feelings. She wanted to believe she and Opal were special. 'But Cass and I are doing quite a bit of painting, so it would be best if you just came at lunchtime, all right?'

'All right.' Angel threaded her hands behind herself, rocking back and forth, then turning her attention to Cass. 'That dude come to yo' house again jus' now. He don't go bangin' on the door this time, though. He bein' all sweet, and nice, and yo' brother girlfriend come out, and they gettin' it on right there on the step.'

Cass's mouth dropped open. 'At *our* place? Rusty made Kiki promise the guy wouldn't come back pounding on our door again. She said he showed up at her work, and the bouncers got him in a corner and told him he better stay away from her or they'd hunt him down and break his kneecaps. It scared him off.'

'He don't look scared,' Angel said. 'And he ain't got no broke kneecaps, neither.'

'I'm gonna kill Kiki!'

'No, you ain't, 'less you know where she boyfriend live. She done took off with that man. She don't lock yo' door neither. We was watchin' yo' stuff, then yo' brother come home, and he ask, "Where she go?" So I told him, and he mad, mad. He throwin' thangs and hollerin'. Ronnie an' Boo runned out back, and I come here. Man, yo' brother got a temper. He askin' where you at, too.'

Cass checked her watch. 'I gotta go.' She bolted out the door, and Angel spun around and followed. I called after them, but Cass only hollered back, 'I gotta go!' and raced down the street.

I hurried to the kitchen to get my purse, and only then realized that Opal was still asleep on the floor with Bobo. Slinging my purse onto my shoulder, I scooped her up and took her to the car, then locked the house, climbed in with Bobo on my heels, and headed down the street.

Opal blinked drowsily out the window as we drove to the apartment complex. Everything looked quiet there.

I found Cass and Angel in the apartment, picking up toppled furniture and pieces of a drinking glass shattered on the floor. 'Is everything all right?' I asked.

'Yes.' Cass looked tired, and much older than twelve or

thirteen. 'Rusty's just a moron sometimes, that's all. I gotta clean up this mess. Mama won't like it.'

'What'chew talkin' about, Mama?' Angel piped up. 'You ain't got no –'

'Shut up, Angel,' Cass spat. 'Just shut up.'

Jerking her chin upward, Angel dropped the drinking glass. It fell to the floor and splintered into more pieces. 'Well, fine. You can clean up yo' own junk, miss big mouth.' She stalked out the door and disappeared.

Opal wiggled drowsily out of my arms and slid to the floor. 'Uh-oh,' she said. Steering her around the glass toward the threadbare sofa, I took in the place where Cass was living. It was even worse than the exterior indicated – just a small main room and a tiny kitchen sparsely appointed with crumbling furnishings. The olive linoleum was brown with filth around the edges and under the furniture. In the kitchen, the single counter leaned to one side, and missing patches of Formica formed divots in which food and debris had collected. Around the sink, the counter had rotted through in several spots, so that it was hard to tell what was holding up the sink. Water dripped continuously from the faucet, leaving a long oval of rust and lime. A sleeping bag on the sofa indicated that someone had been using it as a bed, and there was dirty laundry everywhere.

Opal climbed onto the sofa, and something brown and torpedo-shaped scampered from underneath, then disappeared into a crack in the floor. A shiver ran across my shoulders, and the sensation was quickly followed by a growing, angry heat. No one should be living like this.

Cass stopped cleaning and watched me survey the apartment. Her expression told me I was telegraphing my thoughts. She looked nervous and embarrassed.

'I can help you clean up.' My mind spun through the barrage of new information, piecing facts together. *What'chew talking about, Mama?* There was no mother living here. *Yo' brother girlfriend come out, and they gettin' it on ...* Opal's mother wasn't a relative; she was living with Cass's brother. Cass was living with her brother, some woman who had an abusive ex-boyfriend, Opal, and most likely no one else.

'I can do it.' Filling her chest with air, Cass straightened her shoulders, then squatted down to rake up ice that had been scattered from a McDonald's cup. 'It's no big deal, okay?'

Opal scooted off the couch, and Cass swung a finger at her. 'Opal, stay there! You'll cut your feet.' Her voice reverberated through the low-ceilinged room and blasted out the door.

I picked up a piece of glass, moved sideways two steps, and set it on the table. 'All right, then, I'll just sit here and we can talk.'

Cass sagged over the McDonald's cup. 'You better go. I'll get in trouble. I'm not supposed to let people in.'

I sat on the edge of a dining chair, folding my hands between my legs. 'Cass, if you're in trouble ...'

'I'm not, okay?' Standing up, she faced me. 'I'm not. You gotta go before Rusty comes back.' The words ended in a stifled sob, both a plea and a demand.

I closed my eyes, trying to decide what to do. Was I

making the situation worse? Could I make it better? 'Maybe I could talk to your brother.'

'No!' she wailed, her tears spilling over in streams that she wiped impatiently. 'Just go, all right? I'm not in trouble. I'm fine. I just want to be by myself.'

I stood up, vacillating by the door. 'Will you and Opal be all right if I go?'

Sagging back to the floor, she answered with a nod.

'Okay then.' *Am I doing the right thing? Is this right?* 'I'll leave, but tomorrow I want to know what's going on.' As soon as the words left my mouth, I knew I'd made a mistake. Her body stiffened, and her face took on a cool detachment.

'Yeah, sure. See you tomorrow.'

I knew I wouldn't see her tomorrow. Not if she could help it. 'Same time.'

'Yeah. Okay.'

'Would you like me to pick you up?'

'No, that's all right,' she answered blandly. 'You better go before Rusty comes back.'

There was nothing more to say but good-bye. I left the apartment feeling defeated and spent the drive back to Plano mentally playing out all the ways tomorrow might develop. None of them were good.

At home, Holly was watching for my return. She was in my garage before I'd finished putting Bobo in the backyard.

The moment I saw her face, I knew something was wrong. 'Where have you been?' She sounded almost frantic, and I could tell she'd been pacing her kitchen, waiting for me for a while.

'Holly, what's wrong?'

'I've been trying to call you for *two hours*.' Her face was red, her forehead beaded with nervous perspiration.

'My cell was dead this morning, so I turned it off after I talked to the insurance agent. They're still investigating the accident, but it looks promising. The other guys can't keep their story straight, so that's good for Christopher –'

'Sandra, Chris is in the hospital.'

'Chris is . . . what?' I tried to process the information, but I couldn't take it in. *Chris is fine. I dropped him at school this morning . . .*

'Chris is in the hospital. Rob's with him.' Holly slipped her hand under my elbow as if she thought I might collapse. 'Get your purse. I'll drive you.'

Blood, and emotion, and warmth vaporized in my body like the moisture before an atom bomb, and I stood in a dry mushroom cloud as I grabbed my purse and started out of the garage. 'What do you . . . what happened? Is he all right?' The day suddenly seemed long and impossible, like a terrible dream. *Chris can't be in the hospital . . .*

Please say he's all right. Please tell me he's all right.

Holly stopped me and looked both ways before we crossed the street.

'Holl? Is Chris all right?'

Holly chewed her lip. 'He's better now. He fainted in the workout room today. They're not sure what happened – whether it's related to the accident, or . . . something else.' The way she said *something else* caught my attention.

'What else? Holly, what do you mean? What else?'

She pretended to be busy getting in her car and cleaning out the passenger seat. 'You really need to talk to Rob. I'm not sure what they've found out.'

'Holly, *what else*? If you know something, I need you to tell me.'

'Rob probably –'

'Holly, *what*?'

Her eyes fell closed for an instant as we backed out of the driveway, then she swiveled to check the road. 'Jacey thinks he took something.'

'Something?' I echoed. 'What do you mean . . . *something*? What *something*?'

Holly's fingers kneaded the steering wheel. She pulled her chin into her chest like she had a bitter taste in her mouth. 'Jacey saw him with another boy under the bleachers in the gym. They had a prescription bottle.'

'A prescription bottle?' I felt sick. I wanted to push open the door, jump out and run away. 'How would . . . why . . . Christopher wouldn't do . . . He knows better than to take someone else's prescription. Why would he do that?'

Pausing at the stop sign, Holly turned fully in my direction and met my eyes. 'Have you *looked* at him lately? Have you really looked at him? He's not the same kid.' She clamped her lips closed, as if she were trying not to say anything more. Finally, she spit out, 'He told Jacey he's afraid you and Rob are getting a divorce. He thinks you've been out finding a new place to live or that you're having an affair.'

The words hovered around my head like a foreign language lost in translation. 'A divorce . . . what?'

Holly swallowed hard, her lips pale and pinched. 'Sandra,' she said finally, 'you're gone all day, every day. You don't want anyone to know where you are. I called the organ donors network. I know you weren't there today. You haven't been there in a week and a half. What's going on?'

Taking a deep breath as one reality collided with the other, I tried to arrange the truth into some format that would make sense. 'Holly, there's something I need to tell you.'

CHAPTER 16

Cass

When Rusty came home at the end of the day, he was hotter than a Fourth of July firecracker right after it blows up. He'd drove around looking for Kiki for a while and even went by Kiki's boyfriend's house, but nobody was there. He asked about her at Glitters, but they said she hadn't showed up for work, and the manager was ticked. She still owed him money, and if she didn't come tomorrow, she was fired.

Rusty finally had to give up looking and go home. Dallas is a big city, after all, and we didn't know beans about Kiki, or where she might go with that boyfriend, or why she'd go with him at all. 'She probably took off with him on a long haul and left us here with her kid,' I said, and Rusty didn't answer. He sat there at the table with his head in his hands. 'What kind of mom takes off without her kid?' I asked. 'And with some dude who knocks her around, anyway?'

'Hush up, Cass,' he muttered. 'I don't wanna talk about it.' Who could say why, but Rusty really had a thing for Kiki. I think he would of been less upset if I disappeared.

I made us grilled cheese, and a box of macaroni and

cheese, and potatoes with cheese, because Rusty liked cheese. I wanted to get him in a better mood. I had something to talk to him about. I'd sat at the table all afternoon and thought it through. It was clear in my mind, but I wasn't sure how to bring it up to Rusty.

I waited till Opal'd finished eating, then I ran a teeny bit of water in the bathtub, and let her play in it, because I didn't want her listening. Even though she didn't talk much, she understood a lot. I didn't want her to understand this. Some things, a little kid just doesn't need to hear. Ever.

Rusty was guzzling down the leftover macaroni, bent close to the pan with the fork moving like the big steam shovel in the coal pits he worked in for a couple weeks one time. He looked up at me when I came back to the table.

I figured I might as well spill it. 'I think we should move on. From here, I mean.'

Rusty shoveled in another mouthful of mac and cheese, like he didn't even hear me. Sometimes he did that when he didn't want to talk. Tonight, he looked like he didn't want anybody around. His face was dark with dirt, and strings of sweat had erased little trails from his forehead to his cheeks, so that you could see sunburn underneath. He'd probably been stuck on a roofing crew today. He hated roofing.

Watching him chew, then stir the macaroni, I tried again. 'I think we should go. Now. Tonight.' In my head, I had it all worked out. We'd get everything packed up and have it ready, right inside the door. Then later tonight, after the Mexican dudes finished hanging out in the parking lot, and after the lights went out in Charlie's office, Rusty could go get our truck, pull it up by the Dumpster, throw our junk in, and we'd take off. We could find a rest stop or a park to sleep in, and then in the morning do what we called a *start-over* – find a place to live, find Rusty a job, figure out the lay of the land.

He turned my way, his pale red lashes shadowing his eyes, so that they looked black, not brown. 'I gotta work tomorrow, Sal. We didn't finish the shingles today. We gotta get done before the rain moves in. Supposed to be some big storms coming the end of the week. Man, I hate crawling around on that stinking tar paper.'

As much as I loved my brother, sometimes I could see why his teachers wanted to ring his neck. Talking to him was like being on a cell phone that was way out of range. Only about every third word came through. 'I think we should head east to Ft. Worth. If Ray John's still in Ft. Worth, we'd have a better chance of finding him from there. We can, like, look in the phone books and stuff. If we get a place close to a library, I can search on the Internet some more, like I did in Lubbock. I think if we could be where there's a library, we could find him.'

Rusty stirred the macaroni, parted it like the Red Sea, and watched it fall back together. He was losing his appetite. Pretty soon, he'd get up, gather his stuff for a shower, and when he was done, he'd crash. We'd be stuck here another night, and another night might be too long. 'You tried that before, Sal. It didn't work.'

'I can try some more.' It was kind of nice that he was

calling me *Sal*. If he was mad at Kiki, at least he wasn't mad at me. 'We need a start-over. This isn't a good place. Nothing's gone right since we came here.'

Pushing the pan away, he sat back in his chair, letting his arm dangle toward the floor. 'We can't just leave, Sal. What about Kiki?'

'Heck with stupid Kiki.' I spit out her name like it was poison. 'If she wants to go back with that jerk, you can't do anything about it. He's one big dude, Rusty. You can't fight him.'

Rusty pushed air between his teeth. 'He needs to find out what happens when you take on someone who can hit back. Anybody like that needs his face knocked in.' An angry heat rose up in Rusty's cheeks and showed in the places where sweat had streaked the tar away.

'You can't fight him.'

'I can handle it, Cass.'

'Mama wouldn't –'

'Mama's not here!' He exploded out of the chair. 'Mama's not here, is she? Mama wouldn't just stand back and let some dude hit a woman and a little kid. You don't know the stuff he's done. You don't know what Kiki's told me.'

'She *went* with him again, Rusty.' I stood as tall as I could, but my brother still towered over me, so that I had to look up. I wished I had on Mama's green shoes. 'Did you ever think that maybe she's just playing you? Did you ever think maybe she's coming up with a big sad story so you'd feel sorry for her? Every day, she's got some new excuse why she can't bring home any money. And last night, when she came in from work, she was stoned, and I know she was stoned. I smelled weed, and she was bumping into everything. She's got money for weed, but she can't pay for food or a place? You ever think maybe she's using us, so she's got a bed to sleep in and somebody to watch her kid all the time? Maybe she just wanted to make that guy jealous. Maybe she likes it with him. Maybe that's where she's supposed to be. You ever think of that?' Even as I was saying it, my mind was telling me, *You're wrong, Cass Sally Blue. You know what Opal was like after Uncle Len showed up. She was so scared she didn't quit crying for two hours.*

Rusty clamped his hands to the sides of his head. 'Shut up. Just shut up, okay? I don't want to think about it right now. I've gotta work tomorrow.'

'Let's just *go*. We can use the money from this week's check to get a new place.' Somehow, I had to talk Rusty into it. This afternoon, before she walked out our door, Mrs Kaye gave me that look – the one that comes right before somebody decides they gotta get in your business and *do something* about you. As soon as she drove off, I started making plans. For things to work, Rusty and me had to get out of here before Mrs Kaye decided to call the police or social services, before sweaty Charlie showed up looking for this week's rent, before Rusty got in a fight, before Kiki and Uncle Len got unstoned and came looking for Opal.

Rusty's lips twisted into a sneer, like he thought I was a stupid little idiot. 'Right! And what're we gonna do about *her*?' He sailed a hand through the air toward the bathroom, and there was Opal, standing in the doorway with bubbles and water dripping down her skin, her thumb in her mouth, and her big sad eyes looking up. She was holding her doll under her chin, and the doll was wet, too.

'Oh, Opal.' I hurried in there, got a towel, and wrapped her up in it. The doorway was slippery, and I almost fell when I lifted her up. She put her head under my chin, like the doll was under hers, and I felt the water from her hair sink into my T-shirt as we crossed the room. 'We'll take her with us,' I said to Rusty.

'We're just gonna *take* somebody's *kid*?'

'She doesn't want her.' I hoped Opal wouldn't understand who I meant by *she* and *her*. No kid should ever have to know its mama wants something else more than she wants her own kid. My mama wasn't perfect, and she had bad taste in men sometimes, but I always knew she loved me and Rusty more than anything. When somebody loves you more than anything, they don't need to be perfect. I could feel that way about Opal. I *did* feel that way about Opal already. 'Kiki'd probably be glad. Then she could do whatever she wants with . . . whoever. She won't have anything to get in the way.'

Rusty looked sad. He watched Opal, and I could tell she was watching him. I felt her eyelashes brush upward against my neck. 'You can't just take somebody's kid,' he said again. 'It's illegal, Cass. It's really illegal.'

I felt my worry spinning into something big and desperate. 'We ran away. We took Mama's truck. That was illegal. We worked it out. We've worked it out every step of the way. Nobody's ever found us. Heck, probably nobody ever came after us in the first place. I bet Roger didn't even bother to call anybody. Kiki wouldn't either, I bet. She wouldn't call anybody.'

Rusty stuck his hands in his jeans pockets, sighed and shook his head. 'We can't . . .'

'We *can*,' I pleaded. 'Come on, Rusty. We can do it. We can take care of her. She'd be like a little sister.'

For a minute, Rusty seemed to think about it. Opal stretched out her arm, and he put his hand up and let her wrap her fingers around it. He had so much tar on his skin, him and Opal were the same color.

My heart beat hard against Opal's body, and I squeezed my arms tighter around her. If Rusty said no, I wasn't sure what I'd do. I couldn't let Kiki take Opal back. I had to keep her safe, but I couldn't leave without Rusty. Me and Opal needed Rusty to take care of us. 'Please,' I whispered, and my eyes started to fill, and I thought, *Don't cry, don't cry, don't cry. You have to seem grown-up. You have to show him you can handle this.* 'That guy'll hurt Opal. He said he'd hurt her. You didn't see him when he was here. You didn't hear what he said. We can take care of her.'

Opal let go of Rusty's hand and wrapped her arms and legs around me, like she understood every word we were saying. She hung on so hard, I felt my ribs squeeze tighter together.

'Sal,' Rusty whispered, and he laid a hand on my hair. 'We can't even take care of ourselves.' His face was long and sorry, and the Adam's apple in his neck bobbed up and down.

'Yes, we *can*,' I told him. 'I'll get a job. As soon as we move, I'll get a job.'

Rusty's fingers squeezed my hair, rubbed it like he used to rub that dog he loved so much. 'You're twelve years old, Sal. You can't get a job. You need to be in school. We can't pick up and run off with someone's kid. When Kiki comes back, I'll talk to her. She knows she's gotta ditch that guy. She said it herself.'

'Just because she *said* it doesn't mean she's gonna.' Opal started to whimper, and I rocked her back and forth. 'Don't you watch the news? Women say they're gonna leave all the time, but they don't. They just keep going back. They just keep doing it. They're not strong like Mama. Almost none of them are like Mama.'

Both me and Rusty knew that when Mama met my daddy, she was fallin'-down crazy about him. He was a horse trainer and a dirt track jockey, and he had a nice place with horses and a little pond out back. He was good to Rusty, and after they had me, he thought I was just it-on-a-stick. He got me a pink tricycle almost before I was big enough to ride it, and he got Rusty a bike and a little four-wheeler to drive, and he took Rusty fishing and stuff. He made Mama laugh, and paid for nice vacations and stuff.

The day she found out he was paying for all those things by cooking meth in a shed on the back of the place, she packed our bags and left. She said she wasn't gonna take a chance on losing her kids for anybody, even him. I was too little to remember all that, but Rusty did. Rusty begged and begged to go home, but Mama wouldn't do it. She told him the three of us had to come first. Period.

'I'll talk to Kiki when she comes back.' Rusty patted my

head, then started off to his room. 'Don't worry about it. We'll work it out.'

I didn't have any choice but to let him go. There was no way I was gonna talk him into packing up our things and moving tonight. I'd just have to keep working on him and hope Mrs Kaye didn't decide to call anybody about us. If I stopped going down to Poppy's house, maybe she'd forget. Angel and the Mexican kids could go there and get the sandwiches on their own. I could have Angel tell Mrs Kaye I took a job somewhere else – the Book Basket, maybe, or I could say Mama was sick and needed me at home. We couldn't have any visitors, because her immunities weren't good . . .

Even while I was making the plans, I felt sad about it. I'd miss Poppy's house, and helping Mrs Kaye, and hearing her stories, and having tea parties at our little table in the summer kitchen. But family has to come first, just like Mama always said. *No matter what else happens, the three of us are all that matters* . . . There were three of us again. Me, and Rusty, and Opal.

'You can't let Kiki take Opal back to that guy's house,' I said, before Rusty disappeared into the bathroom with his sweats.

He didn't answer, just nodded, then shut the door.

I sat down on the sofa with Opal, pulled the sleeping bag over us, and held her while her breath turned long and even. After a while, I fell asleep with her. When I woke up, the apartment was dark, and Rusty's door was closed. I could hear him snoring softly in his room. The other bedroom door was still open. Opal was wiggling around and poking me on the sofa, so I carried her in and put her in the bed, then went back to the sofa and laid there a while, trying to get back to sleep.

I was sad about tomorrow. It'd be weird, not getting up and going to Poppy's. It'd be boring, and it'd stink knowing that Angel and the other kids could go down there, while me and Opal stayed home. If Mrs Kaye came by our apartment, I'd have to holler through the door that Mama was too sick to have anybody come in. I'd feel bad telling her that, after she was always so nice to us. It'd be like when I had to cut loose from the Waffle Shop waitress in the oil patch town, but you gotta do what you gotta do.

In the morning, by the time I woke up, Rusty was gone. I jumped out of the sleeping bag, thinking me and Opal better hurry and head off to Poppy's house before Angel, Ronnie, and Boo came out. Then I remembered we couldn't go today, or ever.

Outside it was cloudy, and thunder rumbled far off. The morning glow around the window was gray blue, and even after I turned on the light, the apartment was dark. I squashed a roach in the corner and left it there, where normally I would have cleaned it up. It didn't seem like it mattered right now.

I tried to read my book, but I couldn't get my mind into it. I wanted to open the window blind, but I thought I better not. If Kiki and her boyfriend showed up, or if Mrs Kaye came by, I didn't want them to be able to look inside.

When Opal got out of bed, she wanted cereal first, and

then she wanted to know when we were going to Poppy's house.

'We're not going there today. We gotta stay home,' I told her.

She pushed her cereal away, crossed her arms, and made a pout lip.

'You better eat that before it gets soggy,' I said, and she twisted in her chair, lifted up her arms, and clamped them back down again. 'All right, but you're not getting any more. That's it. You either eat it or you can just be hungry till lunch.'

Opal squeaked and stuck her tongue out at me. I wanted to touch the pepper shaker and pinch that tongue, like Mama used to with Rusty. The pepper taste broke him of sticking his tongue out, that was for sure.

Instead, I shook my finger at her. 'You can sit there until you decide to eat, Opal. Don't you get out of that chair until you finish your cereal. I'm gonna go take my shower.'

I left her there pouting, which was just what Mama would of done. Opal blew a raspberry across the room at me, and I slammed the bathroom door. She whined louder. When I didn't come back out, she came over and tried to open the bathroom door, then screamed and banged on it like a mini Uncle Len.

'Stop that!' I hollered. 'You go back and eat your cereal!' I felt a big lump coming up in my throat, and all I wanted to do was get away. I didn't want to think about Opal screaming, or Uncle Len pounding on the door, or Rusty looking for Kiki on his lunch hour, or what might happen if he found her, or Poppy's house, or the summer kitchen, where our picnic table would sit empty with yesterday's hollyhock dancers slowly drying in the sun.

I turned on the shower and got in. When I closed the curtain, a beetle fell off and landed by my feet. Skittering away, it tried to crawl up the side of the tub. The shower stream caught it and swirled it toward the drain, then around and around while it flailed its feet and tried to grab on. Every time it started to get a hold, the water caught it again and dragged it under. Finally it wasn't strong enough anymore, and it just quit swimming. The water pulled it down and it disappeared.

The lump in my throat burst open, and I wanted Mama so bad that the wanting squeezed around me until the hot steamy air was too thick to breathe. I pulled it through my throat in a long, slow sob, sat down under the water and let it rain over me, so that I couldn't tell what was the shower and what was tears.

Like all the other times, the tears came from someplace I didn't understand, and then they drained away to that place again, a tide rushing in and washing away the sand, then going out again. When I got up, the water was freezing, and Opal was quiet outside the door. I shivered through washing my hair in the cold water, then got out, the air warmer than my skin. My teeth chattered, and I rubbed hard with the towel until my skin was red and raw. The towel smelled like cigarettes, like Kiki. I threw it in the tub, washed it and hung it up to dry.

When I turned off the water, I heard someone knocking

on the front door. By the time I got to the living room, Opal'd dragged a chair over and was trying to open the lock.

Fear went through me like lightning. 'No, Opal!' I whispered, then hurried across the room and pulled her off the chair. We listened to the knocking together. It was soft, and coming from down low, and I figured it was just Boo.

'We're sick,' I hollered. 'We got the crud in here, and if you don't want to catch it, you better go away.'

CHAPTER 17

Sandra Kaye

Christopher spent the first five days of his summer vacation in the hospital, after showing irregular heart rhythms and difficulty breathing the day he collapsed at school. Under normal circumstances, he would have been released sooner, but Rob insisted he remain until we knew exactly what was in his system and how it got there. His insistence came with the silent insinuation that I wasn't adequately supervising Chris at home – that since the car incident, I should have been picking him up every day after school and keeping him prisoner. The insurance agent felt so bad when he heard Chris was in the hospital, he stepped up efforts to clear Chris's name, and came by the hospital personally to tell us the investigator was making progress in debunking the false claims, and he felt certain that everything would be cleared up soon.

Even so, there was still the question between Rob and me of where to lay the blame for Christopher's current problems. Rob insisted that he needed to be on a tighter leash. 'He has to know he can't just do whatever he wants,' Rob asserted in a whisper as we stood in the corridor near Chris's hospital room, waiting for him to get dressed to go home. We were both grasping at straws, trying to figure out why Chris would have done something so foolish as to take a combination of medications – Ritalin he got from a friend so he could stay awake and study all night for finals, along with Xanax and OxyContin from our medicine cabinet to take the edge off his emotions. He'd heard about potential combinations from kids at school, who, according to Chris, thought nothing of sharing meds.

During Chris's time in the hospital, Rob and I had received a crash course in what kids casually referred to as *pharming*. According to Chris's doctors, the problem of teenagers gleaning prescription medications and then using or trading them was rampant, especially in the suburbs, where medicine cabinets were rife with pills. Because the medications were prescriptions and available at home, kids thought of it as okay.

After several days of discussing Chris's problems in clinical terms, we now had to consider what lay underneath and how we were going to prevent it from happening again. Rob's solution was to crack down, take greater control. 'He has to be made aware that his actions come with consequences. This could have been deadly, Sandra. We're lucky all he did was pass out at school.' Rob's face went white, as if the realization of what might have happened had struck him fully.

'Like you made Jake aware?' I spat, and Rob looked wounded. 'You heaped the responsibility for Poppy's accident on Jake until he couldn't take it anymore, and now where is he?' All we'd done the past four days was argue, but so far we were filling in a paint-by-number to which even Chris didn't seem to have the color key. We were groping for explanations in the dark – heavy class load, depression over Poppy's death and Jake's disappearance, guilt about the car accident, Christopher's perception that Rob and I were falling apart . . .

'We're not talking about Jake.' Rob's eyes were bloodshot, sagging into deep circles at the bottom. Underneath the anger, he looked apprehensive and exhausted. 'It's Christopher we're talking about here. He needs a calm, stable environment. He shouldn't be worrying about whether the two of us can hold it together.'

'No, he shouldn't.' But the gulf in our family was growing every day. Of course Christopher saw it. He wasn't blind.

Rob looked down the hall, his lashes narrow over soft brown eyes – Christopher's eyes. Those eyes had caught my attention the day Rob and I met, and they were the first thing I noticed about Christopher when a neonatal nurse placed him in my arms. He had his father's eyes. Rob's beautiful golden brown eyes. The day Christopher was finally released from preemie care, there was so much joy, both Rob and I cried when we carried him into the house. All the emotion had scared Jake. He didn't know what to make of it.

How had we ended up here? Like this? I looked into Rob's eyes now, and there was nothing in them but weariness, as if he were dealing with a medical case so complex he couldn't figure out how to solve it. 'Rob, we need . . . something . . . counseling or something. This isn't us. This isn't the way we're supposed to be.'

As usual, the suggestion that we couldn't handle our family problems on our own fell on deaf ears. Physician, heal thyself. 'Counseling won't keep Christopher home, instead of hanging out at school or running off to friends' houses,' Rob said flatly. '*We* have to do that. He needs you there. He shouldn't be worrying about . . . where you are.' The words, the look of accusation, caught me like a left hook. After Chris had woken in the hospital, I'd explained to both him and Rob that my absences lately had only been because I was having some repairs and updates done at Poppy's house, and that Holly was going to take care of things there for a few days until I could get back to it. It wasn't the whole truth, but now hardly seemed the time to bring up Cass, Opal, and the evergrowing sandwich project.

'I told you I've been doing some work at Poppy's. There's nothing for Chris to worry about.'

Rob studied me, searching my face as a nurse passed. Was he wondering if there was something more going on? 'Chris needs you to be . . .' Pausing to retract whatever word was in his mind, he replaced it with another. 'Present.'

An indignant flush rose in my cheeks. *What about you? Where are you? You're the doctor, the one who takes care of everybody. Where were you when we needed you to take care of us?* 'Maybe what he needs is for the two of us to wake up and see what's going on. Maybe he's waiting for us to notice that he's given up everything he used to love. Maybe he's medicating himself because he's trying to pass a bunch of classes he hates so he can make you happy by becoming Jake. Maybe he thinks if he fills the gap, things will be like they used to be.' It was hard to believe *used to be* was only a few months ago. A few months ago, Rob came home at night from work, Chris played music, Jake and Poppy drove over for family dinners. Rob and I shared glasses of wine and talked about our next vacation, or the boys' activities, or some triumphant lifesaving moment Rob had experienced in the hospital. We didn't get as much alone time as we should have, and busy schedules often stood in the way of romance, but there was always the sense that we were partners, a team in raising our children.

Now I looked at Rob and I realized I had no idea what he was really thinking or feeling.

'Because Christopher is finally growing up and taking an interest in college prep, he's trying to be Jake?' Lifting his hands in the air, Rob snorted, delivering a sardonic smirk.

Normally I would have stepped back, tried to find a painless balance between what Rob wanted to hear and what I wanted to say. Something that wouldn't cause conflict. But this time Christopher's well-being hung in the balance. 'He's given up playing sports – it's baseball season, for heaven's sake, and he's not out there with the team. Doesn't that seem strange to you? Does that *seem* like Christopher?'

'He needs the space in his schedule for –'

'For what? So he can take online courses and rack up early college credits like Jake did?' My voice echoed down the corridor in a hiss, and I took a breath, reminded myself of where we were. Christopher was just down the hall, more fragile than ever, now that he'd failed to live up to expectations once again.

Rob took a few steps away. 'If he's going to go premed, he'll need –'

'When have you ever known Christopher to show an interest in premed . . . before, I mean? Before Jake left?'

Rob slid a hand into the pocket of his lab coat and fiddled with a pen. *Click, click, click, click.* 'His priorities are changing. That's to be expected.'

'Expected? Why is that to be expected? According to whom? According to some article you read in a medical journal? According to some presentation you listened to at a conference? He's our *son*, Rob. He's a *person*, not a case study. Have you noticed that he never plays his sax anymore? It's been sitting in the band hall broken for months, and he doesn't even care. His guitar has an inch of dust on it. When would that ever have happened in the past?'

Rob's lips pursed. 'I don't see what one thing has to do with the other. It's perfectly natural that as we mature we have to . . . give up things . . . surrender some impractical fantasies.'

'Who says Chris's music is an impractical fantasy? Why is it impractical? Why is his idea of playing baseball in college impractical? He's wanted that since he was a toddler standing on the sidelines of Jake's Little League games.'

Rob answered with another sardonic puff of laughter. 'I wanted to be an astronaut, but there came a point when it was clear that wasn't likely to happen. Giving up the fantasy is part of becoming an adult. Christopher's seventeen. At some point he has to understand that sports and music aren't a future.'

'Why?' I looked at Rob, so pragmatic, so steady in his emotion, so certain of black and white. All the things that once attracted me to him – the fact that he could be counted on, the fact that he was a decision maker, the fact that he took charge of everything and made me feel safe – frustrated me now. In his mind, there was only one way things should be. 'Why? Why does he have to understand that the only future is the one *we* pick for him? Because we say so? Because *you* say so? Because now that Jake's gone, the line of Dr Dardens will end if Christopher doesn't come through? What if his future is supposed to be something totally different? What if Jake's was? What if we pushed so hard toward our vision, that's why he finally left – because he couldn't breathe anymore?'

'He left because of Poppy. I take responsibility for that. I shouldn't have been so hard on him about it, but –'

Rob's pager beeped, and the conversation ended abruptly. The emotion on his face, whatever he'd been about to say, was quickly cloaked behind the doctor's mask. 'I'll see you at home. I'll be back for a few hours this evening to pack before my flight.'

I couldn't answer at first. It hadn't even occurred to me that Rob would still go to his annual medical conference in Canada. 'Are you *serious*?' I choked out, feeling wounded, abandoned, pushed aside. 'You're still leaving for the conference, with everything that's going on?'

The pager beeped again, and Rob sighed wearily. 'I don't have any choice. I'm presenting, remember?'

I don't care! I wanted to scream. *I don't care if you're going to*

275

a meeting with the president of the American Medical Association. We need you here. But there wasn't any point in saying it. Rob was already disengaging from personal issues, cloaking everything behind his professional facade. He checked the pager impassively.

Maybe I don't care. Maybe I don't care if he goes or not. The idea scratched the surface of my mind, sharp and painful as he turned and started down the hall. No question about whether or not he should take the page, or fly to Canada the day our son was released from the hospital. There never was.

I went in and helped Chris gather his belongings.

'You guys were fighting again,' he muttered, his face turned away as he pushed a pair of sweats into his duffel bag.

I rubbed his shoulder blades. 'No, we were just talking.'

He put the strap over his shoulder and we started toward the door. 'I'm okay. The pills were just a dumb idea. Lots of people do it. I thought it would . . . help.'

Smoothing my fingers over his hair, I followed him into the corridor, steering him with my hand as if he were a child. 'We need to talk about some things after we get home.' While Chris was gone, I'd cleaned out the pain pills left over from Rob's back problems, along with every prescription bottle in the house. Still, I wasn't naïve enough to believe things were fine just because Christopher said they were, or that he couldn't find more pills if he wanted them. 'We need to set up some counseling for you, to help get to the bottom of what's going on.'

'It was just the finals – all the pressure and stuff. I don't need a counselor.' Chris's head hung between his shoulders, as if he were trying to disappear so that no one would see him leaving the hospital. 'Does everyone know why I passed out at school?'

'The kids think you had the flu, but we did tell the guidance counselor about the boy giving you his Ritalin. The school has to deal with that issue.' I felt Chris's shoulder blades rise and fall beneath my fingers. 'We need to talk about why it happened. And I do want you to get started with a counselor down at Family Central. Some things have to change so nothing like this takes place again.'

'It won't happen again.'

'It's not as easy as just saying that. You need to tell us what's going on, Chris. What you're feeling. When you keep it bottled up inside, that's when problems start.' *You're a fine one to be giving that advice, Sandra. You've been hiding all your life, afraid that if you said what you meant, the world would come to an end.*

'I'm really tired.'

Chris watched the floor. His shoes squeaked on the linoleum, and long sandy curls fell over his eyes as we walked down the hallway.

I waited until we reached the car before speaking again. Chris didn't ask to drive, but climbed into the passenger side, laid the seat back, and closed his eyes, a pointed indication that he was too exhausted for further conversation.

'Chris, I need to ask you something,' I said finally, trying to sort out the next words so they would sound exactly right.

Sunlight exploded through the windows as we pulled out of the parking garage, and Chris threw an arm over his face, hiding in the crook of an elbow. 'Can we talk later? I'm sorry about all this, okay, Mom? I really am. I screwed up. I understand. I won't do it again. You and Dad can drug test me every day it you want. You won't find anything again. Ever. It was stupid. I get it. I just had a lot going on with finals, and it . . . got to be too much.'

'Are you all right now?' I wanted him to say *yes*, to hand me the simple answer, but at the same time, I wanted him to finally tell the truth, to let out all the pain he'd been keeping inside. So far I hadn't found the key that would unlock him. I wasn't having any better luck with him than I'd had coaxing Cass into the open. Hopefully, with Holly going to prepare the sandwiches in my place, some progress could be made where there had been a stalemate. Holly could talk the bark off a tree, and she was especially good with teenagers. 'Chris, I don't want you to feel like you have to keep it to yourself if you're struggling.'

Chris nodded, his face impassive, but the long, sinewy muscles in his arm tightened, as if he were clenching a fist on the other side of his body. 'I'm fine, Mom. I told you.'

'You know your grandmother's history.' From the time the boys had grown old enough to understand it, I'd been honest with them about my mother's substance abuse and the legacy of alcoholism and addiction in our family. The boys would have figured it out eventually, anyway. Grandma Palmer was never the same person twice. 'When addiction runs in your family, you can't take chances. You can't try it once to see what it's like. One time can be the beginning of something you can't stop.'

'I know.' The answer was labored and weary. Glancing

from under his arm, he tried to see where we were – how much longer he'd have to remain trapped in the car with me. 'You and Dad can drug test me anytime you want,' he repeated. Rob had already made known that, along with a long list of new rules and regulations, he intended to include regular drug testing in Christopher's regimen.

'I'm not talking about drug testing, Chris. I want to get to the bottom of why you felt like you needed to do it in the first place. I think spending some time with a counselor at Family Central might help you sort things out.' In between caring for Poppy's house and all her normal activities, Holly had taken time to bring me a list of services from Family Central, the counseling arm of our church, where she'd attended a support group after losing her mother.

Chris groaned. 'Mom, I told you. It was just the finals and stuff. If I go to Family Central, everybody'll think we're, like, messed up or something.'

Oddly enough, he sounded much like his father had when I'd suggested we try counseling. 'Chris, the truth is nothing to be embarrassed about.'

'I don't see you and Dad going to Family Central.' His voice trembled. 'Maybe you guys oughta go.'

I drew in a sharp breath, suddenly feeling vulnerable. 'Did you tell Jacey Riley you thought your dad and I were getting a divorce?'

He grimaced, his nod almost imperceptible.

'Chris, why would you think that?'

His silence lingered so long that I wondered if he would answer at all. It was an embarrassing subject, difficult to talk about. 'I just . . . you're gone all the time, and it's like it's some big secret. I asked if I could come to Poppy's with you, and you blew me off. I just figured . . . I thought . . . Jacey's got a big mouth. I only asked her if she knew anything, like, from her mom.'

'You should have asked *me* before you asked Jacey.' I hit the blinker, waiting to turn left, toward home.

Chris raised his elbow, his eyes wide, mortified. 'Mahom! I don't want to talk about this.'

'Me either.' Glancing in the rearview, I found an empty spot in traffic, hit the gas, and pulled back onto the road, tires squealing. My mind spun ahead, solidifying an impulse into a plan of action.

Chris popped upright and looked around. 'What are you doing?'

'We have somewhere to go.' I glanced at the dash clock. Over an hour until lunch. If we left now, we'd arrive at just about the right time. According to Holly, in the six days since school in Blue Sky Hill had ended for summer, word about the free sandwiches had spread through the neighborhood. The sandwich customers usually started coming around eleven thirty.

Parting the hair on his forehead, Chris rubbed the lines that had begun to form there. 'Can you drop me at the house? I just want to crash.' Glancing in the side-view mirror, he swiveled, looking longingly toward home.

'Well, we're not crashing.' *We're not. No matter what it takes, we're not crashing. This family is done crashing.* 'There's something I want to show you.'

Pinching his forehead, he stretched the skin toward the center until his eyes were buggy on top. 'What?'

'It's a mystery.'

The answer garnered a double take from Chris, and for an instant I saw the bright, curious eyes of the little boy who loved the after-school drives that began with *It's a mystery*. Sometimes, in reality, we were only going to the grocery store or the cleaners, but the fact that our destination was *a mystery* made it more fun. I'd take alternate routes while the boys asked for clues and tried to guess where we were headed. *It's a mystery* would get them in the car without even so much as a minor argument about whose turn it was to ride in the front seat. They both knew that all mystery trips eventually ended at the ice cream parlor.

Chris looked suspicious now. No doubt he knew we weren't headed for ice cream. 'Where are we going?'

'I can't say.'

'You mean you don't know?' Perhaps he thought my plan was to keep driving until we'd talked things through. He sagged in his seat, tired out by the idea.

'I have someplace in mind.' I hoped I was doing the right thing. *Please, please, let this be the right thing.*

As we pulled onto the highway, Chris looked mildly panicked. He wasn't up for a major car trip with Mom. 'Dad said he'd be home in a few hours. He was going to try to get out of the hospital early, to come home and pack.'

'I know.' The odds that Rob would actually show up any earlier than he had to were slim. As usual, someone else would need his time, require it in a matter of living and dying, which would put all other issues on hold. 'We have time.'

Stretching to look out the window again, Chris clicked his teeth together contemplatively – a habit he'd had since childhood. 'Are we going to Poppy's?'

'It's a mystery.'

Settling into his seat, he gazed out the window, lost in whatever private place he traveled to so often now, the one we couldn't reach. Jake would have known how to find that place. Jake always knew. But there must have been a hidden place inside Jake, too – one none of us suspected. Somewhere inside, in the part that remembered the forgotten language of his childhood, there was the little boy who was left in the marketplace. A boy who so narrowly escaped disaster, who was almost sold into a life none of us wanted to imagine. Even years later, thinking of that life, thinking of Jake there made me sick. I never wanted him to know what he'd come from, but perhaps I should have told him, after all. Perhaps we had protected him so completely, cleaned his world so carefully that he felt the need to go off on his own to discover all the dirty truths beneath the shiny surface.

In trying to give Jake and Chris a childhood different from my own, perhaps I hadn't let them carry enough weight to strengthen them. I didn't want them to be what I had been, what I saw when I looked at Cass and Opal – tiny adults, for whom the Edens of childhood had been spoiled by bites of bitter fruit.

'Chris, do you remember when you used to come down with croup?' I asked.

Beneath lowered brows, he thought about it. 'A little. Yeah, I remember a little, I guess.'

I looked at the road, thinking into the past. 'It always made me so angry when the pediatrician wouldn't give you medication for it – an inhaler, antibiotics, cough medicine, something. I thought he was so ridiculous and old-fashioned. I kept taking you in and asking for something that would fix it, and every time Dr White would smile and tell me medicating it would only make it worse. You just had to go through it and grow out of it, and when you were done, you'd have good, strong lungs.'

'I don't remember that.'

'Those were some long nights.' My mind flashed back to lying on a pallet beside Chris's toddler bed, listening for every breath, startling from scraps of light sleep to hold my fingers near his face and feel him breathing. 'I used to open all the windows and we'd sleep in the cold, to reduce the inflammation. Sometimes, if it was bad enough, I'd bundle you up and we'd sit outside on the porch steps.' In the crisp air, I could see every breath, watch it rising as his tiny fingers lifted skyward, pointing out the moon and stars. 'The cold and the dampness always helped.'

Chris's face opened. 'I remember,' he said with a sudden fascination. 'We used to find the Big Dipper and the North Star.'

'We did.' The one thing I'd learned from my stepfather in all our years of living together was how to spot the constellations. On clear nights, he'd be out on the third-story deck with his telescope, stargazing. He'd set me on a deck chair and let me look, his hands steadying me in an awkward, embarrassed fashion. It was the only time we were ever close together.

I never realized, when I was pointing out the constellations to Christopher, that I'd learned their names from my stepfather. I'd never considered that he'd contributed anything lasting to my life. In general, I only resented him for not protecting me from my mother, for not dealing with her addictions. He was an adult, after all. He had no right to be so impotent.

A memory tickled my thoughts like a feather. 'One night when I couldn't get the coughing stopped, we went out there, and Jake woke up and came, too.' I felt Jake close now, his body warm and soft in his Batman pajamas as he snuggled under the quilt next to me. 'He pointed out that it was a half-moon, and you looked up at it and started to cry.'

'I did?' Chris's face tipped curiously.

'You looked up and said, "The moon broke! The moon broke!" You wanted me to fix it.'

Chris scoffed at his former self. 'What a dweeb. Jake probably laughed at me.'

'No, he didn't. For days, he tried to explain the solar system to you. He got out books and tennis balls, and he played teacher. When he was done, he would ask if you understood now, and you'd say you did. Then as soon as the moon came up, you'd be at the window, having a fit.'

Chris slanted a suspicious glance at me. 'Was I really that dumb?'

'You weren't very old.' *Not much older than Opal. Did anyone ever take Opal out to look at the moon?* 'You forgot about it, eventually.'

'Jake probably got through to me about the solar system, after a while.'

'Actually, I waited until the moon was full again, and I took you outside and showed you. You thought I'd fixed it.'

Christopher smiled, his grin straight, white, impish, his eyes sparkling. 'I guess that's a little like hanging the moon, isn't it?'

It was meant to be a joke, or a compliment, but the words left me hollow. I considered the power I'd had in their lives without ever fully realizing it. 'I think I fixed the moon more often than I should have.' A palpable uncertainty hovered at the end of the words. It's always hard to know whether to be honest with your children about your own imperfections. It can't be easy to find out that the person steering your ship doesn't know where all the rocks are.

Chris seemed to collect his thoughts. 'What Jake did wasn't your fault,' he said quietly, then looked at me. 'He did it because of Dad. They're both jerks.'

A swirl of conflicting emotions twisted around me like a tangle of multicolored thread – blue, black, gray, bright colors. It was hard to know which to reach for. 'Try to go a little easier on your dad and your brother, Chris.'

'Jake isn't my brother. If he *were* my brother, he'd be here. He wouldn't have taken off.' His cheek tightened, a muscle twitching at the side of his mouth. He swallowed hard and looked away, his fingers gripping the armrest. I laid my hand over his, bleeding from the same wound, wishing I could heal it with Mycitracin and a Band-Aid, the way I'd tended skinned knees and scuffed elbows when he was little. How could I offer wisdom when I was so lost myself?

Tightening my fingers, I held on. 'Honey, the farther you go in life, the more you realize that most people aren't trying to hurt anybody. They're just trying to . . . get by. People don't always make the right decisions – even the people we love. I know Jake loves us. He's just trying to . . . find his way right now.' *Please, please, let that be true. Please, God, bring my son home.*

Chris shrugged, as if he knew the words were more of a hope than a certainty.

We drove on in silence until finally he recognized the exit. 'We're going to Poppy's.' His voice held greater anticipation than he usually allowed himself these days. Coming here was more important to him than I'd guessed.

'You solved the mystery,' I said.

'Do I get an extra scoop of ice cream?' Chris grinned, knowing that the first one to discern the mystery destination always got an extra scoop.

CHAPTER 18

Cass

Opal and me laid low for days. Every time the door rattled, I was sure Kiki and Uncle Len were back to take Opal, or it was the police or CPS coming to get all of us because Mrs Kaye had turned us in. But every time, it was just the wind, or the kids next door. I kept telling them we had the flu and they better go away. I was gonna tell Mrs Kaye that, too, but she never showed up. All I could figure was once she saw the mess in our apartment that day, she didn't want to get mixed up in our problems. That hurt my feelings in a weird way, but it was for the best.

After five days, I'd read *Where the Red Fern Grows* so many times I felt like it was my dog that'd died. Opal was even starting to know the story, too, because I'd read it to her over and over. I changed the end part for her, though. It was kinda funny, because I'd be looking at the words where Old Dan and Little Ann die, and I'd be saying something like, *And Dan slept for two days, and then Ann came over and licked him on the nose, and he woke up. He felt a lot better after that. He got stronger and stronger every day, which was good, because it was time for a big raccoon hunt again . . .*

Opal didn't know what a 'gak-coon' was, so I drew her one on a piece of paper. She liked it a lot, which was fine, because in my version of *Red Fern*, they didn't kill the raccoons, either. Stories are a little like mind places. You can do whatever you want with them. I want my stories to have happy endings, where nobody hurts anybody. There's enough hard stuff in the real world. You see it whether you want to or not.

I was giving Opal a bath, and when I washed her head I felt something under the edge of her hair. I'd never noticed it before, but I had her tip her head forward, and under her hair I found three little white scars. There wasn't much way a kid could get those on her own. Someone had to put them there. I saw a show like that at the blind lady's house in Fargo – *Grey's Anatomy*, I think. The doctor figured out some kid was abused because he had little round marks. Cigarette burns. Kiki smoked. Uncle Len probably did, too.

Opal didn't know how long the marks had been there. She didn't even know what I was talking about, but then she couldn't see the marks.

That night, I made Opal show Rusty. She didn't mind, because she figured it was something cool, and she liked Rusty's attention. In the evenings when he came home, she'd run at him like a linebacker, and he'd turn her upside down and hang her by her feet while she squealed.

When I showed him the scars, I told him again that we needed to pack our stuff and do a *start-over* someplace else.

I didn't care if we went to Ft. Worth, even. I could look for Ray John on the Internet from anyplace. I just didn't wanna be here, wondering where Kiki was, or if she'd show up again. The day before I found Opal's scars, Rusty'd drove around looking for Kiki, and he went by Glitters, but it was like she'd disappeared off the face of the earth.

It went through my mind that maybe the guy had killed her and dumped her in a ditch, but I didn't like to think about it. Even though I didn't want Kiki here, I didn't want her to be dead, either. Opal asked about her some, and I said she had to go to the doctor, but she'd be all right. I figured, once we got a start-over, Opal would ask less and less, until finally she didn't ask at all. But Rusty wouldn't pack up and go, even after he saw the scars.

'I just got a bunch of overtime work, Sal. Tomorrow night, I'm gonna go with Boomer to pick up a flatbed load of shingles down toward Houston. I get paid time and a half every hour it takes to drive there, get the load, and drive back,' he said. 'We need the money. We couldn't make a new start right now if we wanted to.'

Rusty was probably right, but I didn't like hearing it. Since we couldn't leave, I had to come up with a plan B. I thought about it that night while I was trying to fall asleep. I decided if Kiki or Uncle Len came, I was gonna hide Opal in the cabinet and tell Kiki we'd dropped her at CPS. As soon as Rusty headed off to work, Opal and me practiced it. We put Wal-Mart bags in between all the pans so they wouldn't make a sound. I decided I better tell Angel, and Ronnie, and Boo what to say, too, so I finally let them in when they came knocking that morning. Like I figured, Angel'd been going down to Poppy's every day to get sandwiches.

'They got a new lady down there,' she told me. 'She makin' them sam'iches now, and she handin' them out right off the po'ch. I help her some. Her name Holly. You wanna go see?'

'I better not.' The idea of Angel being down there when I couldn't go really bit, but I still couldn't take the chance of Mrs Kaye getting in our business anymore. 'Opal's just gettin' over that flu. She shouldn't be outside. If anybody asks about us, just tell them we're sick, but if Opal's mama or her boyfriend shows up, tell them Opal's not here anymore, we dropped her at CPS.'

''Kay.' Angel looked at the sofa, where Opal was showing Boo the Candy Land game. 'Hey, you keep Boo fo' me and I'll bring you some a' them sam'iches today.'

I watched Boo and Opal and thought about it. I didn't want to be stuck here babysitting while Angel went down the road, but the truth was we needed the sandwiches. Opal and me had used up too much food, being stuck at home all the time. 'All right. He can stay.'

Angel looked real happy about that. 'Ronnie, too? He in the way down there.'

Ronnie was standing by the door, ready to go with Angel. He gave her a dirty look.

'I guess,' I said.

Angel pushed him out of the way and couldn't get the door open quick enough. I stopped her before she went down the steps. 'Hey, did Mrs Kaye . . . I mean . . . did she, like, ask about us or anything?' Even though I knew it was better if Mrs Kaye forgot about us, I kinda wanted a *yes*.

I got ready to have my feelings hurt when Angel shrugged. 'She ain't been there. Holly said her boy in the hospital.'

'Christopher?'

'Guess so. The new lady nice. She bringin' Little Debbies, and she cleanin' up some big pans from the basement. She talkin' about givin' hot dog *or* sam'ich. School bein' out, they got lotsa people want a free lunch. They gonna put some tables in the yard, so people could sit, if they wanna.'

'Mrs Kaye said that?'

'No, I told'ja, that new lady, Holly. She say so. I gotta go now. I'll come back after while. Tell Boo I say be good.' She didn't wait for an answer, just lit out toward the storm ditch.

I wanted to run and catch her to ask some more questions, but I figured I better not. I couldn't get over that feeling that Kiki and Uncle Len might be right around the corner. I went back inside, locked the door again, and sat there trying not to think about Angel being at Poppy's house. I hoped she wouldn't find the secret room in the summer kitchen. It was selfish of me to feel that way, but I couldn't help it. It was pretty hard, staying in the apartment with three rugrats, while Angel went down the road and had all the fun. I didn't know how I was gonna keep them quiet if Len and Kiki showed up.

By eleven, I was about to go nuts and Angel still wasn't back. The kids were whining and I couldn't just use all the food to give everybody lunch. I figured I was gonna have to do something, or go crazy. I decided it'd be okay to go to the bookstore, but there wasn't any way to know if it was open, so I made up a plan that we'd head down the storm ditch and come up behind the old white church. We could hang out in back of the building where no one would see us while we checked if the Book Basket looked open.

I got shoes on Opal, Ronnie, and Boo, and put our books in a Wal-Mart sack, and Opal grabbed her doll. I sent Ronnie outside first, like a spy, to see if anyone was in the parking lot. He came back and said there wasn't anybody, and so we headed out the door, all running and holding hands in a chain till we got to the ditch.

I made the kids run all the way down the ditch until we were out of sight of the road. They didn't mind it. I think Opal was as glad to be outside as I was. When we got to the little white church, we hid behind the tree in the prayer garden while I tried to figure out if MJ was in her store. The next thing I knew, Teddy was there with a bucket of dirt in his hands. We scared each other half to death, he threw the bucket in the air, and dirt went everywhere.

'Hey, Cass-e,' Teddy said, after he stopped stumbling backward. 'I doin' the fo'wers. Got some dirt with Mir'cal Grow.'

'Cool,' I said, and tried to swallow my heart back down. It was up in my throat like a bat trying to beat its way out of a cave.

'Where you gone?' he asked, and looked toward Poppy's house.

'We're goin' to the Book Basket,' I said, and held up the book sack. 'To get some books.'

Teddy frowned. 'Where you been gone ye-terday?'

I clued in to what he was asking. 'Oh, hey, Opal's been sick.'

'Ohhhh.' He got a worried face, then looked at Opal. 'She all better now. You gone Mit' Kaye house?' He pointed toward Red Bird Lane. 'I gone, in a min-it. Mama gone come in the car. We gone help at Mit' Kaye house, givin' the Lil' Debbie, and the sam'ich, and the juice.'

Everything in me wanted to go. Teddy was a big guy – even bigger than Uncle Len. If we were with him, we might be safe . . . As soon as I thought it, I knew it was a bad idea. 'We can't. We gotta get some books. See ya, Teddy.' I grabbed the kids, and we took off through the churchyard, hit a gap in traffic, and ran across to the Book Basket.

When we got there, I turned loose of everyone's hands so I could try the door, but it was locked, so I rang the bell. Sometimes MJ would come out from the warehouse when I did that. She had a big room back there, and she rented it to a long-haired dude who made clay pots and painted pictures. He didn't like to be bothered, she said, and all I knew about him was that I'd seen him come and go a time or two.

While I waited by the door, Opal stood under the tree with all the glass beads and bottles hanging in it. Looking up at the bottles, she threw her arms in the air, tossed her head back, and twirled round and round with her doll in the colored light, singing a little song. It was something about Old Dan and Little Ann, the red fern, and gak-coons. The high, light sound of her voice mixed with the bottles clinking and the beads jingling, leaves rustling and the wind singing low in the mouths of the bottles. The street noises seemed far away, and for a minute, I just watched her.

Ronnie and Boo pointed like she was crazy, but I let her go right ahead and dance. She looked like a little fairy princess, with the light sprinkling down on her.

Boo took off all of a sudden and ran in circles, stopping to put his feet in the patches of light and look at the colors on his skin. Finally he stood in the place where there were the most colors, and he reminded me of Joseph, with his coat in the Bible. I wished, when we left Bismarck, I'd took Mama's Bible. I could read them that story about the coat. They probably never heard it before, ever.

I knocked hard on the door and rang the bell again, and finally MJ showed up. When we went inside, I asked her if I could trade *Red Fern* for a Bible.

'Sure,' she said. 'Help yourself. The Bibles are free, though, so you can pick out another book to trade for *Red Fern*.'

I stood looking at the stack of Bibles, thinking if someone swore on that monster, they'd sure enough better be telling the truth. 'They're free?' I asked. 'Any of 'em?' There were some nice ones with leather covers, crosses and stuff, and except for being dusty, they looked in good shape.

'Churches give them to me when they're left in the lost and found too long, and I pick some up at estate sales. I end up with quite a few.' MJ looked up from the notebook she was busy with.

'Huh.' I tried to imagine having something nice like that, and just leaving, and not going back for it. 'Can Opal have one, too? There's a kids' one here.'

'Sure. Help yourself,' MJ said, which I did. Then me and Opal picked out our book trades and went to the counter with Ronnie and Boo.

I looked at the pad of paper MJ had on her desk. There were pages and pages of writing that ended where she'd laid down her pen. 'What's that?' I asked, and pointed to it.

'Another story.' She looked at the pad out the corner of her eye while she finished making my ticket.

'What kind of story?' I tipped sideways and tried to see it, but I couldn't read from there.

MJ handed me my ticket. Her eyes were warm, like chocolate. She didn't wear lots of makeup, like Kiki, but she was beautiful anyway. Today, she had her hair wrapped up in a turban again. She looked like the ruler of some country way off – a storybook queen with magic in her.

'Where did this one come from?'

'A friend shared it with me,' MJ answered. 'I'll share it with you, if you like. The best stories are the ones we share.' Her eyes settled on me very directly, like she might be seeing my story without me wanting her to.

Ronnie, Opal, and Boo wandered to the door. Ronnie pushed it open just a little.

'Don't mash your fingers,' I told him.

'I ain't,' he said through his buckteeth, then he pushed the door open farther. 'I wanna see da bottles.'

'Stay right by the door,' I said, but Ronnie had his mind on Opal's book. He took it from her, and they went out the door, and stopped on the step to look it over. The door hung open a minute, and I watched to make sure they weren't fighting.

'My mama says my grandpa was a good storyteller,' I told MJ while she put her ticket book aside. 'She said he kept everybody in stitches at weddings and funerals.'

MJ chuckled. 'Then I do suppose you might have a story in you.'

Some things you can't tell other people, I thought, but I didn't say it. *Sometimes you gotta keep your business to yourself.*

'Mama always said I was just like my grandpa.'Course, she also said, "Cass Sally Blue, you'd be in a lot less trouble if you'd quit giving me a story and just spit out the truth." '

MJ laughed, which made me feel good. I liked MJ. Maybe, at least until I got Rusty talked into going for a start-over, I could hang out at the bookstore some during the days and help MJ organize books. It wasn't a tea party in the summer kitchen, but at least it'd be something to do.

I leaned back and looked through the door again. The kids had got quiet and let the door close, but Ronnie was still right there with the book. He was sharing it, at least. He'd squatted down so the others could look, too. I could just see the bushy top of Boo's head by Ronnie's elbow.

'How is your mother, by the way?' MJ looked at me like Rusty's dog used to look at the baby mud birds that got careless and toppled out of the nest on the porch. Didn't take Missy long to figure out those birds couldn't fly yet.

I knew I'd messed up again and mentioned Mama like she wasn't here anymore. Sometimes when you got to talking to folks, it was hard to remember everything. 'She's a little better. They changed her treatments some.'

'The dialysis?'

Geez, MJ remembered more than I thought. 'Yeah, I guess so.'

I switched the subject and leaned across to look at her notebook. 'So what's this story about?'

'A fish. I heard it from a man named Michael, who preaches to the street people under the bridge. He came here for a book, and I traded it for a story. It's a good trade, wouldn't you say?'

I had to think about that a minute. 'It sounds like you got took. He can make up another story anytime, but you've gotta go out and *buy* more books.'

MJ winked at me. 'But the story I get to keep, and no matter how many times I share it, I still have it.'

'I guess that's true enough.'

'I'll share it with you, very quickly.'

'Cool,' I said, and waited to see what was in the notebook that was worth the trade for a book.

MJ didn't bother to look at her writing. I guess she knew the story already. 'Once upon a time, there was a grandfather catfish who lived in a big beautiful stream. He was the largest of all the fish, and so he was the ruler of the stream. Everything was under his control, and he was very proud of this.'

MJ moved her hands slow, like a big daddy catfish swimming along, looking over his territory. 'One very hot summer, there was no rain, and the streams began to dry up until there were only pools with long passages of rock between them. As time passed, the pools began to grow smaller, and smaller, and smaller, until the fish were trapped together in very tiny places.'

MJ spread her hands along the counter, her long fingers moving as if she were drawing the stream. 'The grandfather catfish knew what to do. Being a wise fish and an important fish, he began to pray for rain. He was certain this would solve his problem. Always in the past, when the stream began to dry, he prayed for rain, and rain came. Because he was very important, he knew God would listen to him. "Father God," he said. "Please send rain to carry me out of this trap." Then he sat in his pool and waited, but no rain came. The pool grew terribly small, so small that the fish could see above the surface of the water.'

MJ stopped and looked up, like she was the fish sitting in its pool. 'One day, he saw a fisherman above the water, who was just a boy. The pool was so shallow that the fisher boy was able to scoop up fish with a bucket. The grandfather catfish was very frightened, and so he hid underneath a rock to keep from being captured, until the boy left.'

MJ made one hand swim under the other, like the fish hiding under the rock. 'Grandfather fish decided God must have missed his prayer, so he said again, "Father God, the pool is getting very small. Please make the river flow and carry me from this trap." But no rain came. The pool grew smaller. The fisher boy came back a second time, and he began scooping more fish with a net.'

' "I'll not be someone's dinner," said Grandfather Catfish, so he hurried underneath his rock just before the net could scoop him. He hid until the fishing boy was gone, and then he came out into the open to find he was the only fish left in the pool. "Ha!" he said to himself. "I'm the wisest of all. God will send the rains, and I'll have the entire stream to myself!" He said his prayer a third time, and he waited, but no rain came.'

MJ frowned, like she was sad for the fish. 'The fisher boy came back again, this time with a line and some bait, but Grandfather Catfish was far too wise for that. He didn't touch the line, even though it sat all day, and he was very hungry and tired. Finally, the boy gathered his line and left, and he never returned. He knew there was no way he would catch the grandfather fish. Shortly after, the stream dried up, and Grandfather Catfish lay in the last patch of mud, gasping his final breath. "God of all things!" he cried. "Why, when I prayed three times, didn't you rescue me from my trap?"'

MJ tapped a fingernail on the countertop, smiling. 'And do you know what Father God said to the fish?'

The answer to the story came to me, and I laughed. 'I bet he said, "If you wanted out of the pool, you should of jumped in the bucket, or swam in the net, or grabbed hold of the line." The boy wasn't trying to hurt the fish, he was trying to take him someplace where the water was deeper, right?'

MJ got a twinkle in her eye. 'You're very clever,' she said. 'Sometimes we become so set on one possibility, we forget that in God's eye the possibilities are infinite. It is not He who needs our wisdom, but we who need His.'

I felt a big smile going across my face, because it was the first time I'd figured out the punch line before the end. 'That's a good story.'

'I agree.' MJ grabbed her pen and made a quick note on the edge of her pad. 'It's worth trading for, don't you think?'

I nodded, but outside Ronnie and Boo were fighting over

Opal's book. Somebody pushed, and somebody landed against the door. I figured I needed to go pull them off each other. 'I better head out.' I took my stuff and started that way. 'See you tomorrow.'

The door stuck when I tried to pull it open. I hoped Ronnie and Boo hadn't tore it up. We sure didn't have the money to pay for a door. I doubted MJ had much either, considering she mostly seemed to give away books.

She came around the counter to help me. 'It does this sometimes. It's old.' Butting the door with her hip, she twisted the handle at the same time, and it came open. I got out front just before Ronnie and Boo were about to knock over a flowerpot.

'You two stop that!' I yanked the book away from Ronnie with one hand, and picked Boo up by the arm with the other. For no bigger than he was, Boo was a scrapper. He kicked me in the shin so hard it hurt.

MJ helped Ronnie get up and dust off, and I pinned Boo to the wall until he quit being a brat. 'We're going home,' I told them, and looked for Opal. I figured she'd be up against the building trying to hide, because she didn't like it when anybody'd get in a fight.

I checked by the front door and the gas pumps, and she wasn't there. 'Where's Opal?'

Boo put both hands up with his palms in the air. Ronnie wiped his nose and did the same thing.

'She was with you two. Where is she?' My voice took on a sharp edge, and Ronnie pulled his shoulders up and ducked his head between them.

MJ and me checked all around the front of the building. We looked behind the flowerpots, by the trash can, on the side of the building where some old gas station signs were sitting. Both of us ran around to the back, yelling for Opal. By then, my heart was pounding, and I felt like someone had a fist over my throat.

'Calm down, now,' MJ said. 'She couldn't have gone far. Let me check inside and make sure she didn't go back in. Keep watching for her out here.'

'Okay.' Tears crowded into my eyes, and I stood on the curb, turning in a circle, not knowing where she could of gone or what to do next. Keep looking? Try to go find Rusty at work so we could drive around in the truck? The construction site was, like, five miles away. It'd take me forever to get there. What would I do with Ronnie and Boo?

Should I call the police?

I couldn't call the police.

What if MJ calls the police?

Settle down. Settle down. Think. Think where she'd go . . .

I couldn't picture anyplace Opal would go – not on her own, especially. Opal never did anything but stick herself to my leg.

'Opal!' I yelled up and down the street. 'Opal! You come out here!' *She's so little. She couldn't go very far. How could she get away so fast? She was here a minute ago . . .*

But a minute was long enough, and now it had been five minutes, maybe ten while we were looking for her. Opal could be anywhere by now. I pictured her running down the street, and I couldn't even breathe. What if she ran out in front of a car? What if she got lost and didn't know where she was? What if she wandered down by the highway bridge where the homeless people hung out?

Another idea hit me so hard it took my breath. *What if she didn't run away at all? What if someone grabbed her? What if Kiki and Uncle Len came back, and they saw her, and took her while Ronnie and Boo weren't looking?*

If Kiki came to get her, Opal probably wouldn't even fuss. She'd just let her mama take her by the hand and lead her away without a word.

CHAPTER 19

Sandra Kaye

'Mom, what's going on?' Christopher stared agape at the collection of people waiting in line on Poppy's driveway. There were groups of young children with older siblings, two elderly women who stopped to talk to Holly and give her a hug as they crossed the porch, a stooped-over man who, judging from his clothes and his backpack, was homeless, and a group of teenage girls, slightly embarrassed and slightly curious, as they eyed the food table with interest. Behind the table, Holly was pouring drinks. The front door swung open, and Angel came out carrying a large aluminum pan filled with sandwiches.

A young Hispanic woman had stopped on the lawn with her children, and they were having a picnic of sorts on a bright Mexican blanket next to the real estate sign, which Teddy had surrounded with transplanted iris, as if it were part of the yard décor. The young mother was taking care to keep her children from crushing the new plants. She gave Christopher and me a strange look as we exited our car and stood on the curb.

'Mom?' Chris muttered, his voice uncertain.

I couldn't formulate an answer. I was still busy taking it all in. How in the world, in just a few days, could a couple dozen sandwiches turn into a line halfway down the driveway?

The answer was simple, of course. Behind the crumbling yard fences, and the windows covered with cardboard and threadbare sheets, and the leaning front porches over-grown with weeds and old plantings, there were people for whom a free sandwich mattered enough to walk down the street and stand in line in someone's driveway.

'Holly didn't tell me there were so many now,' I muttered. Over the past few days, communication between Holly and me had been rushed and limited. I was preoccupied with Christopher's problems, and Holly was busy. Obviously.

'So many ... what?' Chris pulled off his baseball cap, scratched his head, and put his cap back on.

'People,' I answered absently, experiencing a rising sense of panic at the idea that the situation at Poppy's house was rapidly snowballing. All I'd asked Holly to do was come down here, check on the kids, and make a few sandwiches. I hadn't intended for anything like this to happen. Even though the action on the front porch was orderly, the situation seemed bizarre and almost surreal. 'She didn't tell me there were so many people.' Every time I'd asked Holly if things were *all right* at Poppy's house, she'd responded, *Oh, sure. Word's getting around now that school's out, I think. Your little friend came by and helped me make sandwiches today. I told her you were busy at the hospital with Christopher* ...

It was just like Holly to keep all of this to herself. She probably didn't want to worry me, but now I *was* worried . . . or in a state of shock. Something big had been set in motion here.

Chris pointed tentatively at Holly. 'Why's Mrs Riley handing out food on Poppy's porch?'

'It's a long story,' I said, and gave a brief history of the restoration projects at Poppy's; the handicapped lady at Wal-Mart; the kids digging in the Dumpster; Cass, Opal, and the sandwiches.

My son's mouth hung open, and he blinked at me as if I'd grown two heads – as if he were certain I'd slap him on the shoulder any moment, laugh, and one of the heads would say, *Gotcha! You didn't really believe all that, right?* We'd laugh at the joke, I'd turn back into his normal mom, and there would be some logical explanation for the mini-horde of people on Poppy's lawn and the serving line on the porch.

'Ha-loo-oo!' Teddy came out the door, spotted us by the curb, and waved. 'Ha-loo, lady. You comin' back. I put the door on closets, ho-kay?'

Chris stiffened, owl-eyed. 'What the heck?'

'That's Teddy. He does the gardens down at the church on the corner. I hired him to help with the yard work.' I'd left Teddy out of the initial story. It seemed best to lead Christopher into Mom's Alien World a bit at a time. Unfortunately, the new reality of Poppy's house and the summer kitchen was rushing out to meet him faster than I could contain it.

'Oh,' Chris murmured, with a cautionary look that reminded me of Rob. I could only imagine, if it were Rob driving up on this scene, what he would say. Now that I'd brought Christopher here, I'd have to tell my husband, too.

How would I ever explain all this?

Holly followed Teddy's wave and spotted us. 'Oh, hey!' she called as she changed out sandwich trays. 'Hey, Christopher, don't you look great! You're back on your feet again!'

'Hi, Mrs Riley.' Christopher returned an embarrassed greeting, and the teenage girls in the driveway glanced over to check him out.

Holly gave her place in the serving line to a woman I'd never seen before. Still sporting a bubbly smile, my best friend trotted down the steps and across the lawn, lighter than air. 'You look so good!' She gave Christopher a hug. 'Your mom didn't tell me you were getting out today.' She turned what was supposed to be a stern expression in my direction. 'You should have told me Chris was getting out. I would have baked him some brownies.' For Holly, brownies were a home remedy for everything from skinned knees to broken hearts.

'Holly, what's going on?' I motioned to the yard. Three more kids had just come from somewhere across the street. The line was growing.

'What?' Holly chirped innocently.

'Holly . . .' Leveling a grave look at her, I pointed to the line.

'We've . . . uhhh . . . grown . . . a little?' she replied cheerfully, then lifted her arms and twisted first to one side, then the other, displaying herself like a fashion model on the runway. 'But not me. I've lost four and a half pounds.

Gosh, this place keeps you busy. I don't know how you did it by yourself. I couldn't keep up after the first couple days, even with the help of your little friend over there.' She motioned to Angel, who was now handing out drinks and telling children in no uncertain terms not to spill.

'Angel's been here helping?'

Holly nodded. 'She showed up the first morning, just like you said she would. She's been here every day like clockwork. Usually she has her little brothers with her. I don't know where they are today.'

Christopher's head swiveled back and forth between Holly and me, his face pinched with confusion. I was baffled myself.

'But where's Cass?'

Holly stopped with her lips parted and a new stream of words about to tumble out. 'Cass . . . who?'

'The girl who was helping me. Cass. About five five, blonde, blue eyes, around twelve or thirteen years old . . .' Holly's expression said that nothing was ringing a bell. 'She always has a little preschool-aged girl with her – dark curly hair, green eyes, kind of quiet. A pretty little girl. Opal.'

'Oh!' Holly's face took on a look of recognition, and I felt a quick burst of relief. Unless something was wrong, there was no way Cass and Opal would turn their territory over to Angel. All the time I'd been gone, I'd been assuming that when Holly said everything was fine at Poppy's house, she meant that Cass and Opal were fine, too. I never dreamed that the sandwich helper had suddenly, inexplicably become Angel.

307

'That must be who Teddy was talking about,' Holly added. 'He kept asking something the first day, but I couldn't figure out what he was trying to tell me. First he was saying, "Where's the girl and the other girl?" And then it sounded like he was asking, "Where's the gas for the Opal?" ' Leaning close, she held a hand beside her mouth and whispered, 'He's a little hard to understand sometimes. I think I confuse him, but he's very sweet. He's been helping with the sandwiches, too. The lady from next door comes over, sometimes, but if we're going to keep this up, San, we'll need more help. I'm not sure sandwiches are the most efficient menu item, though. I've been counting up the food costs a little, and I was thinking, if I brought the catering dishes, we could cook big batches of . . .' Holly stopped to study my face. 'What? I don't like that look. Now you're worrying me.'

'I can't imagine why Cass and Opal wouldn't be coming by . . . ,' I muttered.

Pulling her lip between her teeth, Holly tightened the bow on the cook's apron she must have brought from home. 'Okay, time out. I think we're talking on at least three different wavelengths. Let's start over. You had the sandwich thing going on here. You couldn't come while Chris was in the hospital, so I came. There was a girl who showed up to help, but it's the wrong girl . . . right? But now we don't know why the right girl didn't come here . . . right?' She ended the sentence by bobbing her head like a marionette. I might have laughed, but I was too worried.

'Hey, we need some help here!' Angel called from the porch. 'The drinks got spilt!' On the table, a half dozen cups had tipped over, and red liquid was streaming onto the floor. In a panic, Teddy was trying to hold back the flood with his hands.

'Oh, shoot,' Holly muttered. Chris and I followed her to the porch and helped clean up the mess while Teddy and Angel stood in front of the table and finished handing out sandwiches. I asked Angel why Cass hadn't been coming.

'Opal got the flu,' Angel answered, seeming unconcerned. 'They been stayin' home. I'm gonna take 'em some sam'iches.'

'Is Opal all right?'

'Yeah, she all right.' Angel shrugged. 'Cass keepin' Ronnie and Boo today, too.'

As I finished wiping the porch floor, I rolled the situation around in my mind, trying to mold it into something that made sense.

I ended up under the table with Christopher and a pile of soggy paper towels.

'Mom . . . ,' he said, but before he could finish, there was a commotion in the yard, and when I stood up, Cass was there. She looked pale and panicked as she tried to hand Boo and Ronnie off to Angel. Holly rushed toward her, and I dropped the paper towels and followed.

Cass met me near the walkway. 'Is Opal here? Did Opal come over? I can't . . . did you see Op . . . Opal? I can't find . . .' The words were tangled in an almost unintelligible jumble of gasping sobs.

I grabbed her hands to hold her still. 'Ssshhhh. Cass. Calm down. Take a deep breath. Tell me what's wrong.'

'Op ...' She choked again on the word, stopped, swallowed, tried a second time. 'Opal's gone. She just ... we were at the book ... at the store. She was only outside a minute. I was watching. I kept looking. Ronnie and Boo got in a fight ... I can't find her! She's gone!'

'Opal's gone?' Her face flashed through my mind. I couldn't imagine her wandering alone in the city. 'Cass, what are you talking about? Where's Opal?'

'I don't know,' she sobbed. 'She went ... she ran off. I don't know if Kiki got her, or somebody got her. I don't know.'

Holly gasped and put a hand to her mouth.

The moments seemed to pass in slow motion as instinct took control of emotion, prompting me to gather details. 'How long has she been gone?'

'Where Opal gone?' Teddy echoed. He'd backed into the flower bed and was nervously pulling the front of his T-shirt. 'Where Opal gone?'

'Mom?' Christopher leaned over the porch railing. His voice probed the silence as I waited for Cass to answer. 'What's going on?'

Cass sobbed out a story about Opal having disappeared during a trip to the Book Basket. She'd been gone at least twenty minutes. 'We looked for her all around the store,' she finished. 'I don't know why she'd run off. She doesn't ever run off. I was watching her. I was!' She collapsed into sobs again.

Holding her shoulders, I looked at her very directly, trying to force her to focus. 'Cass, you have to be calm. You have to settle down so we can find Opal. She can't have gone far.' The words sounded convincing, but in reality, my mind was whirling with terrible possibilities. 'We need to call the police.'

Cass's eyes flew wide. 'No! No! We'll get in trouble. They'll take Opal away. We can find her. She's got to be here.'

'Cass, we have to –' The desperation in her face stopped me, even though I knew we'd have to make the call.

'Is there anyplace else she'd go?' Holly interjected. 'Anyplace between here and there? You know how kids are. They get distracted.'

'The creek!' Cass flashed a glance toward the little bridge and the old park next door. 'We drop cereal off the bridge and watch the fish eat it. Opal's always trying to go down there.' She spun around and dashed across the lawn, leaving us and a group of confused sandwich customers behind.

Teddy lumbered after her in an uneven run, calling back, 'I gone see Opal!' Christopher vaulted over the porch rail and the flower bed and jogged after them with Holly and me close behind. By the time we got to the bridge, Cass was leaning over one curb and Teddy over the other. Christopher was at the end of the bridge, looking for a way down.

'She was here! There's her doll.' Cass pointed as I skidded to a stop beside her. On a sandbar, the little Raggedy Ann was lying alone, the small black orbs of her eyes staring blankly up at the sky.

Holly leaned over the edge next to me. 'Could she have fallen in? It doesn't look very deep, though.'

I thought of all the times Jalicia and I had played in the

creek as children. 'It's never been more than a foot deep here.' Even now, in spring, when the rains were plentiful, the creek was just a trickle in the middle with lazy tide pools languishing in curves along the sides. It didn't seem possible that someone, even someone as tiny as Opal, could fall in and be swept away, or that the people next door at Poppy's house wouldn't have heard if she cried out. 'She has to be near here somewhere,' I said, then I called Opal's name. Teddy and Holly joined the call until the air was full of noise, and we couldn't have heard Opal if she'd answered.

'Maybe she's in here.' Christopher was over the vine-encrusted chain-link fence and into the old park in two quick movements. He disappeared into the growth of dried sunflowers, Johnsongrass, and brambles.

'Maybe Opal gone there,' Teddy echoed. He proceeded to the gate and pulled on it until the hinges gave way. After setting it aside like a toy, he went in. Holly and I made our way through, and Cass climbed over the left side of the bridge to check up and down the creek.

The search was over almost before it began. Teddy discovered Opal curled up in the middle of the merry-go-round with her thumb in her mouth, fast asleep. Summoned by Teddy's call, we all stood looking at her, watching her breaths come soft and even, her body twitching in a dream. Around her, faded streaks of yellow and blue fanned out like a distant memory of sun and sky. Overhead, the swaying tree branches painted dapples of light, softly covering her skin and causing the rhinestones in her pink shoes to twinkle like diamonds.

312

'I'm gonna kill her,' Cass muttered. She stepped onto the merry-go-round, and, off its axle, it listed to one side. In the center, Opal jerked and smacked her lips.

'Just be calm,' I said. 'It's all right now.'

Cass gathered Opal and we started back to the house, Opal blinking drowsily in Cass's arms. Crossing over the bridge, she whined and reached for her doll.

'I'll get it.' Chris hopped over the edge and landed flat-footed on the sand below.

'Christopher!' I scolded, then realized how long it had been since I'd protested one of his crazy, impulsive acts. This was the real Christopher, the one who plunged into every situation with boyish confidence and landed on his feet like a cat.

'Got it!' he said, scooping up the doll in one fluid motion and grinning impishly, delighted to have an audience.

Opal giggled, and Cass gave Chris an admiring 'Whoa' before he disappeared up the bank. He ran back around to the gate and joined us again as we reached Poppy's yard.

''S my doll.' Opal reached for her Raggedy Ann. Chris held the arms and legs, working them like a puppet's, making the doll walk toward her.

Opal's gleeful squeal caused Cass to give her an irritated frown. 'You shouldn't even get it back, Opal. You can't just run off like that. If you ever do it again, you're not gettin' your doll back, ever, and . . .' She stopped talking as a late-model car crossed the bridge and pulled up to the curb. 'Oh, man, I forgot about MJ. She went the other way to look for Opal after we couldn't find her at the bookstore.' With Opal

313

bouncing on her hip, she jogged to the curb to talk to the driver. Judging from the hand motions, she was describing how and where we'd found Opal. After the story was finished, the woman turned off the engine and got out. I watched with more than idle curiosity. Her clothes were as eclectic as the collection of colored bottles and beads outside her bookstore. She was tall, regal in a way, dressed in a turban, loose cotton pants, sandals, and a tunic-style shirt with an African motif. Holding Opal's hand, she bent close and said something, then stood up, took in the last of the lunch customers now picking up their belongings and wandering off, then focused her attention on me. Briefly, I had the sense that we'd met somewhere before, but there was nothing familiar about her, other than that Cass had told me about her on occasion. I couldn't imagine anyplace I would have met someone like her.

Cass brought her across the yard and made introductions. MJ was pleasant enough, beautiful, earthy, and exotic. She seemed completely comfortable in her own skin, yet the way she watched me gave me an off-centered feeling. As we began cleaning up the lunch mess, she remained on the fringes, talking with Opal and Boo.

Holly followed me into the kitchen while the kids picked up cups in the yard. 'So . . . uhhhh, what's with the lady in the Africa suit?' she asked.

'Not exactly sure,' I admitted. 'She owns the bookstore down the road.'

'Is she hanging around for a reason?'

'I'm not sure of that, either.'

'Huh . . .' Holly shrugged, handing me the foil pans so I could dry them. We finished the dishes in silence, then stood together in the kitchen.

'Holly, thanks for taking care of things here,' I said. 'I know all of this must have seemed really . . . strange.'

'I didn't mind,' she replied, slipping an arm over my shoulders and hugging me. 'You could have told me sooner, though. You know I'm the queen of crazy plans. You could have let me in instead of shutting me out. Does Rob know?'

I shook my head.

'You haven't told him anything?'

'No.' The implications of that and the reasons for it were too complicated to consider, standing there in the kitchen. Years of psychoanalysis could probably be spent on the issue. 'I didn't . . . plan any of this. It just . . . happened. Working here took my mind off Poppy's death and Jake's leaving, and I just kept coming back. I never meant for it to . . . get out of control.' *It is out of control. It's completely out of control.*

From the look on Holly's face, I could tell she was about to ask what my eventual plans were. I'd have to admit that I had none. I didn't know where my impromptu lunch program was going and I had no exit strategy.

She seemed to carefully consider what to say next, which was unusual for Holly. 'We could do this, you know.'

'Do . . . what?' I was almost afraid to ask. Holly had that force-of-nature look in her eye.

'We could open this place up for real.' She pressed the tip of her tongue to her teeth and raised a brow, assessing my reaction. 'Put in some tables and serve actual food.'

315

'Holly!' I protested, and she lifted a hand to shut me up.

'Just listen to me a minute. I've been thinking it through. Do you know there's *no* summer food program within ten miles of here for the kids who are out of school? There used to be one, but now there's a condo complex where the community center was. With school out, these kids can't even count on school lunch. Some of them go hungry *all day*. We could do this, San. We could. I've got all the dishes and the tables. We could make this work.'

I stood gaping at her. So much for *me* being out of *my* mind. Maybe it was the paint fumes in the house, but Holly had lost hers, as well.

'Holly, we –' I heard someone coming into the kitchen and turned to find MJ in the doorway. Her dark eyes watched me intently from beneath the turban, and again I felt a flash of familiarity.

'I see the secret room is still there,' she said, her lips parting in a smile.

'Excuse me?' *I know that smile. I know her . . .*

'The summer kitchen.' She motioned toward the back-yard. 'It's still where we left it.'

Where we left it . . . The summer kitchen . . . Her smile, the slight familiarity in her features, tripped a switch in my mind, electrical current raced through the connections, and suddenly everything made sense. 'Jalicia?' I gasped. I could see traces of the little girl in her now, the shadow of the playmate with whom I spent hours pretending in the secret room, exploring along the creek, and looking for the tramps' marks along the backyard fence. 'Jalicia? Is that you?'

Her eyes sparkled. 'Marley Jalicia,' she said, and then I remembered how much she'd hated that she'd been given her grandfather's first name – a boy's name. 'MJ sounds more exotic, don't you think?'

'Oh . . . oh, it is you!' The words rushed out of me in an excited squeal. I stretched out my arms, and we rocked back and forth in the embrace of long-separated friends. 'I haven't seen you since we were . . . what . . . thirteen or fourteen? You moved away somewhere, didn't you?' In truth, I couldn't remember why I'd stopped spending time with Jalicia. As I'd drifted into my teen years, boyfriends, slumber parties, and social plans with school friends overtook spending time at Poppy and Aunt Ruth's. I just remembered going for a visit and learning that Jalicia was gone.

'We lost our house and had to move away,' MJ said against my ear. 'But I came back. This is my neighborhood.'

MJ and I released each other, and I was aware of Holly watching us with her mouth hanging slightly open. 'Ummm . . . not to be a buttinsky, but can somebody tell me what's going on . . . exactly?'

CHAPTER 20

Cass

It was weird to think that MJ and Mrs Kaye were friends from way back a gazillion years ago. Even when they talked about it, I couldn't come up with a mind picture of them being little girls and finding the secret places before Opal and me did. But they had stories about the hideout under the porch, the brick pile behind the shed where the blue-tailed lizards hid, and the summer kitchen. MJ showed me a hidden door in the back room closet. It opened into a steep little stairway to the attic. I sneaked up there later, when everyone was busy. I kneeled on the rafters with the light coming in the little attic windows around me, and I said my prayers all the way through for the first time in a long time. It seemed like, if I said my prayers, maybe that would help a good thing stay good, you know?

But there was always the devil in the corner of my mind, whispering that good things never stayed good, not for Rusty and me, anyhow. It couldn't keep working out that we'd do the sandwiches at Poppy's house, and Opal an' me would get up every day and go there, and Mrs Kaye would give us all the sandwiches and juice and hot dogs we wanted to take home, and Rusty and me'd have enough money to buy groceries *and* gas, and we hadn't seen hide or hair of Kiki since she took off with her boyfriend – not the days we hid in the apartment, or the week since we'd been back working at the café. It was like something you'd dream, and it'd feel so good, and then you'd wake up and find yourself right back where you expected to be.

One day, when we were serving hot dogs with chili, MJ said sometimes the problem with people is expectations – she asked me if I knew that word, and I said of course I did. She said what you expect, you create, just like the frogs in the bucket of cream. If you expect to sink, you'll sink, but if you believe you've got the power, you'll keep swimming until the cream turns to butter, and you can hop on out.

MJ told the frog story to the kids after lunch that day. Monk and his gang had showed up, of all things – once it was hot dogs and chili instead of PBJ sandwiches, they got interested. After the story, B.C. said the little frog just got lucky, but MJ told him he'd missed the point. The little frog wasn't lucky; he was determined. She winked at me when she said it.

It was cool that MJ told stories to the kids after lunch. She brought books and read to them, too, and kids could take one home, then bring it back again to trade, if they wanted to. Story time was on the grass in the front yard the first few days after Mrs Kaye came back, but then when we hit a rainy spell, the whole café moved indoors. Teddy and Christopher set up tables in the front room while Holly, Mrs

Kaye, MJ, and Elsie, the old lady from next door, served up the food. Most days, the tables were full, and people sat on the floor around the edges, too. Holly said we needed more tables.

Even Rusty pitched in. He came on a Saturday after work to help Christopher fix a few things. After he'd looked the place over, he told Mrs Kaye he could bring some scrap lumber from the construction site and build a counter along the walls in the front room, like a diner had. That way there'd be more places for people to eat. Mrs Kaye told him thanks, but she didn't think we better do anything permanent.

When she said that, the devil stirred up the corner of my mind. He pinched me hard and said, *See, nothing lasts, if it's good.* He looked around the pink house and pointed out that everything – the folding tables and chairs, the big warming pans and the juice dispenser in the kitchen, the cups, plates, and napkins, even the little iron table in the summer kitchen, where Opal and me could sneak away from everybody, could be moved in no time.

You could come here one day, and there won't be a thing. Poof! the devil said. *What did you expect? Nothing's permanent.*

When Rusty came back the next day, Sunday afternoon, to work on the burglar bars, he brought his friend, Boomer, from work, so they could tack weld one of the hinges. Mrs Kaye had Christopher with her, and after they got the bars fixed, the guys shot hoops out front with a basketball Holly'd brought from home. She'd also brought a bunch of toys and some clothes for Opal. She said it was silly to keep those things, since she wasn't going to be having any more babies. I couldn't figure why anybody would want six kids in the first place, but Holly liked kids a lot. She was always hugging the customers and teaching Opal patty-cake and stuff.

I'd forgot how good Rusty was at basketball until I watched him playing with Christopher and Boomer. He was better than both of them put together.

'Wow, he's good.' Mrs Kaye sat down beside me on the steps, because she'd locked up the front door already. All that was left to do was put the basketball in the shed and close it.

It was cool that Mrs Kaye noticed Rusty. It made me feel proud of him. 'Yeah, the basketball team went undefeated last year, back in Helena, and it was mostly because of him. Then the English teacher flunked him on his essay, and I thought the coaches were gonna pop a cork. The principal got in on it, and they made her let Rusty redo the essay. They said, with Mama bein' sick and all, the English teacher shouldn't be so hard on him, but really they just wanted him to play basketball. They figured if they could keep him going, by next year the team would be really good.'

'Oh.' Mrs Kaye watched Rusty go right over Christopher's head and dunk one.

We sat there for a while, and then she told me she'd be late tomorrow because she had to help get food ready and tables set up for a funeral at her church back in Plano. Holly and Christopher would come on, open the café, and get things started.

'I hate funerals,' I said, and thought of Mama's – all those people walking around the church hall looking sad, hugging on Rusty an' me, and shaking creepy Roger's hand, saying how lucky we were to have somebody to look after us. Really, they were just glad *they* didn't have to worry about what would happen to Rusty and me. The basketball coaches were afraid we might of got shipped off to foster care somewhere outside the district. I heard them talking about it over in a corner. They said they didn't want to see us have to go live with strangers, but really, they were thinking basketball. If they didn't want us to go away to foster care, they could of took us, couldn't they?

At Mama's funeral, I found a table with a long cloth, and when nobody was looking, I crawled under it and put my head on my knees like I was doing now, watching Rusty play basketball.

'Well, I don't think anybody likes funerals,' Mrs Kaye said.

My mind came back to Poppy's house. 'All those people who were never even nice to you come around and hug on you and tell you how sorry they are and stuff.'

Mrs Kaye chuckled. Her eyes caught the pink sunlight and sparkled. 'I don't think they're all that way. Hopefully, a funeral is a chance to celebrate the good things people have done with their lives.'

'Like the café?' I looked over my shoulder at the house. It bugged me to think that Mama's funeral didn't celebrate anything, so I changed the subject. 'And all the toys and bikes Poppy used to fix for people.' Mama didn't start a place to feed people, or fix bikes so they could be used again. She just went to work, and came home, and tried to take care of us kids. Maybe that was why people didn't have much to say at her funeral. Those weren't very big things.

Sadness broke loose inside me and ran all through like cold, gray paint. I felt it dripping down, icy and thick. I wanted Mama to be alive, so she'd still have the chance to do something big – start a café, or give away books and stories. Back home, probably nobody even thought about Mama anymore.

Sometimes I wondered if Rusty thought about her. Mostly he just seemed mad that she died and left him to take care of everything.

I felt Mrs Kaye's fingers brush my cheek and catch my hair. She pulled it back and tucked it behind my shoulder.

'Do you want to tell me what's really going on?' Her voice was quiet and soft, strange with the basketball bouncing and the guys talking trash on the driveway. 'Sooner or later, you're going to have to confide in somebody, Cass.'

I felt like a person on the edge of the ocean, watching a wave come closer and trying to decide whether to run back to shore or jump in. *Maybe it wouldn't be so bad . . .*

Or maybe you'd get caught in something you couldn't get away from . . .

When you see the wave get closer, it's easiest to do what you've always done. 'I don't know what you mean, I guess.'

Mrs Kaye's hand rested on my hair. She gathered it in a ponytail and held it there. It felt so much like Mama, I closed my eyes and let my mind wander off for a minute. I was back on our porch with Mama. I leaned over and put my head on her shoulder, and she slipped her arm around me.

'I can tell there's something wrong,' she said. 'You have to trust somebody. I think I can help.'

'Mama ... ,' I whispered. Everything inside me wanted her to really be there.

'What about your mom?'

My mind came back to the porch. I knew it wasn't Mama there with me. I knew it was Mrs Kaye. What would she say if I told her about Rusty and me? What would she do?

Maybe she'll take care of us. She probably has a big house somewhere. Maybe she's like Holly and wants more kids. I let the idea start inside me like a pencil sketch, the lines kind of light, so you could erase them in a hurry if you needed to. Rusty and Christopher were getting on real good. There was an empty place in Mrs Kaye's house where Jake used to be. If he didn't want them for his family, maybe Rusty and me did. But then I thought there was no way Rusty'd go live with parents again, even nice ones. He liked being out on his own like an adult, doing what he wanted to do. I couldn't go stay someplace without Rusty. Him and me were still a family, first of all.

I heard Opal's shoes on the porch before I saw her, and there was the second problem with the sketch in my head. If I told Mrs Kaye about Rusty and me, what would happen to Opal?

I didn't have to think hard to answer that question, and I erased the pencil lines in a hurry. CPS would come get Opal. They'd give her back to Kiki, and if they couldn't find Kiki, they'd send Opal off to some foster house. She could end up with someone like creepy Roger. Everybody back home in Helena thought creepy Roger was just fine to take care of us kids. They didn't have a clue what he was really like . . .

Opal climbed on my back and wrapped her arms around my neck. I held on to them like a necklace. They were so tiny, I could wrap my fingers all the way around. *Somebody could hurt her so easy . . .*

I thought about the little burns under her hair, where nobody'd see them.

You can't tell, Cass Sally Blue. You can't ever tell anybody. 'Oh, you know, Mama just doesn't ever feel good enough to do much, with all her treatments and stuff,' I said. 'It makes me kind of sad sometimes . . . for her, I mean. It's like there's no way she'll ever get to be part of anything . . . real important.'

Mrs Kaye frowned. 'Real important?' she repeated, like the words could mean a lot of things.

I thought about them for a minute, those words 'real important.' No matter what it took, someday I was going to do something bigger than the regular stuff – bigger than just going to work and coming home, and trying to make enough money to keep the lights on and buy two loaves of bread at Wal-Mart. Not that I wanted to be president or anything, but one of these days I'd be the lady at the checkout line, with a couple extra bucks in my pocket to buy some kid a pair of pink shoes. 'You know, like start a place to feed people, or give out books and stories, or even like you brought Jake here from some other country when he didn't have a family and stuff. I think my mama would of loved to do something big like that, but she never got the chance. She was too busy raising kids on her own and keeping Rusty out of trouble.' Too bad Mama didn't get a doctor for a husband, like Mrs Kaye had. I'd never seen him, but he must have a ton of money for her to keep buying all this food for the café and him never telling her to quit. 'And now Mama's sick, of course.'

Mrs Kaye watched the boys playing basketball. 'I think raising two children and doing a good job of it is pretty significant. It sounds like your mom has made a lot of sacrifices. Not all parents do that.' Her lips pushed together, and for a minute it was like my thoughts were hooked into hers.

'Like your mom?' I said. A couple days ago, I'd heard her and MJ talking about how they used to hide under the porch to get away from Mrs Kaye's mom, and how she'd show up mad, messed up on pills or booze, and stand in the front yard, hollering at the top of her lungs and calling MJ the *n* word. 'I heard you and MJ talking about her the other day.' *The old witch still alive?* was what MJ'd said. Mrs Kaye told her *the old witch* was living in Seattle with Maryanne, whoever that was. *Seattle's not far enough,* MJ said, and then she asked if Mrs Kaye remembered when *the old witch* caught MJ under the oleander bush, grabbed her arm, then whipped her with a stick and told her not to come back, ever.

Mrs Kaye said she didn't remember, but then, she'd *blocked out a lot of things.* There was a terrible, sad sound in her voice.

I felt like, all in all, even though I wasn't rich like Mrs Kaye, and I didn't own a bookstore like MJ, I'd got pretty lucky. My mama loved me more than breathing, and she told me I was something special, every chance she got. I never knew anything but to believe it.

Mrs Kaye looked surprised that I'd heard all that stuff about her mom. I probably shouldn't of let on. Sometimes I forgot for a minute that I couldn't talk to her like I could with Mama. Mrs Kaye was just a friend. You've gotta be more careful with friends. They can pick up and move on whenever they want.

Right now, Mrs Kaye looked like she might get her stuff together and say it was time to go on home. She probably didn't want to talk about her mama hitting MJ with a switch or hollering the *n* word in the front yard.

'I shouldn't of been listening in,' I said, real quick, because I wanted to stay there a while longer and watch the boys play basketball. Opal ran down to play with them, and Christopher told her to come shoot a basket. 'I didn't hear anything much, anyway. My mama used to call me *Nosey Posey*, because I'd sit under the tables in the fellowship hall at church, and I'd hear stuff people said. It's not polite to listen in on other people's conversations.' I didn't want Mrs Kaye to think Rusty and me weren't raised right. By the basketball hoop, Rusty used a swear word just then, and if I'd had a rock, I'd of thrown it at him. 'Mama taught us not to swear, too.' I burned a laser hole in Rusty's back. Sometimes he didn't have the sense of a goat. 'Rusty's been down at that construction site too much.'

Mrs Kaye looked Rusty over, but not in a mean way. 'It sounds like he works quite a bit.'

'As much as he can,' I told her. 'We need the money.'

'It was nice of him to spend his afternoon off fixing the door.'

'He doesn't mind,' I promised her. It'd come to me that, maybe when he had more time off, Rusty could get a little work at Poppy's, fixing some of the trim that was rotted on the outside of the house, maybe doing painting, or repairing the faucets that leaked all the time. Rusty'd had so many different jobs, he knew a little bit about a lot of things. 'He could come do some more stuff here.' Then again, was Mrs Kaye really so rich she could keep shelling out cash forever?

'How old is Rusty?' Mrs Kaye asked out of the blue.

A fire alarm went off in my head. I couldn't remember if she'd asked me that question before, or what I'd said. 'He's nineteen,' I answered, quick as a whip. It's never good to say eighteen, because then everyone thinks you're lying, just to be legal. I was afraid Mrs Kaye wouldn't believe twenty-one, because Rusty didn't look much older than Christopher, just taller.

She nodded. 'He must play basketball quite a bit, to have stayed so good.' Rusty'd just blown in a three-point shot from the end of the driveway.

'Nah, he doesn't get the time anymore, since he's working.' In a way, it was hard to believe that, just last year, Rusty was carrying his team right through the scheduled games. There was talk that, the way he was playing, this might be the year they'd win state, and if they did, there'd be colleges all over the place offering Rusty scholarships. If he could keep from flunking English, first. He had to write a paper about *A Raisin in the Sun*. He didn't want to read it, so I read it for him and told him what to write.

'That's a shame.' Mrs Kaye watched Opal fall down in the driveway, then get up.

'Well, you know, you gotta do what you gotta do.' What else was there to say, really? You hit a point where some dreams just aren't gonna come true. It doesn't seem so important to read about *A Raisin in the Sun* when you are one.

'I'd have guessed there was more difference between your ages.'

I wasn't really listening to Mrs Kaye. I was thinking about *A Raisin in the Sun*. I didn't much like the way it ended. The people got gypped out of their money, and they had to start over, and I thought that was pretty sorry. I wanted them to win the lotto, or find a wallet with a million dollars in it, or something. 'Five years,' I said, and it took a full minute before I clued in to the fact that I'd screwed up big-time. *Seventeen*, the voice in my head hissed. *You're supposed to be seventeen. Seventeen to nineteen, two years.* I laughed and added, 'Seems like. Sometimes, Rusty acts about twelve years old.' *Twelve to seventeen, five years. Good math.*

I didn't look at Mrs Kaye. When you say something and look at people right after, they know you're wondering if they swallowed it.

We sat a while, and finally Mrs Kaye gave a long, low sigh, her shoulders sinking with it. Folding her arms over her knees, she stared down the street, her eyes flickering like candles in the freckled light as the tree branches swayed apart and came together again. 'You know, if we're going to be in business together, I'll need you to be honest with me.'

'Business together?' Out of the two sentences, that seemed like the least dangerous bit. Part of not having to lie is figuring out what things to talk about. Most people'll let you take a conversation wherever you want.

'The free lunch café.' She nodded toward the house. 'Holly and I have been talking about giving the place a name, trying to get some sponsors or grants, and going forward with it. We're serving so many elderly people, and families with babies and toddlers, I don't think school starting in the fall will make too much of a dent in the numbers here.'

'Really?' All the worry fell off of me like dead weight, and I felt like I could float right across the yard. 'It's not really a business if it doesn't make any money, though.'

'Not so. A business delivers a product or provides a service. The reward doesn't have to be monetary.'

'Monetary's nice, though.'

Mrs Kaye laughed. 'True,' she said. 'If we move forward with making this an official business and applying for grants and fellowships, we'll need social security numbers from everybody.'

'Oh, sure. We've got those at home.' When we moved to Dallas, Rusty'd got a social security card from a guy downtown, so he wouldn't have it happen again where the people he worked for found out he was seventeen. He could probably get me one, too. 'You don't have to pay me to work here, though. I know you need money to buy the food and stuff for the café.'

Mrs Kaye squeezed my hand, then held it. 'We'll talk about that when we get further along. There are a lot of details to work out yet, but for now, I think we need to level with each other, all right?'

''Kay.' Inside, the bird started beating my ribs. This was a trap – the talk about the café, the promises about working here, the stuff with the social security numbers, even Mrs Kaye holding my hand. It was all a trap. No matter how nice people act, they always want to get in your business . . . 'There's not a lot else to tell, though.' I tried to look like I wasn't worried. 'What you see's what you get, pretty much.'

Mrs Kaye gave me the look my sixth-grade teacher used to. *Crap*, I thought.

'Opal isn't really your cousin, is she?' she asked, as Opal stole the basketball and ran away squealing while the guys pretended they were trying to get it from her.

My mind zoomed round and round like a screaming whistle on a string. *What should I say? What should I tell her next?* I thought about what Rusty'd said – *You can't just take someone's kid and keep it.* If Mrs Kaye knew the truth, would she make us call CPS and tell them Opal's mom had left her and not come around for, like, all the days Opal and me pretended to have the flu, and now another week since we'd been back at the café – almost two weeks altogether?

Mrs Kaye's eyes found mine. If I lied, she'd know it. 'Well . . . no. She's Rusty's girlfriend's kid, but the apartment only lets family be there, so we have to *say* she's our cousin.' *Don't look at her right away. She'll know you're making it up.*

I felt her wrap my fingers between hers and hold them

tight. From the corner of my eye, I saw her lean close. 'How about the real truth? You can trust me, Cass.'

The bird pounded so hard against my chest, I couldn't hear myself think. All I could hear was the beating. 'Well . . . ummm . . . she's not exactly Rusty's girlfriend. I mean, they're just friends, kind of. He's, like, trying to help her out. Her boyfriend messed her up some, and she didn't have anyplace else to go.'

Mrs Kaye sucked in a breath, and I couldn't help it, I looked at her. Her eyes were wide and she looked afraid. 'Cass.' Her lips hung open a minute. 'This doesn't sound like something the two of you should be involved in. Things like this – domestic problems – can be dangerous. Even the police are afraid to get in the middle of domestic situations.'

I thought about Kiki's boyfriend coming and beating on the door, and the little scars in Opal's hair. If Mrs Kaye found out about that, everything would be ruined. She'd call the police so fast, Rusty and me wouldn't even have time to get the stuff in the truck for a start-over. 'Oh, no, it's okay now.' I rushed out the words. 'They're, like, broke up. He kicked her out, and they haven't talked since then, and they're not gonna. He moved away, I think. He's a trucker, and you know they don't ever stay in one place long. Once Kiki gets enough money together, she's moving into her own apartment. She's almost got enough now.'

Mrs Kaye smoothed a piece of reddish blonde hair away from her face, looking at me. 'Are you kids on your own down there? You and your brother, and this Kiki, I mean?'

'Oh, no, ma'am. Mama's always home . . . unless she has a treatment.'

The phone rang in Mrs Kaye's pocket, and I was never so glad for anything in my life. She got up and walked to her car to talk. She didn't look happy, and when she came back, she said she and Christopher'd better head home.

Before she left, she handed me a card with her cell phone number on it. 'I want you to keep this where you can find it.' She looked me straight in the eye. 'If there's ever a problem, you call me. Night or day, all right?'

'All right.' I got up off the porch and tucked the card in my pocket while she told Christopher they had to go.

I didn't bother reminding her that we didn't have a phone.

CHAPTER 21

Sandra Kaye

'Dad's home,' I informed Christopher as we left Poppy's.

Chris checked for oncoming cars, then swung into the left-turn lane and waited for a gap in traffic before speaking. I'd started letting him drive on our trips to Poppy's – a silent sign of confidence, a bridge between the two of us to let him know I believed he wasn't to blame for the accident. We'd probably never know for sure, now that the other parties had dropped their claims and disappeared. The sequence of events would always be their word against his, but officially the accident had been ruled no-fault.

Over the past week, there had been a strange and silent compact between the two of us, Christopher acting like the old Christopher, making his silly jokes, helping at the free lunch café, bringing the basketball goal from home and setting it up in the driveway so the kids could play, performing Frisbee displays with Bobo on the lawn while customers waited in line for lunch. He'd brought his guitar and started showing some of the older children how to finger the chords. He'd even begun to lure Monk, B.C., and a few other

teenagers who showed an interest in the guitar and the basketball goal. Chris and Teddy had made plans to mow the
grass in the park and put the merry-go-round back on its
axle as soon as Rusty could procure the welding equipment
from work again.

It was as if we'd been on an odd sort of vacation these past
days, Chris and I. We were bank robbers on the lam, both
of us aware that we were only stealing time.

'Did Dad call from the airport or from home?' he asked,
squinting one eye, as if he felt something heavy over his
head and was just waiting for it to fall.

'He got home about a half hour ago.'

'Great,' he mumbled, not sounding the way a son should
when his father returns from a business trip. Perhaps there
always comes a point at which fathers and sons have a col-
lision of the minds, and Rob and Christopher had reached
that point.

'You can talk to him, you know. If you have something to
tell your dad, you need to get it out in the open.' More than
once on our drives home I'd tried to encourage Christopher
to open up about his future plans for medical school, his
music, his feelings about Jake's leaving, his issues with his
dad. Chris didn't want to talk about it. He was like a tourist
overextending his credit card on vacation – if he didn't discuss real life, it didn't exist. Instead, he talked about the
people we served at Poppy's, the ways we could improve the
place, how the kitchen could be renovated and expanded,
the plan for cleaning up the park, his idea of getting some
cheap guitars and teaching kids to play in the afternoons.

They don't have anything to do all day, he observed. *That's why they hang around the streets and get in trouble.*

Each night after Chris and I ate supper, he filled our house with music again. Life was relaxed and comfortable.

'Dad doesn't listen.' A bitter shadow darkened Christopher's eyes as he looked over his shoulder to change lanes. 'He doesn't care.'

It bothered me to hear Chris talking that way, even though I knew it was his reality, and I could understand it. Growing up, I'd felt as if I were an actor playing a part, and if I failed in my performance the consequences would be dire. I didn't want that for Chris. 'That's not true. Your father cares about you very much. He just doesn't know . . . what to do about it. He didn't come from a very . . . flexible family. Certain things were always expected of him, and, in general, he set the same expectations for you two.'

How could I explain to Chris that Rob's way – *our way* – of protecting the boys had always been to make sure they never deviated from the safe and steady path we'd planned? 'You know how Grandma and Grandpa Darden are, and I can promise you they've always been much looser with you and Jake than they were with their own kids.' Even though they only flew in from Florida a couple times a year, Rob's parents had always tried very hard to be good to the boys. 'Grandpa Darden is a brilliant man, but he's always been very distant and set in his ways. There's never been anything touchy-feely about him. It worked out all right, I guess, because he and your father are a lot alike.'

The corners of Christopher's mouth turned downward, and he blew a puff of air through his nose.

'You need to tell your dad how you feel, Chris.'

'Nobody can talk to him.' A muscle twitched in his cheek. He blinked hard, then rapidly. 'Jake couldn't talk to him.'

The comment surprised me. In Rob's view, Jake had always been the perfect son. Smart, cooperative, easy to control, mild mannered. 'Your father and Jake had a pretty good relationship. They wanted the same things.'

Chris rolled his eyes, his mouth a sardonic line. 'Jake didn't want to be premed. He didn't ever want to go to medical school.'

Struck by the words, I jerked back against the seat. 'What?' Never in Jake's life had there been a discussion of anything else. From the time Jake was small, Rob had insisted on enrolling him in biology camps, accelerated courses, summer gifted and talented programs designed to introduce him to the study of science. Jake was a sponge, absorbing it all, always looking for something more to learn. 'Jake never talked about anything else.'

'Jake just said those things to make you guys happy.' I had the sense that Christopher was finally being completely honest. 'He stopped wanting to be a doctor when he was, like, in the fifth grade. He wanted to be a teacher. He always wanted to be a teacher. He wanted to go back to Guatemala and teach kids who were orphans, like he was.'

My body went limp, and my arm fell against the door, triggering the automatic locks, imprisoning the words inside the car. 'Jake said that to you? When?'

'I've known it forever.' Christopher glanced at me, turned ashen at the look on my face. 'I shouldn't have said anything. Never mind.'

'It explains ... a lot,' I choked out. My thoughts raced through the connections – Jake always playing school in his room as a child, setting up tables and chairs and forcing his little brother to be his student, doing his book reports on subjects related to Guatemala, volunteering at the rec center, where he could work with disadvantaged kids while he completed premed coursework, insisting on enrolling in educational theory classes that weren't required for his major. And finally his leaving. He hadn't gone off into the world to escape his grief over Poppy, or to find a new family. He'd finally broken free and traveled where his heart had been leading all along. He wasn't wandering aimlessly; he was executing a plan.

'When was he going to tell us?' My voice, just a whisper, seemed too loud in the car.

'He wanted to,' Christopher answered. 'He said he didn't think you guys could find room for it.'

'Room for what?'

'The truth.'

I reached across the car and touched Christopher's hair, thought of the little boy who not so long ago fell asleep believing his mom could fix the moon. He was growing up, leaving all the prepackaged expectations behind, becoming a person unto himself. There was nothing to do now but stand back and watch him unfold. 'Christopher, there's room for it. We'll make room for it.'

Resting a hand on his shoulder, I closed my eyes and thought of Jake. If only I could have had this conversation with him. If only we'd let him be himself. We were so busy trying to mold him into who we thought he should be that we never really considered who he was.

No more, I told myself. *No more pretending.* It was time to make a life that wasn't shiny on the outside but hollow on the inside. We could be so much more than what we had been, if only Rob would see it. If only he would listen. If I could find the words to say what needed to be said.

All my life, I'd been afraid to try for something better. I'd never understood why Rob loved me in the first place, why anyone would. *You're just lucky, Sandra Kaye,* my mother had pointed out the day Rob and I married. *Be careful not to screw it up for yourself. If this marriage fails, don't expect our support. You won't be coming back here to live, just remember that . . .*

She was drunk when she said it. Drunk on champagne, in my stepfather's study after our wedding reception. She wanted to give me a mother-daughter talk before I left on my honeymoon. I wanted to keep her away from the guests until they were gone. Rob understood. He told friends and family members good-bye alone and made excuses for us.

When we drove away from the house, he laughed and pointed out that I could finally leave her and my stepfather behind for good. They hadn't managed to foul up the wedding – not my mother, with her overconsumption of Valium and champagne; not my stepfather, with his loud, long-winded diatribes on subjects that had nothing to do with the wedding.

We'd won. We were free.

Did Rob realize that both of them were coming along even though we couldn't see them? They followed me like pieces of baggage that were invisible, yet weighed everything down.

You're forty-nine years old, Sandra, I told myself now. *It's time to cast off the dead weight.*

Jake was fortunate to have figured it out when he was just nineteen. Sooner or later, you have to shed your family's expectations and run the race on your own.

'We'll talk to Dad together,' I told Christopher. 'I want you to be honest with us, and with yourself. It's not your job to fill the space Jake left behind. It's not your job to please us, or make us feel better, or carry on the line of Dr Dardens.'

Chris blinked and swallowed hard, his Adam's apple moving slowly up and down. 'I don't want you and Dad to get divorced.'

'Fixing things between your dad and me isn't your responsibility. We have issues to work on, but you don't need to worry about that.'

Chris's gaze jerked my way, his face stricken. 'I don't want to make it worse.' The words were filled with emotion, with fear.

'You're not making it worse, and you can't fix it by being a perfect kid, by working toward premed and whatever else you think *we* want.' I looked very directly at Christopher, at the young man he'd become. 'You don't want to major in premed, do you?'

340

His lips trembled at the corners, then he pressed them flat. 'No.'

'You miss your music.'

He nodded, but didn't speak.

'We'll talk to Dad together,' I said again. 'We'll start there, all right?'

He nodded, and we drove several miles in silence. Finally, Chris cleared his throat. 'Are you going to tell him about Poppy's house? About the café?'

The question landed in my stomach like a lump of uncooked dough. That issue had been so easy to avoid with Rob gone. 'Yes, I am.'

Worry drew lines beneath the wisps of blond hair on Chris's forehead. 'What do you think he'll say?'

'I have no idea.' A hot flush burned into my skin as I tried to imagine the conversation. I couldn't fathom where to begin. The café was so far outside the scope of our normal lives. It was like nothing I'd ever done, yet I felt as if I'd been meant to do it all my life. I couldn't let it go, but I couldn't keep hiding it from Rob, either.

'You know what he'll say,' Chris pointed out glumly. 'That's why you didn't tell him before. That's why you didn't tell anyone until I ended up in the hospital.'

'Partly,' I admitted. 'But everything at Poppy's just happened. It took on a life of its own.'

Chris considered the answer. 'I think it was Poppy's idea. He'd like that the kids come to his house.'

'You're right. I've thought about that.' There was healing in the fact that Poppy would be pleased with the café, that it was something he would have approved of. There was closure in the café – a slow shift from dwelling on the way Poppy had died to celebrating the way he had lived. 'Poppy would be very proud. He loved that neighborhood, and he wouldn't have wanted to see it slowly fall apart.'

Chris smiled. 'We can talk to Dad about it together – about the café, I mean.'

'Yes. I guess we can.'

Chris cranked up the radio, and we drove the rest of the way home suddenly a team.

We could see Rob at the kitchen window when we pulled into the driveway. Chris and I glanced at each other. He smiled, but looked as if his teeth hurt. 'Are we going to talk to him *right*away?' he muttered, sounding nervous and uncertain, and suddenly very young. By the car door, his leg jittered up and down, the muscles seeming to be debating fight or flight.

I considered saying, *Let's leave it until morning. Dad's probably tired.* But it would have been an excuse, my typical pattern of avoiding potential conflict. If I'd been a general, my armies would never have gone to war. They would have stayed safely in camp, keeping everything calm, and clean, and freshly painted, while our territories slowly shrank until there was nothing left.

You're not the powerless, scared little girl anymore, I told myself. *Nobody's going to whip you with a dowel rod and put you in your room. It's time to grow a backbone.*

All the same, as we pulled into the garage, a small, frightened part of me remembered the way the dowel rod feels when it hits your skin. The thin pipes of wood were left-overs from one of Maryanne's science projects, a model of the universe. They found their way all over the house, lay hidden in convenient places where they could be easily grabbed when Mother needed to straighten a picture high on the wall, or when she was in a mood . . .

Don't muss your dress, the little girl whispered from some-where in the dark.

'Now's as good a time as any,' the woman opening the door said.

Rob was in the kitchen, in a good mood, as was usual when he returned from a conference. The time away from the hospital always did him good.

He greeted me with a kiss on the cheek, which surprised me, then he patted Christopher on the back and offered him a slice of cheesecake from a box he'd picked up on the way home. Chris rolled a bug-eyed look at me behind Rob's back. I had no idea how to respond – to Rob, or to the cheese-cake. I hadn't seen Rob this euphoric in a long time. Even on the best days he had a million work-related issues pressing on his mind.

Turning with a dessert plate balanced against his chest and the fork poised, he smiled at the two of us. 'I have some news.'

He's heard from Jake. The thought spun through me so quickly I couldn't catch it, couldn't contain it before it filled me with expectation. *He's heard from Jake, and it's good news. Jake's all right!*

Christopher slipped onto one of the stools by the island,

his face grim, as if his premonitions of the news weren't nearly so good.

'Well, tell us,' I said. 'Don't keep us in suspense.'

'Want some cheesecake?' Rob joked, delaying purposefully, allowing the anticipation to build.

'Rob, for heaven's sake.' His expression made me laugh. He looked so pleased with himself – as if he were waiting for us to open the gifts he always sneaked away to buy on Christmas Eve. 'We're hanging on edge here.'

He took a bite of the cheesecake, chewed it and smiled. 'I've made a decision.'

'Really?' Something ominous crowded my thoughts, despite Rob's smile. *This isn't news of Jake.* 'A decision about what?'

'I've been offered a position at Johns Hopkins University, and I've decided to take it.'

Christopher fell back against the bar stool, his head whipping toward me, his lips parted in a silent imitation of my next words.

'Wh . . . what? What do you mean . . . you've been offered a position? I didn't even know you were applying.' Over the years, Rob had occasionally received feelers about med school positions, but there was always the issue of a change in income and leaving behind friends, family, and the boys' school for a new location. The discussions never went very far.

Today, he was beaming. 'It's a bit of a backdoor offer right now, not official, but it will be.' As usual, he was confident, but filled with exuberance, also. He focused on me, seeming to forget that Chris was in the room. 'It'll be perfect, San. I won't be tied up night and day, Christopher can finish high school in Baltimore and start undergrad, and when it's time to apply for med school, he'll have an in. After everything that's happened, we can all use a change in location.' There was the quick flash of something serious in Rob's eyes, making it obvious that he'd considered this offer at length. Of course he had. Rob never did anything impulsively. He'd analyzed every angle. He'd sent feelers into the university market, and he hadn't even bothered to discuss it with us.

'When did all this come about?' A simmering started deep inside me, like a pot that had been cool for a long while suddenly finding heat underneath.

Rob set down the plate as if he sensed that holding something breakable wasn't a good idea. 'Within the last few weeks, in general. I've been considering the idea longer, but given Christopher's ... problem ... it's good timing for a move. Word of what happened ... with the pills ... is bound to get around. It won't help him.'

Christopher hunched forward, looking down at the countertop.

Don't talk about him as if he's not here, I wanted to say. *He has ears. He has a mind of his own. He's not an object you can move from here to there, position in whatever way you want.* 'Christopher isn't interested in medical school,' I said flatly. 'We've just been talking about it, as a matter of fact. He has some things he'd like to say, and he'd like you to ... hear him out before you answer, all right?'

Rob's chin did the jitterbug of a bobble-headed doll. Brows lowered, he squinted at me like a man trying to make out objects in an unfamiliar room where the light was too dim.

Christopher's chin jerked up, and he gaped, wide-eyed and ashenfaced. 'Mom, now's not . . . it's okay, we can . . .'

Now or never. Time to grow up and stand on your own two feet. No matter what, I wasn't going to let Christopher do what I'd done at his age – bend to the wishes of everyone around me until I didn't know who I was anymore. 'This is the time, Chris. Tell your father what you told me in the car.'

Chris surveyed the countertop, his fingers fiddling with a discarded twist tie, and his knee vibrating until the stool clacked dully on the tile.

'Christopher.' Standing beside him, I rested my hand on his shoulder. 'It's all right. You don't have to be afraid to tell us how you feel. More than anything else, your father and I want you to be happy.' I turned to Rob, catching his gaze. *Please just stand there. Please just listen to him. . . .*

Clearing his throat, Christopher began forming the twist tie into a knot, then spilled out, in one quick paragraph, the truths he'd shared during our drive home. He bypassed the revelations about Jake's reasons for leaving. Perhaps he was focused on himself, or perhaps he was afraid of making things worse than they already were.

When he was finished, Rob seemed confused and stunned. Beneath my hand, Chris's muscles went slack, as if he'd just run a cross-country race and used everything he had.

Rob didn't answer, just stood there looking shocked.

'Chris, why don't you go on upstairs?' I suggested quietly. 'Your dad and I have some more things to talk about.'

Chris flicked an uncertain glance my way.

'It's all right,' I told him, and he stood up quickly, as if that were enough to convince him to bolt for the safety of his room. On the way out, he avoided looking at his father. Perhaps he didn't want to know what Rob was thinking. Maybe Rob didn't want him to know, either. He waited until Christopher's footsteps had crested the stairs before he spoke.

'Where's this coming from, all of a sudden?' he asked finally.

'I don't think it's all of a sudden. I think he's had it on his mind for a long time. He's been scared to put it out in the open. After everything that happened with Jake and Poppy, he was afraid that if he didn't play the perfect son, we might fall apart, too.'

Rob jingled the change in his pocket, then turned two coins over and over in his fingers, producing a softly rhythmic, metallic sound. 'Did he say as much?' His tone, his expression, conveyed doubt, as if he believed I was being too emotional, allowing myself a reactionary response to typical teenage swings of opinion.

'Yes, he did. He's already lost his grandfather, his brother is gone, and now he's afraid his parents will get divorced.' The words felt strange in my mouth. They hovered in the air like a thunderhead.

'Where would he get that idea?'

I was forced to pause and gather my thoughts. Could this

man, whose mind dissected even the most intricate details of the human body, possibly be so blind to the workings of the human soul, to his own family? 'Rob, do you think he doesn't notice that you're only here one or two nights a week anymore, and when you are here, you sleep in front of the TV? You don't want to talk about anything. You don't want to talk about what's happened with Poppy's case, or looking into family counseling, or where Jake might be, or whether he's all right. You avoid the whole issue, and you avoid us. It's as if we're just another appointment you have to keep.'

He drew upward, offended. 'I don't think that's valid. Just because I'm not hovering around wallowing in it doesn't mean I don't feel it. Just because I don't mollycoddle Christopher doesn't mean I'm some kind of dictator who couldn't care less about how he's feeling or what he wants, or that we need to sign up for some kind of family talk therapy. Chris knows I have his best interests in mind. I want him to have all the tools he needs to be successful.'

'Your kind of success,' I countered. 'Your definition.' My hands rose palms-up in a plea. 'Rob, there are all kinds of success. Titles, and diplomas, and a six-figure income are only part of it. We shouldn't be telling the boys to live their lives to keep up appearances, or to make someone else happy. It's hollow. It's meaningless.'

'That's what I'm trying to fix!' Rob exploded, his face uncharacteristically passionate. 'With the new job. With a new start for Christopher. He can leave it all behind. Nobody will know about the problems he had here ... about the

348

pills. We won't have Poppy's death and everything else pressing in on us.'

Shaking my head, I looked away from Rob, watched the last rays of sun disappear behind Holly's house. How could I make him understand? '*Chris* will know. We'll know. All the stuff that caused him to try pills in the first place will still be with us. We don't need another artificial life in Baltimore or anywhere else. Chris deserves the chance to pursue a life that's authentic to who he is. He's trying to tell you that. He's been trying to tell us that – he and Jake both have – but we haven't been listening, and now Jake's gone. I don't want Christopher to be next.'

'This has nothing to do with Jake.'

'It has *everything* to do with Jake.' My voice had gone quiet. Even now, it was hard to force out the truth about Jake. Rob would be wounded to the core. He'd always thought of Jake as his protégé, an extension of himself, plucked from a grim future in a third world country and carefully groomed for success. 'Did you know Jake didn't want to go to med school? He wanted to be a teacher. He wanted to go back to Guatemala and teach. He didn't run *away* from us, he ran *to* something he'd been keeping inside himself for a long time.'

Rob's head curled upward and angled, as if he were trying to gain a view of something that made no sense. 'Jake told you this?'

'He told Christopher.'

'When?'

'A long time ago, apparently. They've both been carrying

349

it around for years. That's why Jake insisted on the double major. He was preparing; he just hadn't figured out how to tell us yet.'

Rob reeled, caught himself against the counter, crossed his arms over his chest and froze like a statue, contemplating the weight of the world. He shook his head slowly, his gaze scanning the cabinets, as if he were reviewing text in a file, trying to connect the clues, analyze the symptoms and come up with a cure that would fix everything.

Finally, I gathered my courage and breeched the silence. Now that we'd begun, there was no reason not to go all the way. 'There's something else I need to tell you.'

'Can it wait?' Rob was off center, suddenly exhausted.

'I think I'd better say it now.' Without allowing myself time to reconsider, I jumped into an explanation of the past weeks, Poppy's house, the kids in the Dumpster, Cass, Opal, and Rusty, the café. Rob didn't react other than to lift his chin and stare at me, his eyes glazed over through the entire story.

'I'm not sure what you want me ... to ... say,' he stammered.

'I don't want you to say anything.' I wondered whether to be comforted or concerned by his lack of reaction. 'I want you to come see the café. I want you to see the kids there, to look at how they live, everything they need. There's so much work to be done. They not only need food, but also enrichment programs, medical care, dental care. Medicaid doesn't pay for dental, and so many of the little kids have baby teeth just rotting out of their heads, and –'

'This is where you've been every day?' He pushed aside the cheesecake and rested his elbows on the island. 'For how long? How long have you been doing this?'

'A few weeks.'

'A few *weeks*?' His mouth hung open. 'Who knew about it?'

I swallowed hard. The truth would hurt him. 'No one, at first. Then Holly . . . and Christopher.'

'Christopher?' His face conveyed surprise and then injury. 'You've gotten Christopher involved in this?'

'Yes.'

'But not me.'

'It . . . took on a life of its own, Rob. You have to understand.' But the truth was that Rob was right. I had chosen not to tell him. He was justified in feeling betrayed.

'It never occurred to you to discuss it with me, particularly before you involved Christopher?'

'Chris needed . . . something. I thought this might give it to him.'

'Christopher needed his mother at home. He *needs* his mother at *home*.' Rob scratched an eyebrow roughly, watched me with his fingers pressed to his temple. 'We're not in any position to take on something so complicated, especially now.'

'Why *not* now?' I countered, growing desperate. If Rob didn't understand, what would I do, where would I go? 'Why not *us*? We have resources, Rob. We have connections here that could be used – through our church, our friendships, the hospital. Right now, the café is feeding over sixty people a day. You can't just stop feeding sixty people a day.'

He closed his eyes, then opened them again, as if he were hoping to wake up somewhere else. 'Has it ever occurred to you that, while these people are willing enough to cash in on a free meal, they were surviving before you came there, and they'll survive after you leave?'

The fire of indignation in my belly flamed up like kindling with a handful of dry straw thrown on top. 'Has it ever occurred to you that they might have been hungry before we came and now they're not? I don't need a medical degree to spot hungry people, Rob. I may not be a doctor, but I'm not an idiot, either. I'd like you to consider that I am capable of doing more than washing clothes, and scheduling the yard service and the housekeeper, and running everyone's errands, and making sure there's sandwich meat in the refrigerator when you *happen* to show up to eat. Has it ever occurred to you that I might be good at this, and that this might be good for me? That it might be good for Christopher – for all of us?'

Rob's eyes, a cool gold in this light, took me in, studied me. 'I've never questioned your abilities. I've never questioned that you're capable of doing anything you want.'

The statement took me back. 'Really? Because you're talking to me as if I'm one of your underlings, and I need you to guide and direct me. I need you to *support* me, Rob. That's what I need. I need . . .' How could I describe what I felt – the sense that, somewhere between Mommy-and-me playdates and the high school banquets, I'd *become* the birthday parties, the school projects, the PTO, the booster club, the soccer snacks, the doctor's wife. I *was* the job I did. I loved the job, but now the job was changing, pieces of *Mom* evaporating like fog on a bathroom mirror. The same sense of change that made Holly wonder if she wanted another baby whispered to me that now was the time to do something new, to do *this*. The young college coed who'd planned to become a teacher, to be the one who made a difference to children who needed help, was awakening like a time traveler frozen in suspended animation. I could feel her catching her breath inside me. 'Jake isn't here. Christopher's almost grown. This could be good for us, Rob. It's been good for Christopher and me. We talk about things . . . new things, instead of grinding the past into finer and finer pieces – instead of sitting here grieving over Jake and Poppy. It's time to move forward. It's time for something new. Isn't that why you were considering the teaching job?'

For a moment, there was a spark of understanding in Rob's eyes, as if I'd touched the part of him that wanted to break free, that felt as trapped as I did. Just as quickly, he closed the door. 'Sandra, I'm all for your volunteering, or going to work, or whatever you want to do. I understand the psychology of a maturing home, but there are dozens of things you can do without driving to the seedy side of town and setting up a soup kitchen. There are things you can do here.'

'What if I'm needed *there*? What if this *is* what I'm supposed to be doing? We sit in that big church on Sundays.' I stabbed a finger in the general direction of Victory Fellowship, just out of sight over the hill. 'And we talk about having a sense of purpose. Well, I've found it. I feel it in

353

every part of me. Nothing that's happened these past few months has been by accident. It's as if I've been pushed out of the nest, pushed toward that house, toward those people. It's as if I've been preparing for this all my life.' I thought of the dreams I'd held as a little girl, the spirit that my mother's addictions had tried to crush in me.

'Sandra, there are social agencies set up to handle problems like this. Volunteer with one of them if you want to.' Rob's voice was like my mother's. *Don't muss your dress, Sandra Kaye. Stay away from little black children. You'll pick up the dialect . . .*

'I've done my research, Rob. I know this neighborhood. Economics, the rising cost of groceries, everything hits hard in a lower-income area like this. The community center had a summer feeding program, but the community center isn't there anymore. The property was sold to a developer. New condos are going in just blocks away, but that doesn't help the people who were there before. It only raises the tax base. They can't afford to stay. They can't afford to go. They can't afford to live. Someone has to fill the gap.'

Rob stared out the window, his eyes narrow. 'I'm sorry, Sandra. I understand economics and urban redevelopment. I understand that other people have problems, but burying ourselves in some quest for social justice won't bring back Jake, and it won't erase what happened to Poppy, and it won't . . . keep Christopher out of the medicine cabinet. I'm not interested in trying to save the world. We've got all we can handle just trying to put our own lives back together.'

I could feel Rob pulling away, slipping through my fingers

like sand. 'Give it a chance, Rob. Come take a look – see what it's about. I need this. I want you to stand behind me.'

Leaning forward, he sighed, combing a hand through his salt-and-pepper hair. 'What, exactly, are you proposing?'

'First of all, I want to buy Poppy's house from Mother. The café has to have a place that can't be sold out from under us. Without a permanent location, we can't even apply for grants, and –'

His gaze lifted in a way that struck me silent, that burned through the seed of hope I'd begun to nurture. 'Sandra,' he said flatly, 'there was a message from your mother on the machine. She just accepted an offer on Poppy's house.'

CHAPTER 22

Cass

The minute I saw Mrs Kaye get out of her car, I knew something was wrong. You can tell a lot by the way a person walks. She was only carrying a couple grocery bags and one of the metal pans we used in the café, but she moved like her body had an extra hundred pounds on it. She didn't even wait for Christopher or Holly to get out – she just headed up to the porch with lines in her forehead big as corn furrows. Christopher didn't look like he knew anything was going on. He shot a basket from right beside the car. Monk and his bunch had been hanging around on the street waiting for him to play a game of two on two and as soon as they saw him, they came like hogs to sooie, which meant Christopher wouldn't be much help all morning. Working with him was about like working with Rusty – he didn't stay on one track so well.

When everyone got out of the car, it didn't look like Holly knew there was anything wrong with Mrs Kaye, either. She was whistling, and she hugged Opal and me around a stack of paper plates.

Opal could tell something was different with Mrs Kaye today, though – lots of times, it seemed like Opal had a feeling about things, even if she didn't know the words to tell you. She knew when people were mad, or happy, or sad, or upset. Maybe she'd had to learn that to get by, living with Kiki and Uncle Len. She figured something wasn't right about Mrs Kaye, and she hung around by the door, looking up at her with a worried face.

It didn't take Mrs Kaye long to send me and Opal to the front room to set up tables. As soon as we were gone, Holly plunked a cutting board down on the stove so hard I heard it. 'Okay, out with it already,' she said. 'What in the world is wrong with you today?'

There was a long pause and then Mrs Kaye turned on the radio by the door. I couldn't hear what she said at first, for 'Old Time Rock and Roll' playing on the radio. I got closer to the door, and then I picked up, '. . . want to say anything with Christopher in the car.'

'Well, it's just us now.' Holly had the knife going. She could do it really fast, like a Japanese chef on the Benihana commercial. She could even talk while she did it, which, considering she always talked with her hands, didn't seem like the best idea. She'd chop, sling the knife, chop, sling the knife, and once in a while point it right at somebody like it was a giant finger. 'Hey, by the way' – the chopping stopped, and I figured she was pointing the knife right then – 'I did a bunch of research last night, and I've got a stack of grant applications printed off, and I thought –' She cut the sentence off right in the middle. 'Good Lord, San, what's *that* look for?'

'My mother accepted an offer,' Mrs Kaye told her. 'She signed the papers yesterday.'

'The papers for what?' *Chop, chop . . . chop, scrape, chop.* 'A new broomstick and a few dozen monkey men? I swear, San, one of these days you're going to get up the guts to tell that woman off. What form of manipulation and guilt inducement is she into now?' *Chopchop-chop.*

'The house, Holly. She sold the house.'

'What house?'

'*This* house. Poppy's house.'

The kitchen went dead silent. It seemed like minutes passed before anyone said anything. I felt the time ticking inside my chest, like the big grandfather clock in the funeral parlor where Mama was in her casket. *Bong, bong, bong, bong . . .* The closer I got to the box with Mama in it, the louder the sound was, until finally I put my hands over my ears and ran away.

I wanted to do that this time, but I couldn't. I had to know what they were saying.

'How could she . . . I thought you were going to tell her to take the house off the market. I thought you were going to tell her *we* wanted it. Teddy took down the real estate sign last week.'

'It *fell* down, Holl. I just didn't have Teddy put it back up. I didn't think there was anything to worry about. There hasn't been a single sign of interest in the house since we put it on the market. I thought that if an offer did come in, the real estate agent would contact me, and then I could approach the issue with Mother. For one thing, I wanted to talk to Rob about the café first.'

'Great. Now what?' It was the first time I'd ever heard Holly sound mad about anything. The knife went wild, *chop-chop-chop-chop-chop-chop*, and nobody said a word for a couple minutes again. 'There must be something we can do. The house isn't worth all that much. Just call the Wicked One and tell her we'll buy it. We'll come up with the money somehow – maybe get a bank loan, or –'

'She sold it to a broker. That's why I didn't hear anything about it until after the fact. Mother had Maryanne call a home-buying company, and she dumped the place for what she could get. I tried to call Mother last night, and I got Maryanne, and you can imagine how that went. She said Mother was in bed with a headache. Maryanne thought I'd lost my mind, wanting to keep the house. She was delighted to let me know the place was gone, period, and there was nothing I could do about it, so there wasn't any point in my talking to Mother. She had the nerve to tell me it was for my own good – that Mother sold the house so I wouldn't have to deal with it.'

'Ohhhh, I hate her.' I'd never heard Holly say anything like that, either. Holly liked everybody. 'I hate both of them. I do.' The knife went wild. 'Real estate contracts take a while to become final. There are inspections and such.'

'It's an "as is" sale – one of those *We buy shabby houses* companies.'

'Well, that's it, then!' The knife stopped suddenly. 'We'll buy it back from the company. Hagatha and Medusa won't have any control over it. It's perfect. We'll get the house, *and* we can stick it to the wicked witches, all at once. What could be better than that?'

'I already called the company. It'll be thirty days or more before the house is available. They inspect and renovate each property they take on, then they rent it out. I had a long talk with the property manager. I even explained what we were doing here. She was actually very nice, but she knew her stuff. We've got more problems than just the sale of the house. This property isn't zoned for anything more than single-family use. Getting that changed would require a huge effort and it's fairly unlikely we'd succeed. The kitchen here isn't an approved commercial kitchen. Sooner or later, the health department will find out we're serving food to the public – free or not – and they'll shut us down. Apparently, you can't just open your doors and start feeding people. People have to go hungry until you've got all the right permits. End of story.'

Holly didn't say anything, which sunk me lower than all the stuff Mrs Kaye'd brought up. When Holly didn't have a plan, things were bad.

'Wildfire' came on the radio. I sat down in a chair and closed my eyes, and went to a mind place. I was the girl on the pony named Wildfire, running and running.

'There has to be a way,' Holly whispered.

I tried to decide whether to keep listening or stay in the mind place. The song went on, the pony busted down his stall and got lost in a blizzard. The girl ran after him in the cold, calling his name.

Did she ever find him? I wondered, but in my mind, I couldn't see the answer. I couldn't stay in the place where things were good. I couldn't stop the voices in the kitchen from mixing with the song.

The girl in the story died, out looking for her pony. She got swallowed up by the blizzard and nobody saw her anymore, and she never rode Wildfire across the prairie with the whirlwind by her side again.

Nothing good lasts. It's a fact. You build a stall to keep the good thing dry and warm. You try to lock it up, keep it safe, but it busts out, and runs away, and you don't even know why . . .

I waited all day for Mrs Kaye to tell me about the trouble with the house, but she didn't. Maybe she was having a hard time dealing. She didn't tell Christopher, either, or Teddy, or Teddy's mom, who'd had her nurse help her make cookies. They stayed to hand them out to the kids. For a little while around lunchtime, the people were eating, and things seemed okay. MJ told a story out on the porch, and the kids sat and listened. Even Monk and his gang quit playing basketball and stood where they could hear. Rusty and some of his buddies from the construction site came over for lunch. They paid for their food, even though Mrs Kaye said they didn't have to. Rusty and Boomer were headed off on another night run to pick up shingles from the dude in Houston, and he didn't know when he'd be home, but probably not until early morning. He said to be sure I locked the door when me and Opal got home, and I said I would. I didn't tell him anything about the café getting sold, because he didn't look like he needed one more problem on his mind. He didn't like leaving me and Opal home alone that long, but they were gonna get a hundred dollars each for the shingle run.

I told him me and Opal would be fine, then him and his friends headed back to work.

After story time was over and the people left, I looked through the window, and I saw MJ talking to Mrs Kaye and Holly. I could tell without hearing the words what they were talking about. All three of them looked upset.

Cleanup for the day went on like normal, except it didn't feel normal. It felt like the end of everything. I guessed it was, but my heart still wouldn't buy it. I wasn't sure what would happen to Opal and me now, without the café to go to every day and without the food I got from Mrs Kaye. Extra food and free lunch every day leave a big hole when you haven't got them anymore, and you've still got three people to take care of.

I tried not to think about it, but I couldn't get to a mind place, even though I wanted to. When you grow up, there's more things between you and your mind places, I guess.

On the way home, I stopped and let Opal drop some bread crumbs in the creek, and then we hung out in the park a while. I sat on the lopsided merry-go-round and remembered all the talk we'd had about fixing up the place. Rusty was gonna get some bolts and a welder for the merry-go-round, and some spray-on stuff that would make the slide slippery again, and some cables and boards for the swing set frame. He'd talked to the guys at the construction site about welding together a teeter-totter and some frames for picnic tables.

It was too much to think about, sitting in the park with Poppy's house right on the other side of the trees, so I made Opal leave and we headed home. She didn't argue. I guess she could tell I was in a mood, because she just held my hand and walked along real quiet, looking up at me every once in a while.

When we turned the corner into the apartments, Kiki was sitting on our steps. By the time I saw her, we were so close I was surprised she didn't hear us. She was just sitting there still as a statue, her knees wrapped up against her body like she was cold, and her head down between them. I froze, holding Opal's hand tighter and tighter. Opal was watching a bird hop along the gutter looking for food, so she didn't see her mama at first. I moved in front of Opal. She tugged at my hand, watching the bird. I felt the pull stretching my arm as she tried to see the bird better.

Run. Turn around and run away, I thought, but I couldn't move. If we ran away, where would we go? Sooner or later it'd get dark, and we'd have to come home. How long would Kiki stay there? Why did she come? Why did she have to come back at all?

I couldn't wait until Rusty could get home and take care of it. He was probably already headed off with Boomer on the road job, overnight. Even if he wasn't, I didn't have any way to get ahold of him now.

'Is a bird go.' Opal's voice pushed back the silence. I caught my breath and jumped, jerking Opal close. The seconds seemed to pass in slow motion. Opal pulled from my hand, I saw her, I saw the bird. One leg was dragging behind it, the claws curled together, useless. The bird wasn't looking for food; it was trying to get to someplace safe. On the steps, Kiki untangled like a ball of string, loose and slow, like she didn't have the energy to stand.

Opal splashed into the water in the gutter, trying to pick up the bird as it hopped toward the apartments. 'Bird. Bird, 'mere bird.' She moved closer to Kiki without even knowing it.

'Stop, Opal!' I ran after her and grabbed her up, swinging her onto my hip so hard she gulped out air.

Kiki turned all the way toward us, and then I knew why she was back. She had a fresh shiner. Her eye was swole almost shut, with a cut underneath that'd bled down her neck and stained the front of her T-shirt.

'Geez,' I muttered. 'What happened to you?' As if I had to ask.

'It . . . went bad.' Kiki's head tottered on her neck, and I was afraid she'd pass out right there on the steps.

Opal saw her and tried to wiggle out of my arms. I felt stung inside. I wanted Opal to turn away, to treat Kiki like she deserved. She didn't deserve for anybody to love her, least of all Opal.

How can Opal even want to go to her, after everything she's done?

Stop it, my mind hollered at Opal. *Quit reaching for her. Don't you know what she's like? Don't you know she doesn't care?*

But all Opal knew was her mama was there again.

I held on to her tight, so she couldn't get away. 'Quit, Opal. Leave her alone.'

'Hey, mmmb-baby,' Kiki mumbled. She was either stoned or knocked silly. She blinked and swayed backward against the steps.

'Go away.' I twisted in the other direction to keep Opal

from her. 'We don't want you here. You can't come in. Go back wherever you were.'

Kiki let her eyes fall closed, and her whole face seemed to sag. 'I ain't got . . . annn . . . anywhere . . . He kicked . . . kicked me . . . ouhhht.'

'You shoulda thought of that before you went back. What'd you think he was gonna do – buy you a Rolls?' I sent the words out like a rock after a stray dog. I wanted to hurt her, to chase her off. I hated her like I'd never hated any-body. 'Go away.'

'I gotta . . . I gotta get Op-Opal. She's . . .'

'You can't *have* Opal!' Kiki was only using Opal to get me to let her stay. If she really wanted Opal, she wouldn't of run off and left her in the first place.

'She's umm-my ba-by.' Her words ran together like drips of molasses.

If she tries to grab Opal, I'll fight her, I told myself, but at the same time, Opal was wiggling and squirming, trying to get free, and calling, 'Mama, Mama. Unna see Mama.'

'C'mere, ubbb-baby.' Kiki smiled on one side and reached out.

'You don't take care of anything she needs!' I shouted at Kiki. 'If you try to take her, I'm gonna call CPS.' Would I? Would I really risk it? Kiki could tell them about Rusty and me just as quick as I could tell them about her. 'Stop it, Opal!' I hollered at Opal, then tightened my arms. She head-butted my shoulder and started to cry.

Kiki pushed off the cement and staggered closer, then fell against the building, and hung bent over like a scarecrow.

Spreading her legs for balance, she cussed a long, lazy string that ended in a sound like an animal would make, lying on the road after a car hit it.

From the corner of my eye, I saw black and white. A police car. Maybe somebody'd called them about the noise. The car passed by slow. I tried to watch without turning around.

Kiki didn't notice it at all. She was hunched all the way over, coughing with the dry heaves.

'Great.' I moved past her, opened the door and set Opal inside. It took everything in me to come back and get Kiki, but if that police car circled around again, I didn't want her to be out there hocking one up in the parking lot.

Inside, I sat her on the edge of the bathtub and handed her a wet washrag. I watched the dried blood turn back to liquid and soak in around the edges as she pushed the cloth against her eye. Her hair was stuck in the blood.

'You shouldn't of gone back with him,' I said. 'Nobody should be with someone like that.'

'He takes care a' umm-me,' she whispered.

There was a little shuffling noise in the doorway, and I saw Opal with her doll, watching us. 'Go on and read your book, okay, Opal?' I moved her away from the door and closed it, because it didn't seem like any kid should see her mama that way.

Kiki watched me cross the bathroom, the swelled-up eye moving under the eyelid.

'You can't go back with that jerk,' I said, sitting down on the toilet lid.

'He takes care ... ummm ... me.'

366

'He hits you.'

'He's good . . . good sometimes.'

I wanted to shake her like you'd shake someone to wake them up from sleepwalking. 'Opal's got burns under her hair. Did *he* do it? Did *he* do that to her?'

She sank forward until her head was laying in my lap. 'I don't . . . I get so . . . I'm so . . . messed-dup.'

I let her stay that way while the water and the blood soaked through my clothes. I felt sick in my stomach, but in my mind, everything was clear. I sat there thinking about it as the sun sank behind the buildings outside the little window over the shower.

The plan played like a movie in my mind.

As soon as Rusty got home, no matter what it took, I'd get him to see that the only thing we could do now was a start-over. While Kiki was still asleep, we could pack everything, then load up and go. We couldn't wait any longer. Even Rusty'd have to see that now.

After I finished helping Kiki clean up, I put her to bed. Opal wanted to get in with her mama, so I let her climb up with the doll and the book. Kiki laid back against the pillow and pulled Opal down, too, but Opal didn't mind. Opal held the book up and started reading it while Kiki's eyes fell closed, and her breaths grew longer and slower, until she was out cold.

I walked away and left them there. I remembered how it felt the last time my mama held me.

I laid on the sofa reading, hoping Rusty'd come home earlier than he said. Sometime after dark, my eyes went to burning and I couldn't keep them open anymore. Finally, I pulled the kitchen chairs in front of the door, just in case Kiki woke up and tried to leave with Opal. Then I got in my sleeping bag, closed my eyes and listened. I heard the partiers drive by cheering and screaming, headed for the clubs down on Greenville. I heard the Mexican guys rattle up in their truck, play their music loud and hang out for a while. I heard the baby cry next door and the mama holler at Angel to get it. I heard Kiki moan in her sleep, and Opal cough, and move around, and settle back down. Then I didn't hear anything.

I dreamed about Mama. We were in a hammock somewhere, just the two of us, rocking back and forth under a clear blue sky. I wanted to talk to her, to tell her about Opal, but I just laid there for a while, because it seemed like we had all the time in the world.

'Mama,' I said finally, and she tucked my head under her chin, like Kiki did with Opal.

'Ssshhh.' Her breath brushed over my hair, gentle like the breeze. Her fingers twined with mine, and I looked down at our hands, but they were brown and white like mine and Opal's.

Thunder boomed somewhere. Mama held me tighter, so I wouldn't hear it.

It got louder again, shaking the ground, traveling through Mama's body into mine, pulling me away. I felt her arms slip free. 'Mama!' I called. 'Mama!' I was screaming, but at the same time, I knew the sound was nothing more than a low moan. I felt my body jerk, heard the thunder rumble, knew the sofa was underneath me, felt the scratchy sleeping bag. Something banged once, twice.

Air came into my body in a big gush, and I jerked up, awake so sudden it hurt. My heart flapped around like a wounded animal trying to find its feet.

Someone was banging on the door . . .

I heard a voice.

Uncle Len's voice.

'Kiki! You come outa there. Y'hear me? You layin' up wit' that boy? You come on out here!'

The bedsprings squealed in my room. The air turned solid in my throat until I was choking on it. I pushed my hand over my mouth so I wouldn't make a sound. My legs tangled in the sleeping bag as I tried to get up, and I landed hard on the floor, then scrambled to my feet with my blood pounding in my ears, screaming to my body, *Wake up! Wake up!*

The bedroom door banged against the wall and lightning flashed, shooting bright strips through the blinds. I caught the blurry outline of Kiki by my room. 'Stop!' I hissed. 'Don't open the door!'

Uncle Len pounded again, rattling the door so hard the wood split around it. The clock fell off the wall and crashed against the floor. The lightning died. The room went dark. I heard Opal squeal and run across the floor like a little mouse.

'You come outa there, Kiki! Get out here! I'll rip this door down . . .' The sentence ended in a string of dirty words, and then everything went quiet. The hinges creaked and strained, the screws groaning against the wood. 'Come on, baby. Open up. I don't wanna hurt nobody. Just you an' me, baby. You an' me, an' Opal. Hey, Opal. Come see Uncle Len. I'll get you a bike. A new bike. You like that? C'mon, open up.' He waited to see if anyone would answer.

Lightning flashed, and I saw Kiki halfway across the floor. Opal was holding on to her mama's T-shirt.

'No!' I whispered. I ran to get between her and the door, hit one of the chairs and sent it skidding into the kitchen. 'Stop. No!'

'Ssshhh.' Kiki's hand touched my face just like Mama's did in the dream. In the strobe of light, her eyes met mine, then she vanished, and I could only feel her hand, then not even that. In the darkness, I heard her bend down and pick up Opal.

My mind raced. I tried to think of a plan, some way to stop her. I couldn't fight both her and Uncle Len.

The hinges groaned again. In another minute, he'd get through . . .

'Ssshhh.' Kiki's voice was barely there. Her clothes rustled as she moved, then she pushed something into my hand. The wall shook. Wood splintered. A piece clattered to the floor. I felt something in my hand. Shoes. Her shoes. I didn't understand at first, then I did. I put on the shoes. The lightning sparked, then she was gone in the darkness again. She put Opal in my arms, and Opal wrapped herself around me, her fingers digging into my shirt, holding on.

The door gave way, jerked against the burglar chain. Wood cracked, high and loud.

By now, someone's called the police, I thought, and then, *He'll be inside before they get here . . .*

Kiki moved us into the space between the wall and the back of the recliner, beside the door. She pushed me down, and plaster sprinkled over us like rain. I smelled wet pavement, heard Uncle Len so close, heard his hand come through the door, try to work the chain loose, then he backed up and hit it with his shoulder again. Plaster rained down. I curled myself over Opal.

'Ssshhh,' I whispered against her ear, the fluff of her hair brushing my lips.

'Just a minute, baby.' Kiki's voice seemed strange, too calm, almost friendly. 'Just a minute. Let me get it.' The sky flickered. I watched her move the chairs, push the door closed. Silence filled the room, slowed the moments, made her breath loud as it trembled inward, then out. Her fingers shook, loosening the chain.

The door opened a crack, pouring a narrow slice of light over Opal and me, then widening into the room.

'Where's he at!' Uncle Len boomed. 'Where's yer boyfriend?'

'He's not here, baby,' she said, sticky sweet. 'Nobody's here but me.'

Uncle Len stepped inside, hovered so close I could smell the sour scents of cigarette smoke, beer, and sweat. 'Where'z Opal?' He snaked out a hand, caught Kiki's wrist. 'I heard Opal.'

Pressing harder against the chair, I squeezed Opal so tight I didn't know if she could breathe. She was stone still in my arms, her heart fluttering against my stomach like a leaf caught in a storm.

Be still, be still. Don't move. Don't make a sound . . .

'No one's here, baby. That was just me.' Kiki leaned into him. 'You can look.'

'Where're they hidin'?' Uncle Len pushed Kiki back but held her wrist, so that she snapped like a ball on a tether. 'You hear me, Opal? Time-da go home. I gotta come git you, you gonna be sorry, little girl. You better come out.'

Don't move. Don't move. Don't answer.

'They went out the back. Let's just go, baby. Let's go on home, okay?'

'They're here. Yer boyfriend's here.'

'It's empty, see?' Kiki backed up a step, drawing him like a dog on a leash.

The space by the door widened. One step, two. Should I try it? Could I make it? What if he saw us? Could Kiki slow him down enough?

He caught his toe on a chair leg, stumbled forward.

I inched Opal higher on my chest, gathered my legs under me like a cat. They shook, rubbery, numb, uncertain. What if I couldn't run in Kiki's platform tennis shoes? What if I couldn't get us out?

Go, Cass Sally. Run. Mama's voice was inside me. *Now. Go now.*

Uncle Len caught his balance. I stood up. The recliner vibrated. Thunder shook the ground and lightning slashed the sky. I bolted into it, raced down the steps to the parking lot. The street was dead, all the apartments closed, the convenience store dark across the street.

'Hey!' Uncle Len's voice roared after us as the thunder died. 'You get . . . get back here!'

I didn't stop. I held Opal and ran, a pulse hammering in my ears until I barely heard Kiki scream.

Don't look back. Don't look back. Just run. Just run.

I felt the pavement pounding underneath my feet, Kiki's shoes, too big, sloshing around in the water. I tripped, caught myself with one hand, got back on my feet.

Run. Just run.

Uncle Len's truck roared to life behind us, then backfired and died. Opal screamed and held on tighter. I bolted over the bridge and kept going. My heart hammered, but my legs felt like all the blood had drained out.

I passed the church, ran for just a second in the glow from the sign out front, heard a shutter slapping against the building. Thunder shook the sky as I crossed over and went by the bookstore. Glass bottles and MJ's wind chimes clattered wildly in the storm, the sound rushing away down the street.

I looked back. The headlights were coming out of the apartments. The truck fishtailed on the wet pavement, hit something and high-centered, the tires squealing. Lightning streaked overhead, then thunder boomed. The truck busted loose and peeled out. Headlights shined toward us, lighting up the street.

Run. Just run. Just run.

'Wildfire' played in my head, and my mind went clear. I thought of the girl in the blizzard, racing after her pony, fighting to get him to a safe place.

I knew where she ran to.

I knew where she hid from the storm.

I ran toward that place as the truck bounced over the curb, hit something and spun out, then finally squealed back onto the road. The engine roared, then was drowned out by an explosion of thunder.

I rounded the corner onto Red Bird with the headlights coming closer. I didn't know if he'd seen us make the turn. Maybe he hadn't seen us.

It wasn't much farther now . . .

CHAPTER 23

Sandra Kaye

A storm blew through sometime in the dark of morning. The crash of thunder pulled me from a light sleep, and I lay watching the room flicker in the glow from the television. I'd muted the sound and let myself drift off to the late show, trying to ignore the fact that I was going to bed in an empty house. Christopher had slipped away to Holly's for an overnight, and Rob had found yet another reason to work late, so as to avoid further conversation about the café. No doubt he was hoping that if he ignored the issue for a few days, I would get over my whim, and life would return to normal. Then we could discuss his taking the job at Johns Hopkins.

A rapid pulse jittered in my neck now, as if something ominous were hiding just beyond view; I could feel its presence, even though I couldn't see it yet. Through the floor, I heard the hum of the downstairs television. Rob must have returned home sometime after I'd fallen asleep, but he hadn't come up.

A flash of lightning and a clap of thunder eclipsed everything. The TV caught my eye as I felt for my slippers under the bed. The image was cockeyed, partially hidden by the footboard. I couldn't comprehend it at first. A news brief was on. There was an image of Cass's apartment complex.

A feeling of unreality swept over me like a sudden bout of vertigo. *It's part of a dream*, I thought, and let the slippers fall from my hand. *You're still dreaming. It isn't real.*

Thunder rumbled outside again as I fumbled for a mental grasp. Blinking hard, I looked at the television again, took in the scene – the apartment complex, police cars, flashing lights glaring against the rain-slick street, a SWAT van, two fire trucks, and drowsy, confused residents standing behind them wrapped in blankets.

Crawling across the bed, I fumbled for the remote, searched for it among the sheets, a burst of adrenaline sharpening my thoughts, fastening my gaze to the screen while I tore at the twisted bedding, trying to turn up the sound.

My eyes cleared, and I could make out the banner at the bottom of the screen. *Hostage crisis.*

I found the remote beneath the covers, ripped it loose, turned on the sound.

A female newscaster was standing under a streetlamp next to several blanket-clad families. The SWAT van and a fire truck provided a backdrop as she attempted to make sense of the story. '. . . began with an apparent domestic disturbance in apartment One-A. Neighbors reported a man pounding on the door sometime after three a.m., the sounds of an argument, then an apparent struggle, during which some of the family members, possibly children, may have exited the home. The man in question, who was not a

376

resident here, then allegedly attempted pursuit in his vehicle, but may have returned to the apartment, and may be inside with at least one female hostage. Police have received no response after repeated attempts at contact, however, and are unsure whether the suspect may have fled prior to police arrival, possibly leaving behind one or more victims. SWAT teams are currently assessing the situation . . .'

My heart and mind stilled. Outside, the thunder halted and everything was impossibly silent. The thoughts that had been crowding in all evening, the issues that had seemed so important, ripped away like watercolors on rice paper, smeared, and disappeared.

I imagined Cass and Opal, either trapped in the apartment or hiding somewhere in the dark right now. Somewhere . . .

This can't be happening. This can't be real. It's a mistake.

I'd had the same thought the night Poppy was attacked. It didn't seem possible that such violence, which seemed vaguely unreal when you saw it on television, could be happening to you, to someone you loved. *This story won't end like Poppy's. It can't.*

I pictured Cass and Opal somewhere safe, allowed myself to think of nothing else. *They're safe. They're safe. They're all right.* Rushing around the bedroom, I slipped on clothes and grabbed my purse, then ran downstairs.

A dim light flickered from the media room as I reached the hallway, reminding me that Rob was home. If I woke him, would he come with me? Would he come because I asked him to, because I needed him?

I rushed into the room, woke him so suddenly he pitched forward, causing the footstool on the sofa to fold up. He caught the armrest, stopping himself from ending up on the floor. 'Sandra, what in the . . .' He blinked, blinked again, trying to clear his vision so he could see the clock on the VCR.

'Something's happened. I need you to come with me.' The day of Poppy's death flashed through my mind. Rob had said the same thing that day, after he'd gotten the call from the police. *Something's happened, Sandra. We need to go down to the hospital. It's Poppy.*

Rob's head swiveled toward the door, his face ashen with sudden panic. 'Where's Christopher?'

'Christopher's fine. He's at Holly's overnight. It's the café, the kids there.'

Rob sank back against the chair. 'For heaven's sake, Sandra. You scared me half out of my mind. I thought something had happened to Christopher. It's five thirty in the morning. Can we talk about this tomorrow?'

'No!' My hands flew up, slapped downward. I turned away, turned back, trying to decide whether to continue attempting to convince him, or just leave. '*Please*, Rob. I need you. Just come with me. Come with me now, and I'll explain on the way.'

He sat up, then hovered on the edge of the chair, studying me in a way that felt painfully cool and clinical. My hopes sank. He was about to say no. He'd tell me this was insanity. I could see the thought crossing his mind, hardening the expression on his face.

'Please,' I said again. 'Rob, I need you to come with me. Please don't say no. Just trust me.'

Brows drawing together, he weighed the possible responses for what seemed like an eternity. An eternity during which I contemplated our future. If the person who was supposed to love me the most didn't believe in me, then what future was there?

'Let me get my shoes,' he said finally, then pushed out of the chair, checking around the base of the sofa. 'What's going on, exactly?'

'I don't know all the details. Please, just hurry.' I felt a sense of relief disproportionate to the act of a man putting on his shoes. 'Let's take your car. You might need your med kit.'

Slanting a concerned glance at me, he grabbed his keys and wallet off the coffee table, then followed me toward the garage. He didn't ask any further questions until we were in his car heading across town. The highways were quiet, nearly clear in the predawn haze. A low fog settled in as I told him about the news report on TV, the situation with Cass and Opal, my fear that one or both of them could be involved, perhaps even injured or trapped in the apartment.

'Let's not think the worst.' As usual, Rob's course of action was to remain rational, wait calmly for all the evidence before making an assessment.

I turned on the radio and searched for news. 'I'm not,' I said. 'I know they're all right. I just know . . .' Emotion choked the end of the sentence, and my mind spun ahead, creating replays of terrible, tragic news reports of children injured or killed during domestic disputes.

Stop it, I told myself. *Stop.*

Please, God, just keep them safe. Take them somewhere safe . . . The prayer repeated in my head, spinning faster and faster like a pinwheel in the wind, the colors flashing in rapid succession. Despite the lack of traffic, the drive seemed to stretch on forever. I felt as if I were in a dream, running yet trapped in one place.

The fog had thickened by the time we exited the interstate. The storm clouds were moving away, allowing a vague slice of light to tease the eastern horizon. I held my breath, counting down the minutes, the distance. Two miles, one mile, a half mile, just past the buildings ahead, and we'd be able to see . . .

I stretched toward the window, craned to get a better look, heard the words like a drumbeat in my head, *Please let them be safe. Please let them be safe.*

As we cleared the buildings, the street in front of the apartment complex inched into view. Where I'd expected flashing lights and chaos, there was only silence and darkness. The fire trucks were gone, as was the SWAT van, the displaced families, the swarm of police personnel. Only two cruisers remained. They were parked near the Dumpster, the flashers off.

'Turn in here,' I told Rob. The scene was eerily quiet as we rolled past the police vehicles and into the narrow strip of pavement between the buildings.

The door to Cass's apartment hung ajar, the lights on

inside. An officer was stretching crime scene tape over the opening, securing it around the frame.

'That's it,' I said to Rob, pointing. 'That's the apartment.'

Somewhere not far away, a siren wailed, and then another. The sound rocketed through me, hot and painful, pushing me forward as I exited the car and ran toward the apartment.

Standing in the dim circle of light, the officer held out a hand, stopping me. 'Sorry, ma'am. I can't allow you to enter. We've asked all residents to remain inside with doors and windows locked until further notice. We have an armed fugitive at large.'

'Where are the children?' I rushed out. 'The children who live in this apartment? Where are they? Are they all right?'

'Are you a relative?'

'Yes . . . no . . . a friend. A close friend of the family. I saw the report on the news. Where are the girls?'

The officer seemed to consider whether or not he should talk. 'Just a moment, ma'am.' Ducking under the tape, he went into the apartment and came back with a female co-worker, who descended the steps holding a notepad.

'Ma'am, we're still trying to ascertain the whereabouts of the residents here. We've transported one adult female to the hospital, and –'

'An adult?' I interrupted frantically. 'Not a teenage girl? Are you sure?'

The officer checked her notepad. 'An adult female, African-American. Blonde hair, hazel eyes. She was found unresponsive when SWAT entered the apartment. That's all the information I have. Do you know anything about the children who live here? Is it possible they might have been away tonight?'

'No. They were here. I saw them go home yesterday afternoon.' Was it possible that they had left before the break-in? Could they have gone somewhere with Rusty? 'There's a teenage boy living here also. Red hair, thin, tall. About six feet four.'

'I don't have anyone by that description.' The officer checked her clipboard again. 'Neighbors report that someone may have run from the scene during the fight. If there were children here, do you know where they might go? Are there relatives or friends nearby, some safe place they might try to reach, somewhere they might be hiding?

Some safe place? Somewhere they might be hiding?

Anywhere they might go?

Someplace safe . . .

The officer's belt radio squawked, and she reached for it.

I turned around and rushed toward my car, yanked open the door, and slid back into the seat next to Rob. 'Go to Poppy's house. Hurry.'

The first rays of dawn sprinkled glitter over the lingering fog and pressed back the leftover clouds as we drove down the street, passing the strip mall, an empty warehouse, the Book Basket, and the little white church, which was hidden in the fog, only the steeple and cross rising overhead catching the light, seeming to promise sanctuary. Any other time, the scene would have been serene, a postcard picture of a night giving birth to a peaceful day.

'Hurry,' I whispered, my fingers tapping rapidly on the console.

Rob glanced sideways at me. 'I'm hurrying,' he said, casting a pointed glance at a police car passing by. 'What's going on? Why are we headed to Poppy's?'

'The police don't know where the girls are. Nobody's seen them.' Putting it into words only made it seem more real. 'Someone thought they ran out during the fight. They might have hidden somewhere. They play in the drainage ditch sometimes, but they wouldn't go down there at night.' Right now, the drainage ditch was churning ominously with several feet of water from the storm. I didn't want to think about what might have happened if they'd decided to try to hide there, or what could happen to two little girls alone in this neighborhood after dark.

Cass is smart. She knows her way around. She'd go to Poppy's house. She'd know they could hide there until it was safe.

We passed another police cruiser, and with it came the obvious question: If Cass was waiting until it was safe to come out, why hadn't she? There were police cars combing the streets. She could run to any one of them.

Something warm touched my hand, blanketed it, stilled the frenzied movement. I felt Rob's fingers close over mine. I grabbed them, hung on. In the past, he would have told me everything would be all right. He would have said it in a tone promising that, whatever the problem, he would take care of it. But this time he just held my hand.

We turned onto Poppy's street, and I looked ahead, counted the houses. One, two, three, four . . . I could see the park. We passed it and crossed the bridge. The creek was rushing underneath, the sandbar where Opal had left her doll now hidden by several feet of floodwater.

Ahead, Poppy's house sat dark and quiet, a little island above the fog that had settled over the creek and the low end of the lot near the back, where the railroad tramps left their marker for a safe place.

A safe place . . .

Rob pulled into the driveway, and both of us exited the car. He followed me to the porch to check underneath it. I peered into the shadows, called Cass's name, then Opal's, and looked under the oleander bush.

'Maybe in back,' I said, trying to maintain hope. 'She knows the key to the shed is hidden in the bushes. She might have thought of that.'

'No way anyone could get into the house with all the burglar bars,' Rob observed, scanning the darkened windows as we went by.

Plants and garden tools cast eerie shadows as we passed through the gate and entered the yard. The gate was open. I always left it closed. I was certain we'd shut it before we went home yesterday. The wheelbarrow lay overturned and Teddy's conglomeration of pots were scattered around by the shed. Had the storm blown them, or had someone been here? By the back fence, the poles from the old washing lines stood like eerie sentinels in the fog, their arms stiff at their sides. Overhead, the pecan trees moaned softly, the ⌐nches heavy with wet foliage, slowly releasing drops ⌐he grass, showering us as we walked underneath.

'Cass?' I called. 'Opal? Are you out here? Are you here?' *There's a fugitive on the loose, Sandra. There's more than one reason the gate could be open.* The thought sent a shudder down my spine.

We searched the yard as the sky brightened, a timid morning glow probing the pecans, pressing occasional shafts of light toward the ground.

'There's no one here,' Rob said finally. 'The shed's locked, too.'

'Wait.' A faint noise caught my ear, the softest rustle of leaves. 'The summer kitchen!' I rushed toward the wall of hollyhocks. The plants parted easily, and I passed through, falling drops of water raining over me as I stepped into the damp green room within. 'Cass?' I whispered, my feet disappearing into the mist. 'Opal?'

Something stirred in a corner the sun had yet to touch. I moved closer, stood and looked down. Wrapped in the pale green lace of the plastic cloth from the yard table lay Cass and Opal. They were curled together against the old foundation, fast asleep. At any other time, the scene would have been peaceful and sweet, but all I felt was a flood of relief.

'Cass,' I whispered, squatting beside her and touching the dampness of the tablecloth, then the warmth of her skin. I let my hand linger there a moment, felt her breaths rising in and out. 'Wake up. It's all right now. We're here. It's all right. Wake up.' All I wanted to do was gather them into my arms and take them inside, where they would be warm, and dry, and safe.

CHAPTER 24

Cass

One night a long time ago, Mama and Rusty and me sat out on the porch watching for shooting stars, and then the clouds rolled over the moon, and it rained soft and gentle. I thought we'd go inside, but instead, Mama got one of the old quilts my grandmother'd made and she wrapped her, and me, and Rusty in it. He must of been about fifteen by then, too big to snuggle, but he sat there with us anyway. We all rocked slowly back and forth in the swing, a little ball of family with the chains creaking overhead.

I didn't hear Mama at first when she started talking. I was listening to the swing sing its lazy song.

Mama'd brought us out there to tell us she was sick again, and it was bad this time.

'I'm sorry,' she said, like it was something she'd done on purpose, then she squeezed us tight against her. 'We'll get through this, okay? No matter what happens, we're a family. Always.' Her tears were wet on my head. 'I'll always take care of you two,' she whispered. 'No matter what.'

I closed my eyes and rested calm inside the blanket of

that promise. One thing I always knew about Mama was that she kept every promise she ever made to us.

When me and Opal ran down the street with Uncle Len's truck after us, I knew Mama was right there. It was her that made him run up on the curb, hit something and get stuck for a second. She kept my legs strong under me, made my feet land steady in Kiki's tennis shoes as I splashed through the water and the wet leaves that had washed over the sidewalk. Mama whispered in my ear where a safe place would be. She kept my mind clear and sharp as I turned onto Poppy's street, my legs pumping and my throat burning so it seemed I couldn't get another breath.

The truck was after us, then. I saw it turn the corner, heard the engine roar as we got to the creek. The water was rushing wild so that the bridge shivered under my feet. I thought the truck might catch us and hit us, knock us off into the water, and we'd wash away and drown, but then we were over the bridge, and I was running through Poppy's yard. The truck bumped up onto the curb, slinging mud and gravel. Uncle Len yelled, but the words got lost in the thunder. I couldn't hear him then. I could only hear the sky. I thought he'd catch us at the backyard gate.

Mama held him back, I know. She came with the angels, and she made him slide down in the mud where the downspout poured off the corner of the house by the oleander bush. She stopped him just long enough for us to get in the yard and slip through the wet green wall of the summer kitchen. Mama hid us down in the corner, real still, in that secret place where nothing bad could come in. Mama kept

Opal quiet as a mouse while Uncle Len tore through the yard turning things over like a hungry lion looking for meat.

He didn't know about the summer kitchen, and Mama wouldn't let him see it, even when the wind bent the hollyhocks and lightning lit the sky. I could see him through the wall, but he couldn't see us. Mama made sure he wouldn't. She folded the hollyhocks low over us, so no one could see us at all.

She was there, just like she promised she would be.

She kept us safe, even after it seemed like Uncle Len was gone. She gave me the idea to wrap the tablecloth over us, and she told me to close my eyes.

She brought Mrs Kaye to find us just as morning was coming, and I knew it would be all right to finally tell the truth about Rusty and me. We went in Poppy's house, and we sat down at one of the tables, and I stripped off all the fake stories, until it was just me, Cass Sally Blue, the *real* Cass Sally telling everything that had really happened.

The funny thing was that Mrs Kaye didn't seem to mind the truth about Rusty and me. She smiled, and stuck out her hand, and said, 'Nice to finally meet you, Cass Sally Blue.'

I felt kinda silly, but I shook her hand anyway. I guessed, in a way, it was like we were meeting for the first time.

'This is my husband, Rob,' she said, and I shook the hand of the man who was with her. He looked a little like Christopher, and I'd figured he was Christopher's dad.

He smiled at me, and I decided I liked him pretty well. 'How about some breakfast at McDonald's?' he asked when

Opal whined about being hungry. I didn't worry about whether he'd want something in return for buying us breakfast. He didn't look like he needed anything. He had on a gold wedding ring with a great big diamond that must of cost a bundle.

'Sure,' I said. 'Thanks.'

At McDonald's, Mrs Kaye broke it to me that we'd have to go back to the apartment now, and see if the police or social services were still there. She asked where Rusty was, because they'd want to talk to him, too, and I said he'd be home anytime. As soon as I said it, a part of me was afraid. I got up to go to the bathroom, and I saw how I could sneak out the side door of McDonald's. It wasn't too far to the apartments from there. Maybe I could find some way to warn Rusty before he got home, and we could jump in the truck and drive away.

I stood by the door and watched Mrs Kaye's husband help Opal cut the last of her pancakes, and I thought about it.

You can't do it, Cass Sally Blue. You can't leave Opal, and run out on Mrs Kaye. Something in me turned a corner then, maybe grew up a little. One thing you gotta learn in your life is that it's okay sometimes to let people in your business. Sometimes the people are there to help, and you didn't even know it at first. There's not a one of us meant to go along the road all by ourselves. That's what I decided, right there in McDonald's.

Mrs Kaye and her husband took us back to the apartments. A woman from social services was there, asking the crippled lady questions. The crippled lady pointed to us when we got out of the car, then she came all the way across the parking lot with the social worker, which was some trouble with her two canes. She looked at me for the first time, and she smiled, and put a hand on Opal's head. Opal was crying and hanging on to me, because she was afraid to go back into the apartment. She thought Uncle Len was still inside our place, probably. The social worker didn't want us to go in, anyway, because *things were a mess in there,* she said, which was why the police had it taped off. I told her we couldn't leave until Rusty came home, because he'd be scared to death, and he wouldn't know where to find us.

'It's all right,' the crippled lady told me, drying the tears off Opal's cheek. 'Y'all come on into my place. We'll watch for him, and I'll make everyone some coffee.'

I looked at Mrs Kaye, and she agreed it'd be all right, and we all went inside. The social worker asked me to sit down at the table with her, so I did. Opal stayed in my lap, Mrs Kaye and her husband sat on the sofa, and the lady made coffee. Her apartment was lots nicer than ours. Everything was clean, and she had pretty curtains on the window. The pretty curtains didn't make me feel much better. I was scared about what was going to happen next, and I looked over at Mrs Kaye.

'It's all right. We're not going anywhere,' she promised, and I was glad she did.

The social worker told me we didn't need to worry about Uncle Len – Leonard Lee Cole, she called him – because the police had just picked him up. They didn't have any trouble because he was asleep in his truck outside Glitters, and before he knew what was going on, he was face-to-face with five police officers, a dog, and a pair of handcuffs with his name on them. Kiki was in the hospital, in pretty bad shape, but it wasn't life-threatening. 'So there's nothing for you to be afraid of here,' she finished. 'We're just going to talk for a while. I don't want you to feel that you need to protect anyone, all right?'

'Okay,' I said.

She asked questions for a long time about Rusty and me, and how we'd ended up here. When I talked, she nodded and wrote things in her notepad, looking sad, like she'd heard it all before. She had mouse-brown hair with a few gray strands in it, tied up in a sloppy ponytail. She was wearing a wrinkled sweater, jeans that looked like they came off some eighties TV show, and socks that didn't match. Her shoulders were round, like she spent all her time bent over her pad, writing terrible stuff in people's files. I was afraid the sad look meant they were gonna haul me and Rusty away and separate us, so I asked. She stopped writing, leaned across the table, and held my hand. 'We're going to do everything we can to take care of you and your brother,' she promised, but when you don't know somebody, you don't know how good their promises are.

'I don't think Rusty'd want to have, like, foster parents and stuff,' I said, because I pretty much knew how he'd take all of this. 'Not after living on our own so long, I mean. We been gonna try to find Rusty's real dad, but we hadn't had much luck.' The lady asked me for Ray John's name, and I gave it to her, and she wrote it on her pad.

'We have some options,' the lady said, and then she told me about a new place where brother and sister groups like me and Rusty could live in a little apartment, and we'd still be a family, but we'd have adults and a caseworker to help us out. Rusty could finish school instead of working all the time. 'You wouldn't have foster parents, exactly.' She pushed a flyaway hair out of her face and tucked it behind her ear, then smiled at me. 'But there are house parents in the building, and we try to match each family group with a sponsor to help you with decisions, and financial planning, doctors' appointments, school enrollment, and other things that may be a little harder to navigate without some grown-up assistance.'

Mrs Kaye piped up and said she'd be our sponsor. She glanced over at her husband, and he nodded, and said, 'Of course we can do that. Whatever's needed. But if the kids need a place to stay –'

The social worker held up a hand and said, 'Let's just take it one step at a time.'

I got a good feeling all of a sudden. I thought maybe Rusty'd even be able to play basketball or baseball again, and maybe he'd get a scholarship after all. He wouldn't have to work so hard, trying to pay so many bills.

Opal burrowed under my neck, falling asleep, and the good feeling left me. As soon as she was out cold, I pulled up her hair and showed the burns. 'Opal's mama knew about it,' I told her, and even with everything Kiki'd done, I felt bad. I remembered how even after Kiki was gone with Uncle Len for so long, Opal wanted to be with her the minute she came back. I guess, no matter what, it's just natural to love your mama. 'She left Opal here for a couple weeks to go off with her boyfriend, but then she came back. He beat her up again and she was kind of out of it, messed up on something. The guy showed up in the middle of the night and started banging on the door, trying to get to her and Opal.'

'Who took care of Opal while the mother was gone?' The social worker looked up at me over the rim of her glasses. They were bent so her eyes seemed uneven.

'I did.'

'Was the mother aware there wasn't an adult living in the apartment?'

'She knew who was here.'

'I see.'

The questions seemed to run out then. We sat for a while, and she wrote on her pad.

'When that guy showed up last night, she gave me her shoes so I could run away with Opal. She kept him busy so we could get out the door.' I wasn't sure why I wanted them to know that. Maybe because Kiki was in a hospital bed somewhere.

'Who did?' The social worker looked at the shoes, Kiki's purple-and-gold glittery hightops, still on my feet.

'Kiki did. So, she must've cared some. She's just too messed up to be somebody's mama.'

The lady nodded and wrote a few more lines – about the shoes, I guess. I wondered if that would make any difference in what happened to Kiki and whether she got Opal back. Maybe I shouldn't of said anything.

'Rusty and me can take care of Opal,' I told the lady. 'When we get one of those apartments like you talked about.' I held on to Opal tight.

'One thing at a time, all right?' The lady smiled at me again. 'Don't worry.'

'What's gonna happen to Kiki?' I was scared to ask, but I was scared not to know, too.

The social worker seemed to think about whether to give me a real answer, or just one that sounded good.

'I can handle the truth. I'm not a little kid,' I told her, and she actually laughed a little.

'I can see that,' she said. 'To be honest with you, Kiki is in a lot of trouble. She's been on parole for a meth conviction. She's missed several appointments with her parole officer, and one of the conditions of her release was no further involvement with former associates.'

I didn't know why she was trying to put it so nice. 'You mean she wasn't supposed to be with anyone she'd do drugs with.' I figured we might as well say it plain, since it was Opal's life we were talking about here. She needed to get away from Kiki for good. 'Will Kiki go back to jail?'

The lady tapped her pencil on the table, watching the eraser bounce off the wood. 'Yes. I'm afraid she will.'

'For a long time?'

'Yes.'

'Rusty and me can take care of Opal,' I said again. 'We're like a family now. She's scared of people she doesn't know.'

'One step at a time.' I wished she'd stop using that line on me. That's what adults say when they don't want to give you a straight answer. 'Right now we're talking about what happened last night.'

'Opal doesn't take up much space.' I could feel the panic growing in me. I pictured how scared she would be if they took her off somewhere and gave her to strangers. What if somebody hurt her again? 'Even if the apartment's small, it'd be enough for us. She doesn't have much stuff, either, and –'

The lady held up her palm, then laid her hand over mine. 'Let's just stay calm, all right? The biggest thing you can do to help right now is to give me all the facts. We'll make sure Opal is taken care of.'

'*We'll* make sure Opal is taken care of,' Mrs Kaye said, breaking into the conversation, and I was glad she was there and on my side. 'We want to do anything we can to help these kids. Whatever's needed.' Both the social worker and me turned to her, but Mrs Kaye was only looking at me. 'Whatever it takes,' she said, and I knew she meant it. No matter what came after this, she'd be there. Being as she was a grown-up, and her husband was a doctor, and they were rich, I figured the social worker would have to listen to them, and I felt a little better.

Outside, Rusty's truck rumbled up. I pictured how he'd look when he got out. He'd be dirty and bone tired, his hands black from loading shingles all night, his eyelids so heavy he'd sit down and fall right asleep. He'd be scared to death when he saw the police tape.

I thought about how he used to come up Mama's steps two at a time, whistling some tune he'd heard on the radio, his basketball under one arm and his backpack in the other. Mama didn't want him to be worn out and weighed down with worry. She wanted a good life for both of us. She wouldn't of liked the way we were now.

The crippled lady went to the door and called to Rusty before he could get up our apartment steps. 'They're over here,' she said, and Rusty came to the door looking like he was about to have a coronary.

'It's okay,' I told him. 'Some stuff happened last night, but we're all right.'

Everyone got up to meet Rusty when he came in the door. I just sat there looking through the opening, far into the distance, where the new day was burning off the last of the clouds and leaving behind patches of blue.

In a little while, there would be more blue than anything else.

I held Opal under my chin and went off to a mind place while the adults started telling Rusty everything that'd happened.

I thought about Wildfire – how the girl ran off in the blizzard calling for her pony until, as far as everyone knew, she died in the storm, running after what was lost.

All of a sudden, I knew for sure it didn't happen that way. She didn't die. Just when she couldn't go any farther, when the cold and the wind got all the way into her bones, she saw a light off in the distance, through the snow and the dark. She finally understood that sometimes, when you're too far away from your old place to get back to it, you have to head for a new place. She ran toward the light, and she found a home that was warm, and dry, and safe. All she had to do was reach out and open the door. When she did, just before she stepped into the light, she caught her breath and looked back over her shoulder. She knew Wildfire hadn't run away, after all. He was running to something. Behind her, in what she thought was only wilderness, there was the path he'd followed. Even though she couldn't have seen it through the storm, even though she never knew it was there, she'd been on that path every step she took.

CHAPTER 25

Sandra Kaye

I heard the investment company planned to paint Poppy's house yellow. The same color they painted all their rentals – a marker perhaps meant to let residents of the neighborhood know they were moving into the area, looking for deals. Sooner or later, the whole block would go, the old homes would be cleared out, and new housing complexes would be built.

Some things are easier imagined than seen, so I didn't drive by Poppy's house after the sale was final. Even when Teddy, Rusty, Christopher, and a gathering of volunteers finished cleaning the park next door and reopened it, I stayed away from Red Bird Lane. It wasn't so hard to do. There were a million details involved in securing a new place for the café, moving equipment, and getting set up.

It was Teddy who solved the problem of finding our new home. In the midst of Holly, MJ, and me cleaning our supplies out of Poppy's house and discussing the possibility of trying to operate from an empty portion of MJ's building – with no kitchen, almost no parking, and no air-conditioning – Teddy popped into the conversation and said, 'Paster Al church got a kit-tchen, and lotta table, and chair, and . . .'

The three of us looked at each other with our mouths open in a dawning eureka moment.

'That's perfect!' Holly gasped, one hundred percent positive, as always. The next thing I knew, she was giving Teddy a bear hug. He was so shocked he dropped paper plates all over the floor.

When Holly released him, he stood snorting and laughing, his face turning red. 'Pas-ter Al church got a kit-tchen and lotta table!' he repeated, and soon we were all headed to the little white church on the corner to find Pastor Al. Within a few days, we had a location for the café in the fellowship hall. Our new space came complete with a commercial kitchen, tables, space in the parking lot for basketball, and even a few church members interested in volunteering. We moved our equipment from Poppy's house to the church, and I said good-bye to Poppy's on a quiet day in early June, then I didn't go back. It was too hard to think about what would happen there next.

If not for the fact that a bit of mail came three weeks later, I never would have returned to the house at all.

The note was waiting in the mailbox at the end of a perfectly ordinary day, when Holly dropped Christopher and me in our driveway. She waved as she pulled away, with Opal yawning and stretching in the back, her arms barely visible above the car seat Holly had saved in the attic all these years, just in case there might be one more little

Riley, after all. As it turned out, the thought wasn't so preposterous. One adult-child Riley moved out, and Opal moved in.

Christopher trotted up our drive to tell his dad about the day as I walked to the curb to get the mail. I stood leafing through it, the afternoon sun warm on my hair. There were bills, advertisements, a newsletter from Family Central, where we'd started attending group counseling sessions on Tuesday nights. A tattered white envelope fell from my hands and drifted downward into the grass like a butterfly searching for a place to land. I finished skimming the outside of the Family Central newsletter, laughed at a cartoon of a teenager trying to coerce the car keys from his parents, then reached for what I'd dropped. The grass brushed my fingers as I picked up the envelope, turned it over, looked at the handwriting and knew instantly who'd sent the letter. The postmark blurred behind a sudden rush of tears, and I sank into the grass, blinking and reading the return address. *Guatemala City Guatemala.*

Inside the envelope were a carefully folded letter and two photos. I clasped the photos in shaking fingers, holding them like something fragile. A smile bloomed from somewhere deep inside me as I took in an image of Jake. He was laughing, holding up a soccer ball, with children all around him. I turned over the photo and scanned the neatly printed caption, undoubtedly meant to be read after the letter explained everything.

Me at the school with the kids, it read. In the photo, Jake's face was filled with joy, his dark eyes alive with light.

Throughout the years, I'd seen Jake smile many times, but I'd never seen him look so completely at peace, so entirely in the moment.

The second image was of Jake and a beautiful dark-haired young woman. They stood arm in arm in front of a waterfall that tumbled from the thick veil of trees. A rainbow had formed in the mist, encircling them.

Waving the letter over my head, I ran toward the house, calling for Rob and Christopher. 'It's Jake! It's Jake! Jake sent a letter!' I was breathless by the time I reached the kitchen and handed the photos to Rob and Christopher.

Rob smiled and shook his head at the picture of Jake with the children. 'Look at him,' he whispered, his eyes growing moist.

Chris snatched the picture of Jake and the girl, turned it over searching for an explanation, then focused on the image again. 'Forget about Jake, look at *her.*'

We laughed together, admiring Jake's new life. 'There's a letter,' I said, then unfolded the wrinkled sheet and laid it on the counter. The letter was written in pencil on notebook paper, the surface smudged and scrubby, as if Jake had composed and erased the text many times, trying to get it just right.

Standing together, we read Jake's note as a family, learned of his new life teaching at a school in Guatemala, and his blooming relationship with Gabrielle, whom he'd met at the school. He explained his reasons for leaving home, his deeply held emotion for his birth country, his need to go, and his inability to tell us about it.

Mom and Dad, please know that I love you both,

the letter ended.

You gave me everything I needed to come here and try to make a difference. Chris, I miss you, dude. Shoot a three-pointer for me. I'll get home when I can. Write me. There's so much I want to tell you about this place.

I only wish Poppy could see it, but sometimes I know he's watching. I think about you often. I love all of you.

>   *God bless,*
>   *Jake*

I set Jake's letter by the bed, let it rest there overnight, and felt his presence in the house again. Even though he was growing up, finding his own way, we were still a family, and we always would be. Families aren't dictated by geography, or biology, or the chemistry of chromosomes and DNA. There is, in fact, no perfect science to it at all. There is only the tie of love, which, in the end, is all that matters.

In the morning, I woke early to look at the pictures. Rob stirred as I reached for them. He wrapped his arms around me, and I snuggled in, letting the photos lie. For now, there were more important things to tend to. The first lesson Rob and I had learned in family counseling was that *we* were the most important thing of all. In order to give Christopher a stable, happy home, we had to be willing to set everything else aside and do the work it took to give him stable, happy parents. In the long run, it wouldn't matter how perfect our life looked to the neighbors, or how well we kept up appearances, but it would matter whether or not we showed our son that it's all right to be imperfect, to admit your mistakes and then move past them.

When I left the house for the day, I took Jake's letter with me, stowed away in my pocket like a secret passenger. As I passed the little white church, Teddy was already busy working on some new gardens around the fellowship hall. Today he'd brought Hanna Beth and her husband, Edward, and they were planting some daisies with their young nurse and her two little boys. Any time now, Rusty would drop off Cass on his way to the morning credit-recovery classes that would allow him to start next year as a high school senior. Cass would help Teddy, and make the coffee, and wait for me to show up. When I arrived, we'd spend some time checking her lessons from afternoon summer school before the others came.

This morning, she'd have to work on her own for a few minutes longer than usual. I had a special mission, and it was for no one but Poppy and Jake.

Poppy's house was silent and dark when I drove up. It seemed strange to see it in yellow, but it wasn't as painful as I'd anticipated. Just as all of us were moving on, it was fitting that Poppy's house move on, as well. Perhaps it was someone else's time to find the secret places now.

A breeze stirred the roses Teddy had groomed so carefully as I tiptoed to the house and slipped Jake's letter underneath the loose piece of clapboard by the front window, where it could remain part of the house, part of Jake and Poppy.

A bit of each of us, a bit of the whole of us, would always be here.

But there was room for something new, as well, space to grow in directions that had once been beyond our imagining. My mind filled with the possibilities, with a sense of power and potential, as I crossed the yard and slipped into my car, feeling that, in some way, the work here wasn't finished, but what would come next wasn't for me. It was time for the little girl who hid beneath the oleander bush to leave the safe places behind, spread her wings, and fly out into the world.

When I reached the old white church, Cass was helping Teddy in front of the fellowship hall. They smiled and waved as I drove up, then they stood very deliberately shoulder to shoulder, hiding something.

'What are you guys up to?' I asked, climbing out of my car.

Cass rolled her gaze upward in feigned innocence, her eyes reflecting the clear summer sky. 'Something.'

'Som'tin' Rusty done,' Teddy added. 'He done it las' night. Rusty did.'

'Guess,' Cass teased. 'Guess what it is.'

'I haven't a clue,' I admitted, trying to see behind them, where something was covered haphazardly with a tablecloth. Cass nodded at Teddy, and he grabbed the corners of the fabric and pulled it away.

'Ta-da!' she cheered, presenting the big reveal like a game show model. 'It's a present from Rusty and me.' Her blue eyes were so vibrant, it took me a moment to focus on the gift. When I did, I was filled with the purest joy, the sort that is rare and precious.

Who could imagine that such joy could come from a simple wooden sign, from three words carved into the polished grain, then neatly painted in the bright pink of Poppy's house? The gift encompassed so much more than a building, or a group of workers, or shelves stacked with food ready to be prepared, or a sense of purpose found, or empty stomachs filled, or lives changed.

'It's perfect.' I stepped forward, traced the words with my fingers, then whispered them aloud. '*The Summer Kitchen.*'

Letting the name settle over me, I considered the wonders that a simple coat of paint on cabinets had led to.

Who could have predicted such possibilities, but then again, nothing really happens by accident. There is a plan, even when we don't see it, even when it's nothing we would have guessed. There is a purpose for broken houses and broken people.

Perhaps the wandering men knew that long ago. Perhaps they sensed it, and so they left behind the symbol of blessing.

Or perhaps the blessing was the beginning of it all.

ACKNOWLEDGEMENTS

The Summer Kitchen was inspired in great measure by real-life events, and so there are some real-life people to whom I owe a debt. To begin at the beginning, thank you to Judith for showing up at a book signing, telling me about The Gospel Cafe, and then being so kind as to take me there to see it for myself on a rainy spring day. To Sherry, Marsha, Curtis, and John, thanks for sharing the place with me and for taking time to answer questions and contribute ideas for the story. To the great folks in the kitchen, thanks for putting up with me as I learned the routine and asked more silly questions. May the sweet light of grace continue to shine down on you and your little blue house as you fill hearts and stomachs. To Ladelle Brown, thanks for sharing the story of your sandwich ministry. The tales about your 'kids' helped to give faces to the children of Blue Sky Hill and to bring them to life.

On the practical side of things, my gratitude goes out to the fine folks at New American Library for doing the hard work that turns stories into books and dreams into reality.

In particular, my thanks to my editor, Ellen Edwards; to Claire Zion and Kara Welsh; to all the folks in marketing and publicity at the Penguin Group, who bring the books to the shelves; and to Megan Swartz for being a great publicist. Thanks also to my agent, Claudia Cross, at Sterling Lord Literistic.

Closer to home, I'm grateful to my family and my community of reader friends, without whom none of this would be possible. Thanks to Sharon Mannion for tireless proofreading and to Janice Wingate for keeping up with newsletter lists. Gratitude also goes out to Ed Stevens for tireless encouragement and endless technical help with YouTube videos and other mind-boggling projects, and to Teresa Loman for being a hilarious long-distance gal pal and for starting my official fan club on Facebook. With you in it, any club would be a hoot, girlfriend!

Last, thanks once again to readers far and near who keep me writing and give my imaginary friends new mind places to travel to. Thank you for passing the books along to others, and for taking time to send notes, good wishes, and encouraging words. These adventures would be nothing without wonderful people to share them with.

May some measure of the joy you've given me be returned to you in this story.